CISTOPIA

HARLEY GRIGG

BASED LIFEFORM PRESS

PROLOGUE

INTERCEPTED TRANSMISSION TRANSCRIPT—EQUALITY MINISTRY
SUBJECT: INSURGENT BROADCAST #256
LISTENING STATION FRIDA
24-10-46 0738 GMT

SENSITIVITY CLASSIFICATION: 8—CLASSIFIED / SANITIZED

VOICE *[terrorist suspect #2408D]*: Look alive! Coming at you hot, all you Heathens, Compound kiddies, Safe Zone subordinates and inner-city slaves. Whoever you are, if you've managed to evade the censors, then great job—you're listening to the Ozcast on Revolution Radio, the frequency of freedom, with me, the Oz-man, the resistor on your transistor, here with your breakfast briefing.

And, *ee-gads*, have you seen the latest propaganda piece in today's netwires? Oh, right—probably not 'cause you're not a brainwashed simp and, let's be honest, you know I'll wade through this detritus so you don't have to. Well, strap in, 'cause this one's a corker!

With the disinformation machine in hyper-drive for election season, the bootlick-media are declaring—nay, *celebrating*—the latest official polls that, *quelle surprise*, suggest the TEP are on course for another landslide victory. They're busting a prosthetic nut over their prognostications that the prime minister and *his-her* cronies can expect the biggest majority our once-proud country has ever seen.

Hey, maybe they're right. I mean, who knows what they'll be doing this year to fix the numbers, man. Plus, we all know who's behind the tech they use to count the votes.

But you know what's funny? Word on the street is the unofficial polls—the ones the censors don't get their claws into—tell a different story. I'm talking about the ones that show the TEP are losing ground when it comes to public favour. Big time.

Sure, most people aren't going to risk voting *against* the TEP. They're afraid. They don't want to be cancelled. They don't want to be forced into an atonement session—or worse. But I'm telling you, man, there's a keg of gunpowder building and it only takes a spark.

Those aren't the only rumours I'm hearing, either. The Oz-man's sources say the powers that be are spooked. Tavistock's pissing her man-sized pantalettes at the thought of people seeing through the lies, seeing the drag king has no clothes, and it's only a matter of time before the whole thing starts to come crashing down.

So what does that mean? Well, desperate people do desperate things, don't they? We've seen what they're already capable of. Don't expect it to slide down a gear now. What I'm hearing—the TEP is gonna have to make a move, have to amp it up, have to find a way to get rid of this pesky democratic masquerade once and for all! I'm hearing they could even be looking to *[REDACTED]*. The monoculture ain't yet mono enough, man. They want it all. No counterpoint. Not even the faintest whiff of critical thought. And once they have that, you know where it goes next...

Mandatory. Embryonic. Manipulation.

Oh, *conspiracy theory!* I hear them jeer. *Typical fear-mongering!*

But, hey—would you put it past them? Britcoin is in the tank, man. City projects are falling further behind deadlines. More people are finding ways to flee the Safe Zones. The Big Reboot is becoming the

Big Relapse. The New World Order is out-of-order. They're losing numbers. It ain't sustainable, Jack. The higher-ups are getting worried. Tell me, dear listeners—when will this regime learn you can't *disappear* people? Deplatforming doesn't work. Just because they cover their eyes doesn't mean we aren't still here.

And if any of you neo-trans-fascists are eavesdropping on this channel, let's get one thing straight—we didn't move underground. You stomped us underground! But we're still breathing. We're still fighting the good fight. The more you seek to ban us, to silence us, we'll find other ways to speak out. You cannot crush ideas. They're bulletproof. *Taze-stick proof.* They can't be arrested. They can't be censored. They can't be silenced.

Come on! Don't you know your history, man? Oops—I forgot. You only study *zistory*. And we all know that's more hogwash than a herd of pigs in a hot tub.

Mark my words, man, there's change in the air and it's lingering. The censors are gonna get dizzy trying to keep reality on lockdown in the coming weeks, even from those supposedly on the inside. *Especially* from those on the inside.

That's all for now, folks. Tune in this afternoon for my lunchtime update. Oh, and I've got an Easter egg coming for some of you later today. Let's see if you spot it…

But for now—stay alert. Stand up. Be counted. Ominous spiritus. Oz-man out.

END OF RECORDING

CHAPTER ONE

"Great Birth-Giver, Tieman! I didn't think you were the type."

"Sarge?"

"That way inclined, I mean. Not that there's anything wrong with it, mind, just—well—I don't see it myself. Don't understand the attraction."

After eleven hours, the shift was coming to an end right around rush hour, Wednesday morning. Uneventful. Only in the dying moments had the dispatch come through of an assault in progress, the suspect said to have been detained by civilians. Chrissie slid up the speed control on the touchscreen dash. Dennehy perked up, itching for entertainment. Digital blue lights throbbed to the scream of a laser gun siren.

"Why would you assume I wasn't the type?" Chrissie asked, the autobile accelerating, manoeuvring itself through the streets, forcing traffic to part.

"Because you're an equality officer, hun. I'm sure it hasn't escaped your notice that most of us back at Central tend to veer away from conservative activities. No offence. I don't get what you see in privs, that's all. We get enough of their like on the job. Enough to put anyone off for a lifetime, I'd a'thought."

I've had enough NeverCold on the job, too. Chrissie thought. *It doesn't mean I don't crave real coffee once in a while.*

Dennehy gave her a side-look. "Don't think I have to remind you it's an offense for someone in your role to discriminate against non-binary folk when it comes to dating, right?"

"That's not what I'm doing, I swear. I just meant I feel naturally attracted to CisHet males. I mean, sometimes."

Dennehy chuckled. "Careful—that's close to sounding problematic. Wouldn't want to have to arrest you." The warning: angled as a joke, couldn't help but carry an undertone. "Hey, I know what would snap you out of it. A little Sapphic action. How about that new cadet? Think I saw her checking you out. Seriously, hun, what I wouldn't give for a minute alone with her in a gender-neutral changing room."

"Go for it, Sarge. Don't have time for dating anyway."

The patrol car hit a puddle, pulled to an inch-perfect stop outside Marylebone station, coughing dirty water in its wake. The pavements of West London, pavements once choked with commuters, conjured oily rainbows, the smell of aerosol and moss from the morning cloudburst. Pedestrians sauntered up and down and across the high street, flamingos in pastel macs, cradling designer handbags, free to dawdle, to window shop.

Chrissie bowed her chin to the voxcom at her lapel. "Juliet Ophelia 621 to Dispatch. We're at the scene."

A hiss of static, an android blip, the calm voice of the operator: "Received, 621."

Dennehy, already out on the curb, let the door wheeze shut behind her. Chrissie's partner was built like a dishwasher, took up the width of the pavement. A butch lesbian trans-ally who spent her evenings watching sports and swilling cider but who had decided against taking the full leap of transitioning to a male. That choice had no doubt set her career back but she seemed determined to make up for the shortfall in sheer loyalty to the Force.

The sergeant scooped the tight knot of her hair under the chequered band of her cap, touched the handle of the taze stick on her belt to gauge its distance, dug her knuckles into the breasts of her stab-proof jacket in a way that made her elbows splay out like goose wings.

"Let's go, Tieman," Dennehy said. Chrissie caught up. "Keep your asp ready and your body-eye on at all times, unless I say otherwise. Sounds like we could have a live one—with any luck."

She flashed Chrissie her ivories. Together they cut through the side entrance, beneath the yellowing steel archway towards the concourse. Chrissie didn't want a live one. A live one only ever meant one thing.

Inside, sunlight broke through the glass roof and the tarmac grey sky beyond, casting glare across the media walls. Twenty-four hour netwire coverage bounced from celebrity gossip to the prime minister's morning press appearance at some local school. Digital ticker tape announced the latest travel updates, the latest Mixed World

Cup scores, the latest headline from the Leo Learson trial—'*Witness testimony rocks Hollywood.*'

It wasn't hard to find the disturbance. A ring of civilians formed near the front of an ersatz coffee shop, their arms linked in solidarity. A single sky-eye hovered above, red beacon blinking. A few metres away, a young non-binary in baggy jeans and a shaved head was being comforted by one of the baristas, a cordial hand rubbing at her back.

"It's okay, we're here," Chrissie said, closing the gap between them. "How do you prefer to be addressed?"

"She/her."

"Are you hurt?"

The victim shook her head, placed a hand to her throat, apparently making a brave effort to steady her breathing. "No. But I am distressed. Very, very distressed."

"Did he touch you?"

"Not physically, but…"

Another female in the crowd burst into sudden, frantic tears. An androgynous individual lurched into the arms of a friend, made like he or she was close to passing out.

Chrissie opened the channel on her voxcom. "Juliet Ophelia 621. We're going to a need a Counselling Team at Marylebone Station, south entrance. Three—four if you can spare them."

She waited for crackled acknowledgement, turned back to the victim. "Can you tell me what happened?"

"I came out of the gate and he…" The vic took a deep breath, eyes tightening. "…He misgendered me. Called me *sir*. When I looked up, he even had the nerve to grin—the bastard! And I wasn't the only one to hear it. He heard it too."

The vic nodded at a lanky male-presenting non-binary bending his ear a foot away, who tossed his hair back, stepped forward. His voice, shrill and accented, some indistinct European origin. "That's right, I heard it too. I'm a *witness*."

Dennehy shook her head. Chrissie poked details into her smartpalm. The officer's immense fluorescent chest puffed out, elbows spread as far as they would go. She approached the crowd.

One of the non-binaries in the circle saw the police had arrived, broke from the chain, pointed an accusing finger, screamed: "There he is! There's the bigot!"

Dennehy said, "I'll take it from here, folks. The city thanks you for your bravery."

The male CisHet—cisgender heterosexual—sat on the floor, his soft features a picture of bewilderment that turned to fear as the officer parted the way. Strawberry blonde. Thirties. Corduroy trousers. The mandatory armband marking him out for what he was. The bystanders who had him trapped made no move to leave. Dennehy made no effort to make them.

"Get on your feet, creeper," Dennehy said.

The priv knew better than to hesitate. He unfurled his legs, pulled himself up, a head taller than both officers. His shoulders collapsed into his chest, willing himself to shrink.

"That individual says you harassed her."

"I didn't." His pitch all over the place. "I would never do that. I was just letting her go ahead of me and—"

"She says you misgendered her."

"I misspoke. It was an accident. She was presenting as sort of—"

"Sort of what? What does it matter what she's presenting as?"

"I know, I know. It was only a slip of the tongue. My mind was elsewhere. I apologised as soon as she corrected me." The pitch up, the words squeaky.

"Are you shouting at me?"

The priv blinked, his cheeks pallid pea.

"No," he said, then softly as he could, "No, officer."

"And what were you supposedly thinking about to make you so careless?"

"My son. It's my day off. I was on my way to see him. It's my allocated day for this month."

Chrissie tensed. That wouldn't rub well on Dennehy. Sure enough, the sergeant's expression dropped.

"Where do you work?"

"The sewage plant." A clammy hand ran through his hair.

The officer's nose wrinkled. "Explains the smell. Photo card and Ally Pass. Now."

The suspect fumbled for his wallet, produced his documentation. The circle of bystanders sent him daggers, arms folded. Two of them embraced each other, sharing in their trauma, shaken by the unsuspected violence to which they had been indirectly subjected. Other cis pedestrians ambled past without a word, not wanting anything to do with the situation.

"Thomas Tate," Dennehy said, reading his papers, spitting the consonants. "You realise you're only allowed inside this Zone because you're listed as an essential labourer and have agreed to a code of ethics? To conduct yourself in a civilised way?"

"I know but I—"

"We don't accept cissexist violence in this neck of the woods, or anywhere for that matter." Her mouth stretched into a thin imitation of a smile as she pulled up his record on her smartpalm. "And what a surprise. Says here you've been in trouble for aggressive behaviour before."

"That was…that was a long time ago," he said. Some of the spectators came in closer, hoping to drink in all the juicy details. "It was a mistake, but I paid my debt for that."

"Another mistake. Of course it was. Says here you once dead named someone…oof. In a court of law, no less."

"My ex-wife. He began transitioning while we were getting divorced. It was stupid force of habit. I couldn't—"

"You spent three months on probation. Phase Four behavioural orientation. Three points against your Ally Pass. Yeah, your family must be really proud of you."

"Look, this is all a misunderstanding. I'll apologise to the lady right now. You won't hear from me again, I promise."

"You've admitted your offense. Not that I need a confession—we have plenty of people here willing to testify. We'll need to run your information over this evening's Awareness Bulletin, see if you've harassed anyone else."

8

"Please." Pale fingers, trembling. "I can't appear on there. I'll lose my job."

Chrissie watched on in silence as her partner massaged the plasticuffs on her holster, watched her savour the hot air of fear she had stoked. Dennehy, as she was so often fond of mentioning to her colleagues, came from a long line of police officers. Grandfather had been one. Both mothers had been one. The sarge liked to think she had inherited a nose for troublemakers, an uncanny ability to be able to tell the good from the bad in ways that could never be undermined by evidence. For an equality officer—known colloquially as an EQO, or *echo*—there was no skill more needed to enforce the law in today's society.

"You think your job is worth more than that woman's emotional wellbeing?" Dennehy went on, closing in on the suspect. "I guess it's true what they say—once a creeper always a creeper."

The officer unhooked the cuffs. Chrissie felt something inside herself erode a little more, knowing what was coming.

A gap opened up in the circle, one of the bystanders moved forward, pumped a fist in the air, urged others in the crowd to do the same— *Cancel him! Cancel him!*

Thomas Tate broke. Without another word, he slipped Dennehy's reach, bolted through the throng of strangers clamouring for his detainment.

The witness screamed.

CHAPTER TWO

"Shit," Chrissie muttered, breaking into pursuit. Her partner whirled, sheepish one moment, boiling with rage the next, stumbling over herself to pick up the chase.

Tate was fast. He swerved through the exit, went hell for leather down the pedestrian incline, took a right at the datapoints towards the dual bypass that led towards Baker Street. Chrissie kept a bead on him, leaned into the run, yelled at civilians in front of her to get the hell out of the way. Her cap disappeared.

Behind her, Dennehy tried to keep up, shunted into pedestrians as they swivelled blindly around to see what was causing the commotion.

Tate didn't have a plan. He was running on primitive fuel, robbed of fight, left only with the instinct to escape. Chrissie knew the more he ran, the worse it would be for him. Goddess forbid he should actually get away from them. His punishment would already be severe. His Ally Pass for the Outer Safe Zone was as good as gone. He crossed a road without looking either way, clipped the back of a moving taxi, span once, drunk-danced back into his escape.

A sky-eye glided in, locked onto the target, followed overhead like a cartoon storm cloud.

Chrissie slowed at the crossing for a double-decker to lurch by. On the side of the bus, a body-positive drag queen, close to three hundred pounds, modelled *Curvy Couture* lingerie. Chrissie took the opportunity to look back for her support. Dennehy was a good thirty yards behind now, feet dragging. Even at this distance her face looked tomato-ripe. The sarge waved an arm out—*Go on without me!*—and slowed to a stop.

More screams, more gasps ahead. Chrissie used them to guide her. Tate came back into view, peeled off behind a shoe store, into the obscurity of a side alley. The officer didn't let up, avoided the mews, continued on, knowing she had a half-and-half chance of gaining ground on the guy if he emerged onto the main road, of at least pinning him between herself and Dennehy if he chose to double back. By then, her partner's inevitable—if wheezy—call for backup would be summoning more officers onto the monorail station. If Tate had any idea of what he had got himself into, he would be praying Chrissie caught up to him first.

She reached the exit to the mews before Tate, found he had tried a far stupider option—attempting to scale a fire exit staircase up the side of a low-rise apartment complex. It could have provided safe haven for a few minutes but there were scant few ways to get off the roof of a building. His feet, through the railings, stumbled up the concrete. She went for the short-cut: onto a dumpster, along the sill of an ancient bricked up window, pivoted easily up onto the lower ledge of the staircase. She followed him up two flights. He reached the fire exit door, discovered (of course) it could only be opened from the inside.

She said, "That's far enough."

The fugitive gave up pounding at the door, shifted back and forth between the railings like a rat in a microwave. One leg of his corduroys were ripped, dark with blood, had caught on something during his getaway.

"There's nowhere to go," she said. "Please, Thomas. Think of your son."

"I am!" he cried back, choking on ragged gulps of air. "I can't let them take me."

She edged forward, leaving the taze stick in its hoop, holding her hands spread out in front of her.

"I'm going to help you where I can, Tom. Is that what you prefer to be called? Tom?"

A metallic purr—the sky-eye descended from the rooftops, nosed in for a better view. They were both being observed.

"You can't help me," he said, hanging against the side, peering back at the drop.

"I can, but I need you to stop running and let me protect you. Will you do that for me?"

A shiver of recognition, a momentary easing of muscles, the hint of surrender. Then Thomas Tate, who had shown himself to be no disciple of smart choices, threw himself over the ledge, tried to swing himself down to the flight below.

The angle was awkward. One hand slid away. Chrissie was on him in a blink, slamming her body against the grating. She seized his wrist, stopped him from losing his grip altogether.

"Help me!" he pleaded. "I can't see! I'm falling!"

His eyes wet, knuckles fish-belly-white.

She reached his other arm through the railing, was able to guide him back to a hold on the bars. When she had purchase, she got up, curled a leg over the balustrade, caught the collar of his jacket, used every ounce of strength to hoist him up to her level.

Tate regained his volatile sense of preservation. He pushed his feet against the brickwork, tumbled over the railing, back onto the safety of the staircase.

He lay on his back, out of breath, made strange animal howls in between lunatic mutterings: "I'm sorry. I'm sorry. I'm sorry."

Chrissie sat slumped against the wall, ignored him, looked at the sky. Her hair had come loose. The weight of exhaustion spread through her muscles. But Thomas Tate was still alive. Thomas Tate Jr. still had a father. Maybe one day he would even get to see him again.

He was handcuffed for his own sake. She marched him back through the mews towards the station, told him to relax, to keep it together.

"Tieman!"

Dennehy, from nowhere, boots spattered with rainwater, wiping sweat from her brow with the back of her arm. The short run had taken it out of her. The freckles around her nose pulsed fiercely. She had Chrissie's cap in hand.

"Yas, qween!" Dennehy said. "You were *fierce*! You okay?"

The constable retrieved her hat, damp and streaked with an unidentified grey residue.

"Never been better," Chrissie said. "He didn't put up a fight. Let's get him back to the car and off the streets."

"See, this is what happens," Dennehy said, stepping in front of them. "We let them mingle amongst us and they always find a way to abuse their freedom."

"He gave himself up," Chrissie offered.

"Not what I saw."

12

Tate, lesson learned, kept his mouth shut.

"He knows he shouldn't have run," Chrissie said. "I don't think he'll be any more of a problem. How about we—"

Her partner jerked her knee into Tate's groin. He twisted double, chilled bones with the wail he let out. His face hit the ground as he went down. His hands, still locked behind him, did nothing to prevent another swift kick between his legs.

The thing inside Chrissie crumbled a little more. She said nothing, took a step back. Beat-downs weren't illegal in most cases. Not even uncommon. Some juries were known to be lenient on perpetrators— privs or otherwise—who'd been roughed up in custody, so not everyone was a fan. The unwritten rule: if you didn't take part, at least deny all knowledge of seeing anything. After all, building a civilised society from the ruins of disaster was a team effort. If you're not on one team, you'd damn well better accept you're on the other.

"You want a piece of this action, hun?" Dennehy said.

"Too tired, Sarge," Chrissie said, thankful to have a rational excuse. "I'll sit this one out."

Dennehy shrugged, unsheathed the taze stick. It thrummed to life in her hand.

Dennehy said, "If time in a re-education centre doesn't help this creeper understand how much of a cancer he is, maybe this will."

The stick went in hard, fried Tate's rib cage. His foetal frame juddered and writhed. White pain bugged his eyes. Cries fizzled into fits of gurgles. Sputum ran down his chin. Still the stick drove into him.

Again and again.

Again.

Dennehy's face a mask of gratification. Same look she would have on the playback. Unlike most other echoes, the sergeant often admitted to leaving her body-eye on when things got rough, liked watching it all back later on her netscreen with a cider in one hand and the other down the front of her jockeys—regulations against bringing footage home be damned.

Chrissie backed away, wandered out onto the road to let her partner get her rocks off in private. On the side of a building, she found one of the public-fund murals. The familiar image of Suarez-Adarsha watched over them, one fist raised in powerful defiance, windswept hair streaming around her irrepressible features. Its slogan, repeated verbatim from city to city throughout the land, stamped in gold block capitals.

TAG AND LIST 'EM. CRUSH THE CIS-TEM.

CHAPTER THREE

The prime ministerial car peeled onto Dillon Street, flanked at each end by armoured duplicates, making its way back to Westminster via an undisclosed route.

Prime Minister Taylor Tavistock *(trans female, pronouns she/her)* strained to see past the empty front seats through the tinted windscreen. The tunnel-vision of Victorian architecture loomed ahead. Autocabs drifted from one set of lights to the next. She loved these last-minute detours. Designed to protect her, but as much an opportunity to reflect—precious few moments to breathe, to take in the sights at street level before being flung back into the circus of politics.

An immense banner flapped above the limo as it passed beneath a thirty-storey office block. The ruling party's sigil; an enormous mesh drape lined with every colour—and every shade of colour—of the spectrum, cluttered with a galaxy of equally colourful geometric shapes that together looked incomprehensible to the untrained eye. The banners were manifest, wallpapering every city in the country. The building itself was crowned uniformly with the non-binarist glyph, merging male and female in wrought metal, designed to invoke pride and identity as much as to strengthen the region's wi-dev infrastructure. The arrangement was effective. The sight of it never ceased to send a tingle down the prime minister's spine.

"Worthwhile trip, Minister?"

Tavistock pulled away from the window, saw herself reflected in the aviator sunglasses of the person in the seat opposite. Despite her chief security officer being a mere ally, she had become a trusted companion. Tavistock welcomed small talk with her, as long as it was tactful, timed right—usually when she wasn't absorbed in her smartpalm or on a conference call.

"More than worthwhile, Hannah," she said, tagging on a smile infinitely more genuine than the stiff display of teeth she conjured for the netwire cameras that morning. "Those children were so eager, so happy to see me arrive at their school gates—it was darling. And their little faces, so alert to my speech. I almost forgot all the other shit I have to deal with today."

"I'm sure they'll take your words with them for the rest of their lives, ma'am."

"One hopes. There's no substitute for a strong role model at that age."

"Speaking from experience?"

Tavistock scratched her beard, remembering her maturing years. "Levine. McBride. Izzard. Just some of the leaders that fuelled my flame for politics. Without their example, I wouldn't be sitting here today."

"It was your destiny, Minister."

"Poppycock. It was my dedication."

"No one could ever question that, ma'am."

"Damn right they couldn't. And do you know?—I'd still do anything, anything at all to encourage the next generation to be as dedicated to the cause as I was. Pick up placards. Form a petition. Coordinate a book burning. Orchestrate a sustained campaign of intimidation against someone who disagrees with us. We must all do our part to help the Trans Equality Party continue to flourish for generations to come."

"You have a long time left in you, ma'am," Hannah said. "You're as brave and as fierce as ever."

"Aw, thanks, hun. But as the years pass, I find I have to remind myself of the enthusiasm I had in those informative days, have to remember what drove me to become the face of the party. It helps me draw strength. And we all need strength in this day and age, when those who dare to threaten our social values grow bolder, as you well know. How are we for time?"

"Twelve to fifteen minutes away, ma'am," the bodyguard said, a swift scan of her voxwatch. Her gaze rarely left the streets. The Inner Safe Zone was never really safe, every passer-by a potential insurgent. Especially this close to the election.

The driverless limo continued on through London's ISZ, the exclusive area spanning from Mayfair to Whitechapel, traversable in under thirty minutes by autobile, and under ten by monorail. Tavistock had herself commissioned the construction of the two-metre louvered steel hoarding around the ISZ perimeter—known as 'The Privet'—painted a pleasant forest green, piggy-backed with a ten-milliamp current. It boasted solar-charged videyes and decorative tines shaped like doe antlers south of the river, fleurs-de-lis to the north. Her own stylistic touch. Appearances were important. In the ISZ, the wares were boutique, the foods gourmet, the concept of exclusivity pushed to its limits.

Tavistock checked the notes on her smartpalm. Today's discussion at Parliament would hear proposals for even more public funding into London's ISZ and those of the other major cities. Ample resources were needed to support those who lived or worked within the boundary. A vital maintenance. The Inner Zones were the buttercream of urban living, solitaire diamonds protected from the unsegregated Outer Safe Zones beyond and, even further beyond, the unmentionable wasteland of the Heaths—or the 'Cistrict', as it was sometimes referred. The OSZ had its own protective boundary from the Heaths. Not as well guarded or as well designed as the Privet, the 'Fence' was a simple barbed-wire monstrosity—brutal, foreboding. Practical. At least, that was the idea.

The PM shook her head.

"Something wrong?" Hannah said.

Tavistock slumped. "The Fence. These intel reports of people finding their way out in the past few months. What do you make of it all—from a security perspective?"

"Personally speaking, I'd say good riddance to them. But if it's the system you're worried about, I'd say it works more than it doesn't. And it's always improving. Our sky-eyes patrolling the border are top of the line. We're rotating patrol teams at every e-gate. The videyes now have a range of thirty yards, clear as crystal."

"I would do anything to protect those children," Tavistock said, her stare locked on the streets sliding by. "I would die for them."

"Of course you would, Minister. You're so brave."

"Am I, Hannah? Sometimes I wonder."

"You mustn't. You only have to read the posts from your Xprez followers. They adore you because you're brave. *So* brave. And fierce."

"Not like you. You took part in operations in the Heaths once, didn't you? What was it like out there? Was it as terrible as they say?"

"Ma'am, if you're thinking of sending troops back in, I would advise against it," Hannah said. The girl was an honest-to-Goddess mind reader.

"But if the Fence ever fails, what choice will we have? I'm already getting calls for us to channel our funding instead towards a renewed ground campaign, to exterminate these rebels directly, like we used to. If we don't do *something*—"

"I can't blame them for suggesting it. Problem is, most of them have no idea of the dangers. They've not been told the stories. And for good reason."

Tavistock had heard a few. The idea of sending any of her adoring soldiers back into that situation made her chew her nails ragged. Still, her options were shrinking by the day.

Hannah said, "You must have faith in the resilience of our existing security systems, Minister. Maintaining our Safe Zone system is critical to future stability."

"What about all these incidents we've had since the summer? Reports of obscene graffiti popping up overnight, of banned books and transphobia left in public places. It's like the early days when the Big Reboot was getting underway. Tell me the reports are wrong. Tell me the radicals aren't still among us."

"A mere handful of troublemakers, by all accounts. The ministry will smoke them out soon enough."

"I just can't stand the thought of *them* coming near us. I mean, look at that over there—any one of those labourers could be a terrorist hiding in plain sight."

The limo circumnavigated a construction lot. A group of CisHet males there, identified by the purple and blue armbands mandatory for those living inside the Safe Zones. They filed into a trench, hoisting heavy beams and tool boxes—men admitted on day-pass work permits so their specialist skills could be put to where they were needed. They remained under constant surveillance. Their hi-vis jackets marked them out like bell peppers in a vegetable aisle, their overalls blotted with cement and mastic. They kept their eyes averted from the roads. Courtesy screens on pop-up frames were being erected around them to avoid any offense to onlookers.

"A necessary inconvenience," Hannah said. "They'll have gone through rigorous checks, believe me."

Tavistock could remember the Georgian building that had once stood on the lot. In recent years, London's skyline had been filled with dust clouds and high-arm excavators, before reblooming into the TEP's grand vision of transcentric urban beauty. Swathes of low-rise buildings had been converted into skyscrapers, capped with bawdy, bulbous extensions to the upper floors, penetrating the sky. Other high-rise buildings had been torn down and replaced with plazas and yonic single-storeys adorned with seashell roofs, triangular porticos, communal ponds. According to regulations, all of them displayed the mandated rainbow flag at all times, turning the cities into giant kaleidoscopes, hubs of sensory psychedelia.

Not only had buildings been rebuilt, many had been repurposed. To her left, Tavistock glimpsed the mammorous dome of Ru Paul's Cathedral, its colossal size marking out the country's largest Queer Wiccan house of worship. Following the ban on patriarchal religions, the change of its name had accompanied a full overhaul of symbolism, the Christian motif replaced with pentacles and moon phases. Mosaic depictions of prophets and saints had been smashed into indistinct fragments, updated with non-secular portrayals of the real revolutionaries and sufferers—Elliot Page, Munroe Bergdorf, Chaz Bono, the Wachowski Sisters. In similar fashion, the Palace of Westminster, Tower Bridge and many other landmarks had survived the rough-edged, choking sands of time by being refashioned to serve as ideological conquests—as if the stuffy old figures of yesteryear had been redressed in ball gowns, pearl earrings and maquillage.

Aside a concrete mixer, a team of non-binary men and women studied roll-out documents across a fold-out table. They wore glitter hardhats, safety jackets tailored to fit over their corsets and catsuits.

One of them called out to the labourers with a clap of hands, directed them to speed things up. Supervisors hemmed and hurried the workers with schoolmistress enthusiasm. The workers proceeded, robotic, downcast. They disappeared behind the screens. The light drizzle of traffic flowed on.

"I want to believe you, Hannah, I do," the PM said. "I just don't think we've gone far enough. Let's be honest—if I feel unsafe at times, then scores of other trans people probably do, too. That's unacceptable."

"Only you can know for sure, ma'am."

Less than an hour later, Big Beth—still housed atop one of the city's surviving towers—struck twelve. Tavistock stood with the rest of the elect for the weekly rigmarole of *Prime Minister's Conversations*.

CHAPTER FOUR

"Order!"

The speaker's singsong voice carried through the chamber. Since the refurbishment—the removal of the stolid, olive benches, the staining of the oak panels in multicolour—the acoustics of the great room had reached magnificent proportions, each sound ringing out an echo like a mystic chant. Before the last incantation died away, every MP sat or reclined on an animal-print cushion or bean bag, settled in for the half-hour of what was, for some, the highlight of their week.

The six-hundred and fifty members of parliament came in all shapes and sizes, though most of these shapes were round, most of the sizes extra-large. Almost all sported dyed hair—electric blue, candy floss pink, atomic orange—the majority donning spectacles with thick black frames, corrective lenses optional, something of an unspoken uniform these days for civilians within the ISZ.

"Chloe Maxwell!" the speaker of the house shouted, summoning the first question.

The TEP MP for Lichfield (*pyramidgender demiriverqueer, they/them*) stood, peered down at their notes through their oversized glasses. "Thank you, Mx Speaker. Unemployment for non-binary people has fallen to one percent, with over five thousand new apprenticeships introduced at the start of the year doing well. I am holding my third job fair next week with twenty-five companies taking part. Would my right and honourable friend agree with me that we've made a good start but we must not be complacent, rather ensure we continue to give trans and genderqueer people every opportunity to take up any career they desire, regardless of cost, training or ability?"

"*Yas, quing! Yas, quing!*" The ruling side of the chamber filled with the clamour, only subsiding when the PM raised her hand.

"I very much agree with my honourable friend," Tavistock said, coming to the Table of the House. "Complacency is the worst kind of flaw and this party will continue to push new measures on companies of all sizes to give the community the best start. Our mandate for one-hundred percent non-binary management has set a bold and powerful example, but we will also be augmenting this mandate by the end of the year with the abolition of job interviews and performance reviews, so the real decision makers of this country need not be slowed towards their path to leadership."

"*Yas, qween! Slay, qween!*"

"Mary Gallard!" the speaker called.

The cheers faded. Only a handful of MPs welcomed the opposition leader to the floor. Mary Gallard *(omnigender spongesexual, she/her)*, leader of the Diversity and Inclusion Party (DIP) lifted herself to her feet. She had no notes. She paused an additional few seconds, enough for all eyes to turn her way, for the faint sniggering to subside.

"It cannot have escaped the attention of those present that in the past few months an increasing number of privs have defected to the Outer Zone. They take with them vital skills and knowledge our society needs, now more than ever."

Unease rippled through the chamber. The camera operators, broadcasting the session on a ten second delay, stiffened, fired anxious glances at each other. The censors stationed beside them puffed their chests, readied themselves to order the cut to the smartnet broadcast.

Gallard went on, "It is this part's belief that in the spirit of diversity and inclusion, we begin moving towards a full spectrum acceptance of all genders and orientations, *including* that of the heterosexual cisgender, in order to help us restore—"

A deafening wail burst from the only chair in the room—a giltwood bergère, specially crafted, sat atop a plinth—the speaker of the house mashing her airhorn. Over five-hundred MPs screamed in agreement with the objection.

"Order!" the speaker demanded, releasing the nozzle. "Mx Gallard, you have been warned about such bellicose sentiments. I apologise on behalf of the House for anyone who may have been offended by what they heard and insist we resume proceedings in a more mature manner. This is after all meant to be a safe environment for discussion."

The noise picked up again, strong this time but comprised of the same recycled phrases.

"Clap her back!"

"How dare she?"

"Internalised transphobia!"

"TERF enabler!"

Gallard sank back into her cushion, bit her tongue.

Tavistock gave her a knowing smile from across the floor. *Know your place, bitch.*

To her right, the minister for equality nodded approvingly.

"Joanne Collins!"

The TEP representative for Barrow and Furness *(saucepansexual lesbian-adjacent queer, he/him)* sat up on his beanbag and shifted his knees to his chest. "Thank you, Speaker. According to studies, rates of teen suicide are at an all-time high among the trans and genderqueer community, no doubt driven by their lack of acceptance within the oppressive Cis-tem. Will my right honourable friend support the demands of the public by significantly increasing funds and access for hormone blockers and gender affirmation therapies for young people?"

"Yas, king! Yas, king! Yasss, king!"

Tavistock waited for the cheers to die down. This was a serious topic, deserving of solemn debate. "From someone who has seen many of our youngest and brightest lost to this needless pandemic—and indeed from someone who cares so passionately about our youth—it personally breaks my heart that a fraction of health care funding should be wasted on anything other than this cause. In fact, should the TEP have its way, it is my plan, and that of the health minister, to make those very changes just as our friends in Canada, Sweden and the United States have rightly done."

Gallard sprang back to the Table, getting ahead of another wave of applause before it could pick up.

"But can't the prime minister admit the driving cause of these statistics is, at best, inconclusive? The diminishing medical progress in this country already owes much to funding being diverted to these causes, not to mention the laws that suppress the opportunities for cisgender people to pursue—even teach—medical sciences?"

Discomfort simmered once more, but Gallard pressed on, speaking rapidly.

"We all know the health service is collapsing under its own weight, a reality caused by the very decisions the TEP has made. Counter-productive tax rates. Ludicrously generous benefits for any non-binarist who doesn't want to work. A refusal to discourage unhealthy eating..."

Protests blistered from the benches. Tavistock boiled.

"...Not to mention the eye-watering budget being allocated to secretive gender affirmation research projects the TEP refuses to even discuss let alone explain—"

The censors pulled the plug. Backbenchers clamped their hands over their ears, began to scream.

"Internalised transphobia! Internalised transphobia!"

Tavistock's eyes flared at the speaker. The airhorn blitzed the chamber, a long blare reverberating into the rafters.

"Order! Order! That is deeply problematic talk, Mx Gallard!" the speaker said. "We do not identify as a country of diminishing progress. Those are dead-facts and you are mis-truthing our reality. I will not warn you again. You will curtail your remarks or face yet another suspension. And we're getting off topic. I will reiterate for the benefit of our esteemed colleagues that such hostile opinions directed towards our progressive policies are bordering on right-wing extremism. They are not permitted within this chamber. They are not permitted anywhere in the ISZ. This is not the dark ages. Let's show the respect to each other we all deserve."

Gallard shook her head, prickled.

The equality minister leaned into Tavistock's ear. "How *dare* she?"

CHAPTER FIVE

The toes of his shoes squeaked all the way from the end of the corridor to his cell door—a small clue he wasn't simply a ghost floating through the halls. His head lolled forward. The polished floor passed smoothly beneath him.

The other thing that told him he hadn't been corpsed in the orientation room was the pain. Between the unforgiving squeeze of their hands beneath his armpits, the sensation of bruised muscle radiating across multiple parts of his body, he still had a crackle in his lungs as he breathed—a reminder of the infection fought off in previous weeks. The healing had been slow, the staff too reluctant to provide him with antibiotics in the early stages of his illness. There was a waiting period, they said, and he was far from the top. Only when the infection had begun to turn into pneumonia had they relented. Deaths occasionally happened in the Cooler, but most of the guards didn't want the hassle of paperwork. Not that he had anyone to miss him. No family to demand an investigation. No courts to approve an enquiry.

The guards stopped at the door long enough for him to witness a bead of blood slide along a trail of saliva from his mouth to the floor. It pooled in a perfect circle. He wouldn't have put it past them to have pulled back in unison, used his head as a battering ram to open his cell. The keycard panel chirruped, the steel rolled back, the jailors grunted. Next thing he knew, he was airborne and turning. The hard mattress of his bunk groaned as he landed, thumped the wind from his chest. The steel banged again. The sound of boot steps faded away.

"Jake."

The voice ebbed into his skull like it was beneath water. Fingers groped his ears, dug deep into the canals, pried the balls of cotton he had fashioned into plugs before his daily behavioural class. The pressure in his head began to release.

"Jake."

The voice, sharper now, cutting through the miasma.

"Looks like they gave yas a pretty generous farewell. Listen, y'only need to be able to walk in a straight line by the afternoon and you'll be a free man again. More or less. Can't say I won't miss ya, mate."

Jake's lips moved, attempted a word. He coughed to free up some space, cringed as the lungs fizzled again. "My…lucky day."

"Ya lip is split, but otherwise y'ain't lookin' too much worse on the outside. As ugly as evah."

"Alfie?"

"Yes, mate?"

"I won't miss you at all."

Jake's cellmate grinned. For a moment, his teeth shone like the top of his shaved pate. He pressed a paper towel to Jake's mouth. "Sit up. I saved yas a last meal. May taste as bad as it looks but 'least they make this shit with *some* nutritional value. Eat up. It'll help yas get ya strength back."

Alfie helped Jake push his back up against the wall, wedged the paper-thin pillow behind his head. Jake scanned the room, tried to shake off the effects of the taze sticks, the swift slaps he'd taken to the head, the swifter kicks to the rest of him. The ersatz edibles in the tray had the appearance of mounds of ground grey mince. A year of eating this fermentation farm slop had him dreaming of dancing rotisserie chickens and green beans bathed in butter, had him waking up some nights salivating.

Still, he ate. The first mouthful had a hint of iron. It didn't go down without a struggle.

Alfie returned to his bunk. "What d'ya plan to do first?"

"Find myself a steak," Jake said. "Not one ferm-farmed in a microbe-brewery or made out of soybeans or ersatz fruit, either. A real one. One that used to walk, shit and moo. One of the magazines going around the contraband pipes had a feature on a steakhouse down near Regent's Park where they still sell real meat. Thought I'd pay it a visit."

His cellmate laughed quietly, not wanting to attract the guards again. "This magazine—was it written on papyrus?"

The mandatory year service in a privileged youth institute took the fun out of most people but Jake's cellmate had somehow held on to his sense of humour, a fact that had helped them both retain their sanity in the face of daily propaganda sessions. *Behavioural orientation*, the government called it. A way to ensure newly adult CisHets could be dealt with early—and a warning to anyone who would dare to test the equality ministry. Still, compared to the re-education centres, the Cooler was said to be a doddle.

"Forget the steak," said Alfie. "In fact, forget imagining London like the way you've read about it in ya bootleg books and mags. World ain't like that no more. First thing ya should do is find a vocation centre and get yerself a job. Won't be fun, but take it fr'me, you'll need to earn some fast scratch. There's the Cis Tax to think about and the Reparations Tax. Not to mention the rate of hyper-inflation these days…"

Jake said, "They'll give me my final inmate earnings on the way out. Reckon I have a day or two of spending credit in that before I have to join the rest of the working horde. Was thinking of digging my toes in some grass, getting some fresh air."

For the last twelve months, he had been building cabinets and tutoring other inmates on how to read and write. Honest work for low wage that mostly went back into buying toothpaste and tea bags. But over that time, he had managed to save a little, maybe even enough to have a few days of downtime.

"Christ, al'mighty, son," Alfie said. "Ya looked out a windah lately?"

This time they both laughed. Of course he hadn't. Neither had Alfie. Neither had anyone else locked up in the facility. Ultraviolet ceiling lights were the closest they had to sunlight since their monthly group march around the courtyard.

Alfie said, "Weather bulletins aren't exactly forecasting blue skies and rainbows."

"I don't care, man. Rain is fine. Snow is fine. I'd go jogging in a hurricane so long as I get out of this grot hole."

Jake put his tray aside, leaned back in the bunk, thought about red meat, a warm bed, whether he would ever see the sea again because there was nothing like seeing the sea after a long time to remind you the world was big and not all bad.

"The women out there," Alfie said, serious. "Don't go near 'em. You'll be tempted to look, probably more. Don't."

"Sure. You're a seasoned old dog. A real wise man of the world."

"No jokes, Jakey. One wrong move, one wrong word, and you'll be in a worse place than this."

"I'm fresh out of getting my organs rearranged by a couple of them. I'm not eager to meet another woman anytime soon."

"Ain't talkin' about the ones roamin' these halls. I mean real ones. Biologically natural ones." He traced an hourglass with his hands. "Ones 'at smell good and sound like 'eaven. Ones who might even give ya a moment of attention—though, personally, I wouldn't know why any of 'em would."

Jake tried to remember what they sounded like, what they smelled like. All the 'Respect' classes in the orientation room hadn't been able to stop him from thinking about biologically-born women in ways he knew he could never verbalise, never admit, let alone act upon.

"Don't worry about me," Jake said. "I've got more important things to sort out when I'm out."

"Your 'rents?"

Jake nodded.

Alfie sighed, said, "I've not wanted to be the one to get ya hopes down, but you should 'ear it from someone—it'll be a miracle if ya find 'em. A lot could'a happened in over a year."

"They'll be in one of the re-education centres. Narrows it down a bit."

"What, think ya can walk coolly up to a data point 'n download that information?"

Alfie was right. He knew it wouldn't be easy. But even to know they were alive would be better than not knowing anything. And on the off-chance they were free—as free as anyone could be who had defied the state in the way they had—would they still be looking for him, too?

Jake said, "Have to try."

Alfie said, "Then take my advice and start earning money. You won't get nowhere in the city with empty pockets."

"Rumours are there are ways to get out of the city, that it's easier than people think."

Alfie looked at the door, his ears tuning, his voice dropping to a whisper. "I've heard 'em. Maybe they're right. So what?"

"So maybe I could get back to the New Forest, see if anything survived of the old place. If some of the other settlers went back, maybe they've arranged better defences or something. Maybe someone there might know where the authorities took them."

"Ya dreamin', son. Been reading too many a'them bootleg novels a'yours."

Patience. He knew of its value. His parents had taught him from an early age, as they'd taught him so many of life's lessons. Everyone these days seemed so desperate to be heard, even when they had nothing to say. While they talked, he would stay quiet. Stay still. Observe. Give his mind the space to spread out. In some ways, he had been trained for life in the Cooler. It was only when he was older that he began to put his opinion forward, only when he felt a little more confident in knowing where he was coming from. And only then, when his opinion counted less than a tinker's curse.

Jake considered what his parents would expect of him now. He had no memory of them telling him to pursue anything in particular, only that they had been intent on giving him the tools to figure it out for himself. Had that been how they were raised? Or had they both been subjected to controls and pressures so restrictive they had vowed to never force their own child down a prescribed path? Had he been a principle personified or merely a test subject?

An intellect, his father had once said, provides the light towards truth, even in the darkest hour. And courage will allow you to follow that light no matter how faint. With those two qualities, you'd never need a damn thing else. His mother had tutted from her corner in the living room, returning her bookmark to its pages—Don't tell him that. It's simplistic. Truth isn't simple.

As a boy, he had no idea what that meant, was too afraid to ask. Even now it didn't make sense to him. Surely there was nothing more simple than the truth.

CHAPTER SIX

"Do you understand now? Do you see what she's doing?"

Zoe Urwin, Britannia's minister for equality *(neurodivergent agender fudgequeer, pronouns zie/zer)*, placed the hunting crop across the great oak desk, allowed zer cherry red nails to trace the length of the fibreglass. Amid crimson silk and goldleaf, zer presence in the room looked as commonplace as an ox in an opera house.

Even after all these years, Tavistock found her colleague's appearance unnerving. The minister had been assigned female at birth but was now entirely unidentifiable in appearance. Hair the same colour as the lip gloss—velvet purple—shaved around the back, coifed on top in a pompadour. Black-rimmed glasses in front of piggish green eyes. Brows pencilled three shades too dark, hovering above a squashed nose. Zoe's brows and patience were the only things about zer that could be described as thin. Zer bulbous frame strained the buttons of a waistcoat, a surfeit of flab souffléd over the belt of zer trousers. With zer shirtsleeves rolled up, zie displayed a hotchpotch of tattoos—an incest of rockabilly pin-ups girls and dolphins. Zer flesh was pasty, zer breath perpetually stale. Yet with blunt resolve and a legendary unwillingness to compromise, zie had served for years as the head of the country's security forces, now under the governance of the Ministry of Equality. Regardless of zer style, Tavistock appreciated the single-mindedness Zoe had brought to the role, the fear zer leadership instilled across all citizens and non-citizens alike.

Tavistock, opposite, folded herself into the high-back armchair, let her power posture melt away. She worried the lines in her forehead were becoming permanent features, ran her fingers over the bridge of her nose in an effort to smooth them over.

"Of course I see it," said Tavistock. "The DIP is becoming a liability. We were meant to have an understanding."

"A lot has happened in the past decade, Minister. Loyalties change. New frontbenchers are proving harder to investigate."

"It was a mistake. Changing the law to prevent members of parliament from being deplatformed. I'm beginning to think we need to revert back."

"Ill-advised. Aside from the risk of leaving ourselves vulnerable, it would be hard to spin that decision to appear as anything but politically motivated. The public need to at least believe in our democracy. Though I do agree something must be done. We can't change the past, but we can control what comes next."

To avoid prying eyes, they kept their meetings away from Downing Street, had instead taken to early afternoon tea at Urwin's office in the building of the Equality Office, twenty paces across the road. Formerly the Foreign and Commonwealth Office—before the Commonwealth was disbanded and most foreign diplomats were indefinitely recalled—the office had a much better view over Horse Guards Road and Activist Park beyond. The vista, even on a day as miserable as this, was unbeatable at reducing stress levels. The building retained its colonial décor, which, despite being a tad problematic, had at least dispensed with the portraits and busts of yesteryear tyrants. In their place were specially created busts of prominent non-binary figures, from Chevalier d'Eon to Coccinelle, beside paintings of the revolution and framed news clippings of the Big Reboot.

Urwin seemed to prefer meetings here. The walls were vetted. Zer personal staff were always to hand. Though zie seemed less relaxed today. Zie fingered the riding crop, that silly accessory zie was never seen without. Normally tucked under zer arm, zie would mimic the pose seen in pictures of old world field marshals. Now the tongue of the crop drummed against the desk's leather surface, emphasising zer impatience.

"It doesn't matter how much we try, she keeps pushing and pushing," Urwin said. "She's not going to stop, Minister. Our parliamentary majority may be too vast for her words to have meaning within these walls, but out there," zie nodded to the window, "they are knotweed. The more we shut this binarist-sympathiser down, the more she's appearing with her publicists, getting her face on the netwires, commenting on things she clearly knows nothing about. Making

31

criticisms of our core values, which is already problematic, if not down-right phobic. She's a living dog-whistle for binary extremists."

"I know," Tavistock replied, trying to stop the irritation from slipping into her voice. "Have you considered my suggestion of promoting a backbencher?"

Urwin's eyes rolled. "I recall you had a vague notion of creating some sort of...super whip? Was that what you called it?"

"One of our most loyal and trusted—someone from the Tribe. Denise, maybe. Or Ezra. They have huge influence over the party. They'd be more than willing to report anyone suspected of wavering—"

"You think that's going to be enough?" Urwin squeezed the crop. "Minister, may I remind you—with respect—we ourselves were the minority once. We started it all with one seat. One. The Diversity and Inclusion Party still has more than fifty. That's not insignificant. The public are forgetting why they elected us to govern in the first place. They're forgetting how bad things were. Silencing this imbecile and her outdated ideas with airhorns once a week is not going to slow her down or stop her from planting her seeds of hate."

Tavistock allowed a finger to drift to her lip, stopped at the last moment from letting it go any further. Chewed nails were not a good look on the leader of the country. The opposition might attempt to use it to undermine her, to somehow claim it as proof she wasn't as strong as she made herself out to be.

The equality minister must have perceived her nerves, could spot most of the tells in a person's body language.

"Dominic!" Urwin said. "The nibbles."

Urwin's personal assistant *(cisgender bisexual crossdresser, he/him)* approached with a tiered tray of bite-sized sandwiches. Salmon, cream cheese, watercress, sans crust. Dominic Kimmel, the only cis ally allowed in the office, headed a staff of four other allies—the only cisgender people permitted in the building. They of course kept within the varlets' quarters, mostly out of sight, but their presence alone was unusual in the ISZ, let alone in government headquarters. After all, the whole point of the Safe Zone system was that no one had to be in the vicinity of privs at all. Yet Urwin commanded special honours in zer role. It was said all zer house staff, those undertaking menial upkeep duties, were comprised of cis males—something from which zie took perverse satisfaction.

Tavistock was conscious of how she tensed up whenever Dominic appeared, wondered if Urwin noticed, perhaps even secretly enjoyed the discomfort he and his like caused her and other guests.

Dominic placed the tray on the desk, fetched the tea, poured equal measures of steaming Lady Grey into a pair of matching Meissen porcelain cups. Without expecting thanks, he retreated to his place by the sideboard, smoothed the front of his skirt, did his upmost to blend into the wall until further instruction.

"At least the polls are strong," Tavistock said, leaning in for her cup. "Even with three months to go, there's no way we could lose so much ground. Even if a third of those backing the TEP are lying about their allegiance."

"Oh, we'll win the election." Urwin took the chain of zer tea strainer, bobbed it up and down as if drowning a silver mouse. Zie reached out with the other hand, pinched two of the sandwiches in one go. "But what then? What about the next one? Or the one after that? The DIP manifesto is stoking the fire of antisocial thinking. The security breaches we've seen these past few months—these outrageous acts of binarist agitation—are happening because the savages suspect weakness within our ranks. Like flies on decay, they're encouraged by the rot of division. If we don't act now, the next generation will find themselves living in a world not unlike the one that existed years ago. Afraid to go out at night. Afraid to trust anyone. Constantly at risk of violation. The freedoms we are building for them today will be eroded." Zie stabbed at the air with melting bread. "If binarists are a cancer, Minister, Gallard is an aneurysm—coming out of nowhere to destroy us while our attention is focused on another battle. The enemy within is always the most lethal."

Pudgy fingers shoved the sandwiches into zer mouth all at once, distending zer cheeks further. Zie munched, dribbled.

Tavistock said, "Has anything new come up from the investigation? The background checks?"

The prime minister was still looking at all angles. She knew she would be expected to ask questions, even if she didn't know what the answers meant.

"Dominic." Urwin snapped zer fingers. "Be a good boy and show the prime minister through the dossier."

"Yes, ma'am-sir."

The varlet ordered the wall-mounted netscreen on, revealed the files already loaded into the console. He waved his hand, swiped through them, pulled up an assortment of examples. There was a time when a Grimsby accent would have been thought of as rugged, but through Dominic, it took on a meek, sycophantic tone, and oozed with such deference it made even Urwin cringe on occasion.

"In short," he said, "we could find nothing of sufficient severity in any of Gallard's history that may disqualify her from a ministerial position. A minor vandalism during her teenage years committed at an end-of-year party didn't end with any charge. A mild altercation with a waitress several blue moons ago, but nothing uncommon about that. And a second cousin, once-removed, suspected of defecting to the Heaths..." The prime minister looked up at him hopefully. "But each hadn't seen t'other in a good while. It would be a hard sell to issue a denunciation on that one without it seeming a stretch. Overall, I'm afraid she appears to be squeaky clean, Minister. Even releasing these infractions to the press would probably do more damage than good given how easily they could be deflected."

Tavistock's lines deepened. She stared at the screen, tried to find something the team may have missed. "Can't be possible. Everyone has secrets they don't want the world to know. What about smartnet history? Surely there's something there."

Dominic adjusted his square frames. "I wish I could tell you that were true, Minister. However, unless she's using a particularly strong encryption, there's nothing there. A post on Xprez a few years ago about her fitness regime—we considered trying to link that to fatphobia. Anyroad, her wording was too careful. It would be a tenuous criticism at best."

"What about baiting her? I thought your honeypots were putting something like that in the works."

"I'm sorry, Minister. She wouldn't go for any of it. She's spongesexual."

"I'm not familiar with that one."

"Means she doesn't engage in sexual activity herself but enjoys soaking up the idea of it from others nearby."

Tavistock tutted. "What other tactics have you taken?"

"We tried getting her to sign up to support a charity on the problematic list. We tried getting her to make a critical comment about some non-binary celebrity or another. A dozen other things that could have destroyed her reputation for good. Nothing took."

"How about making some bloody thing up? Isn't that what you normally do?" Tavistock threw her hands up in frustration. The teacup shuddered on the armrest.

Urwin waved Dominic away with a flick of the wrist, let him shutdown the netscreen, return to his place against the wall.

"These are games," the equality minister said. "Tricks and tales won't solve our problem. A stronger medicine is required. Imagine if today's debate was the last one to ever entertain her toxic opinions."

"If it's even a possibility, Zoe, I'm all ears."

Urwin slid a drawer open, retrieved a smartpalm, set it down with a ceremonious flourish. No different from any other. Urwin looked at the PM, said nothing.

"What's that?" Tavistock asked, giving in to her curiosity.

"This?" Urwin ran a finger over the touchscreen. "This, Minister, is merely one of the latest novels produced by the Equality Ministry. A political thriller. Entirely fictional but also highly enjoyable, if I do say so myself. Would you like to hear the plot?"

Tavistock sensed the change in the air. "Go on."

"It tells the story of a conspiracy. One to silence an evil and bigoted political figure. It goes into a great level of detail about the mechanics of it all, from the method of execution to the many considerations that the daring conspirators must take to see their plan through successfully. But succeed they must. For if they do—and I shan't spoil the ending for you—they will be able to ensure the sanctity and direction of their civilisation for centuries to come."

The silence lingered. The smartpalm lay between them, inanimate and dangerous.

"A novel?"

"Any similarities to living people or places is purely a coincidence."

"Is this novel likely to be published?"

"Not on any large scale, Minister. Perhaps only for a handful of people who ask for a personal copy. At present, this is the only one in existence. The election trail can be boring at times. I thought you might like to borrow some light reading to help pass those long sky-trips."

Before Tavistock could respond, Urwin slid the pad in front of her. The PM couldn't stop herself reaching for it. Its surface was warm. She pressed the screen. The title of the book appeared in block font.

"*Cockleshells?*" Tavistock asked.

"You'll understand if you read it," the EQM said, her shoulders shaking. "The main antagonist is quite the *contrary Mary.*"

A snort came from Dominic's direction, his amusement snuffed by a scornful look from his boss.

"By the way, Minister," Urwin said. "You look really fierce today."

"Thanks, Zoe. You too."

"And badass, qween."

"*You're* badass."

"So you'll read it?"

Tavistock turned the smartpalm in her hands, avoided eye contact, looked at the walls. The oil painting above the fireplace bore a depiction of the nation's most popular non-binary icon.

Maria Suarez-Adarsha.

Not just one of the early party members but an activist and orator. Outrageously beautiful. Beautifully outrageous. The painting captured the spirit of the moment amid her attempted assassination of the Conservative prime minister on the steps of Trafalgar Square, almost twenty years to the day. The event sealing her position as the face of the next step in human civilisation. Though the hit failed and saw the would-be killer imprisoned, the act divided the nation. Tavistock was proud that one of the TEP's first actions in power had been to overturn the conviction, providing a full pardon. Doing so meant Suarez-Adarsha became their Guevara. Their Lenin. Their Malcolm X. Even now, long after her self-imposed isolation had begun, she was everywhere. Plastered on the walls. Echoed across the netwaves. As role models go, it would be a tough ask for anyone to match her status.

Not that she wouldn't try.

Tavistock knew she had inherited a huge responsibility. To allow society to slide back into its old ways would not only be a national disaster but a personal one.

And yet, if she wasn't strong enough, it could happen.

"Yes, Zoe. I'll read it."

CHAPTER SEVEN

The hour came. Jake shaved with a disposable.

"Lucky bastard."

"Alfie, if anyone can stick another month of this out, it's you," Jake said. "Get in touch when you're on the other side."

"I will. Provided you 'aven't gone and got yerself into trouble."

Jake left Alfie his economy shower gel, his dominoes, his collection of contraband paperbacks he kept concealed behind a tile in the shower room, all of which made his friend smile more than Jake had ever seen in a year of sharing the same cell.

When the bang at the door came, the voice behind the food slot said, "Brody. Merrick. Prepare to exit."

"Christ, what they want with me now?" Alfie said.

They turned, put their hands against the wall. The door swung. The guards stepped in.

"Brody, you're due at the seg-gate for processing," they heard the warden say. "Merrick, you're to report to medical immediately, no questions."

The warden cuffed Jake for the last time. He exchanged the briefest of nods with his cellmate before they spun him, shoved him into the corridor, walked him along the length of Row J.

The place reeked of sickly orange-scented disinfectant and polish. Jake listened to the echo of doors clanging shut throughout the far-reaching halls of the complex, of distant conversations through the concrete blocks where the rats had carved out their own tunnel system. Spotless on the outside, rotten deep down. They descended through three flights, followed the gleaming floor, rubber soles squeaking with each step.

At the seg-gate, two more androgynous officers were waiting to take over. They were heavy-set, had scraped back hair, ill-fitting uniforms. They looked like they wanted Jake to think they were tough. He recognised one of them as having cuffed and tazed him in his first month at the Cooler, had fractured one of his ribs for asking for an extra blanket.

The warden signed him over, told her colleagues to make sure he got processed out. She said it in a threatening way, as if discussing a whitehead she wanted popped. The barred door rolled back. Jake went through.

The guards dug their fingers into each elbow, marched him to the exit, jostled him like an impertinent child. At the end of the corridor, they shoved him into a small room that held nothing but a concrete bench and a carpet. He was told to change out of his jumpsuit, bang on the door when he was done. A plastic bag left on the bench contained the clothes he had worn when he had first arrived. Months of push-ups, crunches and unappetising food had streamlined him. The jeans were a little looser around the waist, the sleeves of his vintage motorcycle t-shirt a little tighter.

When he was ready, he was ordered to go to the checkout desk. The officer in the booth—a trans male—picked crisps out of a family pack, watched a small netscreen. He didn't notice Jake arrive. Jake hadn't seen a smartnet broadcast in a good while so he leaned up against the window, watched along with his jailer. It showed a live US courtroom trial. The defendant, a decent looking bloke, consulting with his team as one of the lawyers cross-examined a witness. The rolling ticker described the 'damning evidence' revealed to the jury. A triangle at the top corner of the screen discouraged the squeamish in yellow letters— *Content Warning!*

The warden eventually realised Jake was there. He eyed him contemptuously through the divide, rolled his chair towards the counter, blocked Jake's view of the screen. He licked her fingers, pulled up Jake's record on the system.

"Brody, Jacob S. Your year of mandatory sentencing required by the Social Reform Act of 2036 is hereby complete. Sign and date at the bottom."

A form was shoved across the counter. The Declaration of Civility, a document consisting of an admission of remorse for being of the 'privileged identity', a legally binding oath to live within the laws of civilised society lest he be subject to penalty as determined appropriate by the state. Jake didn't have to read it. Everyone signed at the end of their cooling or they went straight back inside. If they refused again, they were shipped out to somewhere much worse. Take it or leave it.

Jake autographed the paper. He was instructed to look directly at the pinhole videye on the booth. It flashed once, turned his vision to stars. They already had his fingerprints, earprints and eyeprints on file from his first day. His hair had grown out since and he guessed he looked more than his nineteen years by now.

The warden slid a tub through the partition, read off the inventory: "One leather wallet. One debit chip—balance of sixty thousand Britcoins, including custodial earnings. One state-issued voxwatch. One leather belt."

Jake filled the pockets of his jacket, put the belt on, an extra notch up. The voxwatch was cheap and basic, but it felt okay on his wrist. The rest of his things—few as they were—were still in a storage lockup. He would send a request for them as soon as he found somewhere to house them.

"Your Ally Pass," the warden said, digitally stamping the card, running it through the scanner. "As long as you commit to loyalty to the non-binary community and maintain a clean record, you are from this day forth deemed a privileged citizen and are permitted to live and work within any Outer Safe Zone within the Union of Britannia. It does not permit you to go anywhere else without expressed permission of the state. Consider yourself lucky. Carry it with you at all times and produce it whenever you're asked. Understand?"

Jake said he did. The liquid crystal display made him look oafish, washed out.

"And wear this visibly at all times in public." She flung a purple and blue armband onto the counter. "*All times.*"

Jake duly pulled the material over his sleeve.

"Well, what're you standing around for?" the warden asked him, a mouthful of vinegar. "Exit's that way. Go and behave yourself."

The warden called Jake a bad word under his breath, turned back to the screen.

Jake said, "How do I get into town?"

"You tell me." A snort, not bothering to waste another glance his way.

Jake fiddled with the voxwatch. The facility's signal jammer was killing the reception and—like eighty-three per cent of the population—he had no smartnet access.

Jake went over to the reception area. A framed poster of Maria Suarez-Adarsha hung on the wall by the front door, depicting her at the steps of the National Gallery from where she had made her famous speech, a rainbow flag clutched in her fist. A preacher of sorts, but no saint, that was for sure. Notwithstanding her violent methods, that activist was one of the reasons he'd just lost two years of his life.

A few yards away, he found an old-fashioned voxchat box. It didn't take credit, but did offer a free line to the local autocab office. He pressed the dial-out symbol, told the automated operator where he wanted to go, got told it would be along in ten, got told it would cost him three hundred Britcoin, and disconnected. The taxi service probably only stayed in business thanks to inmates leaving the facility with no one to pick them up.

As he waited at the box, he could feel the two guards at the exit booth looking him over. He took all he could of that for no more than a minute, approached them, presented his pass. They buzzed him through, disdain so palpable he felt it pushing him through the last security gate.

The gate boomed closed behind him. A thick mist clung to the treetops. A drizzle in the air, the kind of day his mother used to call a *soft day*—a poetic term for horrid weather. Rain you could barely see, dancing on the breeze, soaking you through without you even knowing.

It was fine. He was out. He could look for them now. He could find them.

He threw his hood up, went down the path to where the lawns ended, where the main road ran wet and empty.

CHAPTER EIGHT

The prime minister thanked Zoe for the tea and left, smartpalm in hand, her staff impatient to whisk her away to her next appointment. A strange sort of quiet came over the room, as if its remaining occupants were listening to music only they could hear.

Zoe fished out the vaparillo from her waistcoat, powered up the filter, took three short puffs, let the vapour roll, let the heady rush of chemicals fill zer head.

After the kick levelled out, Zoe said, "Your thoughts?"

Dominic loaded the porcelain onto a tray. "You were right to begin planning, ma'am-sir. When she sees how logical it all is, step-by-step, there should be no question of her approval. Your strategic mind is surely one of the sharpest of our times and no doubt statues will one day be built in your honour."

Zoe tapped the vaparillo, dragged the edge of zer tongue across the mouthpiece. "One of the sharpest?"

His face flashed white. It wasn't often he put a foot wrong in the endless minefield of zer company, so when he did, he knew it would sting.

He said, "Well, I mean, next to Suarez-Adarsha, of course. That was all I meant. In the early years, that is, before she…"

"I know what you meant, boy." Zoe sucked again on the filter, coughed. "That will earn you extra time with Jezebel tonight."

He winced, a reaction trained into him on hearing the name.

"Speaking of time," zie said, "shouldn't our guest be here by now?"

The vintage grandparent clock seemed to think so. Dominic compared the hands to the display on his voxwatch. "Still a few minutes. Let me check with reception."

Alone now in zer office, at the window, the empty courtyard of Horse Guards Parade across the way. No guards these days. No Royal Family to protect. Not even horses—the nearest at the stables at Hyde Park, the ones that housed zer own beloved pony, Jules. One of these days zie would find time to learn how to ride, to use Jezebel to keep something other than Dominic in line. Until then, merely possessing

Jules was satisfaction enough. Zoe pulled slowly at the vaparillo, pushed another toxic cloud towards the glass. Elsewhere, officious people prepared the streets in advance of Non-Binarist Pride Day— stringing lights, installing colourful standards on lampposts, lining curbs with barricades, setting up platforms that would bear oversized netscreens and speakers. No expense spared.

Zoe wondered if Tavistock had noticed the effort, had even bothered to consider what was on the line. It seemed strange to zer that even with all the PM's experience—her knowledge of underhanded tactics, her years of knowing what it took to not only break the glass ceiling for trans people but to trample the shards beneath her heels—that there should be any hesitance. Great accomplishments were the offspring of risk. Those who had ruled in the past had understood the need for it, had in fact thrived because of their willingness to lose everything. Nowadays, everyone was bred to avoid risk, to take the gentlest road possible. When nothing was done without the consensus of the majority, hardly anything was done at all. And so the country was slipping, teetering closer to collapse than the public knew. Emergency repair the only answer.

Granted, it had been a long time since they had been forced to make such a radical decision. No one liked the idea of turning on their own to root out weakness, of cutting off a limb to prevent the infection from spreading. The notion was incongruous. Unthinkable.

Necessary.

Only a week until the country would be celebrating Suarez-Adarsha, the person who had left them their most important lesson: to sacrifice is not always to forfeit, merely a way of passing on the torch to someone else—the individual never as important as the community. Amid its social fever, the public had become absentminded about taking its medicine. And now, the recent attacks on their hard-earned community proof enough the Resistance was well coordinated, that it was building towards something. These bouts of mischief cropping up around towns and cities were not simply taunts—they were tests of their defences.

How dare they?

Zoe would show them defences, would show them what it cost to pull the tail of a lion. Or a lioness for that matter. Zer father had been the first to make that unpleasant discovery, all those years ago. Zoe saw his ghost in all of them. A patronising smile on every cis male face. A bullying rebuff in every baritone voice...

Zoe would show them.

Dominic's latest intelligence, a step in that direction, even if its analysis was tame, its conclusions wrong. Much good could still be made of it. All it required was a little hands-on work, getting back in the trenches, leading by example. It had been too long since zie had fronted a police swoop. How quickly would it take to dust off the rust?

Zer voxchat burbled. Dominic, calling from the foyer, informing zer that their Two-Fifteen had arrived. Zoe told him to bring their guest in, dumped the empty vapour cartridge into one of the porcelain cups, picked up Jezebel, tucked her beneath zer arm. It was crucial their guest understood the importance of this assignment, of the danger it would present, of the remarkable new beginning its success would bring to the country. It required someone loyal to a fault. Someone who would follow without question. Someone willing to act decisively when the time came, without remorse, as zie would expect of zerself.

It would require someone far enough down the ladder to remove, untroubled, should the need arise. The survival of the regime more than enough of a reward.

Zoe took out another smartpalm from the drawer, identical to the first, its nursery rhyme designation blinking from the screen.

Dominic showed the officer in.

"Have a seat, Sergeant Dennehy," Zoe cooed, approaching for a hug, a peck on each cheek. "So glad to see you again."

44

CHAPTER NINE

Access to the Inner Safe Zone had been rum cake.

Sure, it had been a long journey, had required months of planning and over a year of living someone else's life to build his credentials. But here he was. In the inner sanctum of society. Trusted. Respected, even.

Already.

A mistake to feel too confident. Slow your roll, kid. Ice your dice. Don't get comfortable, whatever you do. Still a thousand ways to slip up. A million. Be careful, son. Let's not get ahead of ourselves.

A day would come when things would be easier. When he would recognise himself again, as he knew he was. That was the idea, wasn't it? Keep the memories, but nothing else? For now he was one of them. And yet, he was not one of them. Not really. Not in that way.

He was a story writing itself. He was Schrödinger's fever dream.

If fate had shifted only a tenth of an inch, if their politics had only evolved a tiny bit differently, maybe those swamp hags wouldn't have brought this on themselves. Perhaps in that world he would even have liked them, walked among them as a friend. Not creeping around like a rat at a banquet.

He knew he had a free pass now. Knew that, if he wanted to, he could just keep the pretence up forever, enjoy all the trappings of freedom. Sometimes he wondered about that. Secretly to himself, mind. He would never mention it to another soul. Only sometimes. When the world was quiet and there was nothing but his thoughts, he would ask himself if he truly was for the cause so much as for what it would provide him. Was anyone? There were people who lived to fight injustice. Others determined to overthrow the system. Others trying to secure a place in heaven. In any case, was it ever anything but the self that ultimately mattered?

Enough of that now. Pointless to wonder. Wind-piss moot. If he was to commit himself—and, Sweet Jesus, he certainly had—all that thinking had to be pushed into some forgotten cellar of his mind. Kept behind that big, imaginary door. Locked away with the rest of the things he wanted nothing to do with these days. He would need to embrace the person they needed him to be.

Doc Sharma hadn't done the best work of his career for him to have doubts now.

A strong gust came barrelling down the street. He braced himself, directed his umbrella against it like a gladiator's shield, pulled the collar of his Burberry coat up, turned against the wind to check his phone again. His contact was in the park somewhere, exact location undisclosed. The latest message advised him to head north until he reached the memorial fountain, follow the path clockwise. The elm trees lining the walk were barren and tumoured. Why the local council would allow such ugly things to survive here was a mystery, especially when they spent so long taking care of everything else in the ISZ.

His experience of the Outer Safe Zone had been a world apart from where he had started. Its sweet foods and fashions and entertainments had dazzled at first. His first dash of synthetic makeup had been transformative, leading to months of experimenting until he had his own style down pat. His first taste of good tapas had been a real mindjob, the spices and sauces of each dish igniting a flamenco across his taste buds. The simple pleasure of going for a walk through the streets and not feeling like he had every pedestrian measuring him up as a threat. Those experiences—experiences that should have been basic rights—had opened his eyes to the value of what he was doing.

To why the operation was vital.

After eighteen months thriving in the suburbs, he had become accustomed. He had his role down Jagger, wore it as easily as a lace garter. Despite the unfathomable danger ahead, he was no longer anxious. When had that happened? When had been the first day he hadn't looked over his shoulder wondering if he was being followed? Probably one of the busy days, when he'd been too distracted by files and schedules and social media dialogues to even think about the past or the future. Working in the constituency office had been dry work, as uninspiring as it was necessary. An all-important step to gaining accreditation in the eyes of 'them upstairs' and access to the political corridors that would lead him…well, here, to London's Green Park, watching water snake off the sides of his umbrella and stain his suede boots.

A billboard ad for the Non-Binarist Pride Day festivities had been erected in the park. The theme was 'Faces of the Revolution'. It depicted the overly familiar iconography of Maria Suarez-Adarsha waving her clenched fist, looking skyward and…

Ha!

…a bulging groin sword protruding from her proud forehead. The red spray-paint outline accompanied two spiky-haired testicles, the shaft jettisoning spunk in the form of a crude dotted arc from its tip. The CRUSH THE CIS-TEM slogan similarly edited: its new recommendation to FLUSH THE CISTERN.

In their boldness, the vandal would have been sentencing themselves to being flushed themselves if they were ever caught. Even seeing it—even being anyway associated with it—could spell trouble.

Best get a jog on, move a little quicker.

He found her beyond the reflecting pool, beneath one of the ornate iron canopies that kept its pinewood bench dry. Not exactly ambiguous. Who goes for a walk in the park in this kind of weather? He told her as much.

"No videyes here," his contact said. "No sky-eyes. Only the occasional foot patrol. And besides, the ducks love it."

The woman pulled a plastic baggy of torn bread from her mac, tossed a little to the waddling birds. A few of them caught on, took to a fast jam around their feet.

"You're not meant to feed them bread," he said. "It's bad for them."

"Who cares? If they don't know what's good for them, they'll have to learn eventually."

"That's perverse."

The agent flashed a smug little smile that seemed to say 'Look who's fucking talking?'.

"Let's move things along," he said. "I've spent so long sitting around on this job, I can't feel my arse."

"The bag under your seat would wake it up. And then some."

"It's all there?"

"Everything you need in raw material, plus some extra goodies that might come in handy. The instructions are taped under the mattress in your hotel room."

"Tell me it's the Dorchester."

"We figured it'd be better if you prepped outside the ISZ until the weekend of the parade. That way you'll fit in with the rest of the tourists and day-trippers. Easier for us, too. No need to bring radio equipment through a border checkpoint. When it all goes down, you'll want to leave with the masses, probably by emergency autobus. The place you're staying in is good enough to lie low for a few days until the others finalise the gig."

"So I'm roughing it?"

"It's not a bad place. Has its charms. Not that I would ever stay there."

"What about when I'm inside—how will I reach you without the radio?"

"Voxwatch in the bag, encrypted. The voxchats at the hotel will be monitored—don't touch them. Honestly, you'll be smart to not try to reach anyone. Do the job and drop everything as soon as you need to get out of the furnace. The question is whether we can trust you to take care of things without us."

"I've made it this far, haven't I?"

"If you get made, Winter, nobody will come get you."

"Que será."

He scooted the bag out with his ankles, picked it up, felt its weight on his lap. Surprisingly light. Waxed cotton. Tartan lining. Deerskin tassels. Adjustable shoulder strap. Brass fittings. Cute.

"All that matters to me is Bonfire Night," he said. "That was the deal. I'll see to my end, you see to yours."

A pair of echoes appeared in the distance like a couple of lazy pigeons, bottom-heavy and glum. They stopped beneath the defaced billboard, looked up, shrieked. One leaned into the voxcom radio on her lapel, calling in the emergency. The other dropped to the pathway, weighed down under her own bewilderment. The vandalism evaporated their professional demeanours. They were both shaking, distressed.

His contact stood up, fanned out her brolly, said: "Go make history, qween."

The woman left in the direction of the fountains, walked right past the echoes like they were nothing.

The bag felt heavier the longer he carried it. He imagined it tearing at the handles, exploding all over the pavement, spilling his secrets in six thousand directions.

Enough of that, kid. Time to make zistory.

CHAPTER TEN

Chrissie gave herself longer in the shower than usual.

After clocking off, she had gone straight back to her flat, left her uniform on the floor, shut the glass door on the world.

Time lost meaning. All she allowed herself to feel were the jets—over her face, between her toes, pooling inside the folds of her ears. She hovered beneath the showerhead without moving, hoping the water would exorcise the day out of her, flush it out through the pores, out of her body, into the drains of the apartment block like a blood transfusion. By the time she was ready to turn the jets off, the bathroom had fogged, skin on her scalp and shoulders raw to the touch.

Voices, coming from the kitchen. Cupboard doors banging. She tied the bath robe at her waist, went out barefoot. Her hair hung in ropes, black wet against the towel in her hand.

The kitchen, a chaos of hemp shopping bags, each overflowing with groceries. Charlotte (*non-binary-adjacent aromantic, she/her*) was in the middle of it, sitting at the island, buffing her fingernails. Andre, her CisHet house varlet, dealing with the groceries unaided, pushing aside items in the fridge to find home for the soy milk.

"You're home," Chrissie said, the words out like a question.

She glimpsed the netscreen playing in the living room, cartoon animals chasing each other. The little guy, absorbed, stretched out on the rug. But it was still early—wasn't it? She looked at her voxwatch.

"Duh. Where did you expect me to be?" Charlotte said, grabbing a box of Choco-Lite biscuits from one of the bags, popping the tab open. "I never work over the Hallowmass holiday."

"I thought that was next week."

"It is. This week, as well."

That's right. Schools were out until early November. That would explain why her sister had swapped her usual suit and tie for sweatpants.

49

"Honestly, Chrissie, sometimes it's like you live on a different planet. Got you a bag of those sampuro balls you like—no, there, on the counter."

"Sorry, these hours sometimes throw me for a loop."

"Uh-huh. Tough day?"

Before she could explain, Daniel emerged at the kitchen threshold, all three and a half feet of him in a maroon frock.

"Aunt Chrissie!"

He bounded into her, trapped her at the waist with his thin arms. She laughed, ruffled his hair, hair that still hadn't quite lost its fineness.

He said, "Andre took me to the park!"

The varlet looked up, his exhausted smile there and gone. He scuttled back to his work.

"He did?" Chrissie said with exaggerated wonder. "I'm so jealous! Don't tell me you went on the swings."

He laughed with delight, at the memory, at teasing his—as he put it—*best grown-up friend.* "I went super high up. Even higher than last time. You should have seen it."

"I wish I had." She let him stand on her feet (he weighed hardly anything), walked him around the floor. "But crime doesn't fight itself, right?"

"Did you arrest anyone?"

"We did."

"What did they do?"

"They, uh…" Her smile fell away. She looked up at Charlotte. "They broke the law. One of them ran away. I had to chase him."

"But what did he do? Did he steal something? Did he hurt someone?"

Charlotte tutted. "Dani, stop bugging your aunt and go play with your dolls."

His face dropped, his voice teetered on a wail. "Why?"

"Because I said so. Unless you want to do Andre's job and put away all this shopping."

"I don't even like playing with dolls."

It was true. Chrissie had heard him complain about it more than once since his birthday.

"Daniel Tieman, as your birthing person, you do as I say. Understand?"

"But—"

"It's all part of the preparation, Dani. You know that."

His head fell into his chest. He hopped off Chrissie's feet, moped back to the living room to sit in front of an endless NetTube playlist.

Charlotte turned her attention to the other subordinate, said, "Andre, hurry up with this mess and then go and draw me a bath, will you."

"Certainly, madam," Andre said, gathering the last of the vac-packed food into his arms. His thin frame shuffled about the kitchen in a way that made Chrissie suspect he didn't eat as much throughout the day as he burnt off looking after her sister's home. She knew it was his livelihood but she couldn't help feel creeped out by his pathetic manner every time she looked at him, at how much he tried to blend into the background while managing everything from the cleaning to the cooking. He spoke as he moved—only as much as was required.

"Ooh," Charlotte said, "And add a few shakes of that new spring fresh oil range I got for my birthday."

"Splendid idea, madam."

Charlotte waited until both males in the flat were out of earshot. "So are you going to tell me or am I going to have to pour us both a beer?"

There were times when the big sister radar was welcome and times she despised its existence. Chrissie didn't know which one she was hoping for today. She coiled the towel around her shoulders, pulled herself up onto a breakfast stool. The pack of sampuro balls split with a satisfying wheeze. "It's nothing. Like you said—tough day. No one claimed this job was meant to be easy."

Her sister joined her at the counter, grabbed herself a handful of the snack. "True, but I don't know if I've seen you happy about it since you earned your badge."

"I wouldn't say that. The work's okay. It's other stuff, really. I just…I feel like there's a hole in my life."

"What kind of shape would that hole be?"

Embarrassed, Chrissie hesitated. The pause told Charlotte everything she needed to know.

"Oh, hun. Really? Great Birth-Giver! We've had this discussion—I don't know how many times. You don't need some privileged, masculine ape with a Y chromosome in your life to be happy. If anything, it's the opposite. You're young. You've got a good career going. You're super fierce. I don't know where you got this silly notion."

"I didn't *get* it from anywhere. I have a normal urge to find someone and that's what I'm attracted to. It's natural."

"Only if you believe in what the binary extremists tell us is natural. Look at me. I don't have that urge and I'm perfectly happy. Is that unnatural?"

"No, of course not. But you're you, and I'm..." She shrugged, already regretting having started this chat. "Look, I can't help how I feel. I want to find someone who has biological parts and who isn't obsessed with their identity at all hours of the day. Someone without muscle implants or a 'shenis' or an Xprez profile. A good cisgender male, that's all."

"Newsflash—there aren't any," Charlotte scoffed. "I'm serious. Do you know even one person who qualifies?"

"That's my point. The only privs I get to meet are so dreary. So proper. They're starched socks."

"Or they're criminals, I guess. Abhorrent Neanderthals who have no respect for non-binarists. Would you rather that?"

"No, but who decided it has to be one or the other?"

"It doesn't. I mean, if it's a partner you're looking for, there are plenty of nonconformist, trans men out there and, honestly, you'd have your pick of them. Not to mention, they're so much more fun and free."

No denying there were plenty—a result of the dwindling number of cis males permitted within the general populace. Chrissie simply didn't find herself attracted to trans men in the same way. She had dabbled at university, of course, where doing so was more or less required, but she had never had a longing for them in the way she had for the traditional variety.

"That's sweet of you to say, sis, but the fact of the matter is, I was born with a different preference. That's all. You know me. I've always found masculinity in a man to be…exciting."

"Oh, Goddess! No. No! Do you realise how problematic you sound right now?" Charlotte was dead serious. "I get it, I do. But you better make sure my soon-to-be daughter doesn't hear you speaking like that."

Daniel was oblivious. They could see him jumping off the sofa, running in circles, duelling imaginary enemies, one of the plastic dolls taking the role of a mock sword. His mother rolled her eyes. Chrissie smiled, caught a sampuro ball in her mouth. It burst with a sweet heat that travelled through her nostrils, teased her tear ducts.

"He's not shown any feminine presentation yet." Chrissie said. "Maybe it's time to just accept he identifies as male—"

"Is that what this is about?"

Charlotte's features hardened. She looked at Chrissie with that same edge she always used to bring out when little sis borrowed her things without asking or came home late from the running track.

Big sis said, "You know, it's the twenty-first century. A lot of kids go on puberty blockers until they can make their own decision. Ask me, all of them should. You'll understand when you're a birthing person."

Chrissie coughed, almost choked on the tiny crumbs she'd inhaled. When she recovered herself, she said, "When did I say I wanted that?"

"That's what you're getting to with all this, isn't it? A CisHet relationship only leads to one thing."

"Charl," Chrissie said, dropping a hand over her sister's fingers. "Calm yourself. I'm not trying to have a kid. Maybe someday but not anytime soon." The air seeped out of the tyres. "But I'm sure if I ever decide to, you'll be there for me."

"Damn right I will."

Dependable Charlotte. Even when they didn't see eye to eye on things—often—they'd rarely fallen out in the twenty years they'd known each other. When their parents had moved down to the coast, they had stayed in London, forged ahead along divergent paths yet always within reach. Getting the flat together had been her sister's idea. Ticked all the boxes. They knew each other's habits, liked the same décor, shared the same circle of friends for the most part. Good thing, too. It meant Chrissie got to spend time with her nephew, to watch him grow, to have something to look forward to at the end of a long shift. Only now the happiness was fading like blue on jeans. It wouldn't be long before the kid started his treatment. There was no telling how that would change things between them. His normal happy self could soon be a blocker zombie.

Charlotte reached over, put an arm around Chrissie's shoulders, squeezed gently, rested her head against the curtain of damp hair.

"Okay, Chrissie, tell you what—tomorrow we'll take Daniel to soft play. We'll dump him in the ball pit and you and I can grab a NeverCold and go through the Ally Single's Register—see who's available."

Ah, yes, the Register. Files on all single cis heterosexuals who had submitted to the standard legal procedures, including comprehensive background checks, ideology assessments and ethical agreement forms. Chrissie had perused it in the past. The feeling of window shopping for a partner pre-vetted by the state left her feeling cold. Not as cold as the idea of disappointing Charlotte. Hell, maybe it couldn't hurt to give it another try, to open up a little more to the possibility. Who knows? Perhaps all the good men were so hard to find because they were being proactive, getting registered, getting snatched up fast by other CisHet women.

"I guess that might be fun," Chrissie said, returning the squeeze. "Quality time, huh? Fine. But tomorrow's a good few hours away and didn't you say something about a beer?"

Charlotte hopped up, circled the island, scoured the bags. "Right! And of course Andre had to go and leave the case in the AV. Andre!...Andre!...Great Birth-Giver! Do I have to do everything around here? What am I even paying him for? Like I always say, if you want a job done right, don't get a CisHet to do it. Watch Dani for me, would you, sis?"

CHAPTER ELEVEN

The boy didn't notice his mother leave. He was transfixed by the screen—a cavalcade of bizarre and colourful puppets danced in unison to a nonsensical rhyme, cartwheeling and somersaulting over each other, talking in a nonsensical language. Nor did he notice Chrissie creep up behind him until she had scooped him up in her arms, spun him upside down across her shoulders.

"Got you, monkey."

He squealed, his laughter immediate, uncontained. He kicked like a swimmer. Charlotte didn't approve of him being physical—*roughhousing* as she called it. She was trying to coax more feminine behaviours. That meant the wrestling matches always took place on the fly, in the short moments when Charlotte wasn't around. When he wasn't enjoying the feeling of weightlessness, he was trying his best to topple his aunt, somehow drag her to the floor. That was the goal. He hadn't quite succeeded yet.

She said, "Is that all you got?"

Chrissie flipped him upright again, swung him by his wrists, gave him the appearance of a tiny trapeze artist. She held him by his waist, gently tossed him onto the settee. He was breathless. She sat on the back of his legs, pinned him against the cushions.

"Aunt Chrissie!" he giggled. "I can't move!"

"Why not? Are you giving up? Because loser gets tickled."

He wasn't giving up. He squealed again. Her fingers dug into his sides. He wriggled away as best he could.

Between teasing him, she glanced up to see the NetTube acrobats continuing their own performance. The gibberish they were singing became distorted as the audio fizzed, returned to normal a moment later. Almost imperceptible. A surge of electricity perhaps, or a solar flare. It barely registered with Chrissie until the screen flickered a few seconds later, the colourful characters replaced by what appeared to be stock footage of the old Britannia flag, unfurled and translucent beneath the sunlight, swelling in the breeze.

"Are you lying on the remote?" she asked Daniel, easing her weight off him.

"Wake up and take heed."

No one appeared on the screen. The disembodied voice materialised over the flag. It came rumbling through the speakers with the gusto of a ringmaster.

"You put us out of sight but we grow in number. You rob us of our land but we toil fresh fields. You strip us of our arms but we forge new weapons. You expurgate our past but we prepare for the future."

Daniel freed his legs, climbed up the back of the sofa, threw his pipe-cleaner limbs around her collar, hoping for Round Two. Chrissie shushed him, her attention fixed on the smartscreen.

"For too long you have paved over our society with your hate and hypocrisy. The new day is in sight. The time has come to consign this unjust repression to the bonfire of history. Britain will rise again. You're listening to the Ozcast, live and exclusive on Revolution Radio, hijacking your airwaves whenever I damn well feel like it. Listen out for my next segment. And remember—stand up, be counted. Ominous spiritus."

The screen flickered again, cut back to the kid's show. The troupe of puppets blew trumpets, spun on stripper poles.

By now, the boy was quiet, resting against her hip. He looked up at her, blinked. "What was that?"

It didn't cross her mind to lie to him. "I don't know."

Neither of them moved. The screen went to an ad break, as if everything was normal, as if the interruption had never happened. She could feel Daniel's chest rising and falling in heavy waves.

"NetTube, stop," Chrissie said. The screen powered off.

Chrissie's voxwatch lit up, a bird chirp telling her she had an incoming call: Dennehy.

"Daniel, I have to take this."

She stood up in a daze, left the boy on the couch, hurried to the kitchen, raised the wrist to her mouth.

"Tieman here."

"Sorry to bother you at home, hun."

"Don't be. I take it you saw that too?"

56

"Saw what?"

Chrissie told her about the strange announcement, tried to summarise what the voice had said, though she wasn't quite sure she was getting it all right. She kept her back to the living room, hoped Daniel didn't overhear. Silence on the other end. She checked to see if her connection had dropped.

"Not the first I'm hearing about one of those," the sergeant finally replied. "They've had a couple in the past week. Censors stepped in, ordered the media not to report on it—'cause that's giving them what they want, right? But it sounds like it won't be long before it'll need to be addressed. It's too frequent."

"Who is it, Sarge?"

"Who do you think? Same binarist filth vandalising the city with graffiti and leaving illegal books and stuff lying around for anyone to find. Pigs."

"They're hacking the netwaves now? How is that possible?"

"If we knew that, it wouldn't be happening. Not that we won't stamp it out soon enough, promise you that."

Thomas Tate's desperate cry came back to her, as though a kitchen door had blown open in the back of her skull, letting in the cold. She closed it, focused on the conversation at hand.

Chrissie said, "So…that's not why you called me?"

"I guess it is and it isn't." Dennehy sniffed. "I had a meeting today. You won't believe who with."

"Try me."

"The equality minister. Yep, none other. She called me to her office."

"Wow. Look at you—mingling with the upper crust."

"I know. Friends in high places and all that. We met at a fundraiser a few months ago and you know me—I like to leave an impression. Anyway, she wants to put me on a special assignment. Both of us, actually."

"Special?" The word heavy, sliding the wrong way through her throat, sinking into her gut. "I don't know whether to be excited or afraid. What exactly does she want us to do?"

"Let's just say we have a lead on something important. Urwin's going back out on the frontline to spearhead the investigation. Part of a PR campaign, I guess. I need you to come in tomorrow morning at ten."

"Why us?"

"Because she knows how dedicated we are. Said she needed a couple of fierce allies she could trust. I vouched for you—told her you could be counted on. What do you think?"

"Well, uh, I think—"

"This could be amazing for our careers, hun. Tell me you've got my back."

The sarge had talked about her dreams of working her way up to superintendent one day. The thought of letting her down made Chrissie's stomach turn.

"Sure thing, Sarge. I've got this."

Dennehy thanked her, signed off. The watch dulled to a black mirror.

Chrissie stood alone at the island, granite cool on her hands. News of the assignment should have sparked her sense of pride. It did nothing but make her feel nauseous, brought her skin to gooseflesh. When her sister came through the door, case of beer underarm, the old radar missed nothing.

"What's wrong?" Charlotte asked.

"Keep it in the fridge. Work called. I'm going to need a clear head for a few days."

"What about our quality time?"

"Sorry, sis. Think my search for romance will have to wait."

CHAPTER TWELVE

The streets, different to how he had pictured them. Not all that much, but enough to feel like the images and accounts he had pored over in the Cooler for twelve months had got their research wrong. The biggest difference was the remarkable vanishing act performed by several of the towers that graced the skylines in those books and magazines, those giant beacons of the city's prosperity. Their remaining footprints strewn with rubble and machinery, clean-up still underway.

The autocab ride into town shed some weight off Jake's wallet. First thing he did was stop by a credit point, check his account. His funds still there after twenty months of stagnation, though just as lean, having earned no interest. His inmate wages hardly made a difference. He transferred the several thousand Britcoins to his spending account, knew they were worth next to nothing in today's economy. Yet he was determined not to have to register at the vocation centre for a few days. Any fun would need to be dirt cheap.

He followed the signs towards one of the monorail stations, felt cloud spittle on the shoulders of his jacket. He pushed buttons on another machine to pay for his travel to Hyde Park, where he'd learnt a Citizen's Data Bureau was stationed—one of those government-built information hubs for those access to the netwire. It was down the street from that place called the Junction, which he'd read would serve him a juicy medium-rare. May as well start his search on a full stomach.

He stalled at the sight of an e-board depicting two obese trans people modelling some fashion brand's winter range. Wished he hadn't. The couple formed exaggerated catwalk poses in leather vests and pork-pie hats before indulging in a passionate embrace, the footage closing in on their bloated cheeks pressed together, their squirming tongues blown up for the big screen. Almost enough to put anyone off the thought of food for life. Almost.

Despite being the middle of the afternoon, there was still a wait for the CisHet carriage. Two trains went by before Jake found room to squeeze himself aboard the third, his view part-obscured by armpits and elbows, damp coats turning the air thick and fusty. He joined the other passengers in peering enviously through the carriage door window. The occupants on the carriage ahead—and probably the other eight beyond—had seats. At least one for themselves, another for their handbags or briefcases. One of the occupants came to the window, pulled the blind down.

Jake tried to ignore the discomfort. Storm clouds flitted past the window. When that bored him, he turned his attention to the poster boards—ads for skincare products and prosecco bars, public notices about showing courtesy to other travellers. One of them warned: *Stare rape will not be tolerated. Avert your eyes.* And in smaller print—*Stares, smiles, verbal harassment, heavy breathing and sly comments towards, about or in the presence of trans and genderqueer people are violence. Any offenders will be prosecuted.*

He closed his eyes. Not because the sign said he should, because the noise and proximity of other people were suffocating. He let the train's trundling progress bounce him like a raft at sea, pictured in his mind an endless ocean, an endless sky. He considered the rumours he'd heard about people finding ways out of the cities, about the ones who risked it all on one chance to cross the Fence, about the ones who had been caught trying. After half an hour in the cattle car, he got out onto the platform, took the stairs down to fresh air.

According to his research, the Citizen's Data Bureau was stationed on the south side with a view of the park—at least it used to be. Gone now, replaced by what appeared to be an art gallery. Jake stood on the opposite side of the road, wondered what the fuck. Worse still, the Junction was nowhere to be seen either. Must be the wrong street. The magazine had given it full stars. Be strange for a place like that to go out of business so fast. Hoping he hadn't come all this way for nothing, he stepped out of the drizzle, under the awnings of an artisan bakery.

Copies of the *Daily Femail*, available to download from a netwire access point by the door. A guy in a bomber jacket nearby was selling e-brollies, cut-rate—the kind that lit up and gave you readings for humidity and temperature and all the other stuff no one needed when all they were trying to do was stay dry.

"Excuse me, pal," Jake said to the vendor, brushing the rain off his shoulders. "You know what happened to the Citizen's Data Bureau? One that used to be over there?"

"Ain't there no more."

Jake let it slide. "I guess no one has a need to know anything these days. What's in there now?"

"Little museum," the guy said. "If you're after a datapoint, they still have one inside. Replaced all the CDBs a while ago. Although the amount of questions you're asking me, I'm starting to think they should bring 'em back."

Jake nodded, feeling a little relief. "Here's another—what happened to the Junction?"

"Ain't there no more."

"Cool. Do you know any other places around here that serve a good steak? I'm looking for real meat."

The vendor shrugged. "I'm a vegetarian."

"I'm not inviting you to lunch, I'm asking you where I can get a steak."

"Mate, you buy one of these brollies, I'll tell you where they serve the best steak on earth."

The sky was so dense it could have been evening already. "Let me guess. Tokyo? I'll take my chances."

He left the awning, went back to where the eatery had been, took a closer look in the window in case there was a sign or something that might tell him if the premises had moved. The CDB booths had been replaced with plywood dividers, plinths with antiques and the like on them. An assistant with a pageboy cut saw him from inside, waved at him to come in. Would have been rude not to.

"Welcome," the assistant said, her black blazer bearing the name of the museum stencilled across the pocket—*Times Gone By*. "Are you interested in having a look around? The main floor is free but we also have a special exhibition at the far end on late twentieth century Britannia."

"Actually, I was kind of hoping to use your datapoint."

"Oh." Her convivial demeanour slipped, exposed a hint of suspicion. "It's in the back. Wait—you have to pay."

"Pay for using a datapoint?"

"Does this look like a CDB? The datapoint is in the exhibition hall. Like I said, this floor is free to browse, although," she glanced at his armband, "the exhibition requires CisHets to pay a small entrance fee."

"What else do I get for my ticket?"

The assistant's smile returned. She handed him a pamphlet. "*Times Gone By* is an experience. With a presence in every major city across the country, we provide pop-up galleries and museums to help bring education and culture to local areas outside the ISZ. Visitors can walk in and learn more about the tapestry of what made us who we are by travelling through centuries of artwork, antiques and artefacts."

"Well memorised," Jake said, glancing around at the display cases. "Not a bad idea—bringing a bit of culture to the masses."

Tell her whatever. He was getting desperate to find the datapoint and see what came up. Aside to that, the novelty of being out in the wet weather was already beginning to wear off.

She said, "You won't regret it."

He said, "You sold me. How much?"

She charged him two hundred Britcoin. Didn't seem unreasonable. Once he tapped his debit chip to the reader, she opened her arms and turned like a coin-operated dancer, said, "Please. Explore."

Jake gave her the tightest of smiles, began to circle the floor.

An archway indicated the start of the walking tour, where the exhibits were housed. Jake ignored it. The datapoint was back by the fire exit—a blocky yellow thing gathering dust. He scanned his Ally Pass, waited, tried not to think about how and where the Equality Ministry was storing his data. When his options appeared on the display, he selected a People Search. He tried *Brody*, found a list of IDs. None were his parents or anyone else in the old clan.

He tried a few of the other names he could remember, friends and neighbours.

Same amount of nothing.

He swallowed, tried his family name in the death records. Found nothing there, either—left him relieved. He thought about trying to run a search on previous locations, but the camp in the New Forest had never had a name, hadn't ever been a legal dwelling, so that was out.

Instead, he narrowed the netwire archives to the past two years, tried a keyword search—*New Forest, raid, illegal settlement...*

Clips and quotes filtered down the screen, links to stories mentioning Amazon force crackdowns, echoes given medals, mass arrests of *binarist extremists* and *fascist criminals*—all *a danger to the public*. The coverage was fleeting, details censored, reporters concerned more with praising the government for its legislations and the brave security troops willing to bring justice to the wild countryside. Reading the column inches brought black memories, gave him an urge to put his fist through the screen for all the use it had been.

He shut down the session, tried to think of another angle. If the datapoints had been censored, he would need to work harder for information. He was thinking about his next move when he drifted back to the archway. May as well get his money's worth.

Among the exhibits was a medley of stone figures and ceramics, some marked as genuine, others reproductions. Each had a little card plaque with a description. He recognised some of the designs from his studies—Roman, Greek, Sumerian—but not others. Close up, he found the theme of each display was centred on genderqueer discoveries. A whole bank dedicated to artefacts from the Persian civilisation of Hasanlu showed photos of tombs of 'third gender' bodies, male skeletons harbouring female belongings. Pots and paraphernalia claimed to depict male warriors in female dress. Jake was frustrated by the narrow lens, felt like he was only seeing a handful of stars in a sky, no sense of direction or narrative to place them on the map.

At the rear of the gallery was the walled-off 'interactive exhibit'. The triangular *Content Warning* sign he'd seen on the netscreen earlier was mounted on a floor stand at the entrance. He went through, picked up a set of the headphones from their peg, listened to the audio guide take him through a brief account of the 'Brutish Empire' following World War II.

"The early half of the century was a time of great hardship and struggle for these small isles, a nation that was then still known unironically as Great Britain…"

Jake observed blown-up monochromes of people in work overalls, families cradling each other amid rubble. They were hung above a diorama of a London street, circa 1944.

"…War blighted Europe and the world afar. A fascist right-wing movement threatened to bring its toxic ideology to the West. The violent urges of both sides were fundamentally driven by binarist philosophy, which manifested in the need to control and to imprison…"

There were poster boards of soldiers marching, of factory workers sitting in rows, stitching uniforms, piecing together mortar shells.

"…Many transgender people were deported to concentration camps, wiping out vibrant community structures. Although the Axis was defeated, binarist-centred hate continued to prevail in the war's aftermath. Brutish society only became a more dangerous place…"

Further on, a series of post-war news prints, looping video reels. They depicted grey-skinned politicians, criminal mugshots, protests. A mannequin stood behind the cordon, dressed in a leather biker jacket, holding a flick knife.

"…At a time when right-wing ideology should have been shown the door, society remained rooted to outdated notions of identity. Liberation represented a grave threat to the fragile patriarchy. For the next several decades, trans and genderqueer people could rarely walk the streets alone without being raped or murdered by roaming bigots…"

A netscreen depicted a strange amalgamation of vague and unconnected images—flash-cut footage of crime scenes, burning buildings, riots.

"…Millions within the trans community at the time—indeed, the figures are believed to be grossly under-reported—were virtually enslaved within a system that despised them. Corrupt police forces, run by this patriarchal structure, ignored the vast majority of atrocities, while cis-controlled governments turned a blind eye, only addressing the persecution and genocide when suggesting that

the problem was overstated or that the victims were simply fabricating their victimhood…"

Jake scratched the back of his neck. He had read history books, had been shown photos and video footage by his parents of his grandparents and great grandparents living through that era with happiness and optimism. He knew a little of female liberation and the civil rights movement, the explosion of rock 'n' roll, the rise of consumerism, space exploration, the nouvelle vague, the Cold War, assassinations, sitcoms, the War on Drugs, the internet, the War on Terror, and a good deal of other events knitted across those years. It hadn't all sounded peachy but it seemed a far step removed from a lawless nightmare underpinned by gender identity. Had they lied to him?

"It was only in the early twenty-first century when voices for social justice grew significantly louder and refused to be silenced. The Cis-tem was not dismantled overnight but began to be eroded slowly and deliberately. Yet still to this day it holds its iron grip around the necks of…"

He left the room in a daze, the spotlights searing his eyes. He put a hand against the wall, steadied himself.

"Did you enjoy your exploration?" The assistant rose from her desk, falling back into her customer-helper mode.

The pamphlet scrunched in his hand. "To be honest, I don't think it made any sense."

Her eyebrows jumped like startled cats.

He said, "And I have to say, it feels like the focus is off."

"Focus?"

"Well— example—you missed out on a lot of the great things about the last hundred years. The technological progress. The music…"

The assistant snorted. "The exhibit is meant to be more about societal developments."

"Okay. But even all the stuff about society, it—well, it kind of made it seem like everything was terrible because of gender identity."

"It basically was. Don't you know your zistory? Until the Big Reboot, this country was unbelievably oppressive and prejudiced. Some would say evil."

"I'm just not sure your people have their research right. Parts of it aren't just wrong, they're illogical. I mean, what does any of that have to do with crime rates…"

"Pardon me? This is a place of education. What's logic got to do with it?" If she'd been a kettle, she would have been whistling by now.

"Look, what you're saying is beginning to sound a lot like cisplaining. Is that what you're doing?"

"I'm only pointing out my understanding of things. They're different to what you're selling here."

She tapped her voxchat screen, the AI helper asking who she wanted to call. "Are we going to have a problem?"

He tensed up. The bell on the door tinkled. He turned to see two women come in, a mother and daughter seemingly more interested in getting out of the rain than into the *Time Goes By* brand of bullshit. It was all the opening he needed.

"I'll get out of your hair," he said.

Before he was a yard away, the assistant was already welcoming her new visitors. "Hello, folks. Would you like to look around? The full floor and the exhibition at the far end are completely free. Please, explore."

Jake manoeuvred around them, wrestled the door open, fell into step with the other pedestrians.

CHAPTER THIRTEEN

"I believe you'll be pleased with our progress," said Doctor Marsh
(*transfeminine demiqueer, she/her*). "We've made some important
findings since your last visit. A number of projects are entirely novel in
their approach."

The small delegation squeezed itself along the corridor, unhurried.
Dominic followed a few steps behind, as was custom. Zoe listened to
the echoes of heavy doors and security buzzers filtering down from
other parts of the facility.

"The Ministry's investments have been significant, Doctor."

"Indeed, Minister, and for that we're thankful."

"Thankful, I don't doubt. Though I'd rather pay for results than
gratitude."

The doctor pulled her smartpalm close to the breast of her lab coat—
the pristine one she probably saved for special occasions.

"Perhaps, ma'am, it would be best for you to see the progress first. I
wouldn't want you to misunderstand the benefits of our research."

Like the school trips of zer childhood, Zoe loved zer inspections of
the country's infrastructure, particularly zer appraisals of the re-
education centres. And particularly the John Money Centre. Visits here
always left her feeling bubbly.

Reinforced acrylic walls—viewing screens, really—exposed room
after room of students, each at varying stages of their course. Some
here for years, others only beginning their re-education. Dorms
designed for two housing five or six students. Privacy, a memory—not
unusual to see one on the lav, pants at half-mast, always good for a
chuckle. No personal effects. No name badges. This time round she
saw the usual mix of attitudes. The ones who turned away, hid in their
bunks, buried their heads. The ones who stared out from the glass,
gaunt and listless. None of them hollered or threatened the visitors,
their defiance drummed out of them long before they reached the
dorms.

"It always strikes me as funny," Zoe said, "how they all start to look the same after a while. And I don't mean because they're all wearing the same uniform."

The cotton jumpsuits came in powder pink—one of Zoe's creative ideas. One of the many little indignities.

Marsh nodded. "Malnutrition and hard labour do have a way of reducing the CisHet male and female form quite indistinct. But I suppose that's the point."

"All smell the same, too. Like a zoo enclosure—that spicy, overwhelming funk. How on earth do they stand it?"

"Evolution left them with an inferior understanding of gender, perhaps it also left them with underdeveloped olfactory organs. Years back, when they were allowed to take part in sports, they would willingly cover themselves in mud and sweat, wrestle each other and pile into segregated open-plan changing rooms together. Left to their own devices, they would pride themselves on their filth and revel in their assigned genders."

Zoe had heard the pitiful stories. They lent further credence to the belief that the beings inside the locked rooms were more bacteria than people, unfit for civilised society.

Zoe paused at one of the screens. The tour group stopped with zer. A student—elderly in appearance but probably quite young—stood at the window, trance-like. Zoe tapped on the glass. His eyes shifted to the noise, to the fingernail. Zoe moved her hand up and down, back and forth, side to side in waves. His head rowed and rocked to its movement. The delegation laughed.

"Look at it dance," Zoe crowed.

Zoe curled a finger at Dominic. He rushed forward with zer handbag. Zie took the Choco-Lite bar out, held it to the screen. Flickers of movement and uncertainty filled the dorm. Other students came forward, edged towards the food hatch. Zie grinned, unwrapped the bar, ate it carefully, took zer time, savoured each chew. Zie opened the external hatch, dropped the wrapper inside, closed the flap. The internal hatch slid open. A fight broke out for the stains and crumbs left inside the foil, CisHet brutes clawing at each other, climbing on top of each other, falling to the floor.

Zoe said, "You should put a notice up. No feeding the chimps."

The delegation laughed it up.

"But," zie went on, "these privs are clearly still showing signs of toxic cisnormativity. It's offensive. Have them all disciplined."

"Yes, Minister." The doc made a note on her smartpalm.

Zoe grimaced. They would probably rape zer if they could. If these walls weren't here. They were all leering at zer, wanting zer, desperate to despoil zer unattainable body. A primitive lust. Disgusting, pathetic things. Their sick fetishistic fantasies. *How dare they?*

The corridor ended in a sliding door, led out onto a skywalk adjoining the dormitory wing to the medical centre. Halfway across, Zoe stopped again, this time to look down at the exercise yard several floors below.

Around fifty privs on outdoor detention, kneeling in the dirt, heads bowed, greasy, jumpsuits stuck sodden to their shoulders. Guards marched up and down the rows, kicked those found to be slouching. Over by the twenty-foot perimeter wall, groups of three were put through posture punishments, forced to adopt awkward stances for hours at a time, the guards probably taking bets on whether they would pass out from pain or from exhaustion. Zoe had a raw shiver of delight as one of the females fell face-first in the muck.

Radiator air greeted them at the medical wing entrance. A little further on, the doc escorted the group into the labs. More screens here. The rooms less functional than the dorms, not even half the size of them, more like cubbyholes with windows.

Zoe peered into one. The CisHet male student inside, curled up in a ball, jumpsuit dirty, rocking to a rhythm only he could hear. Zoe flicked open the intercom. Through it came a recurring guttural sound, an autistic giggle, something that his mind—whatever was left of it—found soothing.

They walked further on, passed zer favourite attraction—the live experiments. First the castrates, ambling about naked, bodies waxed, patchy with white scar tissue. Then the more creative tests. One with his mouth stapled shut, hands removed, shuffling about mindlessly. One in the sleep deprivation tank, eyes red, scraping at the walls. This one here, strapped to a gurney, skull cap removed, cables hooked up to soggy grey matter, still awake. And the newest research subjects—the trans-species participants. One with wings sewn to its back. One with fur grafted over its flesh. Others with transplanted horns and antlers and fins. Some crawling on the floor, unable to make their limbs work as they once did.

"My Goddess. They look like mythological creatures," Zoe said, her nose fogging the window.

"Gradual elimination of the outward signs of biological anatomy revealed some interesting results," Marsh said. "Surgical enhancements combined with specified exercises to encourage targeted muscle development. Restricted diets. Careful hormone transplants. Not too much to lose all semblance of human form, of course, but enough to bring us close to a more evolved end of the gender spectrum."

Great Birth-Giver. "Otherkin. *Physical* otherkin."

"We call them *therianthropes.*"

"And the behavioural effects?"

"So far…well—they behave."

A few of the tour group were pale, fidgety. Dominic's eyes near shut, the little wuss. Not Zoe. Skipping from one viewing screen to the next reminded her of being a kid, being taken to a sweet shop or bakery, seeing the particoloured treats lined up in their display cases. Liquorice rope. Sherbert dips. Fondant fancies. Cream buns. Pink-iced donuts…

Only one, her father would tell her.

The bastard.

Look at me now you binarist oppressor. Can't tell me what to do anymore can you I'll have it all my rules my treats fuck you you're lucky you're not still here or I'd—

"What's this?" she said, her attention drawn to the people behind the partition that housed the operating theatre.

A young priv in a wheelchair, arms strapped to the armrests, being prepped by a group of masked-up physicians. He fidgeted in the seat, clenched his fists, glanced up at the one-way glass. Healthy-looking enough. Already shaved on top. Zoe edged closer, hunger growing. This was the fudge sundae. This was the triple truffle mud cake.

"Transferred out of a youth institute this afternoon," Marsh said, checking her notes. "Three months' shy of release. He's shown resistance to classes, maintains a defiant attitude. They even found him with contraband when they went to collect him."

"What ya doin'?" the priv asked the medical team. "This ain't where I thought we was going. Why are you—"

One of the surgeons shushed him, told him he wasn't permitted to talk.

"No, I don't want this!" he cried out. "Let me go! Please!"

A doctor approached behind him, pulled a strap around his head, between his jaws, buckled it in tightly until the screams muffled. His shiny head thrashed.

Marsh said, "Such a specimen is ideal to see for this sort of gender affirmation research. The process begins with shearing, cleansing and administration of the sedative."

The surgeons washed their hands, applied latex gloves. Stainless steel pedestal carts were dressed, loaded with rubber tubes, syringes, plastic clamps, all manner of unidentifiable instruments. The subject's gown was removed. He jerked and strained. The doctor ignored the fuss, swabbed hot wax onto his knees. As they worked, other attendants wheeled in a trolley, carrying what looked to be either a dead or sleeping goat.

Zoe breathed on the glass. "What's the objective for this one?"

"Legs, tail and horn transplant. Our first attempt at a faun."

Zoe sighed. "I wish I had time to watch, but we really must move on."

"Whenever you're ready," Marsh said, scanning her biometric card to the doors of the natal lab.

Zoe instructed the others to wait for zer, then went through. An array of small, transparent boxes were lined up around the unit, a miniature version of the main lab.

Marsh flipped the fluorescents on. Anticipating the question, she said, "Cultivation and implantation of the male and female zygotes has been progressing. We've made some headway on fusion, giving the subjects gonadal tissue of both types but won't know if self-fertilisation is yet possible. This time last year, we couldn't harvest one. Now, we've produced more than thirty."

"What about the ready-made ones?"

"I'm afraid the ectogenic phase has hit a wall. The resulting foetuses have been, uh, less than ideal, harbouring all sorts of defects and disabilities. Samples are only surviving a few weeks at a time."

Zoe observed the specimens—mousey pink bodies submerged in electrolyte solution, locked inside clear plastic bags. The broods were weak, misshapen, most only days from death.

"What's the problem?" Zoe asked.

"For one, our research is split between three different objectives— removing the need for parental donors, developing true gonadal intersex individuals, and being able to carry out the entire process in vitro. I would elect to refocus on one objective at a time—"

"No, we need all outcomes together. One solution. No defined gender. No childbirth. No biological parents."

"Minister, with great respect, we're working off a huge gap in knowledge and experience. Years of lessons and material have either been lost or destroyed. In essence, we're having to start from scratch."

"As the country's chief scientist, you're lack of confidence in our work is beginning to sound problematic, Doctor." Zoe spoke with a smile, but nothing zie said was meant to be taken lightly.

"We need more time."

"Don't we all. You know how busy I am these days. It would be such an inconvenience at this stage to have to break away from my duties to look for your replacement."

"But Minister—"

"And failing to meet the requirements of the Ministry could be identified as treasonous. I wouldn't want you to have to deal with all that hassle."

Marsh's words struggled. "We'll try harder. We'll cancel leave, double headcount on night shifts."

"What would you do with more funding?"

"More funding?" She cleared her throat, thinking. "Depending how much more, we could hire more researchers. Buy more processing power. Run more simultaneous samples…"

"And that would progress things more quickly?"

"It might."

"It might?"

"It would, yes. Of course it would."

Zoe tapped on the lid of one of the boxes, seeing if the foetus would respond to the noise. "You'll get all the funding you need, Doctor."

CHAPTER FOURTEEN

It wasn't raining much at all but the drops were big and fat and no less wet. Two blocks on, Jake's hair was matted. He didn't know where he was going. An old-fashioned sandwich board sat out by the curb, chalk lettering crying pastel tears. It advertised all day breakfasts, fresh NeverCold at mid-range prices. It wasn't the Junction, though it still sounded better than the slop he'd existed on behind bars.

It was, but only just. The pale slab of meat resisted his knife, felt like rubber on his fork as he prodded it for signs of life. No wonder he was the only one in the café.

"You want any sauces?" The guy in the apron was cook and waiter in one, a finger painting of brown streaks daubed down his front.

"Yeah. All of them," Jake said dryly, sawing the cords between gristle and flesh. "What kind of cut is this?"

"Reconstituted mealworm."

Jake stopped chewing, slid the food against one side of his mouth. "Mealworm?"

"Yeah. A bug burger."

Jake resisted the urge to gag, swallowed hard instead. "I thought you served the genuine stuff out here? Beef? Lamb?"

The cook laughed unnecessarily loudly, retreated to the counter. "Beef, he says! *Ya salaam.* That's funny."

Jake shrugged. "Is it?"

"Haven't had real meat out here in the OSZ for six months. Don't you watch the netwires? They're running out of the stuff. Not enough open land to rear cattle. Not enough willing people to breed or butcher them."

"Can't you import it?"

"From where? Country's stopped trading with just about every nation on the planet with a cow pasture. How big's the rock you've been living under?"

If Jake had known the Junction had become an ersatz café, he may have skipped it. As of now, he was too hungry to complain. On the plus side, he had a plate of organic animal protein rather than something scaffold-printed in a fermentation farm and deliberately drained of flavour. Despite a distinctive chemical-like taste, the food had enough moisture to rouse his taste buds out of their collective coma. As he ate he developed a greater appreciation of fasting holy men. Deprivation of simple pleasures intensifies them when they're rediscovered…

But that's not always true. What about an object or a person or a place held sacred to your heart for years, only to find it disappointing in retrospect? And what of those things you always want but have never had? Are they sweeter on the first taste, or the second, so many years apart? He wanted to believe the latter. Otherwise everything would only ever get worse the more he experienced it and that thought didn't sound cheerful.

He pushed the condiments aside, opened the digital copy of the *Daily Femail* blinking from the screen embedded in the table. Most news was heavily censored but he could at least try to get some idea of what was happening in the world. The netwire's front page was election coverage. Vid-clips of the prime minister shaking hands, kissing babies. He swiped right. A full spread on fashion: *from activist wear to fetish gear*. Swiped again. The court case he'd seen earlier on the guard's netscreen. Some Hollywood star on trial for hate crimes and violently assaulting a colleague. According to testimonies, the actor had become drunk on his own fame. Like the smartnet coverage, the clip was plastered with content warnings, detailing the man's alleged misconduct. All the quotes provided were cropped from social posts on Xprez, opinions of random people, all mirroring the same sentiment, backing the same narrative. Jake smeared another morsel of his maggot meat with English mustard.

He grazed on the showbiz news, not able to place most of the faces of the rich and famous for their work. Artificial couples on a red carpet seemed to be miming an impression of happy people. One handsome man in a velvet suit and a glue-on smile stood with a squat trans person, gender indistinct, who wore a crystal gown and a pug face, maybe twice his age. This person clung to his arm, pouting for the cameras. It was a hostage situation.

Further on, Jake skimmed an editorial about the growing demand for research into something called psychoendocrinology. The columnist sounded furious. Universities weren't progressing this field of study fast enough, she claimed. No mention of her medical background but she seemed adamant she knew what she was talking about.

In the single page dedicated to international news, he learned of the US president urging Western allies to renew their domestic production commitments or risk further shortages of goods and materials. A summit was to be arranged. It was as if the rest of the world didn't exist.

Nothing in the film review section interested him. An animated family movie about a gender non-conforming gerbil. A couple of big budget superheroine flicks. A documentary about the transcore punk music scene. About the sum of it.

He turned the screen off. Rain made rivulets against the café window. He finished his grub steak.

Jake left the building thinking about women. Not the ones he had known from the Cooler and not the ones that had been created in an operating room—the ones he hadn't ever known, ones who he saw sometimes in the streets, walking by him from time to time. He was still thinking about them when he looked up from the pavement. There were five wholly different types of women at the far end of the street. The sound grabbed his attention: a hollow, scraping sound. Wood on stone. Didn't think much of it at first, but it wouldn't stop. Whatever it was, it was getting closer.

A man ran out into the road, forced an autobile to skid to a sensor-triggered halt, ignored it, kept going until he disappeared across the Common. A flock of birds abandoned a tree like seeds being kicked from the head of a dandelion.

Another man broke out in a sprint, came towards Jake. A theft, maybe. Muggers fleeing from the scene? But the man who steamed past him appeared scared and was empty-handed. Jake called out to him. The runner kept on running.

The group of women were coming towards him. He could see now they were non-binarists, their arms still muscled by organic testosterone, bone structures still dense. Unlike the fleeing men, they moved at a steady, lumbering pace. About two blocks away, Jake saw they were similarly dressed—t-shirts and hoodies cut off at the belly, hair dyed an array of colours. The scraping sound was a result of the wooden bats they each carried, the ends dragging against the paving stones. The danger didn't register with him until he saw the umbrella vendor step out from under the bakery awning to see what was causing the commotion—only to turn in a panic, stumble over his own feet, land on his hands.

The leader of the group rushed forward. In the second that followed, her hoodie fell away, unbridled a ferocious mohawk, a Ben and Jerry's logo emblazoned on her chest. She swung the bat at the vendor, struck him across the back. The vendor fell flat, rolled over, gasped for air.

Stiff as hyenas, they encircled him from all sides. Jake could only see glimpses of him between pairs of industrial platform boots. He had his hands up, protecting his face. It didn't do much good. The bats rained down on his arms and legs. The crack of bones snapping reverberated along the street. The man screamed. He didn't stop screaming.

Mohawk called the others off, stood over him, planted her feet on either side of his head.

"Crush the Cis-tem!" she bellowed, lifting her bat to the sky. She brought it down like an axe on firewood. A sound like an apple splitting. He stopped screaming.

Jake was stationary in time. Tendons wouldn't move. Ligaments wouldn't budge. He could hear nothing but his pulse beating in his temples.

The trans gang were leaving their victim on the street, dead as dirt, turning back towards him. They were crossing the road now, twirling their weapons with the unwavering focus of a marching band. One of them raised her bat towards him, her mouth opening, rallying. They had seen him.

They had seen him and he couldn't move.

They had seen him and they were coming his way.

Rough hands grabbed Jake by the arm, wrenched him out of his stasis, pulled him back through the door of the café.

The cook clicked the lock into place, flipped the welcome sign, turned to him, said, "Come on, help me with this table."

Jake gripped the other end, helped heave the table in front of the door. He followed the guy's lead, crouched to keep a low profile. They headed for the kitchen.

"They just killed that man," Jake said out loud, trying to come to terms with what he'd seen. "What the fuck? They corpsed him right there on the street."

"You were about to be next, standing out there like that," the cook said, his back against the oven. "Keep your voice down."

"Who are they?"

"Really? You visiting from Mars?"

Jake wiped his eyes with the back of his hand. "Near enough."

The cook shifted his weight, sat himself on the floor. "TRANARCHY gang. Thugs. Any CisHet they find, whether they have an Ally Pass or not..." He drew a finger across his throat. "They hate us. Think we're animals."

"We need to call the police," Jake said. He reached for his pocket.

"*Ya lahwi!* You don't have a clue, do you?" The cook looked at Jake with raw pity. "The police won't do anything. They ignore them. Yeah, they say it's illegal but they don't do nothing to stop 'em."

The cook stiffened, pressed his finger to his lips. The scraping sound returned, loud now, outside the front of the café.

A lump rose in Jake's throat. The lock and the table wouldn't be enough to keep them out. There was another exit at the back. He started towards it, only for the greasy hand to seize him by the arm again.

The scraping continued past, became fainter. Whether they knew he was there or not, they weren't stopping to look.

The cook exhaled. They sat there on the floor for a long time.

When the sun was going down, Jake left the café. No sign of the umbrella man's body. No sign of anyone else.

He walked for an hour, nowhere in particular. The chill was setting in, the rain hadn't let up. Jake didn't care. Eventually he found an old hotel, went inside, tracked water onto the wooden floor. The place would once have been nice and rustic. Not now. Now it was dusty and dank and the receptionist behind the desk sat in a hole-ridden cardigan and offered no smile to welcome his guest.

In the room, Jake tried to bathe himself in tepid water, left his soaked clothes over the radiator. He got into bed, pulled the blanket about him up to his ears, stared at the glow of the streetlight on the ceiling.

CHAPTER FIFTEEN

Birmingham's Hyatt Regency presidential suite had everything Tavistock needed. Apart from a punching bag.

The short flight up from London had been the first time she had taken a sky-trip without the usual flutter of nerves. In fact, she had barely registered the journey. She had become lost in Urwin's novel.

The encrypted book sat on the coffee table, its content like a stick of dynamite in the room. The first few chapters of *Cockleshells* revealed to her a path she had not considered before. It was all she could think about.

Now, in the hotel suite, she found herself unable to prep her speech for the morning's campaign rally. Her speechwriter had helped her put together a few words about the future of education and housing. The hard work done. She needed to know her pauses, her inflections, when to play for laughs, when for applause. That was all. Easy in principle.

Curled up on one of the sofas in a fresh terrycloth robe, her notes before her, she was forgetting the words. A scented candle gave the room a hint of vanilla. Soft music played from the speaker dock. None of it was helping.

The book was calling to her.

As she stared at it, a knock at the door made her jolt. Tavistock pushed the smartpalm away, checked the peephole. Hannah, her security chief. Even with the silver cloches and compartments all carefully checked, Hannah had commandeered the room service cart. Only she could be entrusted to bring anything into the suite.

"Much appreciated," said Tavistock, as the bodyguard set the trolley by the baby grand. "Do please order yourself dinner from the executive menu this evening. I think it's well deserved."

"Thank you, ma'am," said Hannah, "but the team has ordered a spread and a few beers. I'll eat later. Want to make sure you have all you need first before I settle in for the night."

As always, Hannah had been given the adjoining room. The rest of the floor and the one below were taken up by other security team members and the prime ministerial staff. Her security chief would not sleep until she knew her employer had gone to bed, when she was sure her crew had the front door and every entrance of the hallway locked down. If need be, Hannah could enter the suite through the emergency side door. It had never come to that. Goddess willing, never would. Knowing she was only ever a few feet away helped Tavistock feel safe, in the way her nightlight had helped vanquish the monsters under the bed when she was still a young untransitioned boy.

"Oh, and my evening plans," Tavistock said. "I trust that's still on the agenda."

"Of course, ma'am." Hannah was already at the door again. "Nine o'clock, as normal."

"Fine. I'll call up first anyway, in case you need additional time."

"What would I do without you?"

If Hannah had ever felt awkward about seeing to these requests, she had never let it show. For that, Tavistock was forever indebted.

The prime minister took the tray to the sofa, set it on the coffee table, tucked into her sole meunière with ratatouille and basil. She paired it with a glass of Bollinger, leaving the rest of the bottle in the ice bucket. More than one glass would be foolhardy, regardless of how much she wanted to forget the day.

For dessert, she treated herself to a raspberry and chocolate meringue. Normally, she would forego so much sugar at once. Now was not the time to impose unnecessary self-demands. As she let a mouthful melt on her tongue, her mind tracked back to *Cockleshells*, to the moral dilemma its protagonists were forced to confront.

Tavistock refused to entertain the notion that society in the real-world was crumbling as much as the fictional civilisation within Urwin's novel. What could not be denied was that the edges were showing signs of wear. She was more than mindful that one loose thread could cause the whole thing to unravel.

She couldn't allow that.

The Big Reboot had been hard won. Timing had been everything. The old regime had not been toppled overnight, but over the course of many nights. Hundreds, if not thousands. The only weapons drawn had been words. The only assassinations successfully carried out were those of the character variety. The only things killed—at least in the early days—were careers. More forceful actions had taken place eventually. But the beginning had been a perfect exercise in soft power.

A fair game. The TEP had simply done what every political party before it had tried to do—play on society's fears, exaggerate the threats, associate counter opinion with extremism, present leaders as parental figures. Tried and tested. Not that it always worked, but when a democracy creates an incubator for freedom, any idea can grow beneath its banner.

It was difficult for Tavistock to place when the turning point truly occurred. Some zistorians cited the ground-breaking research of Kinsey or Money, though she considered their work more a starting point than a turning point. More practical thinkers claimed it to have been the introduction of the Don't Say Anything Bill, when criticism of the LGBTQ+ movement itself was banned, first informally—creeping press regulations, media blackouts, amendments to workplace rules—and then by criminal law. Under huge pressure from lobbyists, a campaign of petitioning, threats of social ostracism, the bill was slipped quietly into the Public Order Act. So, maybe that had been it.

Textbooks didn't dwell on the legal episodes. Why would they? The implications were problematic—to suggest that CisHet people had been the ones to have enabled the change, had relinquished their control of the country rather than losing it in the face of a powerful gender-non-conformist uprising? Such detail would contradict the established narrative. Responsibility had to be placed elsewhere. On the petitions. On the protests. On the leaders hyping the revolution.

In truth, they had done little.

Truth. The word alone left Tavistock nauseated. And yet truth was a teacher she could not ignore.

The old system had tumbled because it had been passive, desperate to please, because it was too arrogant to take the emerging threats seriously. And because its decision-makers had been threatened with social ostracism if they failed to bow to the altar of progressive ideology. She didn't need *Cockleshells'* prologue to remind her of that.

She had obsessed over the faltering of her own system for months, wondered if it had already begun to crumble. It was her pillow thought, the ringmaster of her daydreams, the poltergeist in her head.

Her voxwatch buzzed—a private contact requesting to be connected. A glob of Chantilly cream slipped from the end of her fork, landed on the robe. Tavistock swore, grabbed a napkin, dabbed at it, hoped the raspberry juice didn't stain and make her appear slovenly. If that was her guests calling up already…

"Minister, I hope I've not caught you at a bad time." The voice was unmistakeable.

"All things considered, Zoe, it could be better."

"I wouldn't call if I didn't consider it important. Are you alone?"

"For now."

"Dominic's sources are reporting that Gallard is planning on ramping up her campaign next week. She intends to hold a rally in the heart of London."

"What are her talking points?"

"We don't know the exact content of what she plans to say, but there's rumour she'll be openly criticising your leadership and calling for major reform."

"That's of little concern. Do what we always do. Close the local roads off. Organise a dozen of our own supporters to attend with airhorns. I trust the censors have already instructed the netwires not to cover it?"

"We can't do that any of that this time, Minister."

Tavistock paused. She had never heard her equality minister utter such words. "I beg your pardon?"

"While we can't confirm the content of her speech, we do know the location."

"Don't play games with me, Zoe. I don't have the energy."

"It's Trafalgar Square, Minister. The steps of the National Gallery. On Non-Binarist Pride Day. A few hours before your public address."

Tavistock could feel her blood bubble. Every inch of her wanted to scream, to hurl the dessert plate at the wall, to turn the coffee table over. Instead, she waited. A count of five seconds, each one working to defuse the pressure.

"She wouldn't dare."

"Wouldn't she? When has she ever shown respect for our way of life? It's going to happen. The train is rolling."

Tavistock, pacing now. She kicked her slippers off, bare toes scrunched at the shag pile. Gallard knew they wouldn't be able to prevent people from attending the biggest event of the year. She would command a captive audience of thousands. Every major netwire would be filming live. Everyone in the country would associate her appearance with the memory of Suarez-Adarsha's brave stand. It was more than problematic. It was despicable. Disgraceful. As devious as any tactic the Equality Ministry itself had ever conjured.

The words came dripping from Tavistock's lips, one at a time. "This is bordering on sedition. I want it stopped. I don't care what it takes."

"We could find a way to stop it, Minister. It wouldn't be easy, but we could probably find a way. Or..."

"Or?"

"We could accept that this is exactly the opportunity we've been looking for."

Tavistock took a moment, breathed deeply.

Zoe said, "How much of the book have you read?"

"A few chapters."

"Have you got to the part where it's explained why the plotters need to silence their rival publicly rather than, say, kidnapping her in the dead of night or smothering her in her bed?"

"I'm busy out here, Zoe. I can't spend all my time reading. Bring me up to speed."

"The spectacle is intrinsic to their plan, you see. The violence needs to be overt and final. There can be no doubt of their enemy's demise."

"But you—" Tavistock corrected herself. "They would be making her a martyr, wouldn't they?"

"They would, indeed. But martyrs are defined by those who despatch them. And if the public think she's been silenced by some other entity, the public will set their ire on that other entity. You see, it's not about getting rid of her—it's about reframing the public consciousness, once and for all."

"I think I understand."

"Is that all you think, Minister?"

"I think I need to finish this book."

"You said you don't care what it takes. Is that true? Would you like me to take care of it all now? You'll not have to lift a finger. I promise it will be so easy you'll wonder what all the fuss was about."

She could barely speak. Even hearing herself say the word felt like a risk. "Yes."

"Yes. That's all you need to say. Now you need to relax. Get some rest. Enjoy your campaign. The people of Britannia need you. Okay?"

"Promise me again, Zoe."

"I've never let you down, Minister. And I never will."

Urwin disconnected. Tavistock was tenser than before the call. She knew she would feel this way for a long time. Until the deed was done. Perhaps longer. The thought of being able to run the country again, uncontested, with unquestioning loyalty from her peers—it should have been medicinal. The terrible thing she had sanctioned was already haunting her. She knew Zoe Urwin well enough to know it would be done, as was planned, to the letter.

Tough decisions. That's what she had signed up for. Couldn't forget that.

She would simply have to work harder to channel the hatred within, refocus it in a productive way. Not her fault, of course. *Their* fault. Her self-loathing was internalised cissexism, the scarification of a youth spent growing up in the Cis-tem. She would need to work hard tonight to find sweet relief—that euphoria that would allow her to enjoy a full night's sleep without waking in the early hours, wondering what she had become.

The voxwatch buzzed again. Her PA with a five minute warning.

In the mirror, she applied her war paint—a touch of eyeshadow, a dab of blusher—and trimmed the edges of her beard. She stood back, looked at herself, one side, the other. Unlike most of her colleagues, she had kept herself in decent shape. Not because she was trying to maintain a body image—that would be problematic—but because slender was how she felt comfortable. Still, the past few years had been unforgiving. Her belly had widened. Her skin was slackening. Her visits to the stylist to top up the strands on her scalp to maintain her signature auburn look were becoming more frequent. She knew it was an honour to age, gracefully or otherwise, but that knowledge didn't prevent her from feeling innately horrified by the process, nor stop her from fighting it whenever she could.

The knock came. At the door stood her guests for the evening. One male, one female. Both sandy-haired and button-eyed. Not yet sullied by the ravages of puberty. They brought nothing with them, had been thoroughly searched before coming within a mile of the building. They were nervous.

Understandable.

"My dears! Welcome."

Tavistock examined them, nodded. Most satisfactory. She stepped away from the threshold. The visitors entered the room, the electronic lock clicked into place behind them.

"Care for some champagne?" she asked. The visitors didn't know how to answer. "It's all right. We can ignore the rules for tonight. I am, after all, the one who makes them."

The children declined, apologised. She poured them two half-measure flutes anyway, put them in their hands.

"Try it," she said. "The bubbles feel magical on your tongue. Just like fizzy Choco-lite."

They each sniffed their glass, sipped at the booze, winced at the sharpness.

The girl said, "You look fierce, prime minister, if you don't mind me saying."

She didn't mind, of course. They had been prepped on what they could and could not say. On what they had to say. Normally, for anyone to comment on her physical appearance without her consent would be a serious offence, but not here. Not tonight.

"Aw, that's so sweet of you."

Tavistock dimmed the lights, lit another candle. In her youth—still that clueless, pre-transitioned boy—she had dreamt about ruling the country. Back then, she had only thought about what she would do in the role, not what she would be. Not how much pressure she would have to deal with, not how much stronger she would have to become. Like other colleagues climbing the political ladder, she had always assumed leadership was easier than it looked, especially with all the perks that come with office. Now, at the end of her third term, she sometimes wished for anything but the life she had been granted. But the perks were still the kicker. The perks she wouldn't give up. Couldn't. And if power meant anything these days, her next term in office would allow the party to finally shape the system towards freedoms she had long craved, allow her to indulge in her true passions without having to sneak around like the roaches living out in the Cistrict.

Enough was enough.

"My dears, it's much more comfortable in that room there," she said. "Come. I have lots of fun games we can play together."

The boy and girl cast a slow gaze to the door. They knew better than to refuse the prime minister.

CHAPTER SIXTEEN

Within the belly of the temple, they formed a crescent a few yards from the ancient granite altar. The great dome above them had been installed with nights like these in mind, allowed moonlight to flow through like an effervescent weir of empowerment. It filled the nave and its arches with a white-blue patina.

With the exception of the high priestess, the initiates were dressed identically—swearing off any outward hierarchy—in cowled cloaks of crushed purple velvet. Their sleeves billowed at the forearms, their skirts pooled on the polished stone, hiding their slippers. No more than forty all together, yet each of them bound spiritually and emotionally. As allegory for the biological rhythm into which they had trained themselves, they moved together, spoke together, drank together, shared each other's appetites. All part of the ritual—a bi-weekly occurrence that demanded no less than full commitment and enthusiasm of its elite members.

With the approach of the seasonal holy day of Hallowmas, the Sisterhood was preparing to induct a new apprentice into each coven. This year, a full moon was expected. A good sign. Some called it the Blood Moon, owing to its sanguine hue. They lauded its correspondence to both masculine and feminine traits. Others called it the Huntress Moon, signifying a more war-like connection to their deity, a time of activism and rage. Either way, there was no doubting that—in spite of an approaching winter—something special was about to happen. Zoe Urwin was sure of it. The syzygy of the earth and its lone satellite was further reassurance that zer quest was sanctioned by the highest powers. By That Who is All and Whole Unto Themself.

Perched on a ring of chaise longue, the initiates swayed in the throes of meditation, their bodies rolling as if caught in a gentle breeze, their eyes flickering back in their heads, drunk on the pungency of patchouli oil. The speaker system played the strains of a mountain dulcimer loud enough to drown out the patter of rain on shingle and glass. In this instant, Zoe glanced up from beneath zer cowl at the great stone representation of Hermaphroditus that dominated the crossing between the east and west transepts.

The Goddess, frozen in glorious dishabille, obscenely posed upon her ten-foot pedestal. A female figure with a himation wrapped around its shoulders and a chiton belted below swollen breasts. The front of its skirt raised in its hands, exposing erect male genitalia beneath, unashamed, unrestrained by right-wing prudishness. And surrounding the Great Birth-Giver's pedestal, set spiralling deep through the marble floors, were narrow stone grooves leading to the baptismal pool. Seeing it at this angle, under the moonlight, always made the hair on Zoe's armpits stand on end.

A gong clanged from somewhere in the parapets. The shrouded acolytes began their prayer in unison.

Lovely Goddess of the Cave!
Radiant Goddess of the Pool!
Of Venus and Mars united,
Thou who wakest in the waters,
When the sun is sunk in slumber,
Though with moon upon my forehead,
Though with heaving breast
And bulging phallus…

They shucked and roiled, bowled their arms, stamped their feet.

…Who the union at night preferest
Unto wedding in the daylight,
With the nymphs into the music
Of the horn—Thyself the child of Hermes…

They clawed at their heads, spun in circles, threw their throats to the vaulted roof.

… Ah, happy maid,
Conscious of man's embrace,

Twice happy youth
And most powerful: I pray thee
Think, although but for an instant,
Upon us who pray unto thee!
Blessed be!
Blessed be!
Blessed be!

As the chant ended, they squealed in delight, sighed as one. Several dropped to the floor, feigned exhaustion, acted as though the intensity of their worship had sent them into some form of celestial delirium. A few of the Cultists went to their aid in grand theatrics of care, fanned their fellow parishioners with wafts of their sleeves, shared acknowledgement that the Deity of All and Whole had indeed been casting his/her keen eye in their direction this night.

Post-worship, the atmosphere shifted to decadence, as was customary to these services. Sweet foods were brought forth, set beside the pillows. The droning music amped up. The attendees engaged in light-hearted gossip. Some took each other by the waist, danced in weaving circles. Some fed others by hand, plucked profiteroles and sticky phyllo from the trays, placed them delicately into eager mouths. Some stripped off their cloaks in mimicry of their Deity, writhed against each other, plunged their mouths on any hint of bare flesh. The air soon grew heady with the stink of incense and syrup and sweat and secretions and digestive gasses, all fused into a bitter perfume that would likely cause most uninitiated to gag.

Zoe inhaled deeply.

Zoe shuffled through the tumult, towards the high priestess (*polyamorous genderfluid cryptid, they/them*), known legally as Unicorn Tsunami—who was blanketed in a cloak of black and gold trim, whose hair was a nest of grey and turquoise. The leader of the Central Coven tapped her staff to the floor, beckoned Zoe to the altar. Their discussion would be between no one but the two of them and the statue.

"The time of induction is nearly upon us, child," Tsunami said with practised gravitas. "The hour grows late for you to select your candidate."

"I believe I have done so, Protectress."

Tsunami gripped Zoe by the shoulder. A row of yellow, uneven teeth presented themselves above the loose flesh of her stubbled jowls— tiny, forgotten tombstones.

"And she is receptive to our needs at this crucial time?"

"The candidate has been briefed on the situation at hand. She is receptive. She is unquestioningly one of us. A worthy acolyte to add to our sacred circle."

"It is one thing to be with us, child. It is another to be prepared for what is to come, or to embrace our objectives with courage and conviction. Anyone can claim to be prepared. It is rare to find even a small number willing to commit to sacrifice at the moment fate presents itself."

"I believe she will, Protectress. She reminds me of myself in many ways. More importantly, she has an ideal position in public life to set our plan in motion. She can get close, access any area. A veritable insider."

"Does she already worship?"

"Yes, at the Notting Hill coven."

"An Out-Zoner?"

Zoe could taste the anxiety in the priestess's voice.

"Yes, a lowly ally. But I need someone with a social ladder to climb," Zoe said. "Part of her reward will be permanent residence in the ISZ. There is nothing to fear, Mother."

The pentagram on top of the staff caught a wink of moon from the skylight. Tsunami ran a large hand through her braids, from the grey at her scalp to the motley dyes of each tightly woven lock.

"Then she shall be initiated here," Tsunami said. "If you vouch for this brave individual, we will delay our plans no longer."

"She already has a new cloak being tailored to her size. It will be a magnificent ceremony. Our congregation will ring with joy. And soon…" Zoe stepped closer to the great elder, so close zie could feel

91

zer own breath beating back from the priestess's furry cheek. "Soon we will finally put an end to our enemy."

"Blessed be, child."

"Blessed be."

A shriek of laughter erupted from the nave. Worshippers sprang to their feet, parted in the aisle. The centrepiece of the annual festivity was on its way. Two of the coven lurched up the aisle in staggered steps, their knuckles, white where the chain-link cables bit into the joints of their fingers. Behind them came the scrabbling sound of smaller, harder steps, flighty, slipping on the polished marble.

The pig—a fully grown Chester White, indisputably male—was as unsure as it was unsteady. It showed no obvious signs of distress. Why would it? It was drugged up to its proboscis on sedatives. Had to be. No one wanted to deal with a wild animal barrelling about in such a sacred venue.

The hog lolled its head from one row of pews to the other, left its ears dangling either side of two wary, watery eyes that already seemed to have been replaced with a taxidermist's marbles. It allowed its attendants to half-walk, half-drag it onto the short platform erected below the Goddess's statue like a theatrical stage. A grotesque juxtaposition. Near enough heresy. But if some considered it a sacrilege, it was one the coven had deemed necessary.

Desensitisation was a gradual process. Had to start slowly. A few months of latex mannequins, then on to surgical mannequins. Now they were on livestock. Warm, breathing, quaking livestock. Because there would be a reaction. There would be some kind of noise, some kind of smell, some kind of mess. Without all that, what would be the point?

From zer vantage at the altar, Zoe could see three letters had been painted in red across the beast's back. Merely reading them released a surge of delight.

CIS

Zoe could feel the same energy pluming off the caped cleric, formed by the spiritual bridge they had forged over the years. Unicorn

Tsunami seemed to purr, hiked her robes, circled to the front of the stage.

"Formless spirits, gather," the priestess said. "Open your eyes and take heed. The Deity truly watches over us this night. I have observed the planets, have studied the portents and have tasted the soil. A great event is taking shape, like the merging of two powerful oceans. The True Era of Change peers now from the horizon with the glow of a bright, new day. And we are chosen by Hermaphroditus's hand to bear witness to it."

The congregation sighed, cried out in joy: *"Blessed be!"*

"Where her seed falls, we shall make a new paradise."

"Blessed be!"

The boar grunted, conceding its own prayer. It hobbled a little further forward. Some of the coven cringed, recoiled as it turned its rear to them, giving them full view of the outlandishly bulbous testicles hanging between its legs like ostrich eggs bundled in a leather sack. They swung in a lewd, hypnotic fashion, slapped at the pink flesh of its thighs.

"But until then, we must commit this porcine martyr as a symbol of our dedication. Its sacrifice will feed her flame, will affix quills to her arrow, will bestow strength to her bow arm, and will grant sharpness to her eye."

"That Who is All and Whole Unto Themself!"

"Come forward, spirits!"

Confronted with such a foul sight, the congregation did not rush to the platform. Soon enough they came together, crept closer, each encouraging the other to see the ritual through. Around the platform, the high priestess lit a ring of fat candles. A slab of gold was placed in front of the stage above an ornate stand, accompanied by a rubber mallet.

Surrounded by light that danced yellow and warm, the pig swayed, still upright, unaware of its place at the centre of this production. It snorted lazily.

The beast's attendants hooked its hind legs with the pair of iron manacles, the links welded to bolts set in the floorboards. Locked in, they steadied the animal, forced its trotters to slide apart to keep from bucking. Now, Tsunami had replaced their staff with another. Instead of a glass orb, the moonlight landed upon the smooth surface of steel, oiled metal forged into a crescent, sharpened with a diligent hand into a formidable sickle.

One of the worshippers showed more fortitude than the others, knelt behind the animal, secured the base of its scrotum in a lasso, pulled the knot tight. The pig felt it. It tried to stagger forward to escape, its asthmatic snaffling growing agitated.

Being on the other side of the stage, Zoe had view of the martyr's face. When it realised it was trapped, zie could swear its stupor evaporated, its eyes flash with something that looked like panic. Zoe salivated, imagining this same view in the future. How ironic such a filthy, untamed animal should be granted access to sacred ground while the CisHets of zer own species remained forbidden. That would change soon. When this performance became ritual across the country, some would be permitted for the first time to play their part.

How good of the Great God/Goddess to countenance such a violation in order to cleanse the world. To invite the Devil into their own home in order to exorcise him. Perhaps it was wild boar that Hermaphroditus hunted in their heavenly forest. Or perhaps their quarry was—had always been—a stranger beast. One more brutish and corrupt and despicable. But no more intelligent! Zoe's imagination ran, galloped, leapt, filling zer with unbridled elation.

Still to this day, Maria Suarez-Adarsha was often likened to Hermaphroditus. Some even implied—without an ounce of irony— that the civil rights activist was in fact the Deity's incarnation on earth. A genuine cosmic manifestation, arriving to lead their people into the New Dawn, only to disappear back to the heavens as soon as they had successfully lit the fires of revolution. Zoe knew better, of course—was one of the few who knew, with certainty, that Suarez-Adarsha had not been as committed to the cause as Zoe Urwin. And she had certainly not flown away on a cloud of her own magic genderqueefs.

If anything, Zoe decided, Zoe Urwin was the worldly counterpart of Hermaphroditus. Was it not zer own masterplan that was to bring forth the Era of Change? Had it not been zer own ruthless pursuit of justice that had shaped the nation's most recent and most aggressive policies? And would it not be zer very self who would be standing at the forefront of zistory when the ultimate solution finally became law?

"Lovely God of the Cave!" Unicorn Tsunami said, positioning the sickle at the swine's undercarriage. "Radiant Goddess of the Pool! Heed our offering! Bring forth the end of binarism! Blessed be!"

A collective shudder through the coven as their elder yanked hard on the staff, thrust their elbows into a sawing rhythm.

Despite the heavy dose of downers, the pig reared into frenzy. A piercing, otherworldly squeal filled the walls of the temple, made every tooth in the building feel like it was experiencing involuntary surgery. Its snout flared, its mouth snapped open, showered slobber. Its coiled tail unkinked and quivered. Its front hooves lost balance in a futile effort to run, sending the beast splashing head-first into the floor, over and over. The smell of iron and urine poured from the altar. The ducts circling the Deity's statue ran dark. Thin rivulets spiralled through the floors, carried unidentifiable lumps of gore to the specially-made drains. The high priestess's face solidified in a state of manic determination.

At some point, the pig's liberated genitalia were hauled up by its bonds, dumped onto the golden slab, where one of the attendants— shaking with either terror or bloodlust—picked up the hammer, raised it above her head. The first blow sounded like a bag of overripe melons meeting a close-range shotgun blast. The testicles shattered into gloopy chunks, added something new and alien to the noxious stench.

Unblinking, Zoe Urwin watched it all. Zie had not known at first how the sacrifice would affect zer. Seeing the collapsed body of the beast, the label of zer enemy plastered across its stodgy flesh, zie was pleased to discover zie had not been disgusted by it. Nor was zie gratified. What zie felt was something zie had never expected.

Arousal. Pure, unadulterated arousal.

CHAPTER SEVENTEEN

The hotel was ten pounds of shit in a five-pound bag. A real nit pit.

The only things it had going for it: low-key and within walking distance from the ISZ. They could have gone a little more upmarket, couldn't they? As somewhere for him to hole up in for a few nights, what was stopping them springing for a place with pure cotton sheets and a king-size?

Not that he'd sleep much.

The guy at the desk was afraid to look at him. Good thing, too. He didn't want to leave an impression. The place wasn't exactly teeming with guests but unwanted attention was a risk. The only other people to have seen him there were the gin junkies at the bar, plus the young fella who had checked into the room down the hall and looked like he'd just got out of the Cooler.

He had taken his time to unpack the Burberry case. It was under the dresser now, its contents residing on the duvet and the writing desk. On the floor, the map laid out showed Stopes' Park, the Palace of Westminster, the routes he had trained himself to visualise at street-level no matter which direction he approached it from.

He had found the manual secreted inside the mattress, its coded instructions lit up now under the desk lamp—a reminder of the rigorous training sessions on fusing, welding, all that other work that left his hair matted and his nails chipped. They had provided the capability, as promised. Now he was to provide his part—the part nearly impossible for them to manage without his involvement.

Access.

The logistics of it all were sticky, sure. Months of living within the OSZ and building his profile had raised him up through only the first few echelons of society. Still much more to do to fulfil his ultimate obligation. Dirtier work than meeting strangers in parks or piecing together greasy components.

The chat show host on the smartscreen blabbered on about her brave and fierce female guests all portraying new 'badass' characters and releasing 'badass' albums. If nothing else, the inane voices were background comfort. The volume remained low enough to hear if anyone was coming up the stairs, if the elevator doors were opening. The window was open so the smell of fumes wouldn't alert someone walking past the room—or worse, set off the smoke alarm. Outside, the strain of autobiles and midnight chatter and revellers pretending they were Demi fucking Lovato, even though they lacked any drop of talent, no matter how hard they preened and sashayed or how good they thought their bloated arses looked in sequined bodysuits or PVC yoga pants...

Think, kid.

No time for that.

He dipped into the Vivienne Westwood Balmoral long wallet purse, retrieved a lipstick—Rich Rosewood, the label insisted. The vanity mirror, his canvas. Waxy lines slid down, up, criss-crossed. Location markings. Estimated timings. Things to get. Things to divest.

He stood back, pondered his notes for a while. He sat at the desk, pulled the magnifying glass clamp closer, looked at the manual, flexed the pliers, looked at the casing, peered at the battery array, held the black wire between prongs, stripped the plastic, looked at the manual, heard the plumbing judder, fired up the welding torch, poked at the activator, thought about his end goal, looked at the dress hanging on the door.

An autumnal dress, emerald green with a floral print, long-sleeved and pleated, a vintage belt to pull it all together. Not anything like the t-shirt and joggers he'd changed into when he arrived. There had been a time when it had felt alien, but skirts and dresses and cashmere jumpers were now just a uniform—something he could tolerate and discard when in the privacy of his room. There would be outfits more to his liking when all was said and done, his paymasters had said. Denim jeans. Tracksuits. Premium suits, once destined for Regent Street. Endless options. If he managed to do what they had hired him to do.

He set the torch down to cool, went to the dress, ran his hand down the fabric. It reminded him of the women back at the Compound. It kept him feeling close to them, stopped him from forgetting what they felt like.

He threw off the shirt and joggers, took the dress off the hanger, pulled it above his head. It smelled like sun-baked grass over his face, felt like cerulean sky falling around his thighs. Perfect fit.

Had to admit, it suited him. They were good, those guys. No bullshit. What would he combine with something like this? Maybe the Burberry handbag. Maybe a pair of audacious hoop earrings. Strap suede heels, of course.

97

Take it down a thousand, son. Calm your farm. You don't always have to be in work-mode.

The amount of items his people had raided off the cargo trucks, it was inevitable they'd have stockpiles of all sorts of luxury items stashed somewhere. Bourgeois sugar, baby. Real pope shit. Not that anyone would know, the way most of them lived.

The markings on the mirror obscured his view. That was better. He didn't want to see his face or anything below the waist. He positioned himself so that only his torso appeared in frame. Then he pulled the cotton away from his chest.

No doubt, Doc Sharma's work was Prime Gucci. He squeezed the flesh, traced a finger around an areola. He imagined he was watching someone else.

He lifted the hem of the dress, felt himself underneath, surprised to find he was already plumping. He allowed his fingertips to goad and massage. Thought about his end goal. Thought about what it would mean, about the world he would live in then. Thought about the person he would be on the other side of it all.

Maybe he would keep the breasts.

Maybe.

CHAPTER EIGHTEEN

INTERCEPTED TRANSMISSION TRANSCRIPT—EQUALITY MINISTRY
SUBJECT: INSURGENT BROADCAST #258
LISTENING STATION EMMELINE
25-10-46 0811 GMT

SENSITIVITY CLASSIFICATION: 8—CLASSIFIED / SANITIZED

VOICE [terrorist suspect #2408D]: What's happening, gang! You're listening to the Ozcast on Revolution Radio, with your favourite blacklisted broadcaster, once again jacking your airwaves whenever I damn well please.

First off the bat, you all know I don't often do celebrity news on this channel, but I gotta say—the more buzz coming out of Tinseltown on this Leo Learson trial makes me wonder why any sane binarist would try to be a part of Hollywood these days.

Here we have a brilliant young actor in his prime, arrested and charged with a hate crime…and on what grounds exactly? Guy signs up to a movie and they make a last-minute change to swap out the romantic lead actress for a balding drag queen. He tries to pull out of the deal. The studio leaks the conversation to the press. Now he's Public Enemy Number One. They're pulling all his back catalogue off NetTube. Dolly Danzig, the cross-dresser colleague in question, claims to have PTSD, says his request to leave the production hit her, and I quote, *as if he had physically punched her.* So then they level abuse charges at him on top. I'm like—stop the world, I want to get off.

Sure, it's easy to laugh at millionaire stars and their passive complicity in turning society into this living nightmare, but remember—Dolly's getting sent enough scripts now to fill her infinity pool, while Leo faces full public cancellation and a minimum of ten years in re-education. And that's if he's *not* convicted. *Cha!* As if *that's* gonna happen. Bro doesn't even have access to lawyers. He's over. He faces the verdict of an all-trans jury next week, which I'm sure will be fair and balanced, winky-wink. No doubt the netwires will continue to ride the Dolly train all the way to judgement day. Good luck, Leo, you poor, poor bastard.

Speaking of netwire coverage, haven't things gone awfully quiet around Mary and the DIP of late? Not unusual in the run-up to an election that's being swung one-way by the media giants. But it sounds like there's more to it this year. Word on the street is Gallard's holding a rally speech on [REDACTED]. And get this—she's doing it in [REDACTED], only an hour or two before *Prime Sinister* Tavistock is due to give her annual lube-job tribute to *zistory zealot* Maria Suarez-Adarsha. Word is, they can't find a way to legally stop Gallard without making it look like they're oppressing a trans person's right to a public platform, so instead the censors are doing all they can to keep public knowledge of it on the down-low. *Squash that bug!*...

But word's getting out in other ways, man. DIP supporters are said to be ready to [REDACTED]. Sounds like things are about to get *spi-cy*!

Ask me, man, Gallard needs to be careful. Don't get me wrong, her politics stink too. The DIP are effectively TEP-lite these days. They hate me and the other binarists as much as the next trans fascist, no doubt. But at least they're not pushing for even more legal restrictions on us. At least they want to extend some sort of olive branch, however twisted that may be. And, hey, whatever annoys the TEP and the Ministry of Equality these days *has* to give us all a little cause to cheer. Right, gang? Even a broken clock, and all that...

Hey—didja hear? Some guy got arrested and sentenced to thirty years for calling the equality minister a fat cunt. Yeah—one year for insulting the minister and twenty-nine for revealing a state secret.

I'm here all night.

Well, more or less. I'll be making more unscheduled guest spots on the NetTube feeds in the coming days, so keep an ear out. Our cyber team are samurai, man. They didn't just get in through the backdoor, they took down a few walls along the way. I *love* it!

So, for now, stay alert. Stand up. Be counted. Ominous spiritus. Ozman out.

END OF RECORDING

CHAPTER NINETEEN

Chrissie had seen the equality minister before. Not only on the posters and smartnet bulletins projected across every block of the city—in person, at parades and netwire press conferences. Just never this close up. Her first impression was a disturbing one.

It wasn't uncommon for suspects and criminals to make her skin crawl but she'd had that same sensation at the early morning briefing when Zoe Urwin's moon-like head appeared in the room and Dennehy introduced Chrissie to the country's most senior judge and law enforcement officer.

Nothing the minister said. Nothing about zer words were anything less than polite and officious. It was something beneath the surface that set Chrissie's teeth on edge. Made her clench her muscles tight beneath her uniform.

Perhaps it was the over-starched pantsuit and theatrical military jacket the minister wore—a get-up barely containing zer hefty frame. Or perhaps the fact that zer features, including the unnaturally stencilled eyebrows and gore-purple mouth, all sat within a small centre of a gigantic pudding of a face. Or it was simply the vicious looking riding crop tucked indiscreetly under one arm.

Whatever it was, a wave of revulsion ran through Chrissie when the minister's synth-leather glove folded around her hand.

"Always a pleasure to meet a young enforcement officer so passionate about protecting the public," Urwin had said, more sickly than sweet.

The grip wasn't firm but it was a vice to Chrissie. When she eventually freed her hand, she resisted the urge to shake her fingers, wipe her palm against her jacket, as if removing some invisible, oleaginous residue.

They travelled in one of the vans, the EQM taking great pleasure from riding in the armoured seat like a member of the regular force. For the entirety of the journey, the purple smile never quite disappeared.

No videye at the dilapidated entrance to Tatlow Heights. The EQM let the officers lead the way through the lobby, stood between them as they rode the lift to flat 15b. Dennehy thumped a fist at the door, held her badge up to the peephole. If need be, they had orders to break the lock.

It didn't come to that. A crack appeared. A CisHet male—perhaps still in his teens—peered into the corridor, blinking the sleep away. Before he could utter a sound, the sergeant shoved at the door, sending him stumbling back.

"Morning, all," Dennehy said with sing-song sarcasm. "Mind if we come in?"

The officers had already obliged themselves. The male fumbled for words. He was rake thin, dressed in sweats, his eyes wide beneath a mop of straw-colored dreadlocks. The air in the flat was an infusion of tobacco, burnt toast, turpentine. There were two other people in the living room—a young CisHet female, as reedy and wide-eyed as the guy who'd answered the door, and another male, a dash older than the first, a well-groomed look about him.

"What's going on?" the first male asked. "We've done nothing wrong."

"Who said you had?"

The man looked at his friends, back at the officers.

"Pronouns?" Zoe said.

"He/him," said the thin man.

"Of course. Mister Johansson, I assume?" Urwin emerged at the entrance, peeling the gloves from zer fingers. "And you must be Felicia Stein? Mister, Miss or other?"

The young woman stayed rooted to the breakfast table, her jaw fish-lolling. "Uhm…Miss."

Urwin nodded, moved inside. Dennehy dropped back, closed the front door, planted her imposing frame in front of it.

"This one I don't know," Urwin said, curling a finger out at the second man, who had sprung to his feet as soon as the officers had entered.

He got "Pete" out with a stammer, edging backwards towards the window. "He/him."

Chrissie had a vision of the man throwing himself through the glass. He didn't seem the physical type.

The EQM smiled as if making a new acquaintance. "Do you have a last name, Peter?"

"Yes."

"And what, may I ask, would it be?"

"Cobble...Cobbleswan."

"Peter Cobbleswan! There you are!" Each syllable seeped treacle. "And you know who I am?"

Cobbleswan nodded. Urwin turned to the other two residents. Their turn to nod.

"Splendid," Urwin said. "How lovely to meet you all. I hope you'll forgive the intrusion. Rude of us to turn up uninvited, I know, but I'm sure you'll understand. You see we have some enquiries to make about some small trouble that's been going on and a little bird mentioned you might be able to help us."

The three of them looked at each other, wordless.

Pete, Glaswegian accent thick, said, "Of course. Anythin'."

Urwin's smile widened. Zie twisted zer shoulders until zie was staring directly at Chrissie. "You hear that, folks? *Anything.* Such a good...boy."

Chrissie took a slow, deep breath, concentrated on not allowing her distaste for this game to show through.

The girl at the table, pale. Her hands gripped the edge of the formica surface as though the floor had begun to accelerate beneath her.

Urwin lowered zer bulk into a battered armchair, laid the crop across zer lap. "Great Birth-Giver! Forgive my impropriety. Please—have a seat. Make yourself at home. After all, this is *your* home, is it not?"

Collective nods, a moment's hesitation. The two self-identifying males in the room sank slowly onto the sofa. The invitation didn't include the echoes. The sergeant covered the exit. Chrissie moved around the perimeter of the living room, casually enough to avoid notice, reading the room—threadbare furnishings, basket of electronics, cables on the cabinet, pile of paint-marked bedsheets in the corner.

"Oh, what's a nice chat without a cup of tea?" Urwin said. Zer eyes fell on the girl. Stein pried herself from the table, went to the open-plan kitchen on sea legs.

Chrissie noted a short corridor on the east side of the flat leading to four identical doors. One would be the bathroom. The others likely bedrooms, though one was possibly a closet. Back in the kitchen, an old-fashioned kettle clicked. Porcelain cups tinkled.

"I don't want to keep you long," said the minister. "I imagine you're all frightfully busy and I can understand it must be rather unexpected to be visited by someone of such seniority as myself. My schedule is hectic too, I can assure you. So, let me get to the purpose of this pleasant little stopover. But first, a question. Do any of you like fresh air?"

The men on the sofa said nothing. They looked at the officers, nonplussed, back at the obese figure filling out their furniture.

"Oh dear," said Urwin, wide-eyed and grinning. "None of you seem to have tuned your listening ears today. *Zzzwip!*" Zie made a twisting motion on zer earlobe. "Or maybe you've all caught a bubble in your mouth." Zie clutched at thin air, drew a fist to her lips—*"Jooop!"*— puffed up zer cheeks even more than seemed possible. "I'll try once more—do any of you like fresh air?"

"Would…would you like me to open a window?" said Johansson.

"That wasn't my question."

"Yes. Yes, we all do."

"Marvellous," said Urwin. "Then I imagine you occasionally enjoy a little walk around town, or perhaps in some of the fine parks our fair city has to offer. Not as nice as the ones we cultivate in the Inner Safe Zone, but green and lush nonetheless."

"Yes. Sometimes."

"Then I would wager—not that I'm much of a gambler, mind—that you may, from time to time, have seen some of the *awful* vandalism that's been occurring around our city in recent months—"

A smash from the kitchen, the skitter of porcelain pieces. The men flinched in unison. Dennehy's hand went to the hilt of her taze stick. Zoe Urwin didn't bat an eyelid. "...Yes?"

"Yes," Johansson said.

"Horrendous, isn't it? Sickening, even. Pray tell—out of curiosity—what vandalism have you seen on your little walks?"

"Uh, a few things. Graffiti, mostly."

"Of course, graffiti. I mean, what exactly has the graffiti said? What messages have you seen written?"

"May-May I ask why you're asking us this?"

The EQM's moon-face remained paused in its approximation of geniality. "What messages, Mister Johansson?"

"Awful things, like you say. Political things."

Stein returned to the room, tea tray in her hands rattling like a china cabinet on an express train. The girl struggled to lower it onto the coffee table in front of her guest, her whitened fingers losing their dexterity. The milk jug rolled on its base, slopped its contents, formed white rings around the mugs.

"Political things?" Urwin gasped. "Are you sure? From my knowledge, they were transphobic things."

"Yes, transphobic things," the man spluttered. "That's what I meant."

"You seem to have some trouble hearing me, Mister Johansson. I apologise if I'm mumbling. What transphobic messages—exactly—have you seen? And I do require you to be precise."

Johansson's tongue flicked at the sides of his lips, mouth drying. His friend beside him had inched away towards the armrest, kept glancing at Sergeant Dennehy and the door beyond.

Johansson's eyes closed. His chin dropped to his chest. "Things like..."

"Not things like, my boy," Urwin said. "Things exactly. I'm sure I didn't mumble that time."

His nails dug into his knees. "They said...*Down with Gender Ideology...Stop Erasing Women...Truth Is Not Hate...Cis Rights Are Human Rights...Allies Are Prisoners...P-Protect Our Children...*"

Dennehy squeaked. The sarge's face turned mauve at having to listen to him reel off these sentiments. A pudgy thumb hovered over the clasp of the taze stick holster. Had the EQM not been running this visit, Mister Johansson would no doubt have been screaming for mercy by this point.

Dennehy wasn't the only one who had heard enough. Chrissie wanted to leave, to get away from this absurd interrogation. If only that was an option.

Instead, she turned her back on the room, moved into the corridor, tasked herself with a search of the property. She didn't know if they had a warrant yet. Wouldn't matter. The EQM could simply write one ex post facto—as zie reportedly did for most searches.

"Where's she going?" Cobbleswan asked.

Urwin picked lint from a sleeve. "You don't mind if my constable makes use of your facilities, do you?"

The three youths said nothing, knew better than to object.

Chrissie opened the first door—a bedroom, an untidy space shrouded in slats of shadow cast by broken window blinds. Nothing of interest there. Nor in the second bedroom, tidier than the first but with bin bags and fruit boxes replacing typical furniture. As theorised, the third door was merely a closet, stuffed with clothes.

Finally, the bathroom. The pipes released a rhythmic wheeze. Unremarkable, enough for Chrissie to close the door, to begin her return to the living room to watch the rest of the one-sided inquisition. She would have gone had it not been for the airing cupboard.

For some reason, she had to open it.

Inside, the boy—late teens, she would guess—had curled his dark, sinewy body into a ball, had wedged himself on top of a shelf. The look of complete fear in his eyes probably matched her own, as though each had caught themselves in a mirror, only to find a stranger staring back.

CHAPTER TWENTY

He had been busted. As Chrissie stood there, halted in shock, she remembered Thomas Tate, the so-called creeper who had fled from the station, now worth nothing to anyone, let alone himself. She had arrested many other cis males for trivial transgressions. They had been sent to re-education centres or cancelled or worse. The minister's voice came Doppler-deep through the walls—mocking, stalking, waiting to…

The cupboard door closed.

Had she done that? She couldn't remember. Her actions were automated, so distant that she knew if someone were to walk up behind her, taze her in the back of the neck, she wouldn't feel a thing. Not one thing. Worse still, she wouldn't have minded.

She backed away, boots tacky on the linoleum.

In the living room, the unfortunate trio shared a sallow look about them. All two hundred and fifty pounds of Sergeant Dennehy stood over them now, itching at her belt. Urwin glanced up. Chrissie shook her head.

The silent lie.

Don't go back there. Please, for the love of Goddess, don't go back there.

"I see," said the minister, taking a loud sup of tea, planting zer empty cup on the tray. "It seems you've provided all the information you have, so our business here must be concluded."

The residents blinked, shot each other glances.

Urwin wrung zer hands, heaved zer heft out of the chair. "So sorry to have interrupted your morning. I hope you all have a most pleasant day."

Zie turned like a planet in chinos, made zer way towards the door. Zie stopped, tapped zer upper-most chin with one bloated digit, turned back. "Oh, heavens. How rude of me. You've gone through all this effort to welcome us and I've left you with all this cleaning up to do."

"It's no—no trouble." Stein's words fought through the tightening passage of her throat.

"I insist. Sergeant, would you be so kind as to give me a hand?"

The sarge squatted, grasped the coffee table at the corners, threw it back. The tray and its contents reorganised themselves against the wall, landed wet and myriad on the floor. The table sprang open at the hinges, revealed spent spray-paint cans, stencils, brushes, all crammed inside the storage compartment.

Dennehy wasn't done. She pulled the armchair cushions apart, found nothing. She ordered Cobbleswan and Johansson up. She dismantled the sofa, uncovered computer hardware and radio equipment.

Stein ran for the door. Dennehy, already a half-step ahead, shifted her weight, dropped a shoulder. The girl took a twist, took a carpet burn to the face.

The males stayed glued, waxen and stiff. Didn't stay that way for long.

Dennehy's stick sloughed the skin of its holster, filled the room with a hum, struck Johansson in the sternum. The man appeared to lift off the sofa, only to crash down again, limbs spasming.

Poor Peter Cobbleswan's turn. He twisted as the voltage racked him, landing him spread-eagle amid the mess of the tea tray, jagged porcelain piercing his back. The noise he made was something else, like a landfill fox caught in a waste baler.

"Whatcha waiting for, Tieman?" Dennehy rumbled, her shoulders heaving, her mouth a black leer. "Get in on this."

At that moment, there was nothing Chrissie wanted to do less. Resign from the force. Take up a life of austerity and abstinence. Throw herself in front of the taze stick and take 15 volts to the gut. Jump from the window like Cobbleswan should have done ten minutes ago. All seemed preferable. She stood gawping at the bodies writhing on the rug. Dennehy yelled at her again to stop standing there like a prime numpty, take out her fucking weapon, fucking defend herself, for Goddess's sake.

Across the room, Zoe Urwin's bulging stare bore holes into her, waited for her to do her duty.

"Your body-eye," Chrissie murmured to her partner. "Don't forget to turn it off."

"Crap, I keep doing that. Thanks, hun."

109

Chrissie was doing it before she knew she was doing it. When she finally felt the grip pulsating in her hand, she was already thrusting it a fourth time into Cobbleswan's right side, in the place where his liver had once enjoyed a peaceful existence, listening to him make that awful sound while his friend convulsed with an even more awful silence.

Sickness came in waves—each time one of the men thrashed, each time one screamed, each breath drew in the smell of searing skin. Somehow she beat it, willed herself to ignore what was happening, to detach from it all.

Whatever part of her managed to look away glanced across the room in time to see the boy in the bathroom take his chance. The lithe shadow darted from the hallway, traversed the corridor in rapid silence, disappeared into the apartment opposite. Urwin and Dennehy too busy lauding over their victims to notice his escape.

For now, he was safe.

Safe because of her.

CHAPTER TWENTY-ONE

Helicopter blades throbbed their deafening beat. The prime minister, still brushing the sprigs of her hair back into place, tousled by the short run to the landing pad, when her companion powered up a smartpalm, talked animatedly into the headset microphone curled into the side of her cheek. Tavistock adapted her seatbelt, pulled her earphones over her pixie-cut to save her hearing, only to have her head filled with an instant stream of panicked chatter.

"…which is why Britcoin isn't going to recover anytime soon, Minister. The longer we try to keep it alive, the worse inflation is going to get. The decision to cancel international trade with any nation that doesn't meet our ethical criteria is starving us. We can't subsist on the handful of countries still left in the alliance. We're down to our last reserves of steel, oil, precious metals, plastics—I mean, the list goes on. And this close to the election…"

"I told you, Amy," Tavistock hollered through the headset. "I don't want to hear problems. I want to hear solutions. That's what I pay you for."

Amy Lovelace's lip quivered. Her cheeks flushed splotchy scarlet. She gawped at the digital statistics flashing across her ample thighs as if staring at the world's hardest jigsaw puzzle. As chief policy adviser *(discogender trans female, she/her)*, one of the most powerful positions in Tavistock's administration, Amy had taken up her role with the unbridled fierceness and bravery expected of every member of the Trans Equality Party. Intervening years had seen her self-confidence drain as quickly as the nation's coffers. She had shrivelled into a real *moaning minnie*. Tavistock had begun having second thoughts about keeping her on the leadership team, let alone within the Tribe.

"But—but that's it, Minister. We're running out of solutions. The rate of success in our STEM projects is abysmal. The core industries are collapsing without a viable workforce."

"We have re-education centres for a reason. Make them work harder."

"The inmates, they're—"

"Students."

"Students. Of course. They're already exhausted. In fact, the cost of keeping the centres running and secure is itself becoming impractical. We're talking millions of people in lockdown, contributing nothing—"

"Our own people, then—the ones in the ISZ. Get them to start doing the science stuff."

"We can't, ma'am. Not at the rate we need. Over ninety five percent of them are studying social sciences. Over seventy percent studying gender theory. And our surveys suggest most have lost all faith in logic-based curriculums, given their roots in the old patriarchal Cistem. I can't stress how dire…"

The prime minister would have switched off her audio had she not already begun to filter out the prattling nay-sayer. The most powerful person in the state wasn't meant to be feeling this anxious.

But last night's indulgence hadn't had its usual calming effect.

Certainly it had taken her mind off things for a few blissful, thrilling, sumptuous hours. As soon as it had all been over—her energy already half-spent from a long day on the campaign trail—the wave of joy had been replaced by the sting of reality, by all its tendrilous tensions. Doubts and warnings churned in the back of her mind. The relentless pulse of a headache dug its claws into her neck and temples, refusing to release.

The *Cockleshells* novel, still heavily encrypted, was with the rest of her luggage in the bird's cargo hold. She hadn't the guts to keep it on her person. Dangerous just to be in its proximity. Now, the grey silhouette of the aircraft slid over the ungoverned forests and grasslands of the Heaths, those parts of the country—her country—that had long been left to moulder, to fur over the years, untouched by council development, harbouring unspeakable dangers. In spite of her anxiety, she imagined the silhouette pluming a spiral feather from its tail, the cabin expanding into a palm tree with sudden, silent ferocity, the whole shape breaking into a thousand smaller versions of itself, descending like dry clods of grass over the canopy below. Then she was falling, twisting circles in the wind, blue-green-blue-green, weightless, on fire, her flesh broiling, her joints snapped and askew.

The splash of hot razors raking the remains of her muscles as she plunges through the branches, her mind blank, preparing for the end.

From the cockpit passenger seat, Hannah looked back into the cabin, her sunglasses hiding her eyes yet still seeming to communicate a look of concern for her leader.

Tavistock nodded. She was fine. It wasn't the smartpalm in the cargo hold that felt like a time-bomb counting down to end her career so violently. No. That book was the key to the future, not the nail in her coffin. Indeed, death would be a relief in comparison to the end of her professional life. She would not—could not—go down in zistory as the woman who oversaw the end of the Big Reboot. *Cockleshells* had to work. It simply had to. Her fear stemmed from the view below.

She said, "What's our altitude?"

Hannah made a show of checking the diagnostics. "Twenty thousand feet, ma'am. Well out of range. We're safe as puppies."

Tavistock was always unsure, always uneasy, knowing how resourceful the insurgents were—how willing to take a chance even it meant giving away their location for an instant. Those terrifying reports from the TEP-sanctioned raids across the Heaths. So often they had ended with the rebels on the ground somehow finding a way to down government aircraft, like ancient tribal archers picking doves out of the air. Until someone got round to inventing molecular transportation, taking sky-trips from one city to the next would remain a risk. Even more so when journeying along one of the surviving operational motorways or rail lines.

"They're getting bolder," Amy said, as counter-productive as ever, her plump body squirming in her seat as she peered through the glass. "Large-scale. Coordinated. Used to be they came at us with clubs and bows and bolo nets. Now they're using shotguns, rifles, pistols…at least, that's what I hear. Using explosives to take out the roads. We've had so many vans and food trucks ambushed, business leaders have been asking questions about our policies, Minister. More have been asking us to reinstate the Amazon armed response campaign."

"You know how that ended last time," Hannah said. "You weren't there. You have no idea what it was like. Do you want to be responsible for losing more of our finest to those primates?"

Amy sulked.

The prime minister pinched her brow, remembered how her soldiers had once invaded with unbridled glee—burning tents, cabins and caravans, shipping most of the occupants off to re-education centres. Until the tough approach failed. The rebels, more emboldened, more vengeful. Reports of skirmishes, of the fate of those captured, were unspeakable. Entire units wiped out. Dozens of brave and fierce non-binary warriors trained in combat and survival had vanished in those forests, never to be heard from again. Some even rumoured to have committed treason to spare their lives, swapping the Safe Zones to live in squalor among the savages. And still, more CisHets slipped through the Fence each week, growing their ranks.

"We can increase our airborne strikes," Tavistock suggested. "It's risk-free."

"Not cost-free," said Amy.

"Not to mention the fact," Hannah said, interjecting, "we don't even know where most of the insurgent camps are based anymore. They're vermin. Hiding is what they do best."

"Then we need smarter alternatives to road transport," Tavistock said. "We can't keep adding armour onto lorries and hoping they make it there and back in one piece."

"I agree," Amy said. "But the projected costs of air shipment aren't any better. You'd need constant flights, a million freight drones, no disruptions. We've been through the figures..."

Tavistock said, "What I don't understand is how they so often seem to know where to lay their ambushes."

A smack on the windscreen. Amy jumped in her seat, fearing the worst.

The first drops of rain hit the helicopter, grazed the glass like shrapnel.

"Minister," Amy said, shrinking back into the leather. "We need to take these considerations seriously. We need a hard, concerted look at the country's finances."

The prime minister's patience had run its course.

"No, Amy. I won't hear it. Not when I'm on the campaign trail trying my damned bloody hardest to promote a positive outlook on Britannia's future. I feel I should've brought my airhorn with me today because you're starting to sound like those fucking idiots in the DIP. And that's problematic, Amy. These dead-facts you keep wheeling around are not conducive to TEP ambition. They are mis-truthing our situation. That makes them hateful. Are you supporting hate facts, Amy? Is that what you're doing?"

The adviser's jaw slumped open. "No, Minister! I would never!"

"Because I could have you arrested for that, you know? Hannah is right here." She jabbed her finger at her security chief.

Hannah said nothing, pretended to check the diagnostics as the autopilot adjusted its settings to cope with the downpour.

"It's the opposite, Minister. I'm saying our problems are...quite clearly due to the actions of cisgenderism. The binarists can't stand to see us succeeding. Which makes all these issues a phobic attack on our way of life. That's what I meant to say."

"Right you are. And therefore?"

"We should...not stand for it. We should crack down further on cissupremacy by cracking down on CisHet liberties."

"Right again! So how do you suggest we do that?"

"Well..." Amy swiped at the smartpalm. "We've discussed raising the CisHet goods and services tax again. And the reparations tax. Perhaps we could recoup some of the business losses by lowering the equality wage?"

"What's the ceiling now?"

"Thirty per cent above the lowest paid trans or genderqueer member of staff."

"We could," Tavistock mused. "And raise the CisHet retirement age a little more."

"From ninety-five to a hundred?"

"It's a start, I suppose."

"The only thing is, if we're too severe, we could end up coaxing more of them to the Heaths and then…"

Hannah shook her head, aviators bouncing the orange lights of the flight instruments.

"Do you not want to be part of the Tribe anymore, Amy?" Tavistock asked her. "Is that it?"

Amy shut up. Amy made a note in her folder to have the new legislations included in the next Budget announcement. Amy kissed Tavistock's arse all the way to Bristol.

CHAPTER TWENTY-TWO

FOR PUBLIC ATTENTION

EQUALITY MINISTRY NOTICE: This material must be read immediately. Disregard will be considered an indirect attempt to silence non-binary people and thereby constitute an act of violence. Offenders will be prosecuted.

From the desk of Maria Suarez-Adarsha.
27 Octavia, 2046

Fiercest spirits,

It pains me that I must write to you from afar all these years, but as you are aware, my self-isolation must be upheld for my own safety. To this day, my life remains at grave risk and I continue to receive countless death threats from transphobic terrorists. But do not fear for me, nor concern yourselves that my teachings will ever discontinue. It is my intention to continue to share my lessons and thoughts as a means of empowering us all. Know that I remain safe and well, praise Hermaphroditus.

You may have recently been exposed to offensive and illegal communications broadcast by a loose terrorist entity, an insignificant outfit no doubt formed of envious, fragile cisgender egos, desperate to do whatever they can to gain our validation. I urge you to not be cowed by this overt display of violent and cistemic cissexism. Give them not one bit of attention. Have faith that our authorities and therapists are ready to protect and brace us. Continue to be the badass queens and qwings I know you to be.

More disquieting than this spike of binarist-perpetrated violence are the murmurings of hostility from within our homes. It is my observation that another type of snake lies concealed in the lush grass of our cities—those quislings who wish to overturn our security and see our society returned to archaic and brutal times. They are undeserving of being called non-binarists, let alone allies. They must be rooted out wherever they show their wicked faces. Do not allow them to poison the spring. Call out even the smallest infractions wherever you encounter them. Remain vigilant and reserve for them the sharpest edge of your anger.

With Election Day soon upon us, it remains with you to continue our stand against the Cis-tem. I hereby again endorse the Trans Equality Party as the only true political entity that represents the rights of our community. They alone are the guiding light in the dim tunnel of binarist oppression. They alone will break our burdensome chains and forge our path ahead.

Be brave, spirits, for our generation and all those that follow. Keep Britannia strong. Crush the Cis-tem.

Yours fiercely,

Maria Suarez-Adarsha

CHAPTER TWENTY-THREE

"Let me guess—you lost your job."

The server slid a glass of water across the bar.

"Worse," Jake said, not looking up. "I got hired."

He'd been up early, had left the hotel, avoided its awful breakfast service for the third day on the trot. There was a vocation centre on the high street. Jake had gone in, queued up behind one of the machines, like Alfie had told him he should. He'd inserted his Ally Pass so a processor could scan his details, assign him a career. Wasn't much point in putting it off any longer. The murder of the umbrella man had rung a bell in him. He didn't have real experience of a city, hadn't appreciated how dangerous they'd become, hadn't learned enough about the things waiting for him on the other side of the walls.

Growing up, he had sometimes resented being sheltered, so eager was he to explore the world. There were days when he had tried to plead to his parents to let him discover things first-hand, without books. Days when he had tried to skip out, hitchhike to the nearest city, see what he was missing. Every time, they found a way to stop him. Now it was becoming clear why they'd worked so hard to keep him away. Wherever he hoped to go, he would be hated. Whatever he wanted to do, there would be someone there to stand in his way.

"So wotcha get?" The waiter said, setting a napkin and cutlery down, resting his elbows on the countertop. He wore a matching armband to Jake's.

Jake had stumbled into Gina's, an eatery with photos of bygone starlets on the wall. Not as much of a dive as the place he'd had to take sanctuary in earlier that week. There was another patron, too—a sad old man at a table on his own, down at the back, eating pasta, tortoise-pace. Jake had found a stool at the bar, sat there for who knows how long, staring at the vocation contract the machine had spat out at him, the way a man might look at the losing betting slip on which he'd staked his life savings.

"Road works," Jake said. "I start on Wednesday. Six in the morning."

"Hey, that's not so bad. I mean it's better than working sewage, right? And probably less dangerous than general construction. You get to keep your feet on the ground. It's safe as long as you keep outta the mixer."

"Not as comfy as making sandwiches."

"Trust me—six days a week serving rude customers, on my salary?" He kissed his teeth. "Don't let it fool you. At least with road works you'll be getting out in the fresh air."

"Sure. I love breathing in hot tarmac all day. Keeps a fella feeling young."

The waiter gave up trying to build some cheer, wasn't paid enough for that. He went off to the kitchen, came back with Jake's plate. The steam brought with it a rich, mapley scent.

"At least the food smells good." Jake said, his stomach waking up. The T-bone was bloody and thick. "Looks good too."

"Something tells me you're not going to enjoy it anyway."

"As much as anyone can enjoy a last meal. Speaking of which, how about one of those strawberry milkshakes to go with it? Might as well."

Jake sliced into the cut, took a bite, found he'd been duped again.

"This is ersatz meat, isn't it?" he said, chewing something that tasted like pulped toilet roll.

"What?" the waiter huffed. "Of course it is. Where do you think you are, the Ivy?"

"It said 'real steak' on the menu," Jake said, slapping his hand on the counter.

"Look. Can you see it on your plate?"

"Yeah?"

"So it ain't imaginary, is it?"

Jake spat the morsel back onto his fork. A breeze rolled in from the entrance. The waiter straightened up. Two equality officers came out of the cold. Regardless of their business, their blue-black uniforms and the asps on their belts prompted instant anxiety. The first, almost as wide as she was tall, puffy, freckled features. She reminded Jake of the guard at the Cooler checkout desk. The officer following behind was about his age, large brown eyes, noticeably better proportioned than her colleague. Jake went back to his meal, ears alert.

The big woman said, "What's good today, Sam?"

"Fresh on the grill, officer. Roast pepper and halloumi." The waiter's swagger had disintegrated into deferential jolliness, a little tremble at the edges.

"Are you saying I should go on a diet?"

The cold air again, though the door was closed. It became so quiet so abruptly Jake thought his eardrums had detached themselves and slid out the sides of his head.

"Uh, no, ma'am. Not at all. We also have the Ploughperson's and the House Club. Regular or extra-large if you want. I mean, with extra cheese and pickle. Or whatever. Whatever you want, I'll make it for you. Half price."

An agonising second passed. Jake refused to look up.

"Yeah," the officer said, alligator slow. "Ploughperson's with extra cheddar and extra pickle. I'll take two of those, actually."

"You've got it," he said, already pulling the condiments out of the fridge.

"Give me a minute, hun," the dumpy one said to her partner. "I need to powder my nose."

She waddled off along the aisle, heavy boots descending the stairwell at the back.

"Would you like a table?" the server asked the other echo, wringing his hands.

"No, to go—we're on the clock." The younger officer plucked a menu from the stand at the counter, laid it out flat. "What would you recommend that's hot?"

"Avoid the steak," Jake said, before realising he'd said it out loud.

She looked over at him, at the food on his fork. She smiled. "Yeah, most synth beef tastes like somebody already ate it, right?"

Jake said, "Should'a tried before I buyed."

He glanced up at her, smiled back, went back to his meal. He'd be better off minding his own business. She settled for a toasted mozzarella and tomato. The waiter fell over himself to make everything as fast as humanly possible. The memory of the murder and the TRANARCHY gang and the words of the scared cook flashed through Jake's mind.

The police won't do anything. They ignore them.

Was that true? Was society so corrupt as to let roving gangs of killers pick on any easy target they came across? Everyone from his parents to his fellow inmates had told him over the years that he had to be careful in the cities, that he was taking the dangers for granted. But he could never believe it was that bad. Not when everything else seemed so neat. So orderly. The place was crawling with videyes, with sky-eyes. Hell, his own settlement hadn't been able to escape the authorities, let alone—

"*Times Gone By*—I've heard of that." The young echo, leaning her elbows on the bar, looking at Jake again, her eyes bright.

Confused, Jake glanced around, looked for whoever she was talking to.

"Sorry, your brochure," she said, pointing at his seat. "I've walked past those places on my patrol. Never had a chance to go inside. Any good?"

The little pamphlet from the museum—still tucked in his back pocket. He pulled it out, grimaced, tossed it on the counter.

"Not to my taste," he said. "Like most things around here."

"Oh. How come?"

"I…wasn't convinced they'd done their research. Feel I'm pretty good on my history and, quite frankly, that place was spinning more lies than a false widow. Uh—in my opinion."

The officer frowned a tad, looked him over with an awkward silence. "*History*? Wow, that's…old school."

"Sure it is," he replied, grinning. "Isn't that the point?"

The server stopped slathering mayo, coughed. Jake got the impression he'd said something wrong. The thought of upsetting an echo reminded him of beatings at the hands of female wardens, of the shock troops that came in the dead of night, broke down doors, set his home on fire. He was paralysed. But the officer's eyes lit up again and she laughed. She actually laughed. The sound was birdsong to his ears.

"I guess that's true," she said, turning to him square-on, the pouches on her belt bumping lightly against her hips. "Don't let my partner hear you talking like that."

Jake didn't know what she meant by *like that*.

He shrugged, said, "Our secret."

The netscreen above the bar played a live netball game on a volume too low to hear. A championship qualifier, according to the ticker graphic. Transwomen in cornflower blue and yellow circled each other, intensity etched on every player's face. Their actions were slow and staggered from Jake's perspective. He didn't see what the fuss was about. It would have been more interesting to watch the old boy in the back slurp his spaghetti. The echo didn't seem all that absorbed either.

"So," Jake said. "Any trouble, officer?"

"What do you mean?"

"I don't know. Isn't that what you're meant to ask police officers when you see them?"

She laughed again. "You're an odd one."

"Don't mean to be. Not used to how things are done in London."

"Well, there's always trouble. Though I'm not sure an out-of-towner can help with our enquiries. Whereabouts are you from?"

"Down south. Not far from the coast."

"What city?"

"Not a city exactly."

The waiter came back, asked what salad she wanted. Arugula it was.

"What was that you were saying?" the echo said to Jake. "For a second I thought you said you weren't from—"

The stocky officer returned from the restroom, tugging at her tactical vest. As soon as she arrived at the bar, she was pinning Jake with a death stare.

"Can we help you, priv?" The words bristled.

"It's all right, Sarge. I was talking to him about the game."

The sergeant glanced up at the screen. Jake thought he saw the constable wink at him. But she wouldn't have done that.

"Well maybe he'd be better off keeping to himself." The sergeant leaned across the countertop, made sure he could see her. "This bar area is non-binary only. You being here is threatening to other customers who want to order their lunch in peace."

Jake, incredulous. "I didn't see a sign."

"I beg your pardon? Does there need to be a sign?"

He could feel the heat cranking. The young constable avoided his gaze now, pretended to focus her attention on the menu, even though she'd ordered. Probably as concerned for her own well-being as he was.

"I'm trying to eat here," he said. "I didn't—"

"I don't think you heard me, priv. You're invading my personal space. Now, fuck off."

His temples pulsed, his nerves hardened, his muscles prepared to act, fists trying to crush the cutlery.

Deft from practice, the sergeant's hand dropped to her belt. Thick fingers gripped the holster of the taze stick. Her thumb hovered over the power button.

CHAPTER TWENTY-FOUR

"You can sit over there, towards the back," the constable told him, planting herself between Jake and the seething ogre. "It looks a lot more comfortable, right?"

He froze. The subtle suggestions on her face, the perfect eyebrows silently voicing a plea. She was giving him a chance. One he probably didn't deserve, but a chance nonetheless.

Deep breath.

Before the squat officer could blow her lid, he slipped down off the stool, picked up his plate and glass, moved away from the bar. The sergeant watched him find somewhere else to sit.

"Further back," the ogre said, shaking her head.

He bit his tongue, continued his retreat.

When he got to a table near the old man, the sergeant turned back to the bar. She exclaimed, loud enough for him to hear, "Disgusting people. No respect."

The old man shrugged at Jake, wiped sauce off his chin with the back of his hand.

Resentment came and went, followed only by dejection and humiliation. Jake wanted to climb out of his skin, wanted to run out onto the streets, scream at the sky. He knew what Alfie had been warning him about now, knew why his parents and the other elders had been so cynical of the city. He let the feelings simmer down, reminded himself he was a cog in the wheel, that things could always be worse. He had a hot meal in front of him. Had a roof over his head for the night. Even had a job in the wings. Who was he to complain about his lot? *Stop inviting trouble. Keep your thoughts to yourself.*

The echoes, still at the bar. He tried to ignore the fat bitch, stared instead at the constable. She seemed sweet, had treated him like a human being, had even shielded him from near-certain arrest. To top it all off, she looked pretty stunning—in spite of the uniform. To cheer himself up he thought about what she might look like underneath it, thought about all sorts of things that would definitely get him into trouble if anyone knew. A shame she was an echo. It didn't suit her.

The server finished swaddling the sandwiches in greaseproof paper, slapped them on the counter. The constable told her partner she'd pick up the bill, that she'd see her in the car. Before she left, the sergeant cast an odious glance to the back of the restaurant.

The pressure fell off Jake a little. He already knew he wasn't going to finish his lunch.

The constable settled up. God, she was pretty. Jake expected to watch her leave. She looked over at him. She began walking towards his table.

Fuck.

Her smile was back, if a little softer than before.

She said, "Hey. Look, I wanted to apologise for my partner. She can be a bit, uh, stringent sometimes. It wasn't you, it was...well, thanks for not making a big thing about it."

Jake didn't know what to say to that. He ran out of time before any words could come to him. She was back at the bar, scooping up her order, saying goodbye to the server. His confidence came flooding back like a dose of adrenalin. He wasn't sure what he was doing but he was compelled to try.

He sprang up, crossed the restaurant to the front of the house, double time. "Officer."

She turned, startled.

Looking into those deep brown eyes, whatever he'd wanted to say wouldn't come to him. He blinked, rubbed at his neck. *Keep your head down*, came the order in his head. Stupid idea, anyway.

Scrambling to cover himself he reached out for the door. "Uh, let me get that for you."

When it opened, the constable hesitated, stepped uncertainly into the street. The sergeant was parked out front. She practically spat her food out when she saw him. The blue light on the panda car flickered once, let out a single, dying whoop.

"Stop right there!"

The big woman, out on the pavement in a flash, trudging back to the café. As she passed the constable, she lowered her voice, said, "Yas, qween. Good play."

Her attention was all on him, a bull to a bloodied sheet.

She said, "What do you think you're playing at? Patronising an officer of the law! What, you think she can't open a door by herself? Don't you know acts of chivalry are illegal?"

Jake's hands went up at his sides, "I don't…I didn't mean any offense."

Her hand shot forward. He cringed as her fingers dug into the tendons above his elbow, a Cooler guard flashback. With a whipping motion, she spun him around, pushed him towards the alley on the side of the building.

The constable looked as shocked as Jake felt. In true fashion, she stayed quiet.

"Maybe you think you're funny," the sergeant said. "Or that the rules don't apply to you, is that it?"

Jake's internal brake line had been cut. He didn't know how to stop this. He allowed himself to be marched off the pavement to where the succulent aromas coming from the kitchen vents wrestled with the sour smells of the dumpsters. He was spun again, felt the rough brickwork scrape the back of his shirt, tear at the skin beneath.

She said, "Harassment is bad enough but towards an equality officer? How dare you? How *dare* you?"

Jake said, "I didn't harass anyone."

The sergeant, practically foaming now. "Shut the fuck up. Show me your Ally Pass."

Jake put his hand in his pockets, came up empty. He patted at his jacket. He must have left it in the vocation centre, in that dumb kiosk machine that had dictated his future to him in under three seconds. He told her as much.

A sickening grin spread across the ogre's face. Again, her hands were on him, cuffing his arms behind his back. "Know what I think? I don't think you're here legally."

"You're insane," Jake said, his own anger welling. The plastic restraints cut into his skin.

"I'm *what*? What did you say to me?"

"I said you're insane."

She whirled him around, got close to his face. "You didn't—"

"You're a narcissist," Jake went on, surrendering to his indignation. "A spoilt child with control issues."

Her sulphurous breath hitting him square in the mouth. "You—you can't—"

"A pathetic lapdog."

"I'll fucking have your—"

"With a seriously bad case of penis envy."

Her eyes bulging now, blisters in an oven. Her mouth gaped, scooped air.

He said, "Oh, and you could stand to lose a few pounds."

That last comment seemed to send every pint of blood into the woman's face. She looked like someone had kicked her squarely in her ample gut. Shaking with fury, the sergeant drew the asp from its holster. It snapped to full rigid length, hummed, pulsated. A steel snake, rasping at him. He could almost feel the venomous current running through its tip.

Sweat gathered at his hairline, blood vessels burst beneath his skin. The image of the TRANARCHY leader caving in the umbrella man's head appeared to him once more. He steadied himself.

The baton swung back.

It happened quickly.

A whipping motion. A spark. A cry, cut short.

The sergeant dropped. The sound of impact—a sack of butter hitting concrete.

For a second, Jake wasn't sure what had happened. He couldn't quite grasp why he was still on his feet, why his body wasn't racked with unbearable pain.

The constable.

She stood fixed, taze stick in hand, near traumatised by what she'd done.

CHAPTER TWENTY-FIVE

The world moved around her, blurred at the edges.

He was talking to her, up close. Waves of warm breath on her face, pores clear on his nose. The words, locked in bubbles of glass, as though she and the stranger were both underwater, sinking slowly but inexorably.

She trembled. His voice pierced through the white noise between her ears. She could hear again. He pushed against her, rocked her with his shoulder.

"Hey! Are you listening to me? Get these off me! Please!"

He turned his back to her. His hands, coarse and strong, a sprinkling of hair on the knuckles, veins like tree roots beneath the skin. His wrists, cuffed together, an old model voxwatch pressed up against one of the polymer bracelets. His fingers flexed.

"Do you hear me? Take these off! We need to get out of here!"

The man twisted his neck to her, his pupils deep wells, imploring, searching for her.

Feeling, back in her legs. A sharp clank of metal on stone. Her taze stick rolled away from her feet. Not far from it, the crumpled heap of her partner lay on the ground.

The world sucked itself back in, fast-forwarded at sixteen times the speed.

The priv edged forward, stared off into the street, looked to see if anyone else had come past. He was poised to run. His voice, above the water now, said, "They'll be coming. Help me."

Dennehy was out, her eyes dead bulbs, the filament rattling in their sockets. A strange snoring sound flowed through her nostrils. Drool escaped down her cheek.

Chrissie patted at her belt, found the key pen in her pouch. She reached out to the man. His fingers relaxed. She waved the pen over the digital lock pad. The cuffs unhinged, hit the ground. She expected him to take off running, to disappear into the city. He turned back to her, massaging wrists.

"You can come with me," the man said. "Come on."

Without a word, Chrissie began to move, an automaton reaction, electrons bouncing off the forces around them. She went towards the street, towards the vehicle.

Thought and reason came back in spurts, as though she was outside of it all looking in, observing them both through a fishbowl lens.

"No." Her voice, alien inside her head. "They can track the car. The other way. Wait!" She turned back, crouched next to the sergeant. Some instinctive survival logic compelled her to remove the officer's body-eye, to switch it off, stuff it inside her pocket. She took the voxcom too, tucked it inside her tac vest. Already the fallen officer was stirring, her breathing changing pattern.

The man was waiting. He had picked up the asp. The sight of it in his grip startled Chrissie at first, gave her a second of thinking he'd had a change of heart, that he was seizing his chance to knock her out. The weapon powered down. He held it out to her in offering.

He said, "You might want to keep this."

With that, they fled, deeper into the alley, where the steam of ovens and heaters pumped through exhausts and cracked drains dribbled endless rainwater. They ran in no particular direction, widening the gap in the little time they had. She could feel him near her, this stranger, moving with her like a pack wolf, bonded to her and to her fate within the blink of an eye.

When they came to the mouth of the passageway on the opposite side of the block, Chrissie barred him with her arm, checked to see if their route was clear.

"I just realised," the man said, leaning against a wall, sucking in air, "I have no idea where we're going."

"Away for now. Far away."

"There are border patrols on every side of this Zone…the Fence…how far are we really gonna get?"

She knew she wasn't thinking straight. Her mind jumped over information in spastic tumbles, tried to find the fastest way out of this mess. He was right, of course. Even getting close to the Fence was a tough ask considering the patrols and surveillance coursing through every main thoroughfare. The longer they were out in the open, the more likely it would be that they'd be spotted. More witnesses. More evidence to throw the book at them. How long would they have before Dennehy awoke, shook off the cobwebs, alerted every echo in the OSZ?

Chrissie swore under her breath. She'd taken the sergeant's voxcom but it dawned on her the patrol car had its own on the dash. Hadn't thought to disable it. Time slipped faster.

No alternative. They needed to bed down, hide themselves away, think things through, let the heat cool off, try to find a better opportunity to slip away or burrow themselves in the ground forever. Whatever they had to do to avoid the unthinkable.

"I can't go home," she said, the thought of it coming to her in the same moment. "They'd look for me there."

Her life, fading like a ghost through a locked door. None of it seemed real.

The young man hunkered down, stared up at the slivers of slate sky between the buttresses and power lines above them. He looked as lost as she felt.

He said, "I got a room at a hotel near here. Your friend didn't get my name. Maybe it'll be safe—for a while, at least."

"Where?"

"Portman Square. Place called the Wheelhouse."

A single pedestrian out on the corner, walking a dachshund. No one else. No vehicles.

She said, "I know it. We'll have to stick to the back roads. Sky-eyes everywhere else. I can track their locations on my nav but we'll need to be careful."

"Lead the way."

She did. Through the folds of the city, darkened by rows of looming buildings and billboards and dissolving stucco. They sprinted along a deserted mews, tried to look natural when they came to the bends, when they were forced to cross busier streets. She kept her cap low over her eyes, let him keep a few steps behind to avoid unwanted attention. Whenever they found themselves alone, they ran.

At a quiet corner, Chrissie took out her smartpalm, brought up the nav screen. It showed her the geometric patterns of sky-eyes sliding over the neighbourhood—orange dots with fire tails moving on pre-programmed routes. On occasion they found themselves only yards away from being seen, could hear the drones fizzing overhead, their under-belly videyes whirring, searching, innards rumbling with a hunger for information.

Their boots became speckled with dirtwater. Every hint of their own movement reflected off a shop window filled them with a jab of fear, tricked them into seeing someone else, running towards them, intent on taking them down. People in the street, all enemies, all scouts for the state. Chrissie's tac vest didn't breathe much. Rain on her back, sweat beneath her clothes, soaked her from the inside out. Heat rose through her collar, steam from her throat. On she went, leading him through the labyrinth, adrenalin diluting fatigue.

Two blocks short of the hotel, Chrissie's voxcom let out a squawk.

"Dispatch to Juliet Ophelia 621. Attendance requested at a domestic disturbance on Homer Street. Can you take that?"

They stopped beneath a portico that had become brittle and red with rust. Pigeons and ravens lined up together along the buttress above in a strange alliance, a platoon of alternating pebble-eyes watching them, quizzical.

"Shit." Chrissie waivered, weighing up their options.

They hadn't been reported yet. That was something. But for how long?

The operator probed again. *"Dispatch to Juliet Ophelia 621. Are you receiving?"*

Had to make up her mind. She thumbed the dial, said, "621 receiving."

The operator repeated the details.

Chrissie said, "Yes, we can take that. ETA, uh, fifteen minutes."

A hiss of static. Nothing.

The man, set in a half crouch to catch his breath, looked at her.

"If I don't respond," she said, "they'll know something's wrong. That might buy us some more time. Sounds like my partner hasn't regained consciousness yet."

The image of Dennehy on the ground, the weight of it pushing through her bones. Her hands, leaden. She couldn't stop them shaking.

"Come on," the stranger said.

His breathing sounded pained. He hastened away again, willed her to react, to follow him now. There was no turning back.

"Come on!"

A thought occurred, sent an alarm through her.

"Your voxwatch," she said. "Ditch it."

He slowed, looked at the device on his arm. He got wise, peeled the strap off, hurled it to the ground, stamped a heel on it until it smithereened.

She snatched at the control tab on her lapel, turned off the locator—the only thing keeping her tethered to the city's network.

It was official. Christina Tieman was off the grid.

CHAPTER TWENTY-SIX

The clerk wasn't at the reception desk but the back office door was open. He was only an over-shoulder glance away from ruining everything. They made their way through the foyer without being noticed, up the stairs to where the man said he had a rented room.

Inside, the smallest feeling of security fell around her, the thinnest of thin blankets. They didn't speak. The man set off coughing, the run having taken something out of him. Chrissie lowered herself into the chair in the corner of the room, stared at the ugly hexagonal patterns on the carpet. After he had cleared his lungs, he sat too, on the foot of the bed, waited for her to say something, gave up, put his head in his hands.

Silence filled the space between them for some time.

After a while, he got up. He moved about the bedroom, the bathroom.

Gradually—ever so gradually—time fell back into its usual pace. The enormity of what she'd done left her with a strange tension, as though she'd lit a match to her own pyre, could feel every part of herself melting and charring. Yet the invisible bonds she'd been wearing for so long were disintegrating with her. Another body was prying its way out through the top, breeze-light and soaring. Whether it was freedom she felt or doom masquerading as freedom, she couldn't tell.

For a long while, the young man waited on the edge of her consciousness, loitering, gentle, giving her the space he thought she needed. Eventually she looked up at him. He had taken the jacket off, thrown a towel around his shoulders. His cheeks were reddened, his hair mussed. He brought her a cup of peppermint tea from the complimentary tray, a towel of her own to use. She'd forgotten about the damp clothes. She was still shivering, from the cold or otherwise.

"Why'd you do it?" he asked, soft as anything.

"I don't know." But she knew that wasn't true even as the words came out. "When you know something's wrong, it's wrong."

He rubbed the back of his neck. "I thought that was it for me. Saw my life flash before my eyes and all that. I haven't even thanked you."

She shrugged. "Didn't have to be you. I couldn't let it happen anymore. I joined the force to preserve social justice. Not this."

"We're screwed, aren't we? I mean, they'll find us. Eventually."

"It's likely, yeah."

The man let out a deep sigh. "Would it help if we gave ourselves up now? Save ourselves the energy?"

Chrissie shook her head. "I can't do that. They'll cancel you for what I did. I know how these things work. They'll want to spin the story right."

"Then let them." His jaw flexed, his fingers clamped tightly together. "Look, I've got nothing here. And you saved me from getting my kidneys scrambled—probably a lot worse besides. Least I can do is take the wrap. I could say I grabbed the stick off you. A moment of madness."

Madness. Is that what had happened to her? Is that why she'd done it?

"No," she said.

"It makes sense. I mean, it was my fault I lost my head back there, said those things I said. You don't deserve—"

"No." The word bounced back across the room. She could never let someone else take responsibility for her decisions, let alone an innocent. Doing that would make her as bad as her employers. A hypocrite. A coward.

"I've made my bed," she said. "If anything, it should be you leaving me here to pick up the pieces. They still don't know who you are. You'd have a head-start on them."

"Nah," he said. "I'm not going anywhere."

"But you could have gone. Earlier, I mean. Right when it happened. Why didn't you?"

He went still for a while, contemplated his feet. "Well, when you know something's wrong..."

"There's no recourse," she said. "They'll make this worse than an assault charge."

"Like attempted murder?"

"Maybe even treason. Ever hear of the Abolishment Act? The state technically considers every non-binary person a queen or king in their own right, and therefore every ally in public service a hand to royalty by default."

"Meaning?"

"Meaning they have the right to charge the crime as a High Court offence. Not that they'd even bother with a trial. Don't you know that?"

He laughed in disbelief at the idea. "I don't know much of anything."

"Best start learning."

"I don't know your name. Learn me that."

Hardly mattered if he knew.

"Chrissie. Christina Tieman. Formerly of the Metropolitan Equality Force." Her body shifted in the chair. "Yours?"

"Jake Brody. Road worker, I guess."

She let herself smile a little—more for his sake than her own.

"So what now, Chrissie Tieman? Whatever we do, I honestly don't know how long we'll be safe here."

"I need to think."

Her mouth, dry. She sipped the tea. The window looked out onto a grey street, the sound of cars passing and voices and laughter humming in the shop fronts nearby.

She said, "I need some time."

The voxcom robbed her of that, crackled inside her vest, blasted a second of static. Another. An empty space in the frequency where she would normally hear a voice. A string of clicks and high-pitched beeps sounded like someone on one end of the channel who couldn't quite figure out what they were doing. Finally, the voice croaked through, no stranger to Chrissie's ears.

"Juliet Ophelia…Juliet…Ophelia 621 to Dispatch."

"Go ahead 621."

"This is Sergeant…Sergeant Abigail Dennehy. I've been attacked…I can't…"

"621, are you receiving?…621, what's your location? Respond immediately."

"Beaumont Street…ambulance…"

"621, standby and await attendance. All available units to Beaumont Street. Repeat. All available to Beaumont Street. 621, are you receiving?…621…"

The clock stopped. That was it. The sarge had sounded the alarm. Chrissie put the cup down at the foot of the chair, gripped the hair about her ears, buried her chin in her chest. The whole city—probably the whole country—would be looking for them.

CHAPTER TWENTY-SEVEN

"How are we feeling, Sergeant?"

Dennehy scooted back against the viscoelastic gel pillows, tried to sit up as a sign of respect to the equality minister. By the look on the officer's face, Zoe's visit had come as a surprise. "I've had better days, ma'am, if I'm honest. It's so kind of you to come all this way."

A speaker system on the sideboard played sounds of ocean waves and distant gulls. The room was adorned with lavender-scented oil burners, orange lighting and earth-toned fabrics. ISZ recovery wards could be hard to tell apart from spa chambers.

Zoe approached the bedside, rested a warm hand on the officer's arm, said, "The cis coward. It breaks my heart to see you like this. You're so brave."

Dennehy nodded. Her mouth tightened. Moisture pricked her eyes. She looked up into her superior's thickset face, gave zer hand a light squeeze.

"So, tell me," the EQM said, "who did this to you?"

"I don't know. He didn't give me his Pass."

Urwin turned to the doctor, who was idling by the door, requested privacy. Alone, the minister pulled forward the chair by the bed, wooden legs shrieking as they scraped against the floor. The sound made Dennehy flinch in her bed, made her cower like a beaten dog.

Dominic went to the sound system, tapped the screen, killed the gulls and whales.

"Sergeant," Zoe said, "I know you've already been through things with the attending officers—I've read your statement—but I'd like you to try to remember what you can for me now that you've had some time to recuperate."

"He didn't give me his Pass," Dennehy said again, less forceful and self-assured than the voice Zoe had heard address the Equality Summit last autumn. The officer's words were full of remorse.

Zoe regarded the officer, aware zer disappointment must have been shining through, clear as day. It wasn't that zie didn't feel bad for her. Far from it. Zie was raging on her behalf, sickened with ire that violence had been perpetrated on one of zer own, on the streets zie had resolved to rid of any and all threats from the savage binarists. Yet zie could not quash the sense of disgust that the sergeant had failed to exercise her powers with the aggressiveness required. Responders had found her beside her vehicle, stripped of her weapon, blubbing like a toddler. Embarrassing to think about. It was policy never to blame the victim, of course—never to even criticise them—but as an EQO, Dennehy was a front-line representative of the Ministry and of the state. An attack on one was an attack on all, even if they were a mere ally. So too that weakness from one was a betrayal of the whole.

For that reason, Zoe had come to the hospital rather than summon the officer to Headquarters. It wouldn't do to have her trail her shame into the building like a foul smell.

"Let's start at the beginning," Zoe said. "If it's not too painful, what do you remember about him?"

"He was young—early twenties at the most. Around five-nine. Kind of scruffy looking. Unshaven. Hair starting to go past his ears. Brown hair, maybe. Dirty blonde? Had on blue jeans and a cheap sort of jacket, khaki green."

"Accent?"

"Nothing I could make out. Standard. Estuary?"

"If we send a composite specialist here, would you be able to put together an e-fit today?"

"I don't know. I can try."

Dominic made a note on his smartpalm.

Zoe leaned in closer. "In your statement you said something about him bothered you."

"Yes. He tried to make conversation with Constable Tieman without her consent. And he sat at the front of the café, right by the door. Deliberately imposing, I would say. There was something about his eyes that seemed angry. Like a wild animal. When I confronted him, they looked right through me. Made me think he wasn't all there, if you know what I mean? Then he threatened me... and..." Dennehy tugged at the white cotton pyjamas the recovery unit had provided her. Her uniform had been bagged for forensics. The responders' report had noted it had been soiled. Another indignity to the Ministry's name. "…I'm sorry, ma'am. My memory is still jumbled. I can't remember much at all."

"It's all right. It will come back to you."

"But Constable Tieman, ma'am! Is there any word yet?"

"Afraid not."

"We have to find her. Please promise me she'll be okay."

"I promise we're doing all we can. Every able officer on the force is out there right now, combing the West London OSZ. He can't have taken her far."

"You need to make him pay for this," Dennehy said, wiping at her eyes. "The longer he has her…"

"Don't worry about that, Sergeant. I'll personally see to it this sicko gets what's coming to him. No jury in the country will go easy on a priv who beats or kidnaps an EQO. He'll never see the light of day again. I won't be surprised if the judge deems chemical castration fit for this one. And if our new policies come into effect in time, his sentence will be severer still."

"I'd like to see that."

"You were saying—this fugitive of ours—do you remember anything about what he said? About where he's from? Where he was going?"

"No, ma'am, I'm sorry."

Dennehy's voice cracked. She let out a spluttered cough, turned to the bedside table, pointed to her can of Pepsi.

The minister picked up the can, began passing it over, stopped. Zie set it down on zer thigh. "What do you remember of Constable Tieman's disposition before the assault took place?"

Dennehy's reaching hand withered, retracted, like a newly hatched bird teased with sustenance only to be denied by her birth-giver. "Ma'am?"

"You said yourself this priv gave off a bad vibe, that he'd tried to engage Tieman in conversation. How did she respond to it?"

"Much the same as me, I think. That is, I could tell she was creeped out. No doubt about that. Even with all our experience, it's hard to ever feel comfortable around these people."

"Quite. And after you returned from using the facilities, did she have any further contact with the suspect?"

Dennehy coughed again. She wouldn't be given a drink until the EQM's thirst for answers had been quenched.

"No. Well...yes. I mean it's possible."

Zoe glanced up at Dominic. He stood by zer side, arms folded. He needed only to chew the side of his mouth for zer to understand what he was thinking.

"Explain," Zoe said.

"I'd gone out to the car while she was settling the bill. It's possible he spoke to her at that point. Maybe he thought he'd try to harass her when she was on her own. She's young—still inexperienced. He might have noticed that, tried to take advantage. You know he even tried to open a door for her?"

"Yes, I read your statement. Patronising little creep. Why would Tieman not apprehend him as soon as he did that? Why did it take you to come back and question him?"

"Hard to say, ma'am. My guess is she didn't feel safe, needed my help so she came outside. Then we were about to make the arrest together."

Zoe passed her the Pepsi. The officer glugged, deep, relieved.

Zoe said, "But you didn't."

A trail of syrupy liquid fell from Dennehy's mouth, onto the cotton shirt. The can hovered at her lips. She took another swig, stared back at her superior, not knowing how to respond.

"No, ma'am. We weren't able to get to that stage before he—"

"Yes, what exactly was it that he did? You had injuries consistent with being struck on the side of the head with a taze stick. How did he get hold of your weapon?"

"I...I don't remember. It could have been Tieman's stick. It's all a blur."

"So he took her weapon off her while you stood there and did nothing?"

"No. I didn't do nothing. I was going to book him."

"What was the distraction?"

"Distraction, ma'am?"

"Distraction, Sergeant. You must have been distracted. How else could he have got away from you during an arrest, overpower an officer, take her weapon and knock at least one of you out? All while he was handcuffed?"

"I hadn't got round to handcuffing him. I don't think. I mean, I couldn't have. I remember he was…he was saying awful things. Insulting me. He said I had…I had…"

"He was insulting you while you were arresting him? An openly hostile suspect and you didn't cuff him?"

"I was going to! I think I remember trying to…"

"A CisHet acting in a violent manner and you didn't take measures to subdue him?"

"I was going to, ma'am, I swear. I drew my weapon. I'm sure of it. It must have happened very fast."

"A shame you weren't faster. A shame for you, and a dear shame for Constable Tieman."

Dennehy's eyes filled again. She shook her head, her hand pinching the suety skin at her throat. "I'm sorry."

Zoe leaned in close to Dennehy's ear, close enough for the sergeant to recoil at the stale breath against her cheek. The voice was whisper and spittle.

"You'll be *more* than sorry if this affects our plans Dennehy. I fucking *vouched* for you, don't forget. You think the Coven will take you if they found out you got put on your arse by a *fucking cis male*? They'd expel you for life. They would make it their personal business to *cancel you* from society. From everything. Even kick you out of the OSZ. You'd be lower than a *priv*. Do you fucking understand me?"

A whimpering nod.

"Do you fancy the idea of living the rest of your short, miserable life getting beaten and abused in the Cistrict?"

A snivelling shake of the head.

"But you're right—mistakes happen." Zoe leaned back, zer words once more dressed in an artificial cheeriness. "You can't blame yourself. Get your rest, Sergeant."

Zoe scooted the chair out, swung Jezebel underarm, gave the officer a smile that had all the warmth of a rubber mask. Dominic followed zer to the door.

"Wait!" The officer bolted up in the bed. "I do remember something."

The EQM paused at the threshold, turned back to the room.

Dennehy said, "I asked the priv for his Ally Pass. He didn't have it. He said he'd left it in a machine at one of the vocation centres." She looked up at them, brimming now with hope, at the thought of restoring her credibility. "Yes. That's what he said! I remember now. I remember clearly that's what he said."

A dam gave way around the hot core of Zoe's anger, a rush of anticipation like molten steel through zer arteries. The synth-leather of zer gloves wheezed as zie scrunched zer fists together.

Zie took Dominic by the elbow, said, "Contact every centre within a twenty-mile radius. If we can't find that passport, I want the names and records of every priv who registered their details that morning."

"Yes, ma'am," Dominic replied, already pulling up the contact list on his voxwatch.

The equality minister returned to the bedside. The officer in the bed pulled herself up on her pillow, buzzing about the prospect of putting her assailant to the sword. It almost brought a tear to the EQM's eye.

"Will you find him, ma'am?" Dennehy said.

Thick fingers reached down, patted the sergeant's head.

"We won't just find him," Zoe told her. "We won't just cancel him, either. We'll erase him. Everything he is and ever was. Every generation before him and every generation after. And we'll make it hurt. I swear to the Great Birth-Giver, the world will have no memory this creeper ever existed."

CHAPTER TWENTY-EIGHT

The blade at her neck, a cold kiss making the skin pimple along the length of her back.

"Are you sure about this?" Jake said.

He hovered behind her, a warm shadow at her shoulders. In his hand, her pocket knife—a snubbed blade that folded out of a stainless grip, its evil edge a threat she couldn't ignore, couldn't fend off if she tried.

"Are you *sure* you're sure?" he said.

"Okay," she replied. Not a 'yes'. Hardly a 'do-it'. Only enough of a prompt to usher him on. Enough to push the blame on him in a perverse sort of way.

He took a length of her hair between his fingers, ran them downwards to straighten it all, tried not to pull too hard. Every movement slow, every breath heavy on her scalp. Seemed he was telling the truth when he said he'd never done this before. The towel around her shoulders didn't stop her from shivering. He paused for a while. Thinking, maybe. Judging the angle. He swallowed. A glint of light bounced off the wall in front of her.

"Wait," she said.

Jake froze. The tug on her skin slackened.

"I can't," she said.

He blew air out of his cheeks. The light dropped down the wall, disappeared forever. He moved away. The springs of the bed rasped.

"Good," he said. "I felt like I was about to mutilate you."

Chrissie threw her locks forward, pushed her hand through them, felt the weight of a blackout curtain, twisted them protectively into a loose braid. She got out of the chair, sat with him on the bed.

"Sorry," she said. "It's probably a mistake but I can't bear to do it. I know it'd help to blend in but..."

"It's unnecessary. There are other ways to hide. We'll be okay."

Both the 621 lapel-mounted voxcoms had been quiet for two hours now, probably killed as soon as the investigators realised Dennehy's equipment had been taken. They had no idea what the outside world was thinking, what it knew, how much chaos was—or maybe wasn't—cycloning in their direction that very second.

They had left the NetTube on, low volume, the latest netwire update running in a background murmur. The gentle volume from its speaker eroded the tension a little. Chrissie cradled her knees.

"You look a little pale," Jake said, "if you don't mind me saying."

"I don't mind you saying. But expressing any opinion of my appearance is against the law. Didn't they drill you on that during your rehabilitation sentence?"

He glanced at his feet. "Suppose you better arrest me."

"Or let you off with a warning."

"I'd pay you a compliment instead but you don't seem in the mood."

"Headache."

"Anything I can do?"

"Water would be good. There are painkillers in the front of my utility pouch."

Jake went to the bathroom to grab a glass. Chrissie popped the blister pack, stared at the little red pills. She didn't wait for the water.

A familiar scene replaced the face of the netwire anchor—the awning of the eatery. Footage of forensic analysts in spectre-white boiler suits picking at the ground with tweezers, dropping specks into plastic baggies. The content warning symbol appeared in the corner of the picture.

"Turn it up," Chrissie said, leaning forward.

"…that has shaken both the local community and the entire country. The incident has left one officer with severe injuries and another missing. The CisHet suspect is believed to have used a vehicle to abduct another equality constable after committing his assault, but no make or registration has been identified. Officers from across the Metropolitan area are…"

"Abducted," Jake said. "They think I abducted you."

"They don't think anything," Chrissie replied. "They're telling the media what they want to hear. Until they find us, they won't want to risk accusing an echo of attacking one of her own."

"Even if they know that's what happened?"

145

"It's not about what happened, only about what they need to have happened."

Chrissie had toed the line long enough to be able to predict with near supernatural accuracy how most of these situations would be presented to the public. And how most of them would end.

"We're all terrified he's still out there," said a transwoman being interviewed outside the sandwich bar. Yellow tape ringed off the entrance. The name on the screen identified her as Gina, the owner of the business. *"My employee on duty at the time said this priv came in, angry and abusive, looking like he hadn't washed for days. Then when the officers arrived, he hid at the back of the bar and followed them when they left. He was looking for trouble."*

Unsurprisingly, the sandwich-maker didn't make an appearance. The story cut to a press conference.

The commissioner, in a crisp uniform, addressing the audience from a podium bristling with microphones: *"We are doing everything in our power to locate the movements of the suspect and get our officer back safely. If anyone has any information that may help us with our enquiries, we urge them to be in touch with us immediately."*

A ripple through the crowd gathered in the press room. An inaudible question fired from somewhere off camera.

"Yes. While we can't confirm anything yet, we are investigating links to recent binarist terrorist activity."

"Terrorist?" Jake said. The colour faded from his face.

CHAPTER TWENTY-NINE

"It's all right," Chrissie said into the silence. "They don't know who you are. If they knew a single damn thing, they'd have already said." She put a hand on his shoulder. "If we can get you out of the OSZ, I can make something up—give them a different description. Claim you were from some other part of the country, talked about going back there. Move the search away from London. Maybe that will…"

Jake stared at the screen, shook his head. "It's like you said, whatever they want to happen will be made to happen. Without any real witnesses to what happened, they'll railroad me."

"I can talk to my partner—tell her what really went down. Beg her for forgiveness. Tell her it was an accident. Or that I was sick or something…that I didn't know what I was doing…"

He shook his head. "No point in dragging you down with me."

He was right. Accident or not, Dennehy wouldn't forgive her. The government wouldn't forgive her. A failure by one was a black mark on the whole. First lesson at the academy.

The screen threw up a final image to close the report—a still of Chrissie with Charlotte and Daniel at a picnic a year ago. Big smiles. Happier times. A photo choice designed to get the public to feel anger towards the priv who had 'taken' her. Or to lure her out of hiding. Seeing it felt like falling into an ice bath, soaking in all the pain at once.

It meant two things. That she could no longer show her face in public and that they'd already been to her home, sat her sister down, told her…well, what exactly? That Chrissie had been abducted? Or that they suspected Chrissie had collaborated with a felon, that any attempt to protect her would result in serious consequences?

Much of her now-worthless uniform lay in a crumpled heap in the corner. The tac vest sat upright against the wall, the limbless torso of her former self. She was already feeling ashamed of it. Any day now— maybe even today—people wearing those same clothes would be breaking down the door, hurrying her into a van, slapping plasticuffs on her, locking her in a cell, walking her into a courtroom, all the time sneering at her, reminding her she was a traitor. They might even be colleagues from the Marylebone station, people she knew, who knew her. They might even…

A thought, one so obvious now she didn't know why it hadn't walked in earlier. The chaos of the moment had slowed her thinking, let her forget the one thing that could still swing things in her favour, sitting with them this whole time. Chrissie bolted from the bed, went over to the pile of clothes and equipment.

"Witnesses," she said with a dry urgency, ripping Dennehy's body-eye from its holster, holding it up for Jake to see. "Maybe we're *not* the only witnesses."

He looked quizzically at the device. "I don't understand."

Chrissie didn't waste time explaining. The netscreen was old but she was relieved to find it still had wi-dev connectivity, allowing it to synch with the cam. It found the device. The screen blinked automatically, displayed a map of the external drive, a mosaic thumbnail gallery of auto-segmented video clips.

"Mine wasn't switched on," Chrissie said, "but it's likely my partner's was. She likes to watch the footage later. Gets some sort of sick thrill."

She put her fingertip to the screen, flicked to the last thumbnail. The time tag on display revealed today's date—the Twenty-eighth of Octavia. Chrissie jabbed it. The frame widened, auto-played.

The screen delivered a juddering, twirling image. Shapes of distorted legs and arms in one moment, close-up fingers the next. Then the alley—the same alley that had appeared moments ago on that same screen, only inverted. Bouncing. Hard to interpret. The sound was an incomprehensible rhythm—sand being shaken in a hollow shell. The image winked to black.

"That's it?" Jake asked, scratching his head.

"No. No, it was on. The eye was on! We need to go back further…"

She returned to the menu screen, chose the all-play option, slid the time bar to play backwards from the last shot. The bouncing alley returned, followed by fingers, followed by limbs. Barely any of it made any sense.

She said, "It must have switched off at some point when we ran. But it was definitely…"

The image quit its jerking, stayed motionless for some time, showed nothing now but a rectangle of pale grey. Not quite a motionless image. The grey streaked, slid sideways, as if a window looking into a smoke-filled room.

Sky. London sky.

A minute passed. Neither Chrissie or Jake pulled their gaze away. The screen tilted, swung, showed Jake's face looming in front of the shot, a brick wall beyond. He was wincing, eyes shut, anticipating pain.

"There!" Chrissie said.

It was exactly how she remembered it, only backwards and from a closer angle than she had experienced earlier that morning. None of Dennehy's reddened face spitting hot revulsion in her ear. She looked instead through her partner's malevolent perspective.

A chill passed over her. Jake fidgeted. They shared the out-of-body experience. On the tape, he looked surprisingly calm, hurling those insults at the sergeant with a suicidal indifference that had shocked her at the time. She relived her own emotions, felt fear vibrate through her like a bolt, only for anger to emerge like the inevitable crack of thunder—right through her arm, through the taze stick, into Dennehy's collarbone.

"Strange to watch," Jake said, cutting through their collective unease.

"You're telling me."

Chrissie could see herself now, at the mouth of the alley. Dennehy's perspective trickled backwards from the restaurant front, back over the curb, back into the patrol car. Throughout, Chrissie's past-self appeared stunned. A glasswork model in blue body armour.

"There's nothing here that exonerates me," Jake said, voice grave. "If anything, all it does is incriminate you. We should destroy it."

"No. There has to be something else. Maybe from earlier, when she went off on you..."

Jumping back further, she found Dennehy at the driver's seat. Close-ups of a chewed sandwich reforming, wrapping itself like a grotesque magic trick, a string of saliva dissecting the frame for a moment before breaking like a cobweb.

Chrissie pressed the rewind button again. Was there enough evidence to show Dennehy had been the antagonist? If a jury could see that, perhaps they would be lenient. The picture stalled, fixed. Chrissie stabbed at the button again. The image jerked, darted back too far—a reversed view of the street through the patrol car windscreen. Chrissie recognised it as the route they'd taken to get to the restaurant.

"We're not destroying this," Chrissie said. "I'll make copies of it as soon as I can and send it to people I can trust. It can help you out of this."

Jake shook his head, unconvinced it would help matters. He got up, paced between the window and the bed.

The image on the screen slowed, froze between two frames. Chrissie stabbed at the rewind button several times, hard. Nothing moved. She pressed play again—still nothing. She was about to disconnect the device, reload the video, when the picture came back to life. A temporary blip. Now the footage was cycling more quickly, moving from one moment to the next in schizophrenic bursts. Almost too fast for her to analyse.

The apartment building: Tatlow Heights. The door of flat 15b. Ghost-like shots of poor Peter Cobbleswan, his doomed band of binarist rebels. The screen flew backward through the streets, through the police headquarters. Chrissie saw herself again—emerging from the locker room in the uniform she had once been so proud to wear. It reminded her of her graduation from the academy, her swollen sense of achievement, the delighted friends and family members who had come to watch her accept her badge from the commissioner. It was a time when she was still an ally. Still safe, still a free woman, still able to walk down the street, go home to her loved ones. It would have been good to go back to that time.

No, it wouldn't, she reminded herself. *Not now. Not ever.*

Given the chance to reverse her life like a digital tape, she wouldn't hit the rewind button.

The footage continued its sporadic dance, all flash cuts, fuzzy edges. Dennehy, alone, fixing her lapels in a mirror. Dennehy's hands, reaching for a water cooler. At the steering wheel of a squad car.

Signing a visitor register at the Ministry building lobby. Walking backwards up a marble staircase.

"Wait," Chrissie said, springing from the bed. "Screen pause."

Jake swivelled towards the netscreen. The picture stuttered, stopped. The repulsive face glared at them.

The chill that passed through them both was fleeting and terrible.

"I recognise..." Jake couldn't find the words.

"The equality minister. We met with her a few days ago. Only..." Chrissie leaned forward, read the time-stamp—14:15. Twenty-fourth of Octavia. "This was earlier. Must be the meeting they had last Wednesday."

Mere hours after they'd arrested Thomas Tate. Dennehy hadn't switched off her body-eye. Maybe she'd forgotten. Or maybe she'd wanted to revel in this moment too. Would she have had the audacity to knowingly record a private meeting with a senior TEP official? Either way, Chrissie couldn't pull herself away from the screen.

Urwin: *"Have a seat, Sergeant Dennehy. So glad to see you again."*

Dennehy: *"Whatever I can do to help, minister."*

Chrissie and Jake huddled together, unable to tear themselves from the screen, watched the pantomime play out in full, heard the words they could barely believe were real. Throughout it all, Zoe Urwin seemed to be watching them through the screen, her gaze never wavering.

CHAPTER THIRTY

"What do you do after the blast?"

Urwin, at a desk, thick fingers rolling either end of a hunting crop, her round face sitting squashed on top of her bulky frame. The toadish appearance as unsettling as Chrissie remembered, the unblinking eyes staring into the lens—into her.

"I take the priv out of the building. March him into the street."

Dennehy's voice, from somewhere in the room. This is her seat, across the desk. Her perspective. An involuntary virtual reality.

"No," Urwin says.

"No?"

"You have to wait a few minutes. There'll be panic after you press the button—running, screaming. No one will notice you if you walk out immediately."

"What if everyone scatters?" Dennehy says. "There might not be anyone left to see."

"The book describes that. Officers and barricades around the entire east-facing perimeter of the One Strand building. They'll keep the crowd kettled in."

Book? Perhaps the smartpalm on the desk, the one visible in front of the slack, tattoo-riddled arms.

"Makes me feel better," Dennehy says. "But what if something happens before I can press the button—say, someone raises an alarm, or a bomb threat gets called in?"

"We get dozens of them every year," Urwin says. "Fucking cis rebels trying to disrupt the celebration. Never genuine. The commissioner will instruct our officers to ignore them, as they always do. Start again, Sergeant. What do you do after the blast?"

"I wait. I give things a few minutes to cool down. *Then* I emerge with the priv in cuffs. Make it seem like I chased him down, caught him trying to escape the square."

"Make a scene. Yell at him. Make sure people hear you. You'll want the reporters to notice."

"And at that point I'll be all over the netwires, yeah?"

"We'll direct the reporters where to go so they capture your best side. When all's said and done, no doubt you'll be invited for an interview with every major NetTube feed in the country."

"Like the officer in the book."

"You'll be a national *shero*, Sergeant. Our very own, modern-day embodiment of fierceness and bravery."

Urwin's chins jiggling below the purple wound of her mouth.

"When do I get my robes?" Dennehy says.

"The Central Coven will grant full and immediate membership within the week. You'll be a true disciple in no time. Did I mention the accolade, as well? The Prime Ministerial Medal for Valour. I'm thinking a full ceremony, broadcast nationwide. Prime time streams."

"It's still a lot to take in, Minister. A little overwhelming, even…"

"I understand," Urwin says, bordering on tender. "But you also need to understand how much we need you—our star of the hour. The legislations we'll be bringing into effect on the back of this must be sweeping and expeditious. The longer the gap, the more time the public has to question the sequence of events, to realise what's happening. You need to champion those reforms during your first interviews. Be as vocal as possible about these changes being the only possible thing that can keep the people safe for the future."

Dennehy, lifting a meaty arm, perhaps scratching her face, obscuring the picture for a few seconds.

"The DIP," says the sarge. "They'll probably try to derail things."

The arm dropping. Urwin still there, still stagnant.

"Maybe," Urwin says. "We believe most will back the reforms. The death of their leader will be incentive enough. Even if she somehow survives the blast, it'll be too late for her opinion to count for anything."

Great Birth-Giver, Chrissie thought to herself. *She can't be serious. It can't be real.*

"And those that don't?"

"Our censors are on standby. We'll simply brand them traitors. The mood of the nation will be one of fear. The public will want an aggressive promotion of security. They'll be begging us to round up every CisHet in the OSZ and anyone who objects will be deemed a binarist sympathiser. The DIP will die with Gallard."

No, no, no.

"Tell me again," Urwin says. "What new policies will you call for?"

Dennehy, fidgeting in her chair, picture jouncing.

"About those. I'm not sure on the details."

"You won't need to know the details. No one will quiz you. You just need to know the policies. Say them."

"Pre-emptive arrest and imprisonment of all CisHet people. Chemical and physical castration of all CisHet people. Enforced physical transition for all convicted terrorists. Immediate prioritisation in funding for u...uh..."

"Uterine transplant research."

"...uterine transplant research. The legalisation of permanent corporal cancellation for crimes against trans people and the state. Pre-emptive embryonic manipulation for all foetuses. And the constitutional establishment of a united front political system led by the TEP."

"In order to fortify our democracy."

"Yes. For our own good. Did I say it right?"

"An inch off perfect."

Praising her like a little kid, the officer probably lapping it up.

"The prime minister," Dennehy says. "She's on board with all this now?"

"Almost."

"I'm saying, we're only a week away, so if—"

"She'll be with us, Sergeant. You worry about doing your job. Now, recite those policies for me again. I never tire of hearing them."

CHAPTER THIRTY-ONE

The local streets, quiet at noon, the rain deceptive. It fell like gentle, grey sea-spray yet it clogged every pore of tarmac, transformed the pavement cracks into a network of rivulets, created rank, curdling pools around the storm drains.

The footage had left them shaken, had allowed them to glimpse the future from their hiding hole. The plans being drawn up would lead the world into the Next Circle of Hell. No use hiding forever. The Devil would catch up to them eventually.

They went together. In spite of the risks, Jake refused to allow her to set out alone. Chrissie didn't know if she could trust him not to disappear, but he was probably thinking the same of her. After discovering what was being planned for his kind, it would be natural for him to become suspicious. Scared even.

She could run too, of course—if her senses were so inclined. Ditch him as soon as his attention was diverted, a duck-and-cover as soon as the next autobile approached, a hasty swivel-and-split the next time they got spooked by their reflections in a storefront window.

Yes, she could bolt. She could scream for help. She could turn the whole situation around on this rough, violent priv vagrant, claim he had forced her into a hotel room at the mean end of a stolen taze stick, claim he told her he would corpse her on the spot if she cried out, claim he did awful, unthinkable things to her before she managed to break away. Easy. There would be no questions, no investigation, certainly no trial, thanks to BANBA (the Believe All Non-Binarists Act). She had taken Dennehy's body-eye with her—its incendiary digital payload the only real evidence of the truth. She could feel it now, cold beneath her fingers inside the satin-lined pocket of her bomber jacket.

Throw it in one of those drains! the internal voice screamed. *Let the rain clean this all away! Save yourself!*

But, no.

The voice faded. In spite of the terror, of the inevitability of their arrest and punishment, the thought of abandoning him filled her more with disgust than comfort. She wouldn't just be throwing him to the wolves, she would be closing the door of redemption on herself, accepting this corrupt and broken society for what it was, allowing herself to be swallowed by its poisonous cement, a brick in a wall of a house of horror.

You're free. Don't forget that. Free for the first time in your life.

For now, at least. Her unshackling from the collective authority brought clarity she had never experienced before, like going cold turkey off some debilitating drug. The freedom pumped numbingly through her, deadened the doubt, cast some of her fear into the dark— not gone, but no longer the sole mistress of her thoughts and actions.

There was still Dennehy to worry about. Would she remember? Taze sticks often left their targets with partial memory loss, didn't they? Chrissie hoped to Goddess the sergeant woke up without remembering anything since entering *Gina's*. Wasn't it about time something went right for her?

An autocab idled at a curb across the main road, re-juicing itself at a charging point. Rather than risk being scrutinised at a pedestrian crossing, they waited for a break in the waxed steel worm of traffic winding towards the city, then swerved between its bumpers. Wet and hot, they threw themselves in the back of the vehicle. The dashboard lit up, sensors chirping their electronic welcome.

The autodriver said, *"Where would you like to go, today?"*

The recorded voice was both deep and effeminate. Blank text appeared on the touch screen embedded on the divider, asked the same question. Chrissie gave it the address.

"Please touch your smartchip to the reader to begin your journey."

"Here goes nothing," Chrissie said. She touched Dennehy's warrant badge to the scanning slate.

An unusually long pause before anything happened—a silent, sinister moment of data exchange somewhere in the capacitors and resistors within the machine's innards. The startling shuck of the doors locking.

Jake let out a low gasp. His breath dived in his chest. He pawed at the door, raked the hard plastic and acrylic glass, left streaks as he failed to locate the handle.

Chrissie reached over, grabbed his wrists, leaned heavily into him, like a nurse pinning down a lunatic patient. "Hey, relax! It's okay. They always lock before they drive. It's the law."

Jake stared at her—into her—seeming not to have registered the words. His arms hung like dead weights beneath his jacket. The slope of his brow pinched into raven wings in mid-descent, his eyes silver bullets crashing into pools of water. He did not relax.

"Please buckle up, sit back and enjoy the ride."

Another mechanical sound—this time from outside. The charging conduit detached from the electrobank, reeled itself back into the cab's belly. Chrissie let go of Jake, did as the system requested.

Slowly, Jake came back to the real world. He blinked. His shoulders sank bank in the seat. He fumbled for his seatbelt instead of the door release. She helped him find it. As soon as it snapped into place, the engine span to life, a near soundless stir. The cab pulled smoothly into the road, becoming another bump in the worm.

She said, "You with me? Jake?"

"Yeah. Sorry. I…I had a moment there."

"I understand."

"If only you did."

"Try me."

"Can't. You've only ever known freedom, haven't you? You've never had that taken away."

"Have I? I'm not sure I've ever been free. Not really."

"You think it's not all bad at first," he said. "That if you can walk around in the open air, you have nothing to worry about. But it's always there. They control us. How we speak. How we think. Act. What we're allowed to know. It's always there."

As sorrowful as his comments were, they helped Chrissie. Her resolve restored, swelled back into her like the rainwater gathering in those potholes outside. He had suffered more than she knew. The plight of those on the receiving end of prejudice had been tucked away, silenced for so long. The rumours of hardship and pain and despair had always been mocked, scoffed at as the melodrama of a privileged few, reinterpreted as the politicking of oppressors and monsters who, after all, could never have known suffering *like non-binary people knew suffering.* But he had. His was true suffering, the type that came only from being criminalised, not by action or inaction, but by natural selection.

"Always there," she said. "I know. I've felt it, too."

He looked up at her. "Chrissie. What we saw on the tape…they can't…can't *do that,* can they?"

"Sounds like they're going to try."

"Then we have to stop it. Let people know or else…"

"Can't worry about that right now. We won't be able to do a thing if they find us."

Her gorge rose. She let out a long, slow breath. The droplets formed in runnels on the glass, changed direction at whim, clumped into fatter, quicker tears.

Do something? If only he was as smart as he was idealistic.

On what world would either of them ever be allowed to do something?

CHAPTER THIRTY-TWO

"I want to reassure you this is not an emergency."

The five cabinet ministers stared at Zoe, the green of their faces complementing the felt of the Cabinet Room meeting table, each burning with the unease of a gambler who had just rolled craps. Crisis meetings were usually held in one of the windowless briefing rooms of the Cabinet Office. Today, the equality minister had made it a point to assemble in Downing Street, emphasising the fact through the setting—this was no crisis. Besides, Zoe liked using Number 10 when the prime minister was out of town. Zie could sit in the big chair. Zie could have the staff tend to zer needs. It felt right.

"If it's not an emergency," said Ezra Kennedy, the trade secretary (*staircasegender chromosexual, he/him*), "it's surely a setback."

"No setback, either," Zoe replied with a lilting laugh. "I've spoken directly with our colleague. She's dazed, yes, though hardly incapacitated. And she remains loyal to the cause. She'll be match-fit when the time comes, I assure you."

"We ought to inform the prime minister," said Denise Jenkins, the health minister (*neurodivergent autistic fairy, she/her*).

Zoe daggered her with a look. Denise's neck shrunk into her shoulders.

"No need for that," Zoe said. "She's busy enough as it is, and as I've relayed multiple times now, this is but a minor interruption. We do not need to distract the prime minister from her campaign. In fact, I forbid you all from mentioning this to her until *Cockleshells* is complete."

Another reason for this discussion to not be held as an official crisis meeting. The last thing zie needed was an excuse for Tavistock to get cold feet.

In contrast, the ministers would be easier to coax. They were members of the Tribe—the TEP's circle within a circle, the party's most loyal and least forgiving leaders. Pioneering influencers during the time of the Big Reboot and now the architects of *Cockleshells* and all that lay beyond. They had been rewarded handsomely for their dedication over the years, were privy to what happened to those who did not play by the rules. Still, the equality minister knew the risks of allowing any doubt to germinate among the ranks.

"The way I see it," Zoe said, flexing meaty fingers, "is we look at this as a blessing in disguise. Our colleague is now not only a front-line protector of our liberties but a survivor of extreme cissexist violence. When the media exalts her as a *shero*, she can also be positioned as a victim—one who fought back. An ally who knows exactly what it's like to be harmed by the patriarchal right-wing and what it takes to defeat it. In many ways, we couldn't have hoped for a more ideal arrangement."

The Tribe seemed pacified by the comment, nodded to themselves, to each other, pondered the proposition with tight lips.

If only zie could convince zerself as easily as the politicians across the table. Dennehy had been compromised, the details of her assault an embarrassment to the city's security forces. They would need to be rewritten.

Zoe considered the new narrative amid the silence, thumbed Jezebel's soft tongue against the felt. The bubbles fizzed in zer can of Choco-lite ale. The digital clock above the fireplace acknowledged another minute. Time zie could have spent shopping, or in a spa treatment, or feeding sugar cubes to Jules. The fury zie had for the sergeant's failure was still there, melting into repugnance that such a person would soon be the face of their new movement. Too late to replace her. Dennehy was already an intrinsic part of *Cockleshells*. She knew too much to be cut loose. Assuming the dimwit could remember what she was hired to do.

"I agree with Zoe," piped up the education minister *(demigoosefluid, they/them)*, who never openly disagreed with any of their seniors. "We can use this incident to bring to mind the old adage that binarists are sharks. They may not all be dangerous at face value, but some of them are Great Whites. Ergo, all must be treated as if they are vicious predators."

"Yes," said the governess of the Bank of Britannia *(marzipansexual ferret-adjacent queer, she/her)*. "And if the public are reminded of this, they'll be prompted to suspect the privs who live in the OSZ. Even those who've been given labour clearance in the ISZ. Any of them could give in to their natural urges at any moment."

Denise nodded. "Trans people aren't safe unless we pre-emptively treat all CisHets as violent criminals."

"I'm glad you understand, darlings," Zoe said.

There. Not so hard.

"But what of this particular Great White?" Ezra said. "He's still out there. Does his freedom not undermine our party's claims to bringing these privs to justice?"

"If he's still within the city limits, he'll be found," Zoe said. "I promise you that. Until then, he'll play the role of our bogey-person. A prime example of the need for stronger punishments, enhanced resourcing, harder policies. Not to mention wider powers for the Equality Ministry."

As if awoken by the conversation, the spherical voxchat screen in the centre of the table pulsed and chimed. The ministers shifted in their seats, put themselves back on guard. Zoe accepted the call.

"I'm sorry to intrude, Minister," Dominic said, his appearance on the screen sending a short but palpable wave of repugnance through the room. "You said to only disturb you if there was a breakthrough on the Dennehy investigation."

"The missing officer," came the blunt reply. "You've found her?"

"No, ma'am. Afraid the constable's locator has been turned off and no witness sightings have come forward yet."

"Then why the fuck are you interrupting my meeting?"

"It's Dennehy's assailant, ma'am-sir. We know who he is. Found his Ally Pass in a vocation booth near Marble Arch. Would you like me to share the details with the room?"

Zoe's spirits soared. "Obviously."

The screen blinked, enlarged. The creeper's permit beamed across the table in high-def, four feet high, six feet wide. His height. His weight. Ethnicity. Clearance level. A 3D mugshot, too. A hard-edged face that would fit right into a prison system. And a name.

Jacob S. Brody.

161

CHAPTER THIRTY-THREE

By the time they reached their destination, the windows had fogged all the way. The vehicle pulled up one street away from Andre's Kilburn-based council flat. The locks popped up, much to Jake's relief. Steam rose from the doors as they opened, shawled the passengers in air as cool as it was welcoming. As with the many privileges bestowed on Equality Ministry staff, the first leg of the ride was free, assuming official business. Chrissie asked the cab to wait for them.

"*I will idle here for five minutes,*" replied the digitised voice. "*You will be charged for this service.*"

"Make it ten," Chrissie said.

It waited for them to step onto the curb, closed the doors, entered hibernation mode.

"You have access to this place?" Jake said.

"Echo access," Chrissie said, digging into one of the pouches on her patrol belt. "Key codes and biometric data are for civilians."

Her fingers emerged clutching a metal cylinder, the shape of a touchscreen stylus.

He followed her to a gate at the foot of a multi-storey apartment block. The climbing plants stuck to the brickwork were lank and leafless, hair in a shower plug.

"My sister's varlet is a little taller than you but not as broad in the shoulder," Chrissie said, holding the device against the scanner at the front door. "You should be able to find something that fits you well enough until there's a better alternative."

"What about you?"

A shrug. "I'll roll up the sleeves."

"Sure you still want to do this? If they catch you disguised in some guy's kegs it's gonna be more than a little hard to explain that away."

"I've told you, Jake, I've made my decision. We're in this together now, all the way. Besides, trespassing and robbery isn't going to add much to my crime sheet compared to what we've already done."

He smiled at that, gave her a grateful look. Her cheeks warmed. She glanced down at the grubby doormat. She heard Charlotte's disapproving sighs.

The scanner made an unhappy noise. The digital lockpick flashed green. Within the same second the latch flipped. The French door swung inward, a spectral moan. Chrissie led the way in, knowing Andre should be at work, hoping his schedule hadn't changed last-minute.

The ground-floor flat, as cramped as it was sparse. The minimal pay of a house varlet didn't reflect the hours it demanded. Peeling wallpaper, worn carpets, cheap pine furniture. A bedsit vibe. For someone who spent most of his life cleaning, the place was a nit pit. Only a handful of personal items—a clock, a suitcase, a yellowing rubber plant that reminded her of Andre's wilted posture. Not much sign of human presence. Andre would mostly use the property to sleep. He was required to be on permanent call, taking care of Daniel, keeping the place spotless, running menial tasks. The single bed boasted nothing but a wool blanket, a pillow of matching thickness. A rack of clothes in the corner—screws long ago bent or lost—propped askew, using the wall to keep it from collapsing. Jake went over to it, flipped through the fabric.

"Not much for colour, this guy," he said. He pressed a sleeve to his nose. "Or for detergent."

Between emulsion-smattered work overalls and a natty denim jacket, he found a raincoat. The inseam, eroded in patches. The fabric stained by an unidentifiable grime. Warm enough to keep him shielded from the elements, long enough to cover most of his regular outfit.

He buttoned up, found a wool flat cap discarded among the pile of old shoes, put it on. "How do I look?"

She said, "Like you could pass for an old codger if you keep the brim low."

"I was thinking it's more retro gangster, like in the old-school flicks. Maybe a little *Godfather* or *Bonnie and Clyde*?" He pulled the brim forward, tucked his hands deep in his pockets, affected a hunch. *"This here's Miss Bonnie Parker. I'm Clyde Barrow. We rob banks."*

"What are you talking about?"

"You know. *Bonnie and Clyde?*"

"I haven't had time to keep up with NetDramas."

"Never mind. It probably fell foul of the Cultural Correction Act a long time ago."

No idea what he was talking about. She turned her attention to the rack. Given the size difference, her options were limited. The coat and most of Andre's shirts and jumpers would have swamped her. She tried the denim jacket, found the shoulders hung loosely around her arms, the hem down past her backside. The sleeves, long enough to require her to roll up the cuffs, caked in dry mud from some outdoor excursion its owner had taken several winters ago.

A wool beanie stuffed in one of the pockets. She drew her hair up, bundled it inside, yanked the hat to her eyebrows.

She said, "I feel like a kid playing dress-up in my dad's clothes."

"You don't look far off it, either," he said, guiding her to the floor-length mirror.

With her hair covered and the shapeless jacket concealing her figure, the only indication of her true gender was the undeniably feminine face peering back above the ragged collar. Any passer-by who didn't get a good long look at her from the front could be forgiven for mistaking her for a slobbish teen boy.

"One addition," Jake said. He flicked out a scarf from the rack, brought it gently around her chin, tossed the ends like he was dressing a particularly fragile Yule tree.

She tucked the ends inside the jacket, found half her face could be covered if she buried her mouth inside the loop. The wool tickled her nose. It smelled of cheap aftershave, of decade-old sweat.

"Perfect," Jake said. "The Bonnie to my Clyde."

"We're already in enough trouble without robbing any banks."

"*Don't you believe what you read in all them newspapers, Miss Parker. That's the law talkin'. Want us to look big so they'll look big when they catch us…*"

"Stop it."

He pursed his lips. He turned her away from the mirror, made her look right at him. "Maybe they won't catch us, Chrissie."

"Why the optimist all of a sudden?"

"Maybe it's the clothes, but I'm starting to feel we might have a chance. Might figure this all out. As long as we stick together."

The autocab rolled south through the streets of Kilburn towards Marylebone, maintaining the speed limit to the decimal. Townhouses belched steam from basement boiler vents. Pedestrians carried sour-faced felines from one lounge café or prosecco bar to another. Giant e-boards flashed high-contrast pixel showers of corpulent female bodies that sashayed and wobbled in all the wrong places. Shop windows paraded rotund mannequins bedecked in faux-punk regalia that listed various pronouns, screeched hollow slogans about having *PRIDE* and being *STRONG* and how *RAINBOWS RULE*.

They were less than a block from The Wheelhouse when the sirens came screaming around the corner.

CHAPTER THIRTY-FOUR

Not one patrol car—a litany. An out-and-out, whole-hog convoy, splashing shop windows in a disco of red and blue. Autobiles stopped in their tracks, veered away from the centre of the road, moved by a collective zombie instinct.

"Oh, god!" Jake whispered, his body solidifying in his seat. "They found us."

Chrissie, no stranger to the sound, swivelled her entire body to see through the rear windscreen. The squad cars were the escorts. Behind them emerged two armoured personnel carriers, emerging like steel rhinos with a grudge against the city.

"Pull in here!" she ordered the cab.

Their ride, already making a swerve for the pavement, obeyed the new command, levelled up to the curb.

"*Is this your final destination?*" the voice asked with inappropriate coolness.

"No. Maybe." Chrissie replied, paying more attention to the echoes now barrelling out of the cars like bloated circus clowns. They blocked off the street, pushed pedestrians back, ordered passengers to stay in their vehicles.

"How many?" Jake asked.

"*I'm sorry, I couldn't understand you. Is this your final destination?*"

"Amazon teams," Chrissie said.

"*What* teams?" he said.

"*I'm sorry I couldn't understand you...*"

"Armed response units. They mean business."

"*I'm sorry, I couldn't—*"

"Shut up!" Chrissie said to the autodriver. "Stay right here."

"*I will idle here for five minutes. You will be charged for this service.*"

"Are you crazy?" Jake yelled. "We need to go now!"

"*Where would you like to go today?*"

"No—wait!" Chrissie said.

They hunkered inside the cab in spite of the privacy glass. Armoured carriers yawned open at the rear. Squads of the city's finest launched themselves onto the pavement, suited in special-force black, rubber boots, high-polished tactical gear. Hints of hot-wash hair dye flicked out from beneath the occasional helmet, lipstick red mouths grimaced above chinstraps. All wielded fully charged taze rifles, scoped and singing from their power packs.

Jake freaked. "Guns? I didn't know you people still carried those."

"They use voltaic rounds. Non-lethal. Like our taze sticks but with a lot more range."

"Oh, well, that's so much better! Listen, I've been tazed before. And I saw what happened to your partner."

"Try to relax. Most Amazon officers are wannabe soldiers playing at being tough. They hardly get any practice in real-world situations."

Mostly trying to make Jake feel better. The Amazon motto may as well have been '*Shoot first, don't even bother asking questions later*'. Amazons tended to be selected from those deemed to be carrying a vicious inferiority complex, giving them a propensity for violence. Many of those who failed Amazon entry did so because of fitness and stamina issues. Rejects usually got inducted into the regular Equality Force, eventually becoming donut-bloated sergeants in the OSZ, venting their frustrations on petty CisHet crims and creepers. Chrissie had seen it first-hand. Dennehy had been one of them. Rumour had it that a few of those who did earn their Amazon badge had been scouted directly out of TRANARCHY gangs under an initiative launched by the Equality Ministry, their hunger for blood considered a valuable asset to the Force. Chrissie pushed herself a little further into the upholstery.

The engine ticked, cooled. Three minutes went by. Sixteen Amazons filed back out of the hotel, looked even angrier than when they'd stormed in. Another individual with them—a limp, hooded captive, carried by wrists and ankles. The arrestee wore a black sack over his head. He bucked, shook like a stunned rabbit. They bundled him into one of the carriers.

In lifting their prisoner, the hood slipped. Not enough to identify the perp. Enough to see the foaming lips, the nose streaming with bloody mucus. Chrissie shrunk away from the rear window. They had come for them but had left with someone else, probably taking him for questioning. A pang of guilt hit her like a poisoned dart. They were catching up. They knew where to look. They probably knew Jake's identity by now. Maybe one of the countless videyes or sky-eyes throughout the city had tracked them. Maybe the Ministry of Equality knew Chrissie had switched teams.

Treason. The ultimate shame a member of the community could bring to their name, worthy of the ultimate punishment: permanent cancellation.

The last of the Amazons trudged out of the building, hauled vac-packed evidence. Even squeezed inside plastic, Chrissie could recognise the dark blue padded ribs and silver adornments of her tac vest. Her old life, removed like the belongings of the dead.

"Missed 'em by seconds," she said to Jake. "A minute sooner and that would be us they're throwing in the van."

"It still could be if we don't clear out of here soon."

He was right. Echoes were filing down the street, stopping at the held-up autocars, tapping at the windows, no doubt telling the occupants that all was well, that justice was being served, one transphobe at a time.

Needed a plan. Needed to go somewhere the talons of the Ministry couldn't reach them. It meant making difficult decisions. Impossible ones, even. It meant leaving herself behind. It meant forever.

"Driver, go," she said aloud. "Take us to—uh—anywhere. As far as we can get."

"*I'm sorry, your credit is no longer recognised. Please try again.*"

Chrissie did try again. But again, the cab refused to move.

"Stupid machine," Jake said with a growl. "Perfect time for you to have a software meltdown."

The penny dropped.

"It's not a glitch. It's Dennehy's badge. They've revoked its privileges. Must have figured out we—" She reached for the handle, pulled the locks up manually, flung the door open. "Come on, before they track this thing. It's compromised."

Jake slipped out behind her, followed her back into the side streets where they had first formed their inadvertent fugitive alliance, back into the uncertain world of the hunted. Behind them, chirping cheerfully under the soft light of late afternoon, the autocab's door closed.

"Thank you for travelling with Britannia's official taxi service. Wherever you are, wherever you need to go, we'll always be waiting for you."

The orange roof light flared and vacillated across the wet asphalt as it pulled away.

CHAPTER THIRTY-FIVE

Gone.

They were gone and he was still here. Somehow.

How?

The sirens had died away. The pulsing lights had vanished. A peek through the blinds—yes. Gone.

Could they have made a mistake? Stormed the wrong room?

No. If they'd been looking for him, they'd have found him. Surely.

Then…what? Someone else?

He moved from the window to the netscreen, flipped the feeds. No reports yet.

When he'd heard them coming, he'd thought it was over. The sight of the monstrous vans pulling up outside the hotel, the armed units charging into the lobby, the squeaking of their boots up the stairwell, a crescendo in his ribcage. The rattle of electrorifle charger packs, the shuffle of tac vests on the landing.

Over. Roll credits. Curtains down.

Through will or through fright, he had sunk to the floor, face down flat, hands behind his head, waiting for the door to be rammed open. They'd taze him for the sake of it. He'd tensed, anticipating the powerful shock. A loud bang had reverberated further down the corridor.

Over.

Then, yes, it actually was over. The sounds. The yells. In their place, voxcom static. Curses. Squeaking boots and floorboards, dispersing into the street.

Shaking. He was shaking. He thought he would be calm but his body betrayed him. Of course it had. It wasn't even his body.

He had looked up, eventually. The emerald dress hung on the back of the door like a crucifixion. He stood, pressed himself against it, ear against the wood, fingers clutching the delicate fabric.

Yes, over.

Tried to put pictures to the sounds that had come and gone. The bang at the end of the corridor, hollow and vibrating—another door. They'd battered their way into someone else's room. Some other enemy of the state. Poor bastard. Right now he was probably getting his—

A rap at the door. "Open up. Equality enforcement."

Shit.

Another rap. Impatient.

SHIT.

"Just a second."

What had he left out in view? Components to the device's remote control on the bed, half-assembled. He folded the blanket in half, trapped it all, rolled the whole thing under the cheap frame. His ID badges lay open on the dresser. He pushed them into the handbag, stuffed the bag behind the corner armchair. Then there was the mirror…

The knock again, more aggressive this time.

…The nylon stockings balled in his fist. Furious scrubbing. Rich Rosewood smears from top to toe.

Don't look relaxed, he told himself. Look worried. Even an innocent person would look worried.

He stripped down, kicked the clothes beneath the bed, threw the dress on, let his hair fall down. He twisted the latch, pulled the door open a crack, peered out wide-eyed.

The echo in the hallway wasn't an Amazon. Her sleeve was bare but for her rank insignia—a cadet, probably a few months on the job, pulling the grunt work. She looked like a biological female, possibly even a CisHet. Fresh-faced, terminally pretty. Too young for the beat to have bloated her. The garish stop-light lipstick didn't look as bad as it did on most of the female allies who wore it.

"Sorry to bother you," the officer said, her stare softening. "How do you prefer to be addressed?"

"She/her," he said.

"Thank you, madam. I wanted to check in. We had some trouble in the building."

"Trouble? Oh, gosh…"

"Nothing to worry about. Just have to make sure everyone's safe."

"I heard the commotion. Have to admit, it frightened me a little. But I do feel safer now that I know you're here."

A touch of suggestiveness into the last few words, letting it hang in the air in the gap in the doorway. He scanned the officer down to her boots and back up like smoothing a length of satin.

The echo stammered. Hard to tell in the poor, artificial light of the hallway but her face may have turned a shade darker.

This could be fun.

"Well, everything's fine now," she said, the words tripping over themselves. "Would you like to take a look around?"

The cadet blinked, her bottom lip drooping a little. "Look around?"

The door peeled back.

"To be sure?"

"Uh…"

The girl didn't know, couldn't think quickly enough. And she was one foot in the room now, before she could understand why.

An awkward, stilted moment.

The echo scanned the room, tried to look experienced. Her gaze hesitated at the smudged mirror. Only a second. She nodded, confirming all was as it should be, as if she had completed some thorough investigation.

"All looks okay."

What was she thinking? Was she wondering who this tall, dark goddess was? Or thinking what a nice t-girl like her was doing in a rat ranch like this? The officer appeared to be breathing fast, shallow breaths…

Oh, yes.

That.

"So, what happened, officer?"

"Nothing to be concerned about."

"How can I not be? All those sirens—and armed police."

"I don't really have much—"

"But they arrested them? Whoever they were looking for? Was it one or more?"

"Yeah, they got him."

"Who?"

"Look, I—"

"I need to know, officer. Was it a hate crime? I mean, I have a right to know if there was a hate crime committed here, don't I? Isn't that the law?"

As if it would ever not be. CisHet suspects hadn't had anonymity rights in years.

The echo looked at the carpet, probably debating whether she knew enough about her own duties, whether she was allowed to say more. "The receptionist. Arrested on suspicion of aiding and abetting a known cissupremacist. They've taken him in for questioning."

"Great Birth-Giver! That's so scary. And the other man, the bigot—is he still at large?"

"We don't believe he poses any immediate risk to the public."

"No?"

"No."

"What did he do?"

"Just another typical transphobe. He won't get far. They have his particulars. He'll be all over tonight's creeper bulletin. Probably a guaranteed cancellation."

"That's good. I'll keep an eye out for him."

"Much appreciated." The officer turned to leave.

"And if I do see him? Or anything suspicious? How would I reach you?"

"Oh, right—my card." The cadet rummaged in her utility pouch, handed over the details.

"Perfect." He took the card, barely glanced at it before folding it in half, tucked it neatly beneath the fabric of his top, snug between the flesh of his breasts.

The cadet's throat flexed, swallowed. Her eyes lingered a little too long on that warm valley.

"How about coffee?" he said.

"Oh, I don't—I'm on duty and…"

"Not now, later."

"Well, I mean—"

"You don't have a problem with trans people, do you?"

"What? No! Goodness, no, I'm an ally. I'm completely—"

"Great, hun. I'll call you."

CHAPTER THIRTY-SIX

"Never seen a church before?" she asked off his look.

"Not like this."

"Rarer every day. City never came to a decision on what to do with this one—tear it down or convert it to something less controversial. Or they ran out of funding to do either."

Looking up at the pale structure sandwiched between redbrick townhouses—a style she guessed was gothic because it sounded right in her head—she could make out a few decorative touches she hadn't seen before. The cross at the top of the steeple had already been removed the first time she was here, part of the purge of old patriarchal symbolism. The plywood screen around the entrance was standard policy. But on parts of the stone façade, still visible between the gaps in the screen, she could see graffiti that must have been recent—TRANARCHY style slogans in red and black.

God is genderless

MY temple is MY body

Higher power? TRANS POWER

The kind of scrawls the Equality Ministry didn't care to remove. The type they would judge selectively to be *creative expression.*

"What a waste," Jake said. "What an insult."

"You should be thankful," she said. "It's the perfect place to hide for the night. No people. No patrols. No sky-eyes. No videyes. Doors boarded up."

"Then how do we get in?"

"Same way I got in last time."

He waited for her to tell him. She looked up and down the street, ducked under the police tape, hoisted herself up the screen wall, tried to be quiet about it. Jake hurried after, finding it easier, landing his feet in the churchyard while she was still straddling the boards. He reached out. She let him help, let herself be lowered into his arms, surprised how easy he made it look, like she weighed next to nothing, like she was a kid.

The sun going down. Just enough light to get spotted if someone on the upper floors of the surrounding buildings cared to look out. Had to hurry. She led him to the side entrance where the barricades had been less rigorously pounded in—a few pieces of aged timber across the old door.

They synchronised, kicked the beams until they dislodged and splintered where the nails once held them. The chain slipped, the door caved in, opened on a hall of cobwebs, dust, stale air, unidentifiable grime.

The inside brought back memories—upturned pews, little chapels with their statuette saints, sad features and open hands, and the ones that had been toppled, turned into beige marble shards, mingled on the floor with the rest of the dirt.

Jake breathed sharply. She turned to see him standing at the end of the nave, looking up towards the altar, at the ornate ceiling, at the broken stained glass window. In the half-light, there in his stolen hat and jacket, he gave her the impression of an alien trying to masquerade as a man.

"Books and films," he said, "don't do these places justice."

What books and films had he seen to have formed an image of a church? The censors had long ago cracked down on that sort of thing.

"You think this is nice?" she said. "I'd love to see you walk into Ru Paul's Cathedral. Or any of the others they reclaimed. Not that they pass much resemblance to what they used to be."

A lot of hiding places in the church—nooks and alcoves she didn't know the names of—places that could be hiding someone or something they didn't want to run into. Chrissie took out her mini torch, cast a wide beam, tried to scan each of them as she went further into the building. Jake's heavier steps followed.

"So you were here before," Jake said a little loudly, not as aware—or not caring—that there was still every possibility they were not alone.

"Raid operation," she said. "A dozen homeless cisgender people lived in here once, tried to exist off the grid but hadn't found a way to get out to the Heaths. We came in, removed them."

"For squatting?"

"For non-conforming."

"I don't get it."

"They weren't actively causing trouble," she said, tugging the edges of her hat. "At least not that we knew. Merely existing independently, outside of the reach of the Ministry, like we're doing now—that's enough to be placed under arrest. They can't stand for anyone to be beyond reach."

"Huh," Jake said, as if he regretted asking.

She wished she didn't have to keep reminding herself of her past mistakes, felt she might need to go look for a confessional booth pretty soon. Strange kind of atonement, that. Admitting to your sins, doing it in private, being automatically forgiven. No trials or re-education or cancellation or public shaming or apology tour, just bang—out the door and you're good to go. Maybe those God-people had been on to something.

The Ministry was all about atonement, of course. Fed off it. Gorged on it. But forgiveness—when did that ever happen anymore? When had a business ever welcomed back a problematic employee? When had anyone's career ever been put back on the rails after an accusation of misconduct? Not for a decade or more.

And when had a rogue echo ever been released back into society after serving their sentence?

Never and then some.

Cancelled cops were expunged, went the rumours. Officers disappeared overnight, erased post-haste, all records removed. She started to think back now about the colleagues she'd known who had transferred without warning, left nothing behind but a memory. That girl from Harrow who came up with her in the academy. That sergeant who joined from the Kilburn station, only seen around for a few weeks. Could they have turned? And if so, had they been caught? Or had they managed to slip the net, find a way out?...

"What happened to them?" Jake said.

"What?"—was he was reading her mind?

"The homeless guys you banged up."

"Oh. A few years of re-education would be my guess."

Or worse, she didn't add. He was at it again. Making her feel like shit, not even realising.

She threw the beam at a little recess in the corner, said, "That's a chapel there. Want to see if there are any candles left?"

There were. He came back with his arms loaded up with them, half a box of matches, told her he lit one first as a kind of prayer, put it beneath the statue's feet. She could see it now, glowing from beyond the columns. It lit up more of the graffiti—statues with black 'X's over their faces, circles and arrows splattered above crucifixes to form the transgender symbol, crude outlines of genitalia and breasts on figures represented in some of the surviving murals.

Transgression not oppression

Hail Hermaphroditus

The old God cancelled. Same as most other churches. Same as the old mosques and the synagogues and the mandirs. Chrissie recalled seeing the purges back when the Cultural Correction Act had passed—books, films, data discs, hard drives—anything deemed *non-representative* thrown into those immense mobile shredders that travelled from town to town. To a young girl, they were metal dragons eating their way across the country, fed by echoes and volunteers, turning problematic material into mince, to powder, to ash.

They laid the candles in a half-circle, pulled up pieces of decaying carpet to use as blankets, curled up under the altar, opposite sides, shivering. A draught, fuelled by the pockmarked window above them, the image of Christ and Virgin Mother an incomplete puzzle, a history lasting thousands of years stamped out in the span of one generation. For an hour or more they listened to the sky-eyes outside the broken glass buzzing over the roofs, around the nearby streets. She hoped none of them came inside, hoped none of the holes were big enough for the machines to access.

"Can we turn the lights out?" she said. "I'd find the dark more comforting."

Like the opposite of a kid listening out for the monsters.

Jake blew them out, one by one.

Chrissie thought of the homeless people she had helped to send packing, not unaware of the cosmic irony, finding herself now as they were, hunted like a dog. She tried to cry without making a sound, tried holding her breath in as the shakes started to come.

"I get why those people would have come here." Jake said from the dark. "Churches used to be sanctuaries. You could hide out in one and no one could touch you. Least that's what I read somewhere."

She sniffed, swallowed, said, "Gone are those days. Longer we stay here, the more likely they'll find us."

"I've been considering our options," he said. "Echoes everywhere. Big old security perimeter trying to keep us in. But I've long heard rumours it's easier to get out of the city than they make you think. Know anything about it?"

"Only that it's been known to happen. They try to hush it up, even from the echoes."

"So the question is, where's the weak spot?"

"I don't know. But I might know someone who does. Think he's connected to the Resistance."

"A friend of yours?"

"Not exactly. In fact, I've never met him. Not properly. He might even have gone into hiding himself."

A mechanical purr grew loud at the window, a black shape lingering behind the despairing mouth of Christ, loitering, probing for movement. A thin spotlight raked the glass, spread for a moment across the floor, across the altar, repeated its sweep in reverse. The shape shrank back, took off again into the night.

"If he's still around," Jake whispered, "what makes you think he'll help us?"

Chrissie let her breath out. "He owes me."

CHAPTER THIRTY-SEVEN

*INTERCEPTED TRANSMISSION TRANSCRIPT—EQUALITY
MINISTRY*
SUBJECT: INSURGENT BROADCAST #265
LISTENING STATION GLORIA
29-10-46 0820 GMT

SENSITIVITY CLASSIFICATION: 8—CLASSIFIED / SANITIZED

VOICE [terrorist suspect #2408D]: Coming at you hot! You're back
with the Ozcast on Revolution Radio, joining me, the resistor on your
transistor, for the latest in goings-on around the shit-pile of what passes
for society these days.

Not all of you, mind. Some of our regular listeners in the OSZ won't
be tuned into this one. Truth is, we lost some of our ability to access
the smartnet recently. No biggie. A temporary glitch. Trust me, we'll
be back on all cylinders soon. Like I've told you before, our cyber guys
are the best. But it's a good reminder we need all the support we can
get, man. The powers that be are trying to hit back, keep you
unplugged and compliant, keep you dumb and docile. Revolution
Radio is a thorn in their side and they're stupid enough to be taking a
chainsaw to the problem. Keep it up, skanks. We ain't going nowhere,
right, gang?

Hey, wanna hear something else making me laugh? Get a load of this
article in today's *Daily Femail*: 'Tech firms form pact against cissexist
thought'. They say a number of leading technology and digital media
companies—including Xprez, Microcast, Slut Wallet, Twitchify,
NetTube and Disney—quote, *'will not tolerate any suggestion expressed by
either their employees or by users of their platforms that there is or has ever
been any negative facet of hormone therapy or gender-affirming surgery. Such
hate speech is false and seeks only to disparage the brave and fierce
contributions of the trans community, and has no place in our civilised
society,'* end quote.

Okay, never mind the fact that only seventeen percent of the country is even licensed to access the smartnet anymore, but whatever. The memo reads, *'if you do not accept this policy, you can expect to part ways with the company or be banned from use of our products and services with immediate effect.'*

See what these bullies are doing? They're engineering the discourse, man. They think they can induce national apathy by censoring counter-opinion and tailoring what you hear, what you can say. Their fantasy is in full swing. They're doing everything in their power to crush us, all based on lies. They tell everyone we're violent, that we're supremacists, that we're nothing more than a virus on the earth. It's so obvious where this is going...

Know what? They may control the discourse but they can never control what people think behind closed doors. Believe you, me. There are a lot of folks out there who don't buy into this ideology, man. They'll ally with us when the time comes. Believe. You. Me.

And when they get caught out in their own web of lies? When the facts are too opaque to see through anymore? Sweep it under the rug, they say. Sure, until the rug becomes all thick and lumpy and you trip over it and—*oh, shit*—there's some bodies under there! Yeah. They can't hide those skeletons forever. You *know* what I'm talking about.

Man, you're fed this stuff and you end up with no logical thought pattern. You're simultaneously holding fractured views of history and opinion and ideology and it's all mixed together like a steaming pot of...

Anyway. Speaking of headlines, d'ya hear about the echo that went missing yesterday? Yep—straight up and vanished after another officer apparently got her bell rung. Ask me, maybe someone had enough, I don't know. And I'm not talking about the suspect, as much as that boy deserves a shout out. Proper warrior that one. No, I'm biting at a different fish, man. Some of my sources think maybe the copper wised up. Think she *[REDACTED]*. Imagine that! An echo breaking her bonds and finally developing an independent thought...

We'll see. Wonder if they'll have to notch this one up to another incident of *internalised transphobia*. I know! What a scam. That convenient term they use when they want to contest the notion there are people out there who don't agree with them. And if any of those people try to point that out, guess what? Yep, *they're* internalising their transphobia, too. Semantic circles, man. You literally can't argue with these people. We're in a post-meaning world. Tell *your* truth, hun—no matter if it's total fabrication. After all, truth is just another binary illusion, right? The ruse of reality! Shoot me in the face, I'm done.

Anyway, the sky-eyes were all over London last night and word was the Fence was buzzing with border guards. Think they've tightened the net. I'm telling you, man, something's in the air.

Whatever's going on, I can tell you this—the people have had enough. The pendulum is swinging.

Oh, and I hear the equality minister is due to appear on the Caitlyn Smurth Show tonight. Not recommending you actually watch that drivel but I'll be interested to see what the censors have scripted this time. I know one thing for sure—if you're playing that drinking game where you take a shot every time A-list-ally Caitlyn gabs about her *you-know-what*, you'll probably pass out quickly. And maybe that's for the best. Ho, ho, ho! What a comedic genius she is…*yeeeuck!*

All I got for now. Ominous spiritus. Oz-man signing off.

END OF RECORDING

CHAPTER THIRTY-EIGHT

The Tatlow Heights building had an other-worldly look to it that morning, diabolical and corrupt, even though she had been there not forty-eight hours earlier when it was still nothing more than a rundown redbrick. It pulsed with the ghost of her old self, was stained by the bilious residue of the equality minister. She shuddered at the stone steps, at the thought of where the occupants of flat 15b were now, the torments they were being subjected to.

The thought unsettled her enough to make her want to retch. Her complicity in their fate was naked to her now. No internal voices feeding her the lies of justification, no great divide forged by the myth of duty separating her, artificially, from her own sense of reason. The tide of guilt was as abrupt as it was crushing, a hot rock tumbling through her bile duct.

She wavered at the portico, put a hand to her mouth. Nothing came. Jake reached out, propped her at the elbow. A deep breath. Another. The moment passed.

Chrissie pressed the buzzer on the intercom for 16a. Unlike the buildings in better parts of town, there was no videye on the front door. Had there been, chances of getting inside would have been slim. The electronic box gargled, said nothing. For a while they exchanged looks, hoping a response would come. She jabbed the button again. Same result. Jake gave her a *what now?* look.

"We'll have to wait it out," she said. "Across the road, maybe. See if he shows up."

"A stakeout?" Jake said, a flash of a smile.

"Trust me. They're no fun."

They were back on the pavement when the intercom finally chirped in response. A distinct *Yeah?*—though distant and hoarse, like the person on the other end didn't get many visitors.

Jake dashed back up the steps, leaned into the speaker, tried his best Scottish brogue.

"It's Pete. Let me up." Line perfect.

"Shit." The box spluttered. Hesitation. "How'd you get out, dude? Are…are you alone?"

"Let me up."

The less he said, the less likely the guy on the other end would detect the lie.

A long pause. Seemed like the bait hadn't been swallowed, like the occupant was smart enough—or paranoid enough—to leave it at that. But the pause was followed by the buzz of the digital latch releasing on the security door. It sounded like a thin sigh of relief.

They took the stairs. The carpet, worn, gave off a musty odour mixed with the faint linger of disinfectant, mouse droppings and foods cooking behind closed doors.

At the door to 16a, Jake nodded once to Chrissie, pressed his thumb over the peephole, knocked three times. It cracked, revealed half the face of the teen Chrissie had found in the airing cupboard. His eyes, bloodshot and tired, darted rapidly, registered the man standing in front of him was not, in fact, his unlucky dissident friend.

A question seemed to want to come out but the teen was mute, rooted to the floor.

Until he saw Chrissie.

Even with her head down, the hat pulled low over her ears, he recognised her at once. That was all it took. His face drained.

"Ah, shit," he mumbled.

Jake tried to storm the room. The teen threw the door closed. It banged against Jake's face. He let out a pained grunt, staggered back, held his cheek. The door swung back in, reverberated on its hinges.

Chrissie barged past Jake, propelled herself inside the flat. The teen charged through a door at the far end of the reception room. He was fast. She hurdled the table, followed him, confident he was more concerned with escape than trying to fight his way out. She made it to the unkempt bedroom. His legs disappeared through the open window.

The fire escape, a rust-riddled set of stairs nailed to the side of the building. It shook and groaned as Chrissie's feet landed on the tread. The clanging of the boy's escape rumbled through the bars.

For a second, she was back in the alley by Marylebone Station, feeling like she was hunting another priv accused of violating some social faux pas. A painful, fleeting memory. She leaned over the railing, tried to gauge how far ahead the teen was getting. Only she couldn't see him. The sound of phantom steps. She spun around. The building went up another six flights.

There he was. Two steps at a time to the sky.

A strange move. Either he'd panicked, taken a wrong turn, or he thought he could hide, make them think he'd fled to the street in an effort to lose his pursuers.

Jake came staggering up to the window, hand still clamped over one side of his face. His words were a growl. "Where is he?"

"He's gone up! Find another way to the roof. We need to cut him off."

"The roof? But—"

Chrissie didn't hang around to flesh out the strategy. She half-ran, half-pulled herself up the steps, launched her weight off the railings, a gymnast attacking the parallel bars.

By the time she reached the sandstone eaves, her heart was pumping hard, lungs and adrenal glands flexing. The view across the rooftops extended down the street for half a mile. Vents and chimneys and generators and electrical access boxes jutted up like a smoking model village cobbled together from industrial metals. The boy gained ground—but to where, she couldn't tell. His lithe, dark frame leapfrogged a row of HVAC units.

"Wait!" she called out to him. "I'm not here to hurt you!"

Her plea echoed across the buildings like broken laughter. If he heard it, he showed no response. Chrissie followed the same route. No other way across. She zig-zagged between the air conditioning pipes.

Halfway across, she stumbled at one of the turns, almost knocked her arm out of its socket, elbow colliding against a sturdy sat receiver. The pain jarred. Her momentum rolled her in a full circle. She steadied herself. A dull thud a few yards ahead. The boy, at an emergency access door, took another run up, battered his shoulder into it. It barely budged—locked from the inside.

He glanced back, saw Chrissie closing in, his hasty plan already unravelling. He gave up on the door, took off again—this time heading to the edge of the building.

No, Chrissie thought. *He wouldn't dare...*

Even as she tried to convince herself, the youth was clambering onto the safety wall. He displayed little of the fear Thomas Tate had shown, none of the effort to negotiate. She slowed to a stop, only twenty yards between them now. The boy stood, looked over the side, back at her, considered which fate would be the least painful.

"Stop!" Chrissie called out, raised her hands to show him she was unarmed. "You don't understand. I'm not here to take you in. I'm—"

His arms spread, a chick raising its wings for its first flight out of the nest. He dropped, disappeared in a half-second out of her sight, so sudden her breath cut out like a blown fuse.

An almighty crash. A cacophony of crystal notes sprayed unevenly across the rooftops. The explosion kicked the air back into Chrissie's lungs. She scrambled towards the edge.

Below, the skylight—a square pane of glass punched out, lying separated in a galaxy of shards on the floor below. Among them, the boy, lying motionless. Dead, she thought.

Until he stirred, raised himself slowly to his haunches, shook his head, made blue splinters fly. He brushed slivers out of his clothes and hair. She glimpsed a trace of blood on one arm. He had a dazed expression as he glanced back up at her. Unsteady, he ambled away, his path clear to take the stairs to the front entrance, to the freedom of the streets.

The boy staggered towards the stairwell, heaved the door open. The sound of a dull smack swam up through the hole in the skylight. The boy flew backwards, landed on his back once more. He splayed out, the lights of his eyes dulled, limbs still flopping, still on the brim of consciousness.

Jake stepped into the corridor, shook his hand like he was trying to wring out a flannel. He stood over the kid, made sure the punch he'd landed on his chin was enough to keep him down, looked up into the light, squinting to find her against the radiant slate of the sky.

CHAPTER THIRTY-NINE

Zoe Urwin still had alabaster dust on zer shoes.

Jezebel had been given a workout that morning, had sailed, had belted the Elliot Page bust with the full force built up in the equality minister's left shoulder, sent it toppling from the office mantelpiece. The face had burst on impact, reduced the head to a thousand self-satisfied pieces. Dominic had blenched, made that face he makes when on the receiving end of Jezebel's wrath. Made it in the evening prior when he took his licks for real.

"Clean them, Dominic," Zoe said, from the back of the limo, zer frame taking up both seats. The failure to find the priv and the echo had ruined zer beauty sleep, anger had zer all hopped up like a caffeine and speed cocktail. Someone was going to pay. Not just Dominic.

The varlet produced a lemon-scented wipe, unclipped his seatbelt, dropped to his knees, scrubbed in little circles, tried to buff the shine up, grovelled as he worked. "Our intelligence was sound, ma'am-sir. We had the right place. He couldn't have been gone for long."

"Stand up, Dominic."

The idiot obeyed. Zoe reached under his skirt, clutched his clackers.

"Don't you dare cisplain at me. Ever."

Zoe squeezed. Dominic clamped his teeth, fought not to cry out. Zoe squeezed harder until he did—a girlish, high-pitched cry—kept on squeezing. His eyes brimmed. His legs gave out.

The bruises beneath his blouse would be colourful now, butterfly-like. Zie could make his hairless gonads turn boysenberry by applying this hold, or crush them all together like those of the sacrificial hog.

His words, gasps. "I…I'm…sorry…ma'am-sir."

"That's for allowing me to break Elliot."

"Sorry…ma'am-sir. I'll…have it…replaced right away."

"The prime minister is going to want answers. This couldn't have come at a worse time."

Zoe released his scrotum. Dominic rocked back on his haunches, cheeks wet, cautious of the crop resting inches from his face, reminding him of the variety with which his mistress inflicted pain.

When his breath recovered, zie had him return to buffing zer shoes.

"Dominic, be honest. Where am I going wrong?"

"Permission…" he wheezed, "…to ask a serious question…my qween."

A faux yawn, a wave of a hand.

"Do you think Dennehy is up to this?" he said. "I fear we may have overestimated her ability to operate under pressure."

"Fear. That's exactly what she's feeling now. Fear is a splendid motivator."

"She's unreliable."

"No, she's perfect. Weak-minded, devoted to her superiors, beyond all degree of independent thought, and it's not fear alone driving her—it's revenge. She detests the CisHet subspecies almost as much as I do. If this latest incident doesn't convince her to play a role in their final downfall, I'll eat my menstrual pad."

He grimaced. "It's just that, working alongside Constable Tieman, we may need to consider the sergeant a tainted asset. What if it turns out the missing officer has…" He searched for the right words, "…switched sides?"

"The videye footage doesn't prove that. Only shows her on the street, in the company of the fugitive. For all we know, she's being coerced. Probably threatened with unspeakable abuse, knowing his kind."

"Possible, but her uniform and equipment were retrieved from the hotel. She discarded them."

"Or he ripped them off her in a fit of toxic lust. That's much more likely. Sadly we live in a world where such things happen all the time. The statistics don't lie—every non-binary person is the victim of cissexist assault. Every. Single. One. So it makes sense that the violence will extend to our allies."

Zoe loved quoting statistics to prove a point. Especially the ones the Ministry had invented.

"I'm only theorising, ma'am."

"Never has an equality officer turned traitor to the state. It would be suicide."

"But what if she did turn, ma'am-sir? What then?"

Zoe's fingers pinched at zer thighs. "I'm not a simpleton, Dominic. It's not as if I haven't considered the possibility. After all, why do you think we're in this car, going to where we're going? My point is that *if*—in the extremely unlikely event—she *was* to be guilty of treachery, we will find her. And when we do, I'll make sure justice is served, cold and with a side of mealworm bacon."

"Could she know about our plans, ma'am-sir? That's my concern is all. That the sergeant let her tongue a little loose and we have a rogue element prepared to blow the whistle."

"Doubtful. I've been nurturing Sergeant Dennehy for a long time. She may be a clod, but she wouldn't do anything to scupper her chances of joining the Central Coven."

"I hope you're right, ma'am-sir."

"*Hope* I'm right? Who do you think you're talking to, Dominic?" Zer eyebrows arched. Dominic apologised, backed away, slid into the seat all slow and deliberate, wincing as he did. Fucking sissy.

"*You have reached your destination,*" the limo's autodriver declared.

The car slowed. The other vehicles in their motorcade—an armoured police van and two patrol cars—pulled up along the curb, ocean lightbars blinking silently. The townhouse was unremarkable, as were the begonias in the window-box and the rainwater spilling off the first-floor balcony. Dominic popped an umbrella.

The apartment door, opened by a small child in a dress. Zoe wrinkled zer nose.

"Hullo?" it said.

"Is your birth-giver in?"

"Yes."

"Out of the way."

The brat retreated. The officers followed the equality minister into the living room. A fresh-faced echo already there, growing slothful in a wing chair. The officer sprang to her feet when she saw who had arrived. The boy's parent on the sofa, comforted by a state-issued counsellor. A young cis male in a service uniform hovered near the kitchen—the varlet, meek and as incompetent looking as Dominic.

"Charlotte Tieman?" said Zoe.

The woman nodded, dragged a hand over blotched cheeks.

"How do you prefer to be addressed?"

"She/her." Charlotte looked up, copped a double-take. "Min—Minister Urwin?"

"My dear, I can't imagine how difficult this situation is for you. Which is why it's imperative that you answer a few questions for us."

Charlotte Tieman's reddened gaze drifted to Jezebel, to the asp holsters affixed to the officer's belts. "Here?"

"Heavens, no. Better if you come with us."

The child watched from the doorway.

CHAPTER FORTY

By the time Chrissie got back down to the apartment, Jake had managed to frogmarch their new friend into the living room. The teen had regained his senses enough to mount a defence.

"I had nothin' to do with it," he said, voice chalky. "I swear."

They sat him on his couch. Chrissie didn't want to slip back into echo-mode again. She perched on the armrest in a way she hoped looked unthreatening. She took the hat off, tried to keep her expression open, relaxed. Jake took up guard duty by the door in case the boy tried to spring again. A storm cloud bruise had formed across the ridge of his right cheek where the door had hit him. He was scowling about it, even though he'd managed to return the favour.

As for the teen, his lip had been swollen by the punch. His spluttering protests pushed a trickle of blood down his chin. He was older than she first thought. His wiry frame and smooth, brown skin gave him a more youthful appearance. His converse shoes were dirty, his vintage rock t-shirt wrinkled at the collar. There was a rip in his corduroys that may have happened sometime during his escape attempt or may have always been there. The rest of the flat wasn't faring much better—the few odd pieces of furniture that had been thrown together were all a few decades older than their owner.

"You remember me, right?" Chrissie said. "From a couple of days ago?" It seemed like a couple of years. A couple of lifetimes.

He nodded.

"You remember what I did for you?"

"Sure. I guess."

"You guess?" Her tone edged away from cool. She took a second, checked herself, brought it back. "I stuck my neck out for you. Had it been anyone but me who'd found you in that cupboard, you'd have been carted off along with your buddies. You do know that?"

The teen said nothing but didn't look away. Some semblance of recognition of her good deed was seeping through.

"We're not here to do that," she went on. "I'm not—well—I don't work for the police right now. In fact, we came here to ask for your help."

"I can't help you. I don't know nothin'."

"So you said. Only I know that's not true."

"It is true. I was, y'know, in the wrong place at the wrong time."

"What's your name?"

The youth ignored the question, pressed his finger to his lip, tapped the blood together between his fingers. Chrissie got up, went over to the little kitchenette, ran the cold tap. She came back with a damp paper towel, handed it to him. He didn't take it outright, had to think about it. But once he did, she figured she'd made some ground.

Chrissie perched down again, this time opposite him on an upturned crate he'd converted into an end table.

"I'm Chrissie Tieman. You watched the netwires lately?"

"You mean the propaganda feeds? No, I ain't watched 'em. You a celebrity?"

"Well, if you had, you'd know my name. I'm not an echo anymore. I'm a missing person. Whole of London's looking for me."

The towel came away from his lip, a strawberry print left on the paper. "Right."

"Damn right. I'd had enough. Like you and your friends. I turned against my own and now you and me—we're on the same side."

"Yeah, sure. You're trying to set me up. Make me say something about those guys next door."

"For what? Your friends are already on a bus heading for a re-education centre. And if the police wanted anything else from you, they wouldn't play games—they'd haul you in. Come on, you know that. Think about it. Besides, when did you ever see an echo look like him?"

She thrust her chin towards Jake.

"Well, maybe he's a rat," the boy said. "But I ain't a rat. Nuh-uh."

Jake stepped forward. "She's telling you the truth, pal. This lady saved my life from the same bullies in blue that rolled through here the other day."

The youth looked at the blotch of red in his hand.

"Yeah, sorry about that," Jake said, sheepish. "Didn't want you running off before you'd heard our side."

"Whatever, Popeye. Fuck off back to your caravan."

"It was a cabin, but I'll forgive that."

"Come on," Chrissie said to the boy. "You know it makes sense. We need your help."

"I can't get in trouble," the boy said. "After what happened, I need to get away from all this."

"And you can, but we want the same thing. What's your name?"

He leaned back into the cushions, letting go of his doubts or maybe tiring of his own evasiveness. "Zeebrah."

Chrissie repeated it, not sure she'd heard it right. "That's a real name?"

"What do you think?" Zeebrah shot back, a small smile appearing either side of the cut.

She straightened up, returned his grin. She introduced Jake, who took his time extending his hand, shook a little harder than necessary.

"All right, *Zeebrah*," she said. "We don't have many friends in this town, so we were hoping to make a few. How connected are you to the Resistance?"

"Whoa. Look, miss—the less I say, the safer I is, y'know. Tell me what you want from me."

"We need to get out of the OSZ. I know there are ways you people travel in and out that circumvent the security gates. We need someone to show us how to do it without being seen."

"You're fizzin'. I don't know that."

"Please trust us. We need a way out."

The teen pondered the idea for a moment, his eyes shifting between his uninvited guests.

He said, "Let's say—theoretically—that I even had that information, I wouldn't be able to tell you."

"Come on, Zeebrah." Chrissie said.

"No, I mean, for real. Wouldn't be possible for you to understand the route. The maps we have only show the options. We don't write down the directions."

"You have maps?"

Zeebrah stood up. Jake tensed, expecting another struggle. The teen walked over to a large poster hanging on the wall—a vintage manga print. He plucked the pins out of each corner, laid it face-down on the carpet. Chrissie and Jake took a look at the glossy paper, moved in closer to get a better look. All they could see was the blank white backing. Zeebrah wasn't done. He went to each one of the windows, drew the blackout blinds.

"What the hell's this?" Jake asked from the shadows.

From the darkness, a violet beam appeared in Zeebrah's hand. He adjusted the lens on the mini torch. The blacklight expanded, raked over the room, fell onto the poster. Chrissie stood, found herself staring down at a multi-coloured neon map—a complex web of thinly drawn lines and circles, all positioned beneath a faint grid outline. There were no words on the map, only occasional number and letter combinations.

"This," said Zeebrah, "is your way out."

"This is London?" Chrissie asked, confused. It didn't look like the city she knew. The roads were hard to distinguish. The Thames was nowhere to be seen. Major landmarks had been omitted.

"Like you've probably never seen it before. Subterranean London."

"The old underground railway?"

"That and the sewers. Oh, and the disused overground lines out in the suburbs. Stretches out beyond the old city boroughs."

Chrissie glanced up at Jake. His frown had disappeared. He actually looked impressed.

She said, "You mean you've been getting in and out by—"

"By traveling right under their noses," Zeebrah said, his chest puffing. "The authorities rarely go down there. When work needs doing, they send in teams of cis men. And they left most of the outside of the OSZ off limits since they cut off the Heaths from all utilities, all them transport links. It's been mostly clear for us to slip through—as long as you happen to know where you're going in the dark."

"Jesus," Jake said. "A modern-day Underground Railroad."

"They'll have their own maps of these tunnels," Chrissie said. "Somewhere. I mean, if they knew this was happening, they could go in there and brick up the exits."

"Maybe," Zeebrah mused. "With an old map, you might get a sense of where to travel, but you wouldn't know where the new tunnels are. Only our maps can tell that." He dropped a finger onto the poster. "And you still wouldn't know where we've booby-trapped some of the routes. That's only known by a few, meaning you'd need a chaperone."

"So where are we now?" Chrissie asked, trying to make sense of an expanse that probably spanned for six or seven hundred square miles.

Zeebrah drew the beam in a circle around an inch of the paper.

"Somewhere around here."

"And you have settlements out in the Heaths? Somewhere safe we could go?"

"I mean, yeah. I know of somewhere, but..."

"Please, Zeebrah. We need someone to take us."

"Shit," Zeebrah said, shaking his head.

"What?"

"I don't know. I could organise it, but I can't guarantee..."

Chrissie reached out, taking his hand in hers. He didn't flinch but his eyes went wide, not used to a woman's touch.

"You know, don't you?" she said. "You know the way."

The kid dropped his head, breathed a heavy sigh.

"Listen," she said. "We have information that could be crucial to your people. We're not just looking for sanctuary. We're looking to help the cause."

"What information?"

Jake scratched his neck. "Show him, Chrissie."

"Your netscreen," Chrissie said to Zeebrah. "I assume it has wi-dev connectivity?"

CHAPTER FORTY-ONE

On foot, they travelled north.

The air had a bite to it. Night was creeping in but the streets were still peppered with life. Pedestrians were wrapped up in heavy clothing—collars pulled up over their cheekbones, hats yanked down around their ears. That made disguise easier. The trio walked with their heads bowed towards the paving, eyes hidden, hoping everyone else would be so intent to find the warmth of a doorway, of a family, they wouldn't even think of slowing down to spare a group of strangers a second look.

Travelling at night in London didn't lend itself to stealth. Streetlights flickered awake above them as they passed, outraged at their presence, screaming their silent amber cries. Sky-eyes buzzed the atmosphere, raked their spotlights along pavements and windows, eyes clicking, innards bleeping.

The fugitives crossed roads, pressed deeper into the backstreets, brushed shoulders against brickwork to avoid being seen. Shadow was their best friend. Aside, of course, to their young guide.

Zeebrah brought no copy of the map. No need, he said. He'd been studying the one at the flat for years, been ushering people to the 'gateway' for some time. If ever he was scrutinised by an echo, he would simply alter his course, circle back an hour later. If he was stopped, he said, if he was questioned, there would be no evidence on him—or on any of his travelling companions—to suggest where he was going. He never kept to a pattern, never took the same route twice in as many weeks. He approached his job as though looking through the mind of an observer, someone trying to find a way to catch him out. If he noticed any tilt-of-hand to his methods, he would adapt, cut it out. So, he claimed, with a glint of pride, they would reach their destination soon enough.

Chrissie wasn't as confident. Mistakes could happen. Everything always worked to plan until it didn't.

They reached Regent's Park. Zeebrah finished gloating about his tactics. Neither Chrissie nor Jake had pushed him for information. The

195

teen had been willing to open up, to revel in the genius of his activities. His smooth features brighter, healthier since his fall through the skylight, the thickened lip adding character.

Good for him to showboat. His growing swagger gave a little fuel to Chrissie's hopes. Maybe she would survive this. Maybe not everything had been lost.

Maybe.

The park, easier to cross than the streets. Zeebrah ignored the lit path, took them across the knoll, cut west towards the vermillion slash of sunset beyond the towers. From there, the trans symbol—Mars and Venus combined—branded the sky in silhouette, fixed like aerials above the porticos and masts, black eyes in crude clown make-up staring through the distance.

The walk went on. Chrissie's feet ached, shins tingled. No complaints. She kept pace with Jake as they followed their urban Sherpa.

Approaching Kilburn, the great galvanised OSZ barricades rose up out of the concrete. Moonlight bounced wet off surveillance pods, secured to the head of each post, each installed ten feet apart and just as high.

The barricades, lifeless, impenetrable as far as anyone knew. The Fence's screening blocked views of the alleged desolation beyond, a land overrun by plants and vines. Unmarked, impassable, the wastelands of the country would begin there, along with all the delinquency and dangers and horrors portrayed so often by the media. Lands she would be entering soon. The idea of it filled her momentarily with dismay.

No laws.

No guarantees of respect.

No authorities to keep them safe.

Was she feeding herself to the wolves? Could there be more mercy at the hands of her own authority than at those of a rabble of angry, disenfranchised binarists? They couldn't be the feral savages the government made them out to be. The ones she had known were, after all, rarely a threat. Yet the others, those in the wastelands, would they not surely be base and cruel, shadows of humanity darkened by decades of isolation?

Before they came to the boundary, Zeebrah signalled for them to drop low. A swarm of sky-eyes passed overhead.

"They out in full tonight," he whispered.

He herded them towards a small copse off the side of the road. He waded between waist-high bushes, delved about in the foliage with his feet. A dull sound as his trainer hit upon metal. He disappeared, crouched in the dark, scraped at the earth.

A soft thud.

He stood up. A thick odour broke through the cold.

"Better not be something living down there," Jake muttered, taking a step back.

"Popeye, all sorts of things living down there." Zeebrah beckoned them nearer, pulled a wad of something from inside his jacket. "Put these on."

Chrissie approached, took one of the dust masks from him, looked at the little round ventilators in the sides. The smell, not as vile as expected, though musty and heavy—like rust and fungus joined forces. She needed no further prompting, tied the mask around her head, smothered her mouth and nostrils. The turf had been shifted, the steel handle sprouting from the grass, as though a large clod of earth had been lifted like a saucepan lid. Under a thicket, a black hole yawned up from the soil.

"I'm going to trust you this is safe," she said to their chaperone.

"Never has been. That's the point."

Zeebrah pulled a strap over his forehead. A small light flicked on, emitted a dazzling beam. It bounced across each of their faces, fell on the opening in the earth.

"You go first," the boy said. "I'll get the door."

Chrissie said, "But I can't see a damn thing."

He adjusted the beam. It widened a little, weakened as the light struggled to penetrate the gloom. He pulled a glowstick from his pocket. It cracked between his fists, warmed to an atomic green, tumbled into the hole. Through the darkness, it bounced, settled somewhere below, on what sounded like wet stone, its artificial light still visible.

"There are stairs straight down, 'bout thirty feet," Zeebrah said. "At the bottom you'll find equipment. Headlamps, flasks of clean water, shit like that. Don't fall or you'll never come back out."

Chrissie took a deep breath. The vents in her mask clicked. She edged towards the gap. The glint of the first steel step—barely more than a rod—and the single hand rail didn't seem like much support into the nothingness below. Didn't help at all that the urge to break off, to run back into the darkness of the city, pulled at her with a parent's grip.

"Are you sure about this?" Jake, at her shoulder, pushing his foot at the roots trailing the edge of the shaft.

"Of course not," she said.

Before allowing herself another moment of doubt, she gripped the railing, stooped down into the hole, balanced one foot on a step as the other felt for the next, then the next. Zeebrah's single beam of light gave them little comfort. It raked across a foot of soil, revealed solid, black brick behind the ladder.

CHAPTER FORTY-TWO

The air, thicker with coppery stink for every metre they descended. A constant, distant rumble came from somewhere beyond the slime-encrusted masonry.

A sprinkle of dirt fell over them. The plate scraped above. The moonlight wished them a farewell, disappeared in a blink. Zeebrah covered the entrance.

Chrissie's grip tightened around the ladder. Thirty feet down, her boots hit ground zero—a concrete ledge from what she could make out, some type of mesh laid down to stop her feet from sliding. Turning, she stumbled backward.

Men around her, seven feet tall, waiting in the shadows, within grabbing distance. The half-light of the glowstick cast an oleaginous sheen across their bodies.

But they remained still.

Nothing more than a row of disembodied boiler suits, hung up along the platform. When Zeebrah finally touched down, his beam exposed the overalls for what they were, each paired with rubber boots, gloves, headlamps.

On his suggestion, Chrissie took one of the lamps, pulled the strap tightly around her ears. Jake did the same. She clicked on the light, observed safer ground. Not that the ground here looked safe at all.

Pools of groundwater and soot had built up on the sides of the ledge. They could see now the glimmerings of oily stone arcing overhead, stretching off into yet more dense black. A drain or leak burbled somewhere to her right. Drops of foul ink played an echoing, discordant song.

"Lovely," Chrissie said.

Her words bounced through the tunnels. She swung the beam up at Zeebrah as he caught up to them.

"They closed up everything outside the ISZ when they first started setting up the Fence," Zeebrah said. "Too hard to guard it all the time. Realised they'd got rid of most of the guys who knew how to keep it all running anyway. A few minutes' walk that way and you'd reach what used to be Baker Street Station."

Jake's beam raked the ground. Sure enough, old steel tracks cut through the tunnel. He whispered something quiet into the dark, sounded like *elementary*, shook his head when Chrissie asked him to repeat.

"Rails are inactive," Zeebrah said. He jumped down onto the track and, as if to prove his point, kicked at one of the strips of metal. "No current. Don't mean you don't need to take care still. Rats and mice down here, along with god knows what else. Long as you stay close and follow my every step, you won't step in nothin' unpleasant."

"Slow down." Jake said, his voice muffled behind the fabric. "Where does this thing lead?"

"Technically speaking, all around the outskirts of the city. Though I wouldn't know the first thing about finding my way round the whole system. This is one of only a few access points we can use. Meant to be defunct. Our people spent a lot of time figuring out the blueprint so we don't run through anything we shouldn't, like the sewer or something. All I know is that this is Point A and we're going to Point B. That's it. Takes us right under the Fence."

"And that access point has been sitting under a bush this whole time?" Chrissie said, amazed the plan was so simple.

"Like I said, we rigged several of the routes with traps. Hidden drops. Pongee sticks. All kinds 'a bad news. So no looking around, understand? No falling behind. Don't wanna get permanently left up shit creek, y'know?"

He chuckled to himself, told them to start walking. They hopped down, followed him in close step. Chrissie held Jake by the elbow in case she stumbled, as much to assure her he was still nearby.

"You're sure you haven't forgotten where any of those traps are?" Jake said, half serious.

Zeebrah said, "Well, time to time I need a moment to think about it. But I wouldn't worry. I'm still alive, right?"

"What if you or one of your guides got found out? What if a squad of echoes marched you down here and told you to show them the way out. Would you do it?"

"You mean under *duress*?" He hissed the word. "Sure I would. What choice would I have? Except we have what you might call a policy in place in case that ever happened. We'll take them down all nice like and lead them right into a pit. Maybe into a landmine. Pro'ly take ourselves out with 'em, yeah, but it would make 'em think twice."

"Really?" Jake said.

Zeebrah's voice dropped a pitch. "Yeah, *for real*, man. This shit ain't no game. Every chaperone makes that pact. What's wrong? You think this may be one a'them times?"

An uneasy silence fell on the group. Eventually Zeebrah laughed, laughed like he'd been holding it in, the burst of noise reverberating off the concave walls.

"Luckily," he said, "I'm not doing this under duress. The stuff on that vid you showed me made me a believer."

To avoid tripping over each other, they fell into single file, Chrissie behind their guide, Jake taking up the rear, like people trying to organise a conga line at a funeral, all silent and shuffling movements. Though the Fence hadn't seemed too distant from the surface, the tunnel seemed to go on for miles.

Every once in a while, Zeebrah would guide them into a turn where the tracks forked, take them into a new branch of the system. He whistled a tune, one Chrissie didn't recognise—a rickety rendition of some old hymn about a vagrant being left on the side of a road and strangers refusing to help him. She didn't mind it. It helped to keep the mood light. The sound of his song became full, mesmerising, bouncing along the tunnel walls. He went on singing his own sporadic musical compilation for what she guessed was around twenty or thirty minutes in the belly of the labyrinth.

She tried to memorise the route, tried to map each turn as a sketch in her mind. Impossible to keep up. Knowing there was no way of getting back to Point A alone was jarring. Panic rose inside her, settled back down as she concentrated on Jake's fingers either side of her neck, reminded herself that Zeebrah wouldn't lead them to their doom or abandon them. He could be trusted. Had to be. The alternative was unthinkable.

Now and then she swore she could feel something brushing against her ankles or move across the walls by her head. Rodents, maybe. Cockroaches. Could have bet money on hearing the sound of paws and tails scurrying across her path, of wings swatting wind at her hair. Each time it happened she stiffened, her teeth clamped, her nerves shorted. May have been nothing there at all, her imagination firing itself up.

"This is it," Zeebrah said into the abyss.

"This is what?" asked Chrissie.

The half-light meandered a few feet further up the track, revealed another junction, an old train carriage sitting on the rails, lit from the inside with phosphorescent bulbs.

"The long road to freedom. Please keep your hands inside the vehicle at all times." He returned to his song.

Moving together, against each other, as if in an awkward dance, they did as they were told, stepped up onto a buffer, climbed into the carriage through a gap where a door would have once been, grabbed hold of the rusting handrails. Zeebrah shuffled up to the front of the carriage where a driver's cab awaited.

His gospel melody carried through the carriage. He pressed a series of buttons, pushed a stick, made the lights flicker. An engine rumbled to life, kicked up a filthy smoke. The train compartment lurched forward. Wheels screeched. The tunnels became narrower. Jake dropped into a dusty seat, seemed relieved to be off his feet, the faint crackle in his breath suggesting his body wasn't built for long distance. Zeebrah's song withered to a soft hum.

Undistracted by anything but the sound of the motor and the screaming wheels and their navigator's faint music, Chrissie's mind wandered into places darker and deeper than any underground passage.

Two days ago you were a career woman, keeping the streets clean. Now you've been run underground. Forced to retreat into a hole. You've become one with the rats. *How the hell did you get into this mess, Christina? What in the Great Birth-Giver's name were you thinking?*

But for every word of doubt, she yelled back into that darkness, waved the flame of righteous fire.

Because that world is far more rotten than this one. Because you were living a lie. Never again. You won't enable their intolerance another day. You'll think for yourself now. You have never been so free as you are now.

This internal row swung back and forth unspoken as the journey went on. The defiant voice, the one that grew stronger, the one that knew it was loud and bell-clear where its adversary fought a losing battle. The further the carriage travelled, the more the voice of doubt subsided, shrank until it became throttled and empty.

"How far have we gone?" Jake said, leaning his head back in his seat, watching the lambent light above him flutter.

Zeebrah didn't respond, maybe didn't hear him over the sound of the wheels.

"We must have passed under the demarcation line by now," Chrissie said.

She could feel the bonds of the city falling away from her. With it went much of the fear still hanging from her heels since the moment she'd looked down at Sergeant Dennehy's unconscious bulk. Yes, it was possible to leave the world behind, even easier than she had thought possible with someone showing her the way.

How many people had left the confines of the city in favour of life beyond the borders? She asked Zeebrah if he knew, made sure he heard her.

"More than I could count," he called back from the driver's cab. "Not all take the tube. Different ways to escape. It's amazing how inventive people can be when they're desperate. Not just London, either. All the Safe Zones be leaking a lot more people now. We got a network in place to help. Hardly any children being born, hardly anyone coming into the country—ain't gonna be long before there's no one left in the cities at all. Not except the In-Zoners, anyway."

"Not what the official reports say," Chrissie said. "We're told the size of the population is always balanced, that happiness ratings are always higher than ever. Never mind all the delayed construction projects and inflation rates and product shortages. It's obvious things are getting worse."

"Careful, officer," said Zeebrah. "That sounded like a fact, and facts can't be trusted, remember? Facts are merely the binarists' efforts to maintain their dominance through scientific reasoning, thereby quashing the more truthful insights of non-binary intuition."

He laughed. Jake couldn't stop himself grinning.

She said, "Well, my intuition says it's bullshit, too. Always has. Back on the force, we'd hear rumours of fugitives breaching the Fence from time to time, finding smarter ways to evade the sky-eyes and patrol squads. We'd get bulletin alerts on people smuggling themselves out with helicopters or boats, some of the guards taking bribes, even defecting themselves. Everyone knew it happened. Everyone knew at least a handful of people—friends, family, colleagues—who'd simply disappeared. No warning. They'd tell us not to file them in the system."

"You didn't ask anyone about it?" Jake said.

"Only thing I knew was not to ask about it. The brass didn't want successful defections reported. Worried it would make others feel emboldened to try the same. Probably worried it would make the Equality Ministry look stupid, too."

"What about the unsuccessful ones?"

"Different story. Charges can be anything from civil disruption to outright treason. You've probably seen the trials on NetTube—big-budget specials, prime-time viewing. The Ministry's willing to do whatever it takes to keep everyone convinced the Safe Zones are the cradle of the future."

Jake said, "I still haven't properly thanked you yet—for getting us out of there. I'm glad that intuition of yours kicked in when it did."

"Don't be hasty. Let's wait and see where we end up. Hey, Zee—"

Zeebrah held up a hand, stopped humming. He brought the carriage to a trundling halt in the middle of a tunnel. He opened the cab door. His beam of light, fading now, swung up at the arches, at the steps crawling along the brickwork.

"Our stop," he called out.

He jumped up onto the walkway. They scrambled to keep up, grimaced at the layer of grime attaching to their clothes and hands as they lifted themselves over the jutting ledge.

Zeebrah threw himself onto the ladder, began his ascent. They raced to follow, felt for the railings, desperate now to reach the surface. Their fingers grasped at each wrung in the darkness. Above them, metal scraped against stone. Their guide slid the cover back. The night sky revealed itself. Moonlight spilled overhead. The wave of cool, fresh air that hit them on the way out was indescribable.

Chrissie snatched the mask away, released herself from the stranglehold, inhaled deep draughts of the brusque night before she even acknowledged her surroundings. They had emerged through an old stretch of road grown wild with weeds. They were beyond the OSZ, that was for sure. Woodland and grassland lay either side. A scattering of gutted buildings leered like the skulls of giants. Abandoned houses. A deserted petrol station, sapped of oil. Disconnected streetlamps, caked with rust.

Zeebrah turned to them, arms spread wide: "Welcome to the other side, ladies and gents."

CHAPTER FORTY-THREE

A deep crack split the asphalt straight down the middle. Zeebrah used the ridges of the fault to navigate forward, giving his followers no time to ruminate on their crossing of the border, of their rebirth into the unknown.

They discarded the masks in an old salt bin by the exit, where boiler suits and equipment had been left for prospective travellers. They walked along the main road amid the rustle of wind and bird calls, where nightfall had added a subtle promise of frost to the air. Then an open expanse, strewn with corroding cable bridges, conduits teeming with creepers. The disused train tracks converged into one immense bottleneck. The husks of railcars strewn in disorder, some burnt out, upturned. Here, Zeebrah stopped, flashed his beam several times in the direction of a long, low-rise building. Chrissie made out the 'Railway Depot' letters faded against the wall.

Another beam of light winked back in greeting from the direction of the building. It grew as it approached them, moving at a steady, unwavering pace. Metal squeaked. The headlight was attached to a type of gerrymandered vehicle—a simple steel platform on wheels that moved along the tracks, powered by a pair of mountain bikes attached to each side. A rear-facing park bench had been bolted onto the platform. Compared to the common autobile, it looked ridiculously antiquated. The bikes were pedalled by two figures—both men—who wore wind-proof coats, hoods pulled up around them.

"New chariot," Zeebrah said to Chrissie. "They'll take you the rest of the way. Don't fight it. Do what they tell you and you'll be all right."

"Thank you," Chrissie said, putting a hand on his sleeve. "We know we sort of forced this whole mess on you but it means a lot that you came through for us."

"Glad I did. Taken enough refugees out here to see what's real in people, y'know."

Jake shook the boy's hand. "Sorry again about the fat lip."

Zeebrah's teeth flashed. "Y'er all right, Popeye."

He waved at the cyclists.

The cyclists disembarked. One of them, slow as syrup, pulled a pistol from his pocket, aimed it coolly at Chrissie's waist. She had only ever seen real guns when they'd been seized in raids, demonstrated in police training exercises. Never had she seen one in the hands of a civilian. Never one pointed directly at her by a stranger. The sight of it set her entire sense of reality on edge.

The other cyclist ordered them to turn around, put their arms out wide. Chrissie's body tensed. She inhaled sharply. A pair of masculine hands patted her down. The stranger showed no concern for law or decorum, no hint he cared about her comfort. Like the presence of the gun, this casual violation was alien. The hands moved around, across, along, underneath every soft edge of her body. The stranger removed Chrissie's warrant badge and wallet, took Dennehy's body-eye from her jacket pocket, put it in his own.

When Jake's pat-down came to nothing, the man with the pistol flicked the gun at the vehicle, said, "Get on the draisine. Nice and slow."

They clambered onto the bench. The other held an old-fashioned radio to his lips, mumbled something through the clicks and static.

"Sit there and wait," the gunman said to Chrissie. "Don't try anything stupid."

Chrissie had no idea what kind of stupid he was imagining. Defenceless, lost, surrounded by pitch darkness, they had no alternative. The strangers mounted their bikes again, one either side. The vehicle slid along the track. Zeebrah, who had been watching them leave, soon disappeared. There was only the gentle squeaking of the wheels, the electric hum of a hundred thousand crickets in the tall grass.

After a while she turned her head to the gunman, who was now pushing rhythmically on the pedals, bellowing steam from beneath his hood. "Where are you taking us?"

"To Rockland."

"Rockland? Is that where you live?"

"Rockland is not a place."

"Then—"

"No more questions, miss."

Jake put a hand on her arm. "They're helping us, Chrissie. Let's allow these fine gentlemen to do their jobs."

No acknowledgement came from the strangers.

She dropped her voice to a whisper, said to Jake, "There's no law out here. They could do whatever they want to us and we wouldn't be able to stop them."

"I don't think they'll hurt us. Besides, I wouldn't let them," he replied, pressing her arm a little more. "I owe you one, remember?"

The moonlight was small and wet in his eyes. She let her gaze rest on them.

"I don't get it," she said.

"Get what?"

"You have a way about you. The way you talk. The way you think. It's like you were born yesterday. I mean—in a good way. Where did you come from? Mars?"

He leaned his head back. The stars were ablaze away from the fluorescent headache of London's streets.

"Nowhere nearly as far," he said. "I was raised down south, in a commune in the New Forest. Not many of us. We lived in little houses and tents and cabins, and for a long time that was all I knew of the country—of the *world*—aside to what I was taught by my parents and some of the other elders. I long for those days."

"Wait—you were born in the Heaths?"

"If that's what you call it. We called it home."

"And you didn't know about the Big Reboot?"

"I knew there'd been a…" He tried to think of the right words. "A *social divide*. Some called it a civil uprising without any of the violence. Guess I was sheltered from it. We had all we needed there as far as we were concerned. Food and water. People to talk to. Books. Even had a little chapel and a school. Every day I learned about history and cultures and philosophies and people. The rest of the time I got to race horses up and down the old country lanes. But I never got to see more than the same trees around me. Too dangerous to go back to the cities, they said. Maybe one day. They never properly explained that part. Didn't say what was so bad if there was no actual war going on."

"Is that why you chose to come into the Safe Zones? You wanted to see what it was like?"

"I didn't choose a thing. One day a load of border troops turned up in armoured trucks and kicked the doors down, rounded everyone up. Arrested my folks and shipped me off to a juvie centre in London. That was the day I found out what was really going on in the world."

Chrissie winced. She had heard tales of communities in the Heaths, discovered and raided, their people press-ganged back into civilised society to help feed the system. Boys were highly sought. They could be re-educated early, put to work. With so many CisHets fleeing the cities around the country in favour of taking their chances in the wilds, and with the birth rate in sharp decline, the authorities would do what they could to target new blood.

"They treated us like crap," Jake continued, "like they couldn't wait to get rid of us. I was there a year and then they graduated me into the Cooler. Another year behind lock and key for being born cis. When I finally got out, I got to see exactly what had happened to society— exactly why my 'rents had wanted nothing to do with it."

"Do you know what happened to your parents?"

The sides of his jaw flexed. "Cancelled by the state. At least that's my guess. The courts were charging them with trying to circumvent the system, and with child endangerment since they taught me things apparently illegal to teach these days. I never got to hear the verdict but I'd like to think they're still out there."

"I can't imagine it. It sounds like hell." Her hand rested on his, gripped his fingers tightly. Every inch of skin between them cold.

"It is, at first. You find ways to cope. Rather than let it ruin me, I kept my mouth shut, spent my time thinking. I don't know, maybe there's something to it. Maybe everyone should cool off for a while these days. If I'd been let loose, who knows how I would've reacted?"

"But they destroyed your family. They locked you up, took away your freedom for no reason."

"Oh, I was free." He tapped a finger against his temple and smiled. "I was always free."

"I'm sorry, Jake."

"For what? It wasn't you who did it."

"It was. I was part of it, at least. I worked for them. I said nothing when I saw things like that happening. I enforced their system. Don't even try to tell me I'm not responsible."

"Ah, shush, will you. You were a victim too. Just took you a while to realise it."

He leaned his head a little against hers. The warmth from his body was welcome.

He chuckled to himself.

"What?" she said.

"Remembering when a wise old man once warned me to keep away from the likes of you."

"He was right."

"No. Not at all."

CHAPTER FORTY-FOUR

The draisine slowed to a stop. Chrissie turned in the seat. Nothing but the fading railway, the sea of black forest on either side, tops of trees swaying under the bronze sky, like immense clumps of oarweed—alive, coolly intelligent. The immensity of them, the fact anything could be lurking within them, brought only dread. Everything here was enormous, unknowable.

The vehicle juddered. Above them, a single shoe hung from a power line by its lace. A marker, she guessed—the thing that told the drivers this was the end of the line. The cyclists stepped off onto the rail bed. Their headlamps flickered on, floated towards the treeline.

"Come," said the man with the gun, not looking back. Not even drawing his weapon.

Before he got too far to see, Chrissie and Jake abandoned the draisine, progressed carefully, ballast crunching underfoot. Ground became grass became moss-slathered dirt. The drizzle released an unfamiliar pungency, a heady fragrance of conifer, of slow-rot and mud. They hooked their arms together. They lifted their feet high as they walked, worried they would trip over the ferns and roots reaching for their ankles or sink into the earth, among needles that shifted loose from the day's rain. They trusted the other to hold them up should either lose their footing.

The men stopped by an old stump, reached down, picked up a roll of tennis tarp, unfurled it, uncovered several lengths of timber. There was the sound of a flip-lighter spring, of the wheel spinning on a thumb, a rush of fire as one of the poles ignited at its end, bringing with it an orange glow for which Chrissie was thankful. An old-fashioned torch, the type she had only ever seen in medieval paintings and NetTube period dramas. She had never known them to have any place in the modern world.

The smell of burning hessian tickled her nose. The men handed them each a torch, lit their own, switched off the headlamps for good. How their guides knew the route with such limited visibility was a mystery

211

to her, but sure enough, just as Zeebrah had led them through the underground system, their march went on without delay.

It went on until the rub of Chrissie's boots advanced to a sting. The ligaments in her legs developed a stabbing twinge. Lights speckled through the trees ahead. A few metres closer, they were everywhere, strung from maple limbs in plastic bottle lanterns. More of the improvised torches encircled the glade where shadows danced across a wide cluster of wooden structures.

"How do you travel?" The voice cut through the night from somewhere up ahead, no more than twenty feet.

The guides stopped, planted their torches into the earth. One of them responded. "By track and twisting range."

"Why do you travel?"

"The great affair is to move."

"That you, Oscar?"

"Evening, Angus."

"How many of you?"

"Four. Wyatt's with me, and two new ones. Man and woman."

"Real or pretend?"

"Real."

"Aye. Come on."

Oscar led them forward. Trenches had been dug on either side of the path, sharpened pikes angled into the ground below. Deep. A fortification of some kind, she assumed.

Ahead, Angus came into view, sat as he was on his raised deck, shielded behind a sandbag wall, a middle-aged man in a heavy coat and a trapper hat. His eyes narrowed as they passed. A rifle, cradled in his hands. He kept it lowered.

Movement now. People—more curious than afraid—coming out with torches and lanterns in hand. What she could see of them between the shadows was their clothes, dog-eared and layered thick. That aside, their faces appeared healthy. Sharp. They didn't speak. Oscar didn't address them, only raised one hand in greeting. In this better light, Oscar was a young man, a small man, one sporting a light beard and a glower. His partner, Wyatt, far harder to judge on age—

his beard long, his hair bleached, chest and shoulders a yard wide, tattoos climbing out of his collar.

Chrissie could see cabins and awnings on either side of the winding path. There was an order to the place. Many of the structures were large, covered with vines and foliage. The fort—or was it a village?—had been here for some time.

One of the structures, guarded by another rifleman at its entrance. Oscar spoke to him, received a nod in reply. The guard whistled. Other men and women appeared, gathered at the door. They relieved all four of their torches. Chrissie was hustled against the wall, rough hands patting her down again.

"Whatever you're asked, you answer," Oscar said. "Remain truthful and there'll be no problem. Play games and I will not vouch for you. Understood?"

He turned before either of them could respond, pushed open the pinewood door.

"Stay close to me," Jake whispered.

The inside, a single room. Chrissie smelt tobacco, something like clover, something else still—a sweet, earthy smell she couldn't place. An iron stove sat against one wall, its warmth casting an inviting spell. Jake rubbed his hands together. Chrissie's skin tingled as her face and fingers thawed.

At the far end of the room, two men stood over a fold-out table. One raised a heavy mug to his lips. They were in conference, pondering a spread of paperwork, maps and open textbooks illuminated by candlelight. When they saw Oscar approach, they stopped their discussion dead.

"Zeebrah's runaways," said Oscar. "Is she…?"

The men parted. One waved a hand towards them. The room was dimly lit but Chrissie could see now a third figure, thinner than the others, leaning against the far wall. When she was close enough to make out the face of that figure, the sight of it rooted her to the spot.

A woman, her hair streaked grey, her eyes hot and young, her arms strong beneath her rolled sleeves. Her features in the dancing light as handsome as they were angry. She moved forward, her right hand dropping to her thigh where a leg holster supported a pistol, her fingertips poised at the catch.

"You searched them?" The woman asked Oscar, all thorns and no roses.

"Sure. The girl's the echo. The one they're looking for." Oscar turned to Chrissie. "Tell her."

Chrissie said, "Who are you?"

"*Tell her.*"

"How do we know you're not allies?" Jake said.

It hadn't occurred to Chrissie until then that it could all be a trap— taken in by some scared teen, sold down the river back into the hands of the very people they were trying to escape.

Jake took a step, as if moving to shield her. The shadow of his frame in her peripheral, the flash of another large object.

Wyatt had the back of Jake's neck in his grip. He squeezed. "Advise you not to test our patience."

Jake winced. His knees bowed.

Chrissie blanched. Escape routes absent. One of the men shoved her forward towards the table.

"Last chance," Oscar said. "Tell her who you are."

Chrissie held up her hands. "What he said. I'm an equality officer. I mean, used to be."

The woman rested her palm on the grip of her gun. "The one who sent that fat bitch to the hospital?"

A strange surge of relief washed through Chrissie at that. No card-carrying member of the Equality Ministry would dare say such a thing, even if they were interrogating a suspect. Such an iteration would have them thrown out of the job, had them arrested. "Yeah, that's me. Your men here—what did they tell you?"

"Doesn't matter what they told me," the woman said, low and slow. "What matters is what you can tell me right here."

Oscar flipped Chrissie's warrant card onto the table. The woman snatched it up in one hand, raked it for information, set her gaze back on her two captives.

"Quite a journey you've had, Constable Christina Tieman," she said. "Must've been difficult."

Chrissie nodded. "Certainly wasn't easy."

"To pull it off, I mean. To find a patsy fresh out of the Cooler and convince him to come with you. To fake a large-scale police hunt to provide you an alibi."

The stove crackled. Chrissie and Jake exchanged glances, trepidation splintered in the space between them.

"What do you mean?" Chrissie said.

The woman drew her gun, traced a languid aim on Jake's heart. "Or maybe you were part of the operation from the get-go, boy. A stooge? Let me guess—they got to you while you were still in the youth institute, said if you helped them out they'd give you an easier ride in the OSZ. Maybe put you in one of the slightly less shitty vocations. That it?"

"Now hang on," Jake said, "That's not—"

"Or did they bung you a Britcoin sweetener? Considering the rate of inflation these days, they would've needed to add quite a few digits to your account."

"He's not a patsy," Chrissie said, brusque. "Or a stooge. This isn't an operation. This is real. We need your help. You have to believe us."

"Pretty sure I don't have to, Constable. I have to believe only two things—my gut and the evidence at hand. Gut's been unsettled on the matter since I heard some echo bitch was requesting safe passage to our camp."

Oscar sidled up, fished Dennehy's body-eye from his pocket, said to Chrissie, "Think this will remedy that?"

"It's all on there," Chrissie said. "Watch it. You'll be glad you did."

It occurred to Chrissie as she made this demand that there may in fact be no way for her hosts to view the footage. They were in the woods, miles from civilisation. These people were burning trees and wax for warmth and light. She didn't know if the place even had access to electricity, let alone a monitor to connect a hard drive. Dear Goddess, she thought. What if they don't see it? What if they don't believe us?

Oscar's fingers released the body-eye. It skittered on the table.

"Doubt it," the woman said. "This feels like a plant to me. Who else thinks we need to cut our losses and ditch these two before this place gets air-raided?"

"Are you serious?" Jake said, teeth gritted. "We came all this way…risked our lives to get here."

"Seems a waste of time since we've seen through your game."

Jake lost it, lurched forward. Oscar tried to body-block him, found himself wrong-footed. Jake barged him sideways, grasped for the body-eye.

Wyatt's pistol arced down, sapped Jake on the back of the head, caught him behind the ear. Jake dropped, plummeted against the table, slid to the floor.

Chrissie sprung, seized Wyatt by the arm, knocked the gun from his grip. Wyatt wrestled her off, shifted his momentum, spun her around, pinned her wrist behind her, twisted her elbow until she cried out, applied almost enough pressure to snap it.

"Take 'em to the infirmary," said the woman. "Keep the door locked and a two-man detail outside. If they try to get out, corpse 'em on sight."

Chrissie winced at the pain shooting up her arm. Oscar heaved Jake up to sitting, dragged him towards the door.

The woman picked up the body-eye, turned it in the light. "For your sake, Constable, you'd better hope Rockland believes what he sees on here or he'll bury you in these woods himself."

CHAPTER FORTY-FIVE

Through the curtain, zie heard the ovation die down, saw the host grin large into the camera, the toothy comedienne multiplied across the screens around the stage floor.

"Welcome back to the Caitlyn Smurth Show. My final guest for the evening is a truly special one. And I know you know who I'm talkin' about! Yes, zie's the empress of equality—the baroness of bravery…"

Green-lit letters above the stage blinked *APPLAUSE*. The audience went back to whooping it up.

"…The qween bee of badassery—the binarists' worst nightmare…"

The show runner said something into her headset, gave zer two thumbs up, a frantic nod. Showtime!

"…Please give a big hand to Britannia's equality minister—Zoe Urrrrwin!"

Zoe elbowed the curtains aside, came out to supernova lights that obscured zer view of the live audience. Zie could hear them—thunderous in their love for zer.

You're a badass!

You're so brave!

Work it, qween!

Badass! Boss bitch! Badass!

So fierce!

You're stunning!

The live band threw themselves into a big swing version of Lizzo's classic, *Juice*. Zoe preened, waved to zer fans, half bopped zer planetoid frame towards the host's desk. Zie embraced Caitlyn like an old friend, *mwah mwah,* both cheeks. When zie took a seat, the applause kept going until Caitlyn had to raise her hands, beg them to calm down.

We love you!

"My Goddess!" Caitlyn said, her mouth a mile wide. "Do you ever tire of it?—No, I'm serious! It's like wherever you go, it's like *'yaaay'*!"

Zoe laughed, gave an ever-so-humble shake of the head. "Oh, I don't know. I think our community are simply happy to see a fellow qween persisting."

That sent the hyenas off again.

"Your thing, maybe," Caitlyn said, struggling over the noise. "The only thing I'm persisting at is trying to keep my vagina smelling fresher than a barnyard. Right, people with vaginas?"

Vagina jokes. Sure-fire crowd-pleasers. The flock roared, its collective delight verging on manic.

Smurth said, "Now, Minister—please, folks—now, Minister, we so appreciate you coming back on the show during such a busy time for you. Election season, huh?"

"That's right. We're in the middle of our campaign and the prime minister's out there as we speak, talking to the good people of this country, truly listening to what they have to say."

"She's so fierce, isn't she? Wowza. And it's so apparent she loves children."

"Absolutely. She understands how important it is to reach the younger generation before they can have their opinions manipulated by right-wing propaganda. She's truly passionate about them. In fact, her nickname within the party is Taylor the Child-Lover."

"That's beautiful! And I know you wanted to come here tonight to address some issues, not least these transphobic messages the public has been subjected to recently. These pirate broadcasts that have hijacked the feeds and spouted the most appalling things…"

Some of the crowd booed. Zoe guessed the ones staying mute probably didn't want the risk of mistakenly being seen to jeer zer, not comfortable enough to act without the prompter signs telling them how.

"That's right," Zoe said. "Fake news is still a real problem and it's important we treat these people as they are—terrorists. Terrorists who want our society to fail because they can't stand to see trans or genderqueer people succeeding."

More boos, the building on vibrate, the crowd a little more emboldened.

Caitlyn calmed them. "You're right. Their propaganda does seem to be as silly as it is dangerous. I mean, really—" She consulted a little smartpalm on the desk, the cue for one of their rehearsed lines, po-faced, building up to the punch. "Tell me, Minister, how did you murder Maria Suarez-Adarsha?"

A stunned silence. A hard second. The audience held their collective breath, eyes bugged, wondering why Caitlyn Smurth had pulled the pin, anticipating the echoes on site to descend, to tackle her to the ground, to drag her from the set.

Zoe ruptured, let off the most natural sounding laugh zie could. It came out well, zie thought. The hint of surprise, of exasperation. Green letters flashed *LAUGH*.

The audience caught up, burst into glee, revelled in the absurdity of the claim, one they had all probably heard by now, the rumours trickling into the illegal transmissions, into anonymous messages and posts on the smartnet.

"They want us to believe you have all this incredible power," Caitlyn went on, sniggering between the words, "and yet binarism is still a threat wherever we look. What will they possibly accuse you of next?"

"Funny you should ask that," Zoe said, restraining zer amusement now, wiping an invisible tear from the side of zer eye. "Earlier in the year I heard I was adopting an alien from outer space. Not only that, but we'd found the Loch Ness Monster and I'm keeping him in an underground swimming pool in preparation to unveil him to the world on New Year's Day."

LAUGH.

Zoe grinned as the audience members threw themselves into fits. It was true—zie had read those nonsense stories and others like them on Xprez, the smartnet's most viewed social media platform. They had been picked up by the media, derided mercilessly. Zoe had enjoyed writing them as much as zie had enjoyed watching the Ministry machine go to work, peppering them around, drawing attention to them, carefully creating ammunition to discredit all other unsavoury rumours, even the ones that were true, the ones that had the potential to undermine zer—maybe ruin zer—if they were to ever be proven.

They would never be proven.

Not with the Ministry pumping most of its annual budgets into PR and Communications, through which the censors were now repressing every word out of step with TEP thinking. An unstoppable juggernaut, trampling facts, muddying reality, until the people would look blindly towards their government for any purchase on the truth.

Let them try to break it. Let them fucking try.

The green letters stayed green. Rows of heads gave themselves sore ribs hyucking it up, over the top, trying to outdo each other, no doubt afraid of what might happen if they appeared one jot less than zealous.

"The Loch Ness Monster!" cackled Caitlyn. "And here I thought I was the only one harbouring an oily swamp creature downstairs. You vagina-owners know what I'm sayin'!"

The idiots whooped, high-fived, stamped their feet.

Zoe laughed with them. Not because the revolting, scripted joke was any less hacky the second time zie'd heard it, but because zie knew zie still had them. Human clay, pummelled, squeezed in zer hands, pledging their souls to zer cause.

"But joking aside, Minister—what do we need to do to defeat these right-wing terrorists? What can each of us do to make a difference?"

"That's a great question, Caitlyn, and I'm going to tell you. The first thing is easy. Wherever you see any transphobia, or anything you think could be cissexism, or any time you get even a whiff that someone you know may be defending cissexism, report it immediately. Call the anonymous citizen's hotline or even the police directly. Don't wait. Do it. Our enemies are everywhere. The second thing is even easier. Log in on voting day and put a big tick next to your TEP representative. Tag and list 'em! Crush the Cis-tem! It's what Maria Suarez-Adarsha wants us to do!"

The crash of hands, deafening.

The host drummed her hands on the desk, her voice battling to be heard over the din. "You hear that, folks? Get to the polling stations! And, hey, speaking of getting a whiff of something…"

CHAPTER FORTY-SIX

INTERCEPTED TRANSMISSION TRANSCRIPT—EQUALITY MINISTRY
SUBJECT: INSURGENT BROADCAST #266
LISTENING STATION TATYANA
30-10-46 0015 GMT

SENSITIVITY CLASSIFICATION: 8—CLASSIFIED / SANITIZED

VOICE [terrorist suspect #2408D]: Evening, gang! You're listening to the Ozcast on Revolution Radio, the freedom frequency. And yeah, yeah, I know—it's a later one than you're used to. I wonder how many of you are actually listening live right now…Well, if you are, I salute your resilience. It's good to know you're out there, still holding the fort, still staying alert.

In the midnight hour…!

Listen, I wasn't gonna broadcast tonight but I received some new intel that, uh, gave me the urge to fire up the ol' system. It's big. Serious stuff, man. I told you they were planning something. I. Frickin'. Told. You.

Didn't know it was already in the works, though. It's legit. They're pulling out the stops, man. My sources are solid. Let's just say I heard it right from the horse's arse. Or maybe not a horse. Maybe something more bovine…

Can't say too much at this point. I know they listen in on these things. Those freaks have ears everywhere. So for those in their listening stations, all I'll say is two words…

Project *[REDACTED]*.

That's right. We know all about your little game. We got the deets. Came to us wrapped in a pretty little package and everything. Thinking right now about what we do with that intel. Wouldn't want to blow up your spot, now, would we? You'll see, eventually. I'm excited! Remember, though—*we didn't start the fire.*

221

Anywho, for the rest of you Heathens and outback agitators, you rural rebels and Safe Zone serfs, I'll update you as soon as we get a handle on our next steps, so stay tuned.

There's something happenin' here... what it is ain't exactly clear...
Nighty night, folks. Ominous spiritus. Oz-man out.

END OF RECORDING

CHAPTER FORTY-SEVEN

FOR PUBLIC ATTENTION

From the desk of Maria Suarez-Adarsha.
29 Octavia, 2046

To my loyal qwings and qweens,

As we prepare to join in spirit to celebrate Non-Binarist Pride Day, I have found myself contemplating our Great Enemy and the challenges of categorisation. Only in being able to more accurately identify our adversary and the many manifestations they may slyly adopt will we have a better chance of defending ourselves from his trickery and violence.

I propose there to be only eight types of cisgenders, simple creatures as they are. Of these, they exist merely as variables of the same spectrum, which I shall list herein.

Cis Supremacist—The innately violent transphobe who advocates binarism and acts in a way that preserves and values cissupremacy. Often engages in, sponsors or promotes binarist terrorism. All CisHets are at risk of becoming the Cis Supremacist if their thoughts and actions are not corrected on a routine basis.

Cis Extremist—The cissexist who shares in the beliefs of the Cis Supremacist but who only supports these actions or states these beliefs privately. By remaining passive and unwilling to challenge the Cis Supremacist, the Cis Extremist is an enabler of binarist terrorism. More widespread than most realise and given that the violence is merely dormant, many eventually become Cis Supremacists over time or when triggered by a moment of anger.

Common priv—A cissexist who may openly and privately critique the Cistem but who still benefits from it by virtue of being cis. May secretly maintain a deep investment in old-fashioned interpretations of 'truth', 'fairness' and 'equality' that normalise cisgender thinking and exacerbate binarist rule.

Cis Voyeur—A cissexist who routinely watches trans people from afar, and fetishizes them for sexual or intimate gratification. Such unwanted attention, even when undetected, is of course harassment. This type of cis may also commonly be referred to as a 'creeper'.

Cis Introvert—A cissexist who eschews trans and genderqueer relations or even communication out of transphobia or fear of transcentric superiority or a general recognition of their weakness as the inferior persuasion. All cis homosexuals are Cis Introverts because they spurn trans relations despite desiring, envying or appropriating trans and genderqueer freedoms, which is a form of cissexism akin to Cis Voyeurism.

Cis Manipulator—An all-too-familiar cissexist who will speak openly about and point out the evil of binarism, but only as a way of trying to ingratiate themselves with the trans community. Seeks validation from us but puts little to no practical energy into raising trans people up or correcting their own cis privilege.

Cis Subversive—A cissexist who actively invests in exposing, marking and subverting cisnormativity and who refuses to be complicit in it. Still guilty of bigotry as this overt behaviour can result in a lack of accountability for the cis privilege they still carry inside them and shifts the attention to themselves, thereby robbing trans people of their place at the centre of the issues.

Cis Abolitionist—A cissexist who changes institutions that are historically cisnormative, dismantles and destroys binarist notions of 'history' and 'facts' and does not allow any form of cisgender privilege to reassert itself. Guilty of cissexism as cisnormativity still exists, proving that the Cis Abolitionist is either unmotivated or ineffective as a result of their own cis privilege. This type of cis may therefore, in fact, be as dangerous as Cis Supremacists.

As you can see, we must remain as vigilant as we are confident in detecting and confronting bigotry. We must trust no one within our lives, no matter how much of an ally they present themselves, for even those closest to us, mingling within our so-called Safe Zones, are prospective deviants, abusers and radicals in waiting. Tag and list them. Crush the Cis-tem.

For now, I wish you a joyous Hallow's Eve.

Yours in stunning solidarity,

Maria Suarez-Adarsha

CHAPTER FORTY-EIGHT

The squeak of trolley wheels roused Chrissie awake. No idea where she was. Her memory entwined with her dreams, hoodwinked her into believing she was still in the city. Was she on shift today? Should she have breakfast at home or grab something on her way to the station?

Canvas walls came into focus, a privacy curtain encircling most of the bed, gold light trying to break through. A divider prevented her from seeing the rest of the room, from giving her something to grasp.

Trolley wheels again. With them came the sharp snap of reality, snippets of unwanted memories born of the past few days. The sadness. The fear.

This is how it must be for most people who wake in a hospital, she thought. Confused by the light and the smell of sanitizer and a little afraid until they see the—

Doctors. Two of them, through the gap in the curtain, across the room. No surgical scrubs—casual wear. They were still identifiable, still gave off the same quiet assuredness of medical practitioners. Men with their hands on their hips, talking in low voices. The darker skinned of them, the one she could see now, had a stethoscope draped around his collar. He turned, made eye contact through the screen, nodded once, hurried off.

Chrissie tried to move. A hard tug on her left wrist. Her arm, handcuffed to the hospital bed. She remembered the struggle as they had taken her in, the guns they had brandished, her panic as Jake had been taken to another tent. She was sore where they had searched her, embarrassed to have been violated in such a way. Her clothes had been replaced with cotton pyjamas, a thick, itchy blanket. Was it the exhaustion that had knocked her out or something else?

The curtain slid along the rail, light flooding in. Oscar's face peered back at her, clocked she was awake, gave her a wink. "Rise and shine, camper."

He carried a mug in one hand, a pile of clothes in the other. He placed both on the side table. He looked less intimidating in his hoodie and cargo shorts.

"How do you prefer to be addressed?" he said.

The question took her by surprise. "What?"

He laughed. "Just kidding. Coffee?"

"I...I don't..."

"Oh, I'm sorry. Let me get that."

He pressed his thumb against the handcuff, triggered the biometric lock, caused it to snap open. Chrissie rubbed the impression it left in her skin.

"A precaution," he said. "We couldn't be sure. But that's changed now. Listen, I've brought you clean—"

"Where's Jake?" she said.

"Doc Sharma fixed him up. Gone out to the quad for breakfast already. Poor guy still has a bit of a hangover and a nice purple bruise to go with the story, but there's no lasting damage. Here."

He passed her the mug. She refused to move, unwilling to accept his pretence at courtesy no matter how parched she felt. Who knew what he was trying to get her to drink? The aroma struck her. A rich, woody smell, a hint of caramel. She sat up, snatched it from him, held it to her nose.

"It can't be." she said.

He nodded. "Fresh, too. Last supply truck we jacked was meant to go to some fancy place in the ISZ."

"Who the hell are you?" she said.

"Bring the mug. Jake's waiting and I need to get you both up to speed. No point in me covering the same shit twice."

"I'm not going anywhere with you."

"You want to stay here all day?" He grinned. "Suit yourself."

Oscar walked away, pulled the curtain closed behind him. Chrissie lay there, gripping the hot mug. What in Goddess's name was going on? The sound of distant people drifted in with the air.

Oscar returned in a beat, same grin still plastered across his face. "I'll be waiting outside. Fresh clothes on the side there for you, about your size. Don't take all day, man, I'm starving."

Did she have a choice?

The morning sun, dazzling as she headed out. The entire area about her speckled with soft light. Chrissie—donning the donated blue jeans and parka—squinted at the sky, found nets had been strung across tree branches, across wooden posts, creating a canopy. Leaves and other debris scattered across the netting offered only glimpses of blue.

"Keeps them from seeing us from the air," Oscar said. "This way, please."

Her eyes adjusted. They traipsed along, the track mottled with shadows from the foliage above. The place was a network of clearings, each encircled with outfitter tents, makeshift buildings of lumber and corrugated metal. The waft of smoke and roasted meat greeted them from somewhere up ahead. People—young, old, male, female, all varying in size and colour—moved between the buildings and trees. Some carried trays of food, jugs, bottles. A young man walked by with a bundle of logs under each arm. An older woman sat by the path, plunging clothes into a broad bucket of water. Further along, a cluster of children screamed with laughter, chased each other.

Chrissie neared the edge of the site. Each of the settlers looked up, watched intently. Not looks of distrust, as had been the case on her arrival. Only curiosity. Perhaps even warmth. The fortress they had entered last night now looked more like a holiday camp.

At the mouth of the clearing, settlers sat shoulder-to-shoulder on rows of picnic tables. Chrissie's eyes danced as she took it all in. Each table laden with piles of food, the size of which she hadn't seen since she last attended one of the annual police banquets. Platters of eggs and beans and mushrooms sat amid mason jars of cereals and dried fruit. Pans of bacon and sausage sizzled on wire racks. A centre board, the width of a tree trunk, displayed loaves of grained bread, cheese, pots of jam. Several grills still on the go, ready to replace the helpings as soon as they ran out. Chrissie's stomach pleaded.

There, standing among the others. He had washed and shaved, a clean-up that brought out his features. Like her, he had been given a clean set of clothes—new jeans, a plaid shirt, a borg-lined jacket rolled under his arm. He looked so different. When he saw her approach, his relief was palpable. There was something else in him she hadn't seen before—a cheerful glow in his cheeks. Probably still dazed from being cold-cocked.

"Jake, are you all right?"

"Hard as it is to believe, I think I am. Other than the piercing headache and the other usual side-effects of being pistol-whipped." His brow knitted. "What about you?"

She shrugged. Remained to be seen. The world she knew seemed to flip on its head every time she woke up. She wasn't all that sure anymore if she even was awake. Still, she was touched by his concern.

She said, "Do you remember what happened?"

"Not much of it," he said. "They filled me in this morning, right after they apologised. Said they'd taken a look at the—"

"You can stand there gawping," Oscar said, "or you can sit yourself down and have some more coffee. What else can I get you?"

Chrissie couldn't believe what she was hearing. Only hours ago, this man had held a gun to her. His partner had hit Jake so hard he'd left him concussed. Now he was taking her breakfast order.

"I'm sorry," Oscar added. "I hope the Colombian Roast is acceptable. We'd normally have fresh tea, but our last crop got root-rot and we're in the process of moving the plantation to higher ground."

Jake said, "You grow tea? I didn't even know that was possible in this country."

"Lemme tell you, man, you'd be surprised what you can achieve when necessity requires. As Rockland says, God can indeed spread a table in the wilderness. Case in point."

He motioned to the nearest bench. Oscar asked some of the settlers to shuffle up. He reached for a stack of clean dishes, began loading them up.

"Is this what I think it is?" said Jake, sniffing his stack of bacon. "Real meat? Tell me this is real."

"Well, look at that. You can take the boy out of the country." He chuckled, passed them both a fork. "Everything we haven't scavenged out of supply trucks is grown organically on our soil or shipped in from one of the other settlements. Place nearby has a pig farm. One further up has cattle. Here, we mostly keep chickens and operate a lot of the corn and wheat for the region. Government tried to choke us out with chemicals a few years back, came overhead in crop dusters and started spraying us to hell, man. So we relocated the produce to, uh, hidden locations. But not before we downed a few of their bastard planes. You'd probably know about that, right?"

Oscar stuck Chrissie with a look. She shook her head, turned to see Jake stab a fork into his helping like he was afraid it was going to escape.

"No," she said.

"Huh," said Oscar. "I would have thought…"

"And you're all living out here off the land?" Chrissie said, trying to bring the conversation back. "What about electricity? Running water?"

"The country's best engineers are Heath dwellers. Our generators run off solar panels, wind turbines, reservoirs, wood, coal, peat, all sorts. For the most part, we like to go back to basics. More than enough wood for heat and sanitation. The rest is pure, old-fashioned know-how. Lessons learned over thousands of years and passed down to our communities."

Jake, his mouth full, said, "I used to live in one of these places but it was no way near as big. Or as advanced."

"It's incredible," Chrissie said.

Oscar grinned, served himself some hash browns. "Lemme tell you, you ain't seen nothing yet."

"So where's Rockland?"

"He'll have eaten by now. Normally wakes early. Though, having said that, I can't remember ever having seen him sleep."

"Take it he's in charge of this place?"

"This place has a name. We call it the Compound. And he's not just in charge here. Rockland heads up most of the local colonies in this region."

"How many are there?"

"Twenty-five in these parts. Across the country—who knows? Several hundred, at least. When the TEP passed the Social Reform Act and started banning CisHets from city centres, we claimed the rivers and hills as our own."

"He sounds powerful," Chrissie said.

"Rockland? He doesn't believe in power, man. He's a civil leader, one of many. They're the people we need for the challenges we face today, willing to disarm the authorities and shame them for what they are. Now you mention it, I'd say Rockland is a special one among them. In my opinion."

"Why do you say that? I mean, who even is he? Ex-military?"

The burble of conversation at the table died down. Settlers at other benches strained to listen.

"Not my place to say. He stepped up and he's making it work. He has a plan. There's going to be…"

Oscar cut himself off.

"You've got my attention," she said.

He wasn't prepared to elaborate, acted instead like he hadn't heard her, said, "The guest cabin they're sorting out for you is usually used for laundry storage and such but you can bed-up in there until you get acquainted."

Oscar poured equal measures of tea into four stainless steel beakers.

"Acquainted as what?" Chrissie asked, taking a deep breath. "Guests or prisoners?"

"Got no reason to imprison you. He believes what you say you are. He took a look at the footage you brought with you. He's seen the netwires. We've been intercepting the police chatter too. Oh, boy, do they want to catch the two of you."

"What are they saying? Do they know we're here?"

"Sweetheart, they don't even know *here* is a thing."

Caught her off guard. Not so much by the news that she and Jake had made it out without being noticed but by his use of the term *sweetheart*. Back in the Safe Zones, that sort of language from a CisHet male would have him automatically stripped of his assets, thrown into a re-education centre. She thought about that, embarrassed again about her role in upholding such oppressive laws.

"So that's it?" Jake said. "You'll let us stay? No further questions?"

He took a swig from his cup, said, "If it were up to me, sure. I'm bored of looking at these same reprobates all day."

People at the bench laughed.

"What about the footage?" Chrissie asked. "About the—you know? What it says they're trying to do?"

"What about it?"

"Are you serious? They're going to try to—"

He held up a hand. "We know what they're trying to do. Clear as day on the tape. But there'll be time to discuss that. There's a lot you need to know before you get all het up about this thing or that."

"Discuss it?" Chrissie said, mystified by the suggestion. "Everything you have here—if they succeed, they'll come for you next. It'll be the beginning of the end. Don't you get that?"

The buzz of conversation died down around them. Settlers listened in, lowered their forks.

Oscar leaned back. "The beginning of the end? And ye shall hear of wars and rumours of wars. See that ye be not troubled, for all these things must come to pass. But the end is not yet." He raised his cup. "Enjoy the grub, kiddos. I'll take you on the grand tour and then you're off to see Rockland. Because, trust me—you'll need to be of sober spirit for the journey that lies ahead."

CHAPTER FORTY-NINE

Oscar was an able guide. He led them through the Compound at a leisurely pace, took unreserved joy in pointing out all the little landmarks dispersed among the trees. The place had its own showering facilities, its own mess hall, its own medical tent with a fully-equipped surgical theatre. It had a church; not anything near as extravagant as the one they'd spent the night in—all wood and cinder block—but it had one. It had a rec room, complete with pool tables and a drinks bar. It had an alarm system to warn them of approaching threats. It even had a childcare centre.

He didn't hurry them, let them idle at the things they found most interesting, explained them in detail, let them touch whatever they wanted, invited other settlers to demonstrate how things worked. He had an easy manner, softened by the pride he took in this world, by the wonders his people had been able to manufacture amid coniferous forest and acid grassland.

"Bream, Tench, Roach, Rudd, Trout," Oscar said, leading them down the path towards the lake. "You ought to take a rod out there one day. Borrow one from the boathouse, there. We farm them sustainably, mind, so if you catch anything, you have to note it in the register book."

In the middle distance, a mass of silver water rippled a thousand times in the breeze.

"I can't believe it," Jake said. "It looks so much like home, only bigger. So much bigger. How long have you been out here?"

"Close to ten years for me. Longer for others. Places like this take time. Some of them don't survive, as you well know."

"I often imagine what my old home looks like these days. Could be they rebuilt it."

"Could be. Ground raids are uncommon these days. Taught 'em a lesson, we did. When people first started migrating to the country en masse, we were vulnerable to government incursions. With the poverty came sickness and desperation. By the time the authorities began actively trying to prevent people from leaving the cities, our settlements had started to form. Civilisation sprung anew and life started to get easier. Nowadays we're strong enough to hold our own. But it's a fine balance."

Ducks bobbed in bunches. A handful of small boats floated unhurried. At the opposite bank, a group of settlers laundered by hand, sheets swelling like sails, piles of clothes dunked wet and fat on the end of poles.

"Who are they?" Chrissie said.

Oscar's apprehension was plain. "Them, there? Just another neighbourhood."

"Another part of the Compound?"

"Not quite. Some folk prefer to keep to themselves and we don't mind that. There are a few different camps out here but the Compound is sort of the centre—looks after them all, keeps them together in a way, but we don't interfere with each other. That's important."

"How many neighbourhoods are here?"

The guide looked at her out of the side of his eye. "A few. Almost every settlement across the country has its own neighbourhoods, its own ways of doing things."

She could see the inhabitants milling around their little township on the water. They moved differently to the settlers she had encountered. As she watched, she realised why they seemed so familiar. "Those ones out there—are they…?"

"Yup," Oscar said. "Trans people. Pre-op and post-op."

"What are they doing here?"

"Same as all of us. They didn't want what was inside the Safe Zones. They see it for what it is—a charade. A pretence of inclusivity that really just masks a reality of conformity to the approved narrative."

"I thought you people believe in binarism," Jake said.

"Sure. That doesn't mean gender dysphoria isn't real. Christ, man, what else don't you get? It's real, and it's a problem for people. That's never been a question."

"Oh," Jake said.

"See, some of those folks regretted transitioning and were ostracised for speaking up or seeking help. Others never wanted a part of any of it in the first place and just wanted their privacy. They came here because they know we don't care what they think they are—we just don't want to be forced to believe what isn't true. That doesn't mean we're not compassionate."

"Then why don't they live with you? With the cis?"

"First of all, we never use the C-word here. It's a slur, designed to ridicule us. Second of all, some of those folks do live with us, just most feel safer staying amongst their own. Often they're dealing with trauma, mental health issues. Real stuff. Not the bullshit those posers in power are performing for the public."

"I had no idea people like that even existed anymore," Chrissie said, unable to hide her sadness.

"Course not." Oscar said. "As if the government would allow you to know."

"Doesn't seem right to me," Jake said. "Like they're here but still kind of segregated."

"Humans are funny, man. Tribalism always exists, no matter how much we try to make things work for everyone. Which is why we need to be careful how we deal with divisions in the colonies. No system is safe. There'll always be internal grabs for power, always someone looking to challenge the Alpha if they smell weakness."

Chrissie said, "I remember, years back, how the conversations started changing. You used to hear all the time about other kinds of oppression—race, class, religion. And some people would be speaking about all of them, like they were one thing. You don't get that anymore."

"They called it intersectionality." Oscar nodded. "It couldn't last. Competing interests. Ate itself good, lemme tell you. And I should know. As a bisexual man myself, there was a time when I would've been considered part of the protected class, when human rights still meant something. But when everyone realised there was power in being a victim, the boundaries blurred. The flags became nonsensical. And everyone started fighting to be the worst off. It was only ever gonna end up a dog's dinner, believe me. But, hey—let's not get into that now. I'm sick of politics. Besides, there's a whole lot of stuff I still want to show off and you curious cats are slowing me down."

They left the lake and the social outcasts, went back up the trail, inhaled the perfume of bramble and pine.

Mid-morning, Oscar took them to see one of the watch towers that had been established around the invisible perimeter of the camp. The naked, log framework criss-crossed upwards through five levels, a roofed observation deck at the top. No telling how old it was. It looked sturdy enough. Two horses hitched at the foot, ears forward, heads bobbing, patient. She kept her distance. Jake, starry, bee-lined for the grey mare, held his hand below the beast's nostrils.

"Go ahead and pet her," Oscar told him. "Doesn't bite, this one. Comfortable with anyone." And as Jake went to town, scratching the horse's neck, asked him, "You ride?"

"Used to." Jake said. "Had a horse back in the old camp. Wish I knew what happened to her. She could run, the old thing. God, this one would look just like her if she weren't so dusty."

Oscar gave both the animals a long, hard look. "Fair point you make there, man. Poor things. I'll give 'em a quick rub down. You folks go on up—check out my rig. Get your VIP behind-the-scenes look at the voice box of the revolution."

Chrissie glanced up at the tower, back at their guide, finally grasped where she'd heard his voice before.

The young man gave her a wink. "Ominous spiritus. Jacking the airwaves whenever I damn well please. Go ahead. Enjoy the view for a while, but don't touch anything, okay? Sensitive equipment."

He handed Jake his monocular, rummaged in a saddlebag for a brush.

Up they went, taking careful balance on each wet step, until they reached the little hut in the sky, parallel with the canopy of trees either side of the trail.

Dry leaves had blown into the old-fashioned radio booth, heaping at each corner of the square floor. A swivel chair, leaking foam, stationed on one side of the hut, next to a table that supported a soundboard, microphones, other antiquated electrical equipment, all rotary dials

235

and LED indicators. An array of smartpalms—the only modern things in the place—sat on a desk next to a small military radio, a pack of playing cards, an ashtray piled with a score of hand-rolled cigarettes. A can of dumped grind filters gave the place a dead coffee fragrance that wasn't wholly unwelcome. A button the size of a fist, wired to one of the pillars, probably leading to the klaxons setup around the camp. A box of vintage glossy magazines, long having lost their gloss, sat on the floor next to a rusting brass bell—presumably a backup in case the alarm system failed.

"This is it?" Chrissie wondered aloud. "This is all it's taken to undermine the Equality Ministry's iron grip on mass communication?"

"Any iron can be ruined by a little rust over time," said Jake.

She grinned. "You're such a bumpkin."

The broadcast tower was peaceful. Looking out at the forest, slashes of yellow grasslands peeked between the branches. Not much of a view beyond the wide path and the gravel road in the distance.

"Trees, trees and more trees," Jake mused from the opposite side of the deck. He looked briefly through the thin end of the monocle, snapped it closed. "When was the last time you climbed one?"

"Too long ago to remember," Chrissie said. "A lifetime ago."

"I'll never get tired of looking at them after all that time staring at the same four walls."

"They're convenient, I'll say that. Be hard to spot most of this place from the air, let alone find it from ground-level."

"Oscar said the authorities don't do much anymore to interfere with the Heaths these days."

"He's right. I'd heard rumours around the station a few months back, said terrorists living in the wild had found ways to shoot down our aircraft. Still don't know if that's true or not. It was never the official story, at least. Haven't heard of many ground raids taking place of late, so something changed. They used to splash their successes all over the netwires to try to discourage any more people from absconding."

"If they'd stopped a year or two earlier…"

Didn't finish his sentence, tapered off, turned back to the forest. He wallowed in his thought. She watched the back of his head, listened to his breathing and the chirrup of the birds surrounding them. Could she have survived as he had, knowing how everything he had once had was probably gone, despite his escape from the world? Knowing he was his own master again but facing that existence alone? Knowing he was free but confined, safe but always under threat?

"Probably wouldn't have made a difference in the long run, Jake," she said. "If anything, this Resistance has made them stronger, given them a reason to enforce tougher laws and harsher penalties. Given them the evidence they need to prove their society is under violent threat of attack. Exactly what they were always after."

Jake nodded. "Like constantly slapping someone in the face, telling them not to be violent, waiting to see how long it takes them to hit back. It's a classic play, I'll give 'em that."

Lowering herself on the edge of the table, the magazine pile seized her attention. A woman on the cover stared back. Unlike the body-positive, dowdy cover models she was used to seeing, this woman was slim, healthy—athletic, even. Perfect makeup in a style more complex and flattering than the layers of cosmetics plastered on most modern women. Her skin was buttercream smooth. She was barely dressed, her svelte figure concealed only by a bathing suit. She was beautiful in the classic sense—in the sense that had long been disavowed and of which depictions had long been banned for being offensive. But the depiction on this magazine would have been beyond offensive by today's standards. Way beyond.

Sports Illustrated, the title declared. *Swimsuit 2007*.

"This thing's older than me," she said.

"What thing? Jake said, wandering over.

"Oh, nothing, just an old magazine. Can you believe they used to print these things?"

She couldn't stop herself from picking up the publication, laying it down on the crate. She flicked opened the page at random, found the cover model inside, posing in her bikini on pristine sand.

Chrissie turned another page. "They're gorgeous."

"Can't deny that."

Chrissie kept turning. More slender women, flaunting their curves. Not one overweight. Not one with body hair or endless tattoos or facial piercings. Not one with a tell-tale bulge in their briefs or rubbery-looking muscle implants. No beards. No moustaches. No surgical scars.

"Amazing, isn't it?" she said, a slight tremble in her hand. "How they got away with this back then."

"What's to get away with?" Jake said. "What's wrong with beautiful women?"

"Nothing at all. I agree. But the reason they banned this stuff was that women like this—they're standards of beauty are unattainable for most—"

"Exactly. That's the point, isn't it? People love to look at the ideal. It motivates them. Makes them feel good. Reminds people the world's a competition. Reminds them it's okay for us to strive for peak forms of beauty. What's wrong with that?"

"Yeah, I'm not sure that's exactly why people would read this magazine, Jake."

"No, you're probably right."

They laughed. He was blushing, struggling not to creep at the scantily-clad models. She didn't mind. She kept turning the pages, running her fingers over the gloss paper. When she looked up at him again, he was looking at her. The hut felt warm and no longer still. Swimming. Pulsing.

"You folks okay?"

Oscar's voice almost sent them through the roof. The magazine scattered off the back of Chrissie's hand, creased on the floor. The guide came clopping up the steps, popped his head above the boards.

"We're good," Jake said, breathing all wrong.

"I was going to give you the grand tour of the rig but I got a call in. I can take you somewhere much more interesting than this old place. Kind of a long way off. Won't be getting there on foot."

Chrissie cleared her throat, steadied herself on the desk, tried to even out her voice. "Railway line?"

He shook his head. "Motorway."

CHAPTER FIFTY

A row of cars sat under a long tin roof. No autobiles. Old-fashioned manual models, complete with steering wheels and pedals, all in fair condition.

"What's wrong?" Oscar asked, pulling open the driver's side door of a mud-splattered Nissan SUV.

"Guess I thought all roads out in these parts were no good for driving anymore," Chrissie said. "I haven't even seen cars like this since I was a kid."

He dropped in behind the wheel, waited for them to settle into the back. He pulled the overhead mirror down, caught the car key in his waiting palm.

He said, "About a half-mile from the Fence we avoid any use of them, particularly at night. Create too much light. Too much noise. Out here, away from the main cities, we put down tyres when we need to. It's not all that safe 'cos the main roads can be seen from above, but most of what we have down here can outpace whatever they can put in the sky. The Heaths are full of slip roads and hunker holes anyway— good for shaking any unwanted attention."

He wasn't kidding. There were hiding places aplenty out on the abandoned A-roads, amid the skeletal remains of townships scattered throughout a part of the country that had once been affectionately called the Home Counties.

"So," Chrissie said.

"So?" said Oscar.

"Are you gonna tell us where we're going?"

"My favourite place."

They rode out along the track, through the woodland, across a field of gravel that was, at one time, a car park. The roads running through the countryside, peppered with cracks and potholes. What hadn't been left to bake or freeze throughout the seasons was covered by vines, mulched leaves, waist-high grass that swallowed crash barriers and roundabouts. Not a single other car passed by them.

An old paper road map was stuffed inside the webbed pocket of the roof. They left it untouched, tracked the journey instead by sight. Jake nudged Chrissie, leaned in, told her he thought they were heading further west based on the sun being mostly on the rear window. She wasn't sure how that knowledge was useful. Oscar refused to give anything away. No signs to read, no obvious landmarks. The eerie quiet of the world was everywhere.

According to the dashboard display, the journey was over in half an hour. The car stopped at the foot of a hill. They disembarked to climb a steep, winding trail.

Gaining height, they walked parallel to the slope, could see much further across the land they had entered—a panoramic view of the Heaths for the first time. An endless, green paradise. Pockets of former towns and villages poked up between the forests and glades. For the most part, nature had reclaimed the country as its own. Clouds passed the horizon like starships, combed the landscape with their shadows. It was glorious. Worth the pain of sunlight in her eyes. They had to hurry to keep up with Oscar, who was unmoved by the view, only wanted to press forward.

They hiked through another corner of woodland, emerged directly in front of a sight even more astounding than the Heaths, at once beautiful and unsettling.

The ruins of a gothic church—at least on first appearance. The entrance, an immense arch made of grey stone, held a vaulted window, divided by two slender stone columns. On either side stood high walls of flint, complete with curvatures and recesses. At its foot was a large empty courtyard surrounded by a wrought iron fence. Oscar opened the gate for them, its hinges squealing. There was little else beyond the windows except more of the hills, more of the forests. The church was nothing more than a façade, and yet the arched entrance clearly led somewhere, its walls pulsing with an amber glow. Oscar picked up a pair of LED lanterns at the threshold, handed them over.

Chrissie couldn't help but wonder at how unquestioning she had become when it came to strangers leading her into dark holes. This time she wasn't afraid. The gust of cool air circling up through the entrance, the strange radiance beyond, the itch of curiosity, all seemed to draw her in.

As in the abandoned Tube network, she found herself descending underground. The tunnel declined gradually. The rock walls so cold they felt wet to the touch. The trail here was shingle. After the first turn, the pale stone glimmered under the spotlight-white burn of the surrounding alcoves.

On they marched, the air sharper with every winding turn.

Chrissie's nose prickled. An arcane perfume. Something like coffee and earth combined. Something from deep within her past.

They arrived in a round expanse. The cavern reached up into the hills like a great shaft. Large recesses carved out of the chalk, beset with classical stone figures, life-sized. At the centre of this area was a spiralling staircase, branching off onto numerous platforms made of steel tread plates. Even more striking to Chrissie were the tiers of shelves that extended into the darkness above.

Everywhere she looked, the place was crammed with books. Old books, varying levels of distress. More books than she could remember seeing since the days of iced lollies and skinned knees.

"Welcome to the Hellfire Archives," Oscar said. He set his lantern on the ground.

Astonished, she turned to the nearest arrangement, ran a finger along one of the shelves as if testing for dust, plucked names like slack teeth. Balzac. Baum. Beckett. Burroughs.

Another tier.

Double Indemnity. The Stranger. Don Quixote. Heart of Darkness.

She had read none of them. As far as she could recall, they were all on the Problematic List, most deemed *non-inclusive*, others *highly offensive*. Their colourful spines and dramatic fonts called to her. Her breath drew short, nothing to do with the cave's cold must.

"Dear Goddess," she said. "Every one of these…"

"I know," Oscar said, suppressing a smile. "A mandatory ten-year sentence for possession of each—and double that on some of the specialist pieces we have in stock."

"You're probably looking at a million years of re-education."

"Worth every second."

"Is that the reason for the quirky name? You're expecting eternal damnation?"

His shoulders shook. "Maybe. Sure as hell they'd burn this place to brimstone if they ever found it."

Jake looked as ravenous as when he'd wolfed his bacon breakfast. He moved rapidly around the bookcases, practically skipping, his lantern bouncing from one corner to the next.

"No way. Chrissie, check it out," he said. He pried a paperback from one of the shelves, held up the beaten bundle with a gleam in his eye. "JK Rowling. *Harry Potter and the Philosopher's Stone.*"

She gasped. "Just holding that is an automatic life term, without parole."

He stopped at one of the statues, frowned, said, "I know this. Hercules?"

Oscar nodded.

"I remember seeing a picture of this scene when I was a boy. He had that club. And this lion here—if memory serves—couldn't be killed by any conventional weapon."

"That's right," said Oscar.

"So Hercules ended up strangling it to death." His attention flitted to the next recess. "What's this one? This one I don't know."

"Dionysus. God of wine and fertility."

"Oh, right. I see it now. Someone certainly has a thing for Greek history."

"Which is appropriate because it's history itself we're preserving here. Not just Greek. All of it. Ah, what am I saying? I'll let the man himself explain."

Oscar turned, lifted his chin to the rafters.

"Professor! New guests!"

A ruffle like a pigeon roosting above. Clank-clank steps on steel. A glimpse of a head peering above a scaffold barrier thirty feet up. The voice, male but reedy, resembling something from one of the kid's puppet shows Daniel liked to watch.

"Hey, come up. I'm in *Art and Culture*."

CHAPTER FIFTY-ONE

The platforms juddered as they climbed the stairs, nut-and-bolt levels creaking under their weight. When they found the man Oscar referred to as 'Professor'—sure enough, in a section boasting an *Art and Culture* sign above the bookcases—he was clearing stacks of papers from a pair of time-beaten armchairs.

An impossibly narrow man. The poncho hanging over his natty jeans clung with desperation to his shoulders. At full height he would have been over six feet but either the cramped conditions of the cave or the weight of his tasks had stooped him. His sunken cheeks were mottled with several days of growth. Black triangles of brow were parted by two deep lines above the ridge of his nose, setting his face into a state of perplexion. He batted at the sprig of grey hair falling over his forehead, extended his hand.

"They gave me some warning before you came," he said, motioning to the radio system at his desk. "Normally we don't invite people in here but when I heard we had a former echo joining the ranks, I insisted."

The hollow-turned-study had been decorated with art from times past—Celtic carvings, canvas paintings, early-century vinyl prints. Impressionist. Pointillist. Pop-art. At least half of it would fall foul of equality regulations, particularly the ample depictions of colonial antiquity, and those of the male and female form. Nowhere, of course, was there room for the legally mandated picture of Suarez-Adarsha and her over-stylised banner wafting in the breeze, the one that took up space in almost every home in every Safe Zone across the country.

"Benjamin Kolbeck," said the narrow man.

"You're a professor?" Chrissie asked.

"Yes. I mean, I was. They cancelled me a long time ago, years before they started to purge the universities and schools en masse." He said it like he was showing them a badge of honour.

"And now you're an archivist of some sort? A curator?"

"Grander words than I would use, my dear. If labels apply, I'd deem myself nothing more than a dragon. An old fossil sitting in a cave, protecting his treasure."

"All this belongs to you?"

"Oh, no. I didn't mean it like that. No one owns this. No one *can* own this. Art, literature—it's ours. Shared history. Belongs to all and no one."

Jake said, "Can't believe someone once told me *I* read too much."

Kolbeck harrumphed. "Read *too much*? Is that a *thing*?"

"Either way, it's incredible. How did you come by it all?"

"Don't think we're sitting out in the wilderness collecting moss. Our society demands we remember. If we forget who we were, what we achieved, and how, we're destined to fail in this world. So we scavenge. Have done since they began expunging the libraries and bookstores and academic institutes. Moral cleansing, they called it." He blew air out of his cheeks, seized by disgust. "They thought they'd destroyed it all. We saved it. Not all, but a hell of a lot. A *hell* of a lot."

"No offense," Jake said, "It's also a hell of a lot of knowledge to keep locked away."

"It would be if that were our attitude. We have banks of scanners churning out paper copies to anyone who wants them. Group book readings are every Monday and Thursday afternoon. If you're interested, I'll see they reserve you a seat."

"Why not digital copies?" Chrissie said. "You have electricity here. Everything on these shelves could probably be stored on a couple of hard drives. You'd save a lot of space."

The professor's mouth tugged into a tight smile, as if deciding whether to humour the question.

"We have more than a few digital backups," he said. "But all that could be erased by an act of God. A flash flood, for instance, or something far less natural, like a well-placed EMP blast. Who knows what those twisted crones will try next. When it comes to preservation, you can't beat a good old paper and glue hardcopy. We do audio transcribing too. In fact, Miss Tieman, you have a lovely, clear voice. Perhaps you'd like to record something for us one day."

"That's nice of you to say," she said, recognising the compliment as he meant it, rather than some subtle attempt to objectify her. "And I'm grateful you and your people are making us feel welcome. In all honesty, Professor, we're not sure if we're staying here. We needed a way out. There was nowhere else for us to go. Even if we want to stay, I don't even know if this Rockland person will allow it."

"With Rockland—who knows? He's bloody difficult."

"Could he stop us from staying? If he wanted to?"

A shadow passed over Kolbeck. He folded himself into one of the natty armchairs, beckoned for them to sit with him.

"Listen," he said, crossing his ankles, revealing a pair of sea-green novelty socks dotted with cartoon amphibians, at odds with the mudwater colours of his outfit. "You don't have to be part of this colony—or any colony—if you don't want to be, and you don't have to clear out either. Rockland leads but we're still a democracy here. Our community is about individuals making their own damn decisions. As long as you're not hurting anyone, no one person has the right to make you leave. Individuality has been trampled on too long for us to abide that nonsense."

The tightness that had been curling its way around Chrissie's chest eased a little at that. Only a little. After all, the society from which she had escaped had claimed to be a democracy too. If final say on their fate didn't belong to Rockland, it didn't mean they were—in any sense—out of the woods. She knew how easy it was for the few to influence the many.

"They talk about him like he's some sort of messiah," Chrissie said.

Kolbeck cleared his throat again. "He's a man of good intentions. You'll know where that often leads."

"Doesn't sound like you trust him."

The professor cast his gaze at the ceiling. "He's all right. We're not exactly on a philosophical parallel, but what does that matter at times like this?"

"Say we're allowed to stay," Jake said. "How long does a place like this have? They drove my people out of our camp years ago. Rounded us up, punished us for daring to reject their rules. I don't even know where my parents are—whether they're even still alive. What makes you think they won't do the same to everyone here?"

"You're right. This place won't last. Something will happen eventually, maybe sooner than any of us imagine. History has taught us that lesson time and again—for those who bother to learn." He gave a wary flick of his fingers towards the books. "What comes after could be better. God, it *has* to be better, doesn't it?"

"Back in the cities," Chrissie said, "We don't learn any of that. We're told how the centuries passed with cycle upon cycle of Cis-temic privilege, all having ascended and declined because of the violence and greed of cisnormative thinking."

"The violence and greed part is true," Kolbeck said. "Though that's more the result of human nature, not of binarists alone. Civilisations are roaring fires that grow hot and bright and have generally been lit by war or revolution, that's true. The tinder that kept them going was only enriched by reason and order, by justice and security, by dialogue and debate, by the mutual support of peers, by the adherence to a natural hierarchy. None of what goes on in the cities today allows any of that. Instead, we—well, you, and those with state-issued licences to exist—have been subject to an utterly insane attempt to subvert the underlying infrastructure of humanity, all within a generation or two. It's doomed. Collapsing in on itself. We're sitting on the cusp of change and, mark my words, they know that. They're terrified. And because they're afraid, they're resorting to violence, as people always have. Violence begetting violence. Positive feedback loops. You hit me, I slap you back, you punch me back, I stab you back, and on and on. Only this is their own brand of violence. It's less visible, but it's the same ruthless operation as when tribes were beheading their enemies and torching their crops."

"The current regime has been doing that too," Jake said, the lamp next to him making his shadow huge against the bookcases. "When they stormed our camp, they set it on fire. I remember watching it as a boy. They burnt the crops, the shelters, the vehicles…."

"Forgive me for generalising," Kolbeck said. "We've been defending ourselves against those same kinds of raids for years. All across the country, there are other settlements like this and the more coordination we've had, the tougher our resistance has become. Not so many raids these days and that's no bloody coincidence, I can tell you. Anyway, all this talk of violence—it's not what I had wanted your first experience here to be about."

He got up, went over to a desk, rummaged around, found a boxy plastic gadget, yellowed with age.

He said, "Afraid I'm a bit of a dinosaur when it comes to music, but let's see…"

He held the device close to his face, his thumb jabbing at the display. From somewhere up in the rafters, notes stirred in the walls, permeating through the bookcases and picture frames and mismatched, ramshackle furniture.

Chrissie had never heard anything like it. A strong, sad bass played under a voice—a male voice—that began gravelled and rough and defiant only to become sweet and mellow and defeated by the end of the chorus. The lyrics were complex, as poetic as anything she had ever identified in the world as beautiful.

"Remarkable, isn't it?" Kolbeck said, sagging against a wall of books. "The things humans can do when we allow ourselves to be free. I'd say the world is more like an elaborate musical composition than anything else. Everything is oddly connected."

"It's more noise than music out there, Professor," Chrissie said. "There's no harmony. People have been reduced to nothing. You're living out here in hiding. Most of the population are treated as slaves and sub-humans. It's hard to understand how we allowed things to go this far."

Kolbeck sprang forward, eyes rolling. "Bloody-minded group mentality, let's try that. *Transtrenderism.* The pretence of uniqueness. Which of course led to mass psychogenesis. State-required rejection of the individual. Abandonment of the merit of one's character in favour of pseudo-Marxist virtue signalling. Censorship of opinion. False victimhood. False outrage. False accusations. Mob mentality…"

Like the song he had played, his speech formed an emotional glissando, pinballing from exuberance to exhaustion—his rhetoric fiery one moment, choked to tears the next. She had lit a fuse in the man that seemed to be entrenched somewhere deep inside him.

"…And it all goes back to the cultural shift away from responsibility. It was never about emancipation or civil liberties as it was years ago. It was about wanting to have it all and not having to do anything for it. The majority are now fugitives, or dead, or detained, all because a tiny fraction refused to grow up and accept they have to work for their damned privileges. It was nothing but a bloody power-play. One that's led to the rejection of biology, to the butchering of children. An utter travesty of everything humanity had worked for…"

His lip quivered. He shut his eyes.

"I'm sorry," said Chrissie, shaking her head. "For everything. I was one of them. An ally. I believed them—for a while, at least. I didn't know. I wasn't told anything else until I experienced first-hand the reality of what was happening. People in the Safe Zones have an idea of you as thugs, gangs of people not much better than beasts, living in squalor, killing and stealing anything you can—even attacking each other."

Kolbeck worked on getting his breath back. When he finally opened his eyes, they glistened.

"I know the lies they've spun about us," he said. "They never anticipated we would find a way to unite. What they deprived us of, we rebuilt. Made use of the fact we had people with huge skills and knowledge. We organised. We housed and fed those willing to get behind the cause. In small, isolated numbers, the government has the advantage. Together, we've proved too much for them. Why do you think we still hold most of the land in this country? They told you it was a wasteland, didn't they?"

"I've seen it now," she said. "It's beautiful."

"And it's ours. But without the cities, it's doomed. We'll always be a nation stuck in an asymmetric war."

"What do you mean?"

"I mean the change that's coming isn't going to happen in the forests and barrens, it's going to happen in the streets. You must realise that?"

Chrissie and Jake looked at each other.

CHAPTER FIFTY-TWO

Again, they ascended, three more spiralling flights, their movements shaking the rivets. The web of scaffolding criss-crossed the cave in a heady, indecipherable pattern. Benjamin Kolbeck took them through a series of narrow walkways, above which a few bits of timber had been nailed together, the word 'History' stencilled on it with spray paint.

"Violence, revolution, war and political upheaval," Kolbeck said with a wry smile. "It's all here in brutal detail. Nothing like the fantasies they peddled to you in *zistory* classes."

Chrissie chose not to meet his gaze, embarrassed by her own miseducation, even if the fault lay on the shoulders of a twisted political elite. The musty books presented a convenient distraction.

Kolbeck stopped at one end of the aisle, ran his finger along a series of tomes. "World War Two. Early to mid-twentieth century. I imagine you've heard of this one, but probably know little about it."

"It tore the world apart," Jake said.

"That it did. Here in this forest you can still see the line of trees they planted to harvest and send to the frontline trenches, as well as the areas they used to hide military supplies from enemy surveillance. I won't seek to present a lecture on it all for you today but if you'll humour me for a moment…"

He reached into the shelves, pulled out one of the thick volumes. A puff of cave dust plumed and evanesced. He flicked through it, landed on a chapter entitled 'The French Resistance'. He spread the pages for them. A monochrome photograph depicted a group of people in trench coats and berets huddled around a table as one of them exhibited a rifle, perhaps explaining its assembly and operation.

"France, early nineteen-forties. The Germans had invaded. Strategically vital to their control of Europe. The French puppet government collaborated with them to save their own skins. Sound familiar? Anyway, all across the board, it was a disaster. Civilian resistance movements sprang up—the *Maquis*—normal people who had been postal workers and shopkeepers and butchers mobilising as an underground force. They wanted to stop this regime and redeem themselves of the humiliation of being conquered by a foreign power. In the years after the war, they were greatly romanticised—'Brave patriots who put their own lives on the line to reclaim the country and turn the tide of conflict.' Only it wasn't like that. The Maquis were next to useless. They weren't coordinated among themselves. Their operations were mostly small acts of vandalism. They were made up of countless splinter groups, all with their own names and emblems, all doing barely a jot to take down an autocratic powerhouse. At most, they were a trifling nuisance to the Germans. Until the British arrived. The Brits knew how to organise. They understood that while the Maquis were largely ineffective, they could perhaps be turned into a real weapon if they had people inside who could teach them tactics, join up their fragmented efforts in line with the larger scale military strategy of the Allied forces—back when the word 'ally' wasn't just some defensive label—and that's exactly what they got."

He turned the page, pointed to a photograph of a group of people parachuting against a grey sky.

"They called them *Jedburghs*. About three hundred paramilitary troops. Men highly skilled in unarmed combat and sabotage techniques, dropped behind enemy lines to lead these ragtag rebels. The Jeds did more for the Resistance than anyone else, even if history became somewhat distorted later on." He snapped the book shut. "You want to know who Rockland is? This is it. He's a Jedburgh. Our most senior one, at least in this camp."

"I hate to break it to you," Chrissie said, "but I've seen your Resistance in action. Looked to me like they bore a strong similarity to these Maquis people. Petty acts of vandalism. Defacing public property. Hacking the occasional netscreen feeds. Nuisances, that's all. Hardly anything the police can't rectify. I'm sorry to disappoint you— your tactics aren't working. If anything, they've given the Equality Ministry more control than ever."

Kolbeck stood there, looked at her with a blank expression that made her think he hadn't heard a word of her dismissive account.

He said, "If you think that's all that's going on, you've been missing the bigger picture."

"Enlighten me," she said, crossing her arms, tired of the people around her feeling fit to keep her in the dark.

"The communities out in the Heaths don't just have a network and a bunch of tents in the woods and a secret handshake. We have a stratagem. Had one for a long time now. The denouement is right around the corner."

"Denouement?"

"We have to do something, don't we? We have to confront the potential for chaos before chaos takes hold forever. How would we ever live with ourselves if we didn't? That's what I wanted to see you both about. I think you could be of great help."

"Professor, what—"

A shrill beeping filled the aisles. Kolbeck sprang past them, a spooked fox, running for the stairs. Chrissie and Jake followed him down, fearing the sound was an alarm—perhaps some kind of air raid signal, half expecting the stone walls around them to explode into rubble. They found the professor at the end of an overlook, hunched next to a stack of upturned crates that propped up an old-fashioned two-way radio, the headset cupped to his ear.

"I copy," he mumbled into the bowing microphone.

He released the transmitter switch. The radio box buzzed like a dying insect.

Kolbeck pivoted back to his guests, said, "You have a lot of questions, Miss Tieman. Fortunately, you can expect them all to be answered within the hour." He leaned over the railing, his reedy voice rolled, bounced into the chasm: "Oscar! Better head on back. He's ready."

CHAPTER FIFTY-THREE

Tavistock took a heavy breath, lowered herself against the work desk, turned the voxchat on. She had been pacing the hotel room for the past hour, half fighting the urge to make the call, half gearing herself up for it. Throughout the afternoon rally—a healthy turn-out in Manchester city centre—she had been unable to shake the feeling of needing to try. She hated the contrarian cow, but she would hate herself more if she'd never made an attempt to prevent it all.

Wouldn't she?

The notion was ruining any fun she had hoped to milk out of the campaign tour. Amid the multicoloured balloons, the cheers of adoration, the sand sliding through the hourglass was as clear as if it was seeping between her toes, between her teeth, between the folds of her delicates. Itching. Insufferable. It robbed her of appetite, left her unable to sit still.

One day left.

Calling it off wasn't an option. Something fundamental would have to change. The antagonising bitch would have to see sense. There was simply no alternative.

"Prime Minister?"

The DIP leader didn't try to hide the surprise in her voice, nor the whiff of disdain. Go in soft, Tavistock reminded herself. This was no time for hard-balling.

"Mary, I hope you don't mind me calling you in a private capacity."

"It's...unexpected, to say the least. But, no—it's fine."

"I need to talk to you, as one leader of the community to another. This is a secure line. No one else with me. Are you alone?"

"What's this about?"

"Are you alone, Mary? This is important."

Gallard squinted into the netscreen, evidently baffled. Tavistock could see a well-tended garden behind her, guessed she was at her home, perhaps in a heated office pod, no doubt busying herself with her campaign preparation. From Gallard's view, she would be seeing the harlequin furniture and synthetic-fur throws of the Dakota's grand deluxe suite, the flickering gas-blue flames of the replica log fire.

"I am," Gallard confirmed, surrendering to her intrigue.

"Good. I need to talk to you about tomorrow. We know what you're planning—the rally in London."

Her political rival paused at length, pursed her lips, shrugged. "Of course you do. You can't know what I plan to say, though. I've not written anything down."

"It wouldn't take a genius to guess its content."

"The censors have no legal grounds to deplatform me."

"I've not asked them to, Mary. I'm asking you, as a fellow non-binarist, to do the right thing."

"Oh? And what's that, in your mind?"

"Deplatform yourself, before it's too late."

Gallard almost let slip a laugh. "Minister, please. You know as well as I do this is a rare opportunity for my party to speak without being shouted down or drowned out. As a non-binarist, as an MP, my voice has a right to be heard. I will never deplatform myself."

"Mary, listen to me. There's another way. I've been thinking about this a great deal and, all things considered, I believe there's an opportunity here for us to come to a mutual agreement. It's a bit radical, but hear me out."

The eyes narrowed again. Priggish little bitch. The prime minister dug what was left of her nails into the palms of her hands, tried to summon a warm expression. She couldn't allow her personal contempt to get in the way now.

"This country is on the cusp of real reformation," Tavistock went on. "The changes we're planning would see non-binarists everywhere seize exclusive, inalienable and unprecedented power. That includes you, but only if you're on the right side of zistory. I'm willing to extend an olive branch—no—more than that—a life line. Join us. Join our cause."

"What?"

"I mean it. I'm offering you the chance to merge the DIP with the TEP, to stand down from this hill you've chosen to die on and reap the rewards that are yours by divine right."

Even as she said it, a lump travelled to Tavistock's stomach. Zoe would throw a tantrum if she knew what was being proposed. So would the rest of the Tribe, not to mention most of the party members.

"A coalition? Why on earth—"

"No, no coalition. A completely new outfit. No more opposition parties. No more parliamentary squabbling. A monopolitical approach to governance, with the aim of a monocultural objective."

"I'm not sure I get what you're saying, Minister. Or why."

"Come now, Mary. What's democracy, anyway? An outdated part of the Cis-tem, invented to keep trans people subjugated. Together, we can build a better system. We're enlightened. We should be beyond the nuisances of elections and all those primitive distractions."

"Minister, this country was built on democracy."

"It was built on oppression," Tavistock said with a chuckle. "Look, you want everyone to be afforded the rights we have? You'll lose at the ballot boxes. Fast. You know there's no hope of the DIP gaining any more seats under a policy of inclusion for *everyone*. In a few years' time, the TEP will stamp you out completely across every constituency—"

"I do not know that. And even if I did, that's not the point of our oppositional stance—"

"Mary, this is your survival I'm talking about here. We're stronger as one. We can keep the spirit of diversity and inclusion going, so long as it never allows CisHet people in. Wasn't that always the cornerstone of the philosophy anyway?"

"The fact you're even suggesting a merger tells me you're not as confident in your voter turnout as you'd have the public believe."

"Don't be silly," came the terse reply. "The polls speak for themselves."

"Then why not wait it out? Why not be satisfied to crush us under your boot, as you claim will be the case? You're worried the public's getting behind our viewpoints, aren't you? Admit it."

"Absurd."

"You want me out of the picture. You think this will be the easiest way to do it."

"Can't you see I'm trying to help you, for Goddess's sake?"

"You'd throw us under the bus at the first opportunity."

"This is compassion, you dumb—"

Tavistock stopped herself. She could feel the sand up to her neck now.

Gallard said, "I will be speaking at Trafalgar Square tomorrow, and I will be speaking my mind."

The prime minister glared at the screen, wanting to put her hands through it, to wring that slender neck. The defiance was an affront to her position, to the future of every non-binarist in the country. Zoe had been right: Mary Gallard was too dangerous to ignore.

"If you continue down this road," Tavistock said, "continue to try to pry open the grip we've built up against the binarists, to diminish what we've spent years making, they'll take every opportunity to re-establish their cisnormative tyranny. Give them an inch and they'll take a mile."

"We need them, Minister. And we're running out of justification to exclude them. Our own convictions have become too contradictory. It's a house of cards."

"Might I remind you that the whole reason we had to reintroduce the Gender Recognition Act was because too many CisHets started circumventing our reforms simply by claiming to be genderqueer. They made the whole thing a circus."

"But this process of labelling and categorising has gone too far, Prime Minister. I've been trying to tell you that, but you won't listen. We've created a meaningless morass of a culture that we can't pull ourselves out of. We can't identify anyone, so no one is held to account. We can't criticise anything, so everything ends up wrong. We have no past to learn from, so everyone walks around thinking they're infallible. We spend millions every month just updating our national flags, for fuck's sake. And the worst part is we've done it all just to create a new dichotomy. Us versus them. We've become the ones obsessed with defining and ostracising others. We've literally created a new binary system."

"We're not like them!" Tavistock screamed, squeezing her fists. "We are not binarists. That's problematic!"

"We are. That's why we have to stand against you, Prime Minister, whether the people vote every one of us out or not."

"No. The real binarists are pitbulls, Mary—waiting for their chance to bite. Let them off the leash and they'll come for you, too. Your rhetoric alone is a dog whistle to violence. It doesn't matter if you're trying to reinstate some semblance. Mark my words, if we allow them a fragment of freedom back, they'll use it to come for you, as much as any of us."

"I'll take my chances."

"Fine," Tavistock said with a baleful smile. "I best let you get back to your work. After all, we both have a speech to prepare for tomorrow."

"Prime Minister."

The voxchat dinged out, Gallard's self-righteous profile traded for sleep-mode animations. Knowing the idiot would be dead in a day suddenly felt less of a burden. *Cockleshells* was an unstoppable train, rolling towards its terminus. Her hands hurt. Her nails had drawn blood, formed little crescents in her palms.

Tavistock stood, went to the minibar to find something cold to suck down, resisting a glance at the expansive mirrors on the way. Between tipping back the mini champagne from the bottle, she used her voxwatch to plug in a message to Hannah, requesting to know when her evening guests would be arriving and for a bottle of Laurent Perrier to be sent up with them. She would need more resolve tonight, a medicinal edge to help her forget the pressures, help her enjoy the only thing that still made her happy.

257

CHAPTER FIFTY-FOUR

Even sitting, he was noticeably tall. Not as brawny as Wyatt but big all the same. A man with slack, sunken cheeks that bore the grain of two or three days of stubble. The rest of his skin taut and toughened, particularly around his eyes—grey eyes, at once hard and liquid, giving away nothing of the workings behind them. He bore a scalp of short, thick hair that had once been dark but was now sprinkled with salt. It had the texture of something like a beaver pelt—neither wet nor dry, combed flat, forward. His getup, a mix of military green and olive, a waxed shell coat bearing the name of some defunct outdoors brand, a pair of hardened hiking boots. In his hands he held a hunting knife, still sheathed in its tanned scabbard. It rotated between his fingers, behind stubbed, broken nails, the tip pivoting on the armrest. Rockland said nothing.

Jake broke the silence. "Mister Rockland, we would like to stay here. For a while, at least."

The woman who had welcomed them so warmly to the Compound the night before leant against one of the pine supports to his right, spliced in shadow. There was no fire now. She looked like any one of the other settlers they had met that day.

The cabin sat at the centre of the Compound, built atop a little hill, hemmed by a stake palisade, guards observing the gate. Chrissie had expected to find a fortified building inside, maybe a bunker of some sort. The cabin was unremarkable—little more than a shack with handmade tables and crooked oil paintings. Sunlight cut through the shutters, left slashes of yellow across the floorboards. The only notable aspects were the man in the chair and the chair itself—a seat chiselled into a large oak trunk with gnarled boughs forming the backrest, a mass of oiled roots forming the base, as beautiful as it was bizarre.

"You saw the footage," Chrissie said. "You know I can't go back to that."

The seated man stared at them. His hand moved to the copper ashtray on the side-table, brought a half-burned cigar to his teeth. A silver ghost rolled from his mouth, escaped towards the rafters. He placed the cigar back in the tray, swivelled the hunting knife again.

When he finally spoke, the words sounded like they were coming through the floorboards. "A cop deciding to run from the law. If that isn't the ultimate double-or-nothing move, I don't know what is."

His expression didn't change all that much but something suggested he was amused by the idea.

"So, you believe us?"

The crow's feet softened. "Why wouldn't I, Constable Christina Tieman?"

"Maybe 'cause your friend here was ready to corpse us," Jake said.

"Please forgive Sadie. We don't always know if the people coming here are who they say they are. Especially not allies. Jesus. Especially not equality officers."

"Ex-equality officer," Chrissie said.

Sadie lowered her gaze, folded her arms, gripped the flesh beneath the rolled sleeves of her plaid shirt. "I'm sorry. I'm not good at trusting people."

"I gathered that," Chrissie said.

"They took everything from me. Had me imprisoned for trying to protect women's rights. Labelled me a TERF. Cancelled my entire family. It took years to…" Sadie looked away. "We have to be so careful who we let in here."

Rockland said, "That we do. But we also have to have faith in the best of people. Without that, this place of ours would never have been possible."

Chrissie eyed him with a caution she once reserved for criminals. Not that he wasn't a criminal, technically speaking. There was something else about him that unnerved her. The way he sat there, impossible to read, twirling his damned knife.

"The footage," she said. "You saw it?"

"I did."

"Then what do we do? How do we stop it?"

Rockland simply looked at the cinders on the cigar, a growing stack of dust refusing to deposit itself on the ground.

"Your people have been hacking into the smartnet," she went on. "I've seen it first-hand. You could have them broadcast it on one of the feeds—send it right into the Safe Zones, into people's homes. They'd see the truth for what it is."

Sadie exchanged glances with the man in charge. For a while the loudest thing in the room was the sound of the settlers outside, beyond the paling and the trees, where voices mixed with the sawing of wood, with the cold banging of nails and the crunch of wheelbarrows. Rockland took another drag of the cigar, undaunted by time.

Eventually, he spoke. "It may help a bit, yes."

"A bit?" The words caught in her throat. "It's clear as day. The equality minister directly plotting to assassinate a rival—a woman— with the help of the police. It's a smoking gun."

"I agree," he said. "It's damning. Further proof of what we know to be the blackened heart of the government and we'll add it to the trove of intelligence we already have that points to the reality of life under the TEP. All being said, it'll do bugger all on its own to sway public opinion in the Safe Zones. The Ministry would simply claim it a hoax—digital manipulation, perhaps. Make up some evidence to show it was just some binarist propaganda, like they always do. The public only eats what it likes the taste of, Christina. The truth isn't appetising."

She shook her head. "No. We need to get it out there. At least if Mary Gallard sees it—or her people hear there's a threat—she'd cancel her appearance. We can still stop this from happening."

"Gallard and her politicians are no friends of ours. You may think of them as the lesser of two evils but their vision of the world still spits, shits and quits on the likes of us."

"You heard it yourself. The Equality Ministry intends to blame the murder on you—on your people. Make you their scapegoats. It's the push they need to see through all the new laws they care to invent. It will galvanise the TEP for years—maybe forever. You can't ignore that." The silence returned. "Mister Rockland, we risked our lives to get this evidence to you."

"We're grateful for that."

Sadie stepped forward, produced Sergeant Dennehy's body-eye, dropped it into Chrissie's stiff hand, shrugged, slunk back against the wall. The battery light on the device had died. Chrissie's heart sank.

"Grateful enough for us to stay?" Jake said. "If for nothing else, the footage proves which side we're on, right? If it's more assistance you want, we can offer that in spades."

Rockland grunted. "So the deal would be your assistance for our protection? And our shelter? And our resources?"

Jake took a breath. The dust and smoke floating in the air smelled thicker. "Whatever we can do."

The knife rotated. "Sounds square and fair to me, Jacob."

"How exactly can we help?" Chrissie said. She had never farmed before. Never chopped wood. Never plucked chickens or fished bream. She could learn these things, she was sure, but she doubted it would be enough.

"Friends, you've come at a strange time. A fortuitous time. Perhaps an ideal time. Depends how you look at it."

"Professor Kolbeck said something about a plan," Chrissie said.

"Ah, you spoke to the doc. He's a great man, isn't he? Wise beyond all our years. But a sentimental man. I worry for him."

"You should worry for everyone. If the TEP corpse their only political rival, you and everyone like you will be condemned to—"

"Relax. The TEP still have plenty of people ready to stand against them."

He pushed himself out of the chair, unfolded to his full, disconcerting frame. He left the cigar smouldering on the table, took the scent of it with him as he strode forward, past them, past the men guarding the entrance.

He pulled open the door. "Oscar hasn't shown you everything yet."

CHAPTER FIFTY-FIVE

They stayed close together, followed him out, flanked by his entourage, away from the palisade walls, along an indistinct trail in the woodland behind the cabin. Rockland moved with fluid steps, his well-set shoulders and oak neck towering over the others. The further they walked, the more the familiar noises of the Compound gave way to those of metal and machinery, to the distant chanting of men in unison.

At the clearing, the source of these sounds stirred a new well of fear in ex-Constable Christina Tieman. Platoons of men and women, jogging around a campground, climbing ropes, scaling walls. They crawled with furious determination beneath wire nets, attacked heavy bags with fists and feet. Knives and machetes hacked at tight bundles of bamboo. Drill instructors barked orders. Wyatt was among them, whistle in hand, his hulking size marking him out. He gave a slow nod as the group came by, went back to enjoining the trainees at top decibel.

Beyond the exercise yard stood a line of sheds, each building as massive as the last. Rockland headed in their direction, cut directly through the grunting militia, barely waiting for his group to follow. The smell of sweat and dirt rose off the grass. Chrissie pressed herself closer to Jake's side. They reached the sheds, where hammers and drills reverberated through the roll-back hanger doors. Rockland extended a hand to Chrissie, crossed the threshold, chivalrous.

"One of our workshops," he said above the noise. "Almost every settlement has one."

A storm of sparks and hot irons. Banks of milling machines, row upon row of them. Open crates covered the floor, each one crammed with ammunition, overflowing like brass pasta. Workers strung cartridges to bandoliers, rolled them into steel carry-cans. Elsewhere, weapon components were wedged between bench vices—buttstocks, iron sights, muzzle breaks.

Rockland called one of the engineers aside, took a finished article off his hands. The modern rifle—something Chrissie had only ever seen in

NetTube movies—gleamed unpainted. Rockland racked the slide, bounced it in his hands like a baby.

He said, "Assault rifles, uzis, pistols, shotguns, rocket launchers, grenades, machetes…they did all they could to rid the country of them years ago but we secured a healthy cache. More importantly, we retained the knowledge and expertise to engineer new ones."

Chrissie edged a step back. "What are you planning to do?"

"Your intel has been more useful than you probably appreciate. We know now that we're working against the clock." He checked his wristwatch. "Less than twenty-four hours."

"I don't understand." Only, she was sure she did understand. She was listening to the nauseating tide creeping up on her, waiting for her to turn, to spot it, before she would admit it was there.

He said, "If all we'd been doing this time is sitting out in the woods, plucking chickens and getting drunk on homebrew, we'd deserve our misfortune ten times over. That hasn't been our way. We're everywhere. We're in the cities, in the OSZs and the ISZs. We're manifest. We've been crouching in the shadows. Waiting. Watching. Preparing to strike."

"Strike how?" The tide, growing louder.

"I'll spell it out for you, love, if only because you risked everything to be here and I admire you for that. We're taking this country back, by hook or by crook. By the time our people get into London, colonies across the country will be moving into all other major cities, trampling the Fences, breaking down the Privets."

Chrissie's breath stalled. She looked to Jake for some sort of help. Jake was unreadable.

"War," Chrissie said, if only because he had not. "You're talking about starting a civil war."

"Where have you been, Miss Tieman?" Rockland said. "The war started years ago. I'm talking about ending it. This is a coup."

"What about *Cockleshells*?"

He shrugged. "Their lazy assassination plot won't derail us. It may even help—sow some seeds of confusion, form a nice smokescreen for us to come through, lay siege while panic rules. Either way, by the time they start trying to lay blame on us, we'll already be in the thick of it. God willing, it may even be over by then."

"You're going to let them do it?" she said, her voice climbing.

He propped the stock of the rifle against his shoulder, aimed the barrel at the ground, peered down the sight. "If it happens, it happens. Other than timing, it doesn't change our plans. We thought we had another week to prep, but hey-ho. There's not much more we could do then that we can't do now."

"You're going to let Gallard die. That's what you're telling me?"

"DIP, TEP, it's all the same. Those transgender Marxist politicos aren't people, they're belligerents. You know that. Anyway, we don't plan on much of a fight. No one else needs to get hurt."

"Then why all this?" She gestured to the arms factory.

"Scare tactics. Keep the public in line when we move in. Don't worry, Constable—you know as well as I do they don't have the firepower, let alone the skills or the stomachs to go toe-to-toe with real men and women, trained paramilitaries. We predict it'll all be over in two days. Three, tops. With the hardware we've amassed, you're going to bear witness to one of the swiftest insurrections of all time."

Great Birth-Giver, Chrissie though. He was probably right.

CHAPTER FIFTY-SIX

"Thomas Tate, you stand before the public court accused of gross cissexism, implicit assault, denial of implicit assault, physical assault of an officer of the law and resisting arrest."

The speaker system crackled, paused. Spectators filled the silence with vicious hollering, venom-ridden insults. They bubbled like water on a hob, undulating together, threatening to go off the boil. They held up their voxwatches, streamed the event live to Xprez. Above them, the break in the clouds over the west terrace revealed a deflating sun, a citrine sky.

The stadium announcer continued: *"You may now admit your misconducts and plead for atonement before the adjudication panel and this citizen-jury. Should it be determined you are not sufficiently remorseful for your actions, the Ministry of Equality has determined you shall face cancellation in the third degree. Should it be determined you are sufficiently remorseful, you shall face cancellation in the second degree."*

The priv's pathetic frame shivered, appeared altogether remote on the stage. He was ordered to his knees. The early evening spotlights lit up, burned at low heat, glowered at the centre of Stamford Bridge field where the week's scheduled atonement session played out.

Zoe normally loved soaking up the atmosphere of the arena on these nights. Now zie was struggling to fully enjoy it. The rows of empty plastic seats in the upper tiers were hard to ignore. It wasn't the wet weather keeping people from enjoying Britannia's favourite pastime of public social justice. The gradual decline of ticketholders represented another embarrassing slide of support for the government's policies, no doubt brought on by that Gallard bitch and her meddling cabinet. The crowds were as thin now as those arriving for the Netball Superleague. It wouldn't be long before rhythmic gymnastics nights were rivalling in numbers.

Zoe sucked the melted cheese off a nacho, tried to focus on the fact zie still had the best seat in the house—Executive Box, centre—thanks to the PM being off on the campaign trail. A taste of things to come, zie told herself, trying to mainline the cheer back into zer night out.

The speaker whined. So did Tate, mumbled into the microphone about how sorry he was, how he was a terrible person, how he would give everything to change what had happened. Zoe had heard the same plea hundreds of times from hundreds of defendants. Zie always found it amusing, like watching people bare their necks to those operating the guillotine. Tate's bare neck already had it bad, the sign hanging around it reading *Cissupremacist*, marking him out as a repeat offender. So much for behavioural orientation. Better he be sent to a re-education centre for good. Of course, that would be for the judging panel to decide, the volume of the crowd acting as their weatherglass.

"S'no need to be so anxious, ma'am-sir." Dominic hunkered in his duffel coat. His focus flitted between the spectacle, the smartpalm in his hand and his employer. "We could retire early to keep fresh for the 'morrow. Perhaps a foot spa would soothe you."

"There are better ways you can serve me tonight," Zoe said. "I need your eyes open, your people in constant communication. Nothing can slip through the cracks."

They could speak freely here, the VIP seats beyond earshot from the common spectators. The warble of the crowd—slender though it was—provided a comforting damper to their conversation.

"Dennehy's no concern," he said. "I've had word come—she's taken up position. Our team are on watch."

"All the same, I won't rest easy until I know she's there on the day."

"We'll make sure of it."

His reassurance was empty. Zie had spent long enough in his company, teasing his flaws, testing his nerves, scrutinising his ticks. He was holding back.

"What's making you twiddle, Dominic? Tell me. Now."

He wet his lips, took a breath, unable to lie to her. "We intercepted a private call to Mary Gallard this afternoon. Our dear leader was trying to petition her to call off her speech."

The jittery little fool.

Zoe should have expected as much. It was plainly obvious Tavistock had become weaker in more mature years. The feistiness had waned, her appetite for the fight eroded. She was the reason numbers were dropping at atonement sessions, why unsanctioned polling numbers showed the TEP losing favour. As a younger transwoman, Tavistock had been the ideal standard-bearer—beautiful and beloved. Now her fatigue was becoming a liability. Perhaps even more so than her private passions. Yet, it was that same weakness that made the prime minister useful, made her easy to manipulate, to inveigle her to act by merely implying her commitment to the cause could be called into question.

Zoe mulled the new information, said, "She didn't expose the plan. No. You'd have told me immediately if that was the case, or if her negotiation attempt had come to anything."

"An insignificant development," Dominic said. "After all, I'm no one to lay any criticism on the PM."

True. It would be problematic for an ally to raise even a word of disapproval of a non-binary leader, private or otherwise. His inference was enough. Dominic was concerned about Tavistock's reliability so close to the endgame. Who could blame him?

Useless to fret over it. The Tribe were still loyal to Tavistock, sickeningly so—thought her still the magnetic idol of yesteryear, even if they had experienced her faults first-hand.

"Nothing we can do yet," Zoe said. "We wait it out. Everyone's term ends eventually."

Dominic's right eyelid twitched, an involuntary action zie had seen hundreds of times. It always left an uneasy impression on zer.

Zoe checked zer voxwatch. There were other loose threads to worry about.

The mob had their say on Tate, their united tirade morphing into a rhythmic stomp. The panel gave their verdict, dropped the big third on him despite his plea. The priv blubbered like a baby. That got the crowd going again—this time a victorious cheer. They cheered again as the gag went in, drank up his tears as the hood came over. Tate was shoved back into the maelstrom, jostled, kicked, spat on as the ushers bundled him back to the holding cells.

He was the last of the privs for the night. The focus shifted to the suspected traitors—the trans, genderqueer and allies accused of committing acts of betrayal against their own kind, of whoring their loyalty out to the enemy. Zoe considered them almost worse than the binarists who stood trial, insisted there was a Special Place in Hell for them. Still, most who repented before the crowd served no more than a year or two in re-education before they would be released. Limited rights and forever branded, but free nonetheless. If the country was going to survive, zie thought, that sort of soft-touch justice would have to change.

A war cry rose from the tunnel. The line of traitors filtered onto the field, bumped, butted by the ushers, by those in the standing yard. They were set upon as soon as they appeared—throngs of banshees circling, clawing, screaming obscenities and denunciations. The accused wore their charges around their necks—display-screens that spelt out their crimes in pixels. They walked as steadily as they could to the platform.

"When are they going up?" Zoe said. "You know I hate to wait."

"That's them, there," Dominic said, pointing to the overhead smartscreen. "At the front. I had them go first, ma'am-sir. Wouldn't want your satisfaction delayed another moment."

Sure enough, the echo's sister and brat nephew were climbing the steps, a posse of ushers prodding them along. They were positioned centre-stage, a metre apart. Not being allowed to hold each other, they hugged themselves, shivered against the breeze rolling in from the open roof. One of the ushers barked an order. They each sank to their knees.

"*Charlotte Tieman, you stand before the public court accused of aiding and abetting binarist terrorists, of denial of aiding and abetting binarist terrorists, and of raising a child to embrace toxic beliefs.*"

The crowd steamed. Someone threw a to-go cup of NeverCold. It hit the child in the head. The brat squealed, scalded. A string of snot and tears swung from his nose.

"*You may now admit your misconducts and plead for atonement before the adjudication panel and this citizen-jury. Should it be determined you are not sufficiently remorseful for your actions, the Ministry of Equality has* determined you shall face cancellation in the fourth degree, and the child shall face the same sentence. Should it be determined—"

"No!" Charlotte Tieman cried out. "She's done nothing! Please don't do this! She's trans! She's about to begin her therapy! She's one of you!"

"...Should it be determined you are sufficiently remorseful, sentencing shall be allotted by the judging panel."

The wind shifted, tussled both the defendants' hair. The adult was silent now, still shaking. The crowd fretted. For a moment, it seemed like she would refuse to take part in the show. She shuffled closer towards the mic. The display screen around her neck swung like a millstone.

"I am an ally," she said, fighting back tears. "I am a TEP donator. My pronouns are she/her. I follow the law. I've always followed the law. I promise you, I don't know what all this is about. All I know is my sister has gone missing. I don't know where she is. All they told me—"

"TERF! TERF! TERF!"

The mob, agitated, angry at the failure to repent.

"I'm not!" the defendant protested. "This is all a misunderstanding. I—"

Zoe didn't like the suggestion of defiance in the suspect, was becoming concerned the pathetic creature's ramblings were about to reveal too much. Zie heaved zerself to zer feet.

Marsh looked up, waited for instruction. Zoe thrust an arm out, gave a thumbs-down. Marsh nodded.

"No, please!" the convicted woman blubbed. "My pronouns are...my pronouns..."

Charlotte Tieman's mic popped, the sound cut out. She went on with her pleas, the vague insect-hum of her words barely reaching the stands. Her son's sobs, drowned out much the same.

The ushers closed in, threw a hood over the boy. His birth-giver screamed. They heard that in the nose-bleeds, felt it travel through their bones.

They hooded her, too. Pulled the bag down tight.

CHAPTER FIFTY-SEVEN

"We have to warn someone."

They were far enough from the Compound to be afforded some privacy, standing amid scots pine, deep enough in the forest to have lost sight of the footpaths.

Jake rocked on the log, stared at the leaves. "Why the hell would we do that?"

"You heard him." Chrissie pulled her arms around her, trapping what little warmth was left. "He's going to let them go through with the assassination. He doesn't even care who else gets hurt. If he doesn't care about that, what do you think his soldiers will do when they get into the city. Do you think they'll control themselves? Do you take them as a compassionate lot?"

"He said it was scare tactics. Even if it's not, he's right—this is already a war. They deserve what they have coming. It's the only way."

"Jake—"

"The government went rotten years ago, right? Raiding and corpsing their own people. The TEP are even planning to murder a rival in front of an audience. You're so worried about Rockland and his army but what else do you think the government's capable of?"

"I don't know, but Kolbeck said it himself when he talked about violence only leading to greater violence. You honestly think this country needs more innocent people caught in the crossfire of this stupid cultural squabble?" She steadied herself against a tree trunk. Droplets shook off the leaves above, peppered her head and jacket. Tears threatened to transform her face into a red, blotchy mess.

"I didn't say that," he said. "Nor did Rockland. They won't need to use their guns unless they have to."

"It baffles me you believe that."

He let out a colossal sigh, looked up at the lattice canopy, thick enough to hide the atmosphere. "Kolbeck said other things too. He said something does have to change and if it means making some tough decisions..."

"These aren't tough decisions, Jake. We're talking about stopping people from being killed. Rockland's soldiers aren't in this solely for change. They're angry. They're not discriminating. Innocent people will lose their lives."

"A lot already have." Jake's eyes flashed. He had the same look about him as when he had challenged Dennehy, coal-red and reckless. "My family. My people. Were they not innocent? Jesus, Chrissie—me and you, even. They'd cancel us permanently if they ever caught up with us. It's a dictatorship. To hell with them."

"If *Cockleshells* happens, they won't just be murdering a politician. Bombs don't discriminate. The blast will probably take out her staffers, her driver, her assistants, stage managers, who knows who else. Maybe the nearby echoes. They might take out people in the first few rows—CisHets among them. Maybe children."

"And if it doesn't happen, the public may never understand what their leaders are truly capable of, or why they need to be removed."

"Jake, are you even hearing yourself?"

"Let me remind you, we're still fugitives. The insurrection could be our only hope of ever being free. We can't jeopardise that."

"I'm not saying I don't want the insurrection to happen. I'm saying there has to be another way of going about it."

"Rockland's way is our best hope."

"Kolbeck doesn't trust him."

"He has a difference of opinion. He's entitled to that. Everyone else—each and every one—have faith in him. That kind of loyalty doesn't come from nothing. This country needs a real leader. He's leading. He's inspiring people. He's taking back control. He's exactly what this world needs."

"His followers are investing in a general, not a leader. He's more dangerous than you realise."

"You may never have been taught about it in your *zistory* lessons but we had men like him in the past. Great men. Men who were willing to make tough decisions to create a just society. Sometimes people get caught in the cross-fire, but often that's a small price to pay."

"You know who would say the same thing? Zoe Urwin. Abigail Dennehy. The prime minister. All the so-called *trans revolutionaries*. They all claimed to be fighting for justice once, too. It's all the same shit, Jake."

"We're past the point of options here, Chrissie."

"Listen—you may have lost all the people in your life, but mine are still out there in the city. I can't sit back and let them get caught up in this."

She regretted saying it as soon as the words had left her mouth. Jake set his hands down on the wet bark, steadied himself as if he had been punched in the chest. He stared off into the distance. He looked tired as hell.

They said nothing for a long time, let the patter of the rain speak for them. Beyond the treeline, some sort of celebration was taking place, a large group gathered at a fire pit. They sang songs, songs that that had long been condemned by the Cultural Correction Act. They played fiddle and drums, sounds accompanied by the occasional waft of wood smoke and cooking.

Chrissie sat down next to him, close. Her hand rested on his fingers.

"I'm sorry," she said. "I know what it's like to convince yourself of something, to want to believe you're doing the right thing to justify all the terrible things being done to get there."

He interwove his fingers between hers.

He said, "Must have been tough. All that time having to enforce their twisted rules."

"It was degrading," she said. "Having to do something you know is wrong, day in, day out, just because of fear. It broke me."

"I know."

"And it was lonely. More than anything, that feeling of isolation was..."

"I know lonely. I know it well."

"We don't have to feel alone anymore, Jake." Her fingers freed, found their way to his thigh.

His arm was around her, hers around him.

"Let it go," he said. "Let's not think about it anymore. Any of it. We can leave it alone, let the fates decide. We don't have to be part of any of it."

"We could…" she said, and that was all she said.

He kissed her knuckles. The smallest warmth.

The music rolled in through the trees, sweet and supernatural, resounded in their blood, awakened in them a primordial intelligence.

His mouth—on hers. Warm again, strange and wet and firm. So firm it hurt. She could feel it even after he pulled away. Then he was back, harder still, his tongue probing this time. She tasted exhilaration where once would have been only distress. The hunger in her stirred. He pulled away.

"We could," he said.

CHAPTER FIFTY-EIGHT

INTERCEPTED TRANSMISSION TRANSCRIPT—EQUALITY MINISTRY
SUBJECT: INSURGENT BROADCAST #267
LISTENING STATION SIMONE
30-13-46 2334 GMT

SENSITIVITY CLASSIFICATION: 10—CLASSIFIED / HIGHLY REDACTED

VOICE [terrorist suspect #2408D]: Hey, hey! It's the Ozcast, it's Revolution Radio, and, yes, it's your favourite Heathen broadcaster, once again.

Stop me if you've heard this one. Two students meet at a re-education centre. One says, "What's your sentence?" The other says, "Twenty years." The first one asks, "Whatcha do?" Second one says, "Nothing." The first one goes, "That's impossible." The other says, "Why's that impossible?" The first one says, "Because you only get ten years for doing nothing."

Ba-boom-tssh.

Wait. Was that even a joke? I dunno. Sounded pretty accurate to me.

I'm trying to keep it light, man. This may well be my last broadcast, at least for a while. At least on this particular channel, in this particular format.

Now, now—no need to get all teary, gang. It was always going to be this way. Besides, I don't plan on being away from your ears for too long. There's been some developments and I'm needing to do some travelling.

You know, when I started this thing years back, I thought it was enough. I didn't have much else in mind other than being a voice they couldn't repress—a way to bring truth to the masses. I thought this little booth and the ability to penetrate government systems were the strongest weapons we had, man. Giving strength to those who had been enslaved. Empowering hearts and minds, and all that. But I've been thinking about things for a while, now, and...

Look. I know it's cliché but don't actions speak louder than words? I don't know, I'm asking. Are deeds stronger than words? I mean, deeds are short-term. You do something and it can have an immediate impact, but the longer time goes on, how much do those actions matter? Whereas words can survive, man. They can inspire many more deeds. My point, I guess, is—ultimately—what's one without the other? Is either one better? Is either one *truer*?

I dunno, I'm probably not making much sense. Anyway, here's the nutshell—this is me thanking you all for listening. If you never hear from me again, remember the lessons. Don't mourn the man, spawn the plan. Save your tissues. This is a positive step. I hope to the Almighty you all come with me. It's time we stop being *wordsmen* and become *swordsmen*. It's time we [REDACTED].

For my brothers and sisters out there who've been with us on the journey already, my advice to you is to wake early tomorrow. Prepare for what you've been trained to do. That's right, I'm talking about [REDACTED].

[REDACTED].

[REDACTED].

[REDACTED].

And to you all—ominous spiritus. Stay alert. Stand up. Be counted. Oz-man out.

END OF RECORDING

CHAPTER FIFTY-NINE

No morning wake-up call for the guest shack. Jake stayed beneath the blanket, content, letting the morning light dance between the gaps in the slats, over his eyebrows. Time didn't matter. He wasn't hungry. He lay there, thinking back to what had happened—to what they had done.

Not how he had imagined. Not exactly. Not far off, either. There had been a craziness to it— disjointed and wild. The actions of two people who had no real understanding of what they were doing, just doing what felt right in the moment. Mimicking the things they had seen, had heard about. Things he'd only ever thought about.

He was still thinking about them now.

How she felt. How she tasted. How she moved. The soft bits and the hard bits. Helping and hurting.

Speaking of which…

Jake wasn't sure if it was the memory or the morning, but he was a rock.

Only one cure for that, he thought, and he rolled over, sat on the edge of the bunk.

She was already up—or, at least, she wasn't in the bed. Her clothes were gone. He was a little disappointed by that but it made sense. Nature had called, probably. Or she wasn't sleeping well, had gone for an early breakfast. She had loved their fruit selection—watermelon and pear and strawberries. All organic. No ferm-farming here. Never again.

Something else was different. This was the first time she had chosen to be away from him since they met, the first time he had been alone since he'd abandoned his grub steak in *Gina's* on Homer Street to talk to her. The moment the world changed was so long ago to him. How long had it been?

This is the land of lost content, I see it shining plain.

One of the many poems his mother had taught him, the ones he had kept reciting to himself while serving time, holding onto bits of home.

The happy highways where I went and cannot come again.

But he had come again. He was back and he was safe and although he hadn't found them yet, there were people here who would understand, would work to get him what he needed.

He sat alone for a while, reminding himself what alone felt like. It wasn't the same as before. It had lost its dredging, hopeless depth. It had lost its control. Because it wasn't real anymore. She was only a short distance away, walking in the leaves, a cup of real fresh-brew coffee cupped in her hands, no doubt thinking about the night before. He wondered what she had enjoyed the most, what had surprised her, what she had learnt about him. About herself. He got up, pulled on his clothes, went out into the fresh air.

It was bright where the branches deviated and still as cold in the shade. It didn't take long for him to see the sparkle in the dirt—shining plain—the glass pupil of the body-eye sitting there like a gemstone someone had dropped.

No. Not dropped. *Discarded.*

And he knew.

Knew he'd been kidding himself. Knew she was more than a short distance away. That she could have left at any point and he wouldn't have heard her go, exhausted as she had made him. By foot, she could have covered a few miles by now.

If they hadn't already caught her.

CHAPTER SIXTY

The Nissan roared as it broke off from the slip road, headed eastwards on the remains of the motorway. An open run from here to the distant blue haze, though pitted with craters and crawling with vines. Paint marking the lanes had all but washed out. The speedometer crept to ninety. The vehicle wove, surprisingly nimble for an old manual motor. She was glad there was no clutch or gearstick to deal with. Had there been, she'd probably still be trying to back out of the Compound.

Chrissie held the wheel tight, unused to the pedals, let alone hitting these sorts of speeds. Every few seconds she was sure the SUV was going to veer into a spin, give the rust-orange crash barricades a last hurrah. Grass had grown shaggy at the sides of the asphalt, thick enough to leave the vehicle little room for error. Disused street lights spanned like twin rows of crucifixes on the Appian Way.

Her plan was half-baked, she knew. No way she could drive through the customs gate. She had no permit, no identity papers. They would have her on a watch-list. Sky-eyes with facial recognition would spot her, relay her location instantly. But like the country's regime, the Fence was full of holes, full of weak spots, riddled by budget pressures. If countless citizens could find a way out—through subterranean tunnels or otherwise—surely she could find a way in.

It was not a question. She had to get back inside the city.

The Fence was out there somewhere, fifteen miles into the future. Maybe ten. She clicked the window button, welcomed the cool blast of air on her face. The roadmap flapped, flew off the dashboard, landed in the passenger seat. No matter. There was only one direction—where the sun was rising. Only it was in her eyes now, mashed like white butter across the cloudscape, heightening her fear that she might hit something. She lowered the overhead visor.

The truck appeared in the mirror, tiny, barely a shape in the distance, but it was there, on the same route, a behemoth approaching. A delivery run, she figured, one of several still risking the Heaths because the loads were too heavy to fly. The occupants wouldn't stop if they saw Chrissie, wouldn't want to interfere in criminal matters. They would be obliged to call in any threat to their cargo before reaching the Fence. Such an alert would fuck things royally. Security would tighten for an hour or two, make it even more difficult to scout access. The north-west gate would be swarming with patrol teams—human and drone alike.

Speed up, she thought. *Get out of sight. Beat them to the punch.*

No. Turn off somewhere. Wait for them to pass. Give yourself more time...

Time Chrissie didn't have. The engine thrummed, gas pedal flush with the floor.

As her focus split between dodging potholes and figuring out what in Goddess's name would be her next move, a thought—a *crazy as shit* thought—dragged itself together.

A bridge. She needed a footbridge.

Half a mile on she found one, bestriding the road, mottled with graffiti. She drew level, hit the brakes, pulled the Nissan across the centre lane so its length blocked the space between a mound of leaves and a pile of bricks collapsing from the walkway.

Chrissie threw the door open, sprinted to the shoulder, clambered the barricade, scraped skin off her hands, scrabbled up the verge through thickets and weeds, prayed she would make it before the truck bore down.

CHAPTER SIXTY-ONE

"I don't agree with it. Though I am curious as to what you think either of us can do about it."

Professor Kolbeck's home in the Compound had nowhere near the amount of decaying treasures as those he oversaw in the Hellfire Archives. The odd shelf and side table offered tell-tale signs of the man's obsessions. A metronome rocked dispassionately, soundless, on an antique desk. The mechanism that produced its internal click had been removed so it seemed to be counting time for no one and no reason. A semi-automatic pistol, some relic of a long-dead soldier, sat on display in a teak box. Garish sculptures from the Americas of the Old World watched the room with reptilian eyes, fashioned from polished pebbles. The cabin was monastic in its own way.

Jake turned to the window, fought to keep the worry from getting the better of him. The lake was on the other side, rippling and smoothing, helping him stay composed if not calm.

"Chrissie's out there," he said, "probably about to get herself corpsed trying to stop *Cockleshells* from happening."

"I admire your friend's courage, but things are more complicated than you appreciate."

"Rockland said he respects you, Professor. Said you're wise. If you tried talking to him—"

"You think I haven't?" Kolbeck said. "Jake, I've spent many a long evening with that man attempting to explain the mistakes of the past and the nature of human conflict. He's steadfast, has his own views built on his own experiences—whatever those may be. So what good is wisdom when there's nobody to bloody listen?"

"He's not unreasonable," Jake said. "No one is proposing we stop the insurrection. All we want is to get a message to Gallard and her people, tell them not to show up. Who knows? It could help the DIP to understand we're not their real enemy. Stopping *Cockleshells* won't have to change anything about the uprising."

"I'm afraid it could."

Jake turned to find Kolbeck had trained his dark eyes on him, the triangular features of the man radiating tension. The professor pivoted his tall, thin frame, relieved the coffee pot from the stove, let the steam wash over his face.

"Rockland's not trying to stop *Cockleshells* because he's callous," Kolbeck said. "The truth is, he's one step ahead. I'm sorry to say, but the TEP's idea for a fireworks show isn't the only one in town."

"Feels like you're about to tell me I should be sitting down to hear this."

The professor motioned to the chair by his desk. Jake ignored it, leaned against the wall.

"What he hasn't told you," the professor said, "is our ground invasion was never the only part of the plan. They have *Project Cockleshells*. We have *Project Gunpowder*."

"Gunpowder?"

"Been in development for over a year. Meant to take place on the fifth of November, a day we used to call 'Bonfire Night'. No accusing the brains behind that of not having a sense of the theatrical, ay? Then again, *Cockleshells* has its own symbolic timing. It's no coincidence that what they call *Non-Binarist Pride Day* falls on Hallow's Eve. Used to be a time when that day was a celebration of the dead. Kind of ironic, I suppose. They've co-opted it since for their pagan wiccan ritual gobbledygook, tried to tie it into their transcentric—"

"Time is of the essence, Professor."

"My point is the schedule has changed. The footage you managed to obtain didn't just tell us the TEP had their own plot, it told us *when*— one week earlier than ours. If that were to happen, ISZ security will shoot through the roof. They'd put the border on full lockdown, scupper any chance of getting our man inside. So, thanks to you, Gunpowder has been accelerated."

"You're talking in code."

"We have an insider in the ISZ, someone who can access the centre of government without raising suspicion. They'll be planting enough synthetic explosive to bring down half of Whitehall."

"Jesus Christ," Jake said. He moved now to the chair, allowed himself to sit. "It's an arms race."

"Not a bad analogy for it. If Gunpowder goes ahead early, Mary Gallard won't even go on stage tomorrow. If she's lucky, she'll be taken away to a secure location. If she's not, she'll be among those who perish in the blast."

The professor handed Jake a mug of hickory—healthier, according to the good doctor. With it, he gave Jake the space he needed to gather it all together. Two bomb plots. Each expected within a day. Gallard caught between them, along with innumerable innocent lives. And Chrissie out there, risking her own, unaware it would all be futile.

"Pointless," Jake said. "The people in this camp alone probably have enough firepower to takeover London as it is. Why bother blowing up parliament at the same time?"

"Their excuse is to call it a strategic measure. Cripple the centre of leadership, throw a response coordination into disarray. My guess, however, is less elaborate. It's a simple act of vengeance."

"You knew about this—about Gunpowder. You're in on this plan? You, who said violence would only lead to more violence?"

"Quite the contrary," Kolbeck said, looking at the floor. "I voiced my opposition to it. Vehemently. Our revolution should be aiming for peace and equality from the get-go. Of course it should. Rockland doesn't get that. His only aim is to win. He doesn't realise a violent uprising won't end the polarisation of our nation. I argued for an alternative until I was blue in the face and because of that they cast me aside, told to go back to my cave and my musty books. It's why Rockland and I don't see eye to eye anymore. It's why I'm not taking part in his bloody-minded plans."

Jake shook his head, no patience left to be sold on a fait accompli.

"You said before something needed to be done," Jake said. "That we had to—what was the phrase you used?—*confront the potential for chaos.* Sitting back and letting things unravel like this isn't going to help. If anything, you'd be as culpable as the people pushing the buttons. Well, almost as culpable."

"I've spent hundreds of nights considering that same thought," Kolbeck said, as if a cloud had descended. "Won't pretend it doesn't keep me awake. Killing people is a line that, once you cross, you can never cross back. It's the Stygian River of decisions. I'll bet most of Rockland's soldiers don't appreciate that. It changes you. You're never the same person. It scatters you. In many ways, it's suicide."

"Chrissie isn't sitting around, juggling ethical decisions. She's trying to do something. She's trying to prevent chaos."

"Yes. A good woman, for sure. Driven by truth and courage. She understands what needs to be done and she's willing to do it. We could use more people like her. The question is, what are *you* willing to do, Jake?"

"She saved my life. I owe her the same. I have to go after her."

"I'd say you're probably right."

"I am? It'll probably get me killed, too. Every echo in London will be looking for us by now."

"Yes, but at least it's your decision. Dare I say the right one."

"Thanks for the approval. The more important question, Professor—is what about you?"

"Me?"

"Yeah. You spout off about how we have to go out and make a difference, yet you're content to stay here and act like you've already done everything you can, and that's that. I expected more from you. I'm sorry to say, you're a fucking hypocrite."

Kolbeck gave Jake a half smile. "You'd be right, if that were true. Only, I never said that's all I was doing. I said I wasn't willing to go along with Rockland's bloody-minded plans. I'm certainly doing something, Jake. Point is, I can't do it alone."

"Do what alone?"

Kolbeck gulped the brew. Somehow the heat didn't melt the man's throat.

"That footage you brought back to the camp with you," the professor said. "Let's start with that."

Jake's hand delved into his pocket. The body-eye felt somehow different to when he had picked it up that morning. Not as cold. Not as dead. The way the professor looked at it when he reached for it, it felt quite the opposite.

CHAPTER SIXTY-TWO

"Keys are still in here."

The security officer stood at the window of the SUV, one hand capped over his eyes, the other bearing a riot shield—extra caution. He was decked out for trouble, armoured from helmet to kneepads. The way he had taken his time edging towards the abandoned vehicle suggested he rarely left the safety of the sleeper cabin.

His partner, sitting driver's side—as if the truck needed a driver—pressed the voxcom channel button. Her voice crackled through the external speaker, allowed her the luxury of remaining secure inside the vehicle. "Are you sure there's no one in there, Stewart?"

"I'm sure."

"Check again."

The male officer swore under his breath, retraced his steps around the other doors, slow, the nervous poise of someone expecting to be set upon at any moment. He looked up towards the truck, shook his head.

"Then push it out of the way and let's get moving."

"You gonna come out and help?"

The trucker chewed her lip, rubbed the back of her neck. "I shouldn't abandon the cargo. It could be an ambush."

"Great Birth-Giver, Melinda! Don't say that!"

"I'll keep the engine running. Take it off the handbrake. Give it a shove."

"What if it hits the barrier?"

"Who cares? Get it out of the way. Fast."

Scanning her surroundings again, the guard on the outside propped his shield up against the truck's enormous steel wedge plow—part of the vehicle's suit of bolt-on armour that made its occupants feel safe if only because they didn't know any better. He hastened to follow the orders. His legs flailed through the door as he straddled the seat to release the parking lever.

Neither of them heard the thud. Or if they did, they showed no sign of panic.

The SUV started rolling. The guard loped back to the truck, wrestled the shield into his arms, threw it into the cabin, scampered up the side of the fuel tank to get back into the warmth. "Go, go, go!"

The exhaust stack coughed smoke. The Nissan clipped the pile of stone debris, came to a crunching halt. The truck was already accelerating east.

Chrissie Tieman splayed herself out flat against the roof of the trailer, gripped the edge so hard her knuckles burned.

CHAPTER SIXTY-THREE

"That echo bitch. I told you. I *told* you we shouldn't have trusted her."

Sadie was roiling, gun in hand, face as red as her ponytail, which lashed like the tail of a bloodhound on a scent. The rest of the men and women in the cabin watched her, chose instead to fume in silence as they absorbed the news.

"Lying piece 'a shit. I should've shot her as soon as I saw her. She's gonna ruin everything. I told you. I said it right from the start." She whirled, marched up to Jake, put her face up to his, put her gun to his ear, put her spittle on his eyelids. "This motherfucker. He brought her here. He's an ally too, I bet. Let me do him, Rock. Let me—"

"That's enough." Rockland, motionless in his oak seat, his fingers clasped together in a tepee, his metal stare unwavering.

"We can't trust him. He's blown the plan. He's—"

"I said enough."

His voice no louder, his tone no different, but everyone sensed it.

Sadie snapped shut. She shook her head. The barrel fell to her side. She looked like she was about to scream again. She swallowed it, backed off.

"Oscar," Rockland said, "You were with them all yesterday, scoped them both out. Tell Sadie what you observed."

Oscar shrugged. "Got 'em to go up in the broadcast tower unsupervised, like you suggested, chief. They didn't try anything with the equipment. No attempt to dial out. No attempt to sabotage anything. Not that they could have anyway, what with the power off. Kept their hands nice and squeaky."

"You showed them the neighbourhood by the lake?"

"Yep. They reacted as you'd expect them too. Nothing strange."

"And no concealed wires? No weapons?"

Oscar nodded. "Brought nothing else with them. We watched them constantly, every minute they were here, just as you ordered. Tried to make them feel free. Nothing on the closed-circuits showed anything to give us reason to worry. Not until this morning, I mean."

Sadie sniffed. "Stealing a car and driving in the direction of London is reason for us to worry."

"True," said Rockland. "Spy or no spy, that girl will sing like a canary if they pick her up before we do. If she doesn't know about Gunpowder, it may not matter. One can hope. Any news from the search party?"

"Hide nor hair," Wyatt said, smoothing his beard, staring at his radio.

"What about him?" Sadie said, looking Jake's way.

Jake eyed her trigger finger.

Rockland said, "He wouldn't have stayed here if he was conspiring with her. Wouldn't make any sense. Isn't that right, Jacob?"

Jake couldn't tell if he was being set up for a fall. He ran a hand over his face. "She's not one of them."

The comment made Sadie bristle.

"She panicked," Jake went on. "Afraid for her family, that's all. She's risking her life to stop them from getting in harm's way, not trying to interfere with your plans."

"Sure about that?" said Rockland.

The only thing Jake was sure about was that he wasn't sure about anything anymore. "Positive."

"Be a shame if that wasn't the case, though, wouldn't it just?"

Jake nodded.

"So, maybe Sadie's right. Why should we take the same risk with you?"

Ice flushed clear through Jake's veins. Rockland's tall frame rose like morning. The light through the windows behind him made him seem half translucent, a distant tower shaped in the form of man. Moving forward past his loyal troops, he walked directly towards Jake, his pale gaze never tracking, never shifting. The floorboards protested. The leather scabbard trembled against his thigh. It seemed for all the world like he would not stop coming forward, would keep marching determinedly on, cut him down with a single swipe of his paw. He felt the others in the room tense, as if all were one.

But he did stop, an arm's reach in front of Jake. He held out his hand. Jake's bones met, squeezed by bear-strength pressure.

"It's all right, lad. I can tell you're not a part of whatever it is she's doing. All I ask is you promise me you'll help put it right."

Jake cleared his throat. "What do you want me to do?"

"I've told you. Promise me. That's all."

"Right. Yeah."

Rockland released the handshake, turned to Oscar. "Friends, need I state the obvious but the hourglass has turned. Not exactly as we'd planned but there's many a slip betwixt the cup and the lip. We move out at noon. Suit up, quick. Leave your troubles in your tents. This is what we've been preparing for."

The men grunted, whooped, piled for the door.

"Oscar, contact Winter. The game has changed and we need the switch thrown by Fifteen-Hundred hours at the latest. He'll know what's expected."

Oscar nodded, disappeared out the door.

Sadie stepped forward, eyeballed Jake. "We should keep him here. Lock him up in the guest quarters or somewhere. Keep him under guard, in case."

Rockland ignored her. "I'm not going to arm you, son. Don't take that personally. But if you'll care to, I'd like you to be with us, to saddle up and watch us take this country back." Then to Sadie: "Jacob Brody rides with me."

CHAPTER SIXTY-FOUR

Birdsong.

Outside the window, even though there were no trees on this street. Were there?

It didn't matter. It was a rich sound, the perfect wake-up call.

The bedcovers in this nit pit weren't the comfiest but in that moment he could envision staying under them all day if he was permitted. The warmth was bliss.

It was close now. Much closer than he'd realised. Tangible. It was happening.

He spied his voxwatch sitting on the stand, didn't fancy looking at it. Blinds still closed from the night before. A good decision. It was probably getting late. The breathing he could hear was not his own—low and profound and content.

Wow. That.

He played it again in his mind, re-trod the steps, re-spoke the lines. He was getting to the good part when her voxwatch jingled.

It took a moment for him to recognise it. Only a handful of people had means to call him and they did so rarely. It had to be important.

Oscar. What the hell did he want? He could hear him coming through the line sounding amper stoked.

A hitch, he was saying. A small change of plan. A possible spook in the Compound. Accelerate the mission, he was saying. Project Gunpower has to happen today, goddamit. Has to happen before Fifteen-Hundred.

That soon. Moving it forward was madness. Barely enough time to make any final checks.

As if it made a difference. The mission was already a shot in the dark.

Project Gunpowder was a ballsucker. Project Gunpowder was fingernail lottery.

Was he ready?

Yes. He thought so.

Be so.

What was that about an intelligence leak?

Forget that. Get moving.

He told Oscar, fine, the final phase of Gunpowder was in motion, cut the line, lay there still for another minute. Another. It seemed like every time he told himself he would move, he would allow himself a few more seconds. What was a few more seconds, anyway? A few more seconds to anything is nothing. And, if you wanted to, couldn't you keep leaving anything for a few more seconds? Time after time, until time lost its meaning and nothing mattered anymore anyway?

He thought about Project Gunpowder and his end goal and the switch in him flipped without him having to think about it and that was the last of the few more seconds.

He rolled to his side, gently as he could. The round of the cadet's hips, the slide of her waist, the adorable dips where her tail bone met that badass backside that had been bounding and rebounding on top of him all night.

Oh, poor thing.

Not so animated now, huh? Out of it. Would probably have the worst hangover ever if she were to wake up. Punch drunk and pretty and purring as she was.

A shame. A nice girl. Kind you could take home to mum.

A shame it had to end, but it was never there to last, was it?

He rolled the other way, reached into the bedside drawer, took the Gigli saw out, the one Doc Sharma gave him right before he'd set out. A simple design. Nothing but razor wire strung between two handles. Good for escape, the Doc had told him. Good for all sorts if you find yourself in a tight spot.

Thank you, he whispered to the cadet. The girl stirred.

Birdsong. Perhaps a nest on one of the balconies.

Get on with it, kid. Gunpowder cannot wait.

Because Project Gunpowder was roulette. Project Gunpowder was Dillinger. Project Gunpowder was locopops.

CHAPTER SIXTY-FIVE

Mauled by the autumn air, Chrissie ran. Her only option. She was a woman without access now—no name, no state, no money.

When the truck had passed through the Fence, she had crawled down between the trailer and the cabin to evade the sky-eyes, bolted over the e-gate, squeezed against the layers of grime built up along the armoured panelling. They had not seen her. With luck on her side, the vehicle had not been pulled over for random screening. Had it been, she imagined she would now be sitting in a cell surrounded by Ministry officials picking her apart like carrion. The thought of her situation—of what it was not—was the only thing keeping her warm. Over time, she told herself, the blood in her legs would thaw, would spread to the rest of her, would alleviate the agony of half-frozen ears and fingers.

On she staggered, once again forced to scurry through alleys and side streets. Her fingers wrung from the cold. Her lungs strained. Pain detonated through her shins with each stride. By the time she made it to the steps of the townhouse apartment, she was ready to drop. She hammered the bell, ordered herself to *hold out, hold out, hold out…*until the door buzzed, cracked open.

"Miss Tieman—what—what are you doing here?"

"Live…I live…here," she rasped, pushed past Andre, made her way to the living room.

"But you're…they're looking for you."

Chrissie made a motion for him to shut the door. She lurched to the window, leaned into it far enough to confirm an empty street, snapped the blinds, sank against the radiator.

Her flat, a mess. No sign of the valet's usual care and attention. A sleeping bag, rolled out on the sofa. Cartons and cups and packets of food lay partially eaten on the coffee table. She wanted to ask him what the hell was happening. Her breath was having trouble keeping up. Deep down she knew she didn't want to find out.

Andre stood on the opposite end of the room, arms pulled around him, tugging at his shirt.

He said, "No one has heard from you. I thought you were…in trouble. There were reports on the netwires. We were all fearing the worst. Why are you dressed like—"

"Where's Charlotte?"

Andre shook his head. "They took her. Her and Daniel, both."

The room hummed. Tendons and joints tingled. She ignored the pain, pawed at the wall, found her feet, tried to regain some semblance of stability. "When?"

"Couple of days ago. They told me to stay here. To let them know if…"

"If you say anything about this, Andre—anything at all—"

"I won't, I swear! I don't want any part of it."

She wanted to believe him. Only reason they wouldn't have taken him into custody with her sister is because they would have sensed his weakness, would know they could trust him to be their scared little messenger boy. It left her with a bad decision to make.

She would have killed to go to the shower, throw herself under a hot one. Zero time for that. She went instead to the kitchen. More mess. She ran the tap. The water, sweet. She slugged mouthfuls, splashed it over her face until her hair dripped. He watched her from the doorway.

Chrissie thought again about Dennehy's footage, about the conversation with the equality minister, the orders security were being given to ignore any bomb threats. Raising the alarm remotely wasn't going to change things. At best, it would flag the system, activate a unit of echoes to descend on the flat in minutes.

"I need you to do something for me," she said. "I need you to book a cab, pre-paid. Have it arrive on the corner as soon as possible. Tell them some other name—tell them it's for…Sadie. Tell them it's to go to Trafalgar Square, or as near as possible."

"Okay, okay." No hesitation.

He hurried to the smartscreen by the kitchen door, opened the voxchat, asked for transport services, said exactly what she had told him to say. The automated voice told him her ride would be there in seven minutes, thanked him for his order, reminded him that *wherever you are, wherever you need to go, we'll always be waiting for you.*

They sweated it out without words. Chrissie fingered the blinds every once in a while. For whatever reason, he tidied, piled greasy pizza boxes and foil trays into the bin. Seven minutes later the voxchat gave a jingle.

"Andre, one more favour." He stared at an empty Choco-Lite ale can on the floor, rolled it with his toe. "A ten-minute head start. That's all I ask."

He didn't look up.

She left the door swinging open behind her.

CHAPTER SIXTY-SIX

The strong aroma of its mane, enough to bring it all back.

Rough sprints through the fields. Daredevil jumps over abandoned stiles. Days of cantering alone, miles from the nearest settlement, the sun on his back.

Jake's heels squeezed against the beast's sides, moved it forward. The old muscles still there. He ran a hand along the pale grey coat, made the hairs turn silver in the light.

Rockland nodded, acknowledging Jake's ease in the saddle. The Compound's leader sidled up on his own mount—a mahogany bay stallion with a fur hide, a bedroll draped over its croup. On Rockland's own back was an automatic rifle. A bandolier swung across his chest. His knife stayed attached to his hip, counter-weighting the handgun on the other side of his belt.

Ahead of them, troops filed past, some in cars, some on motorcycles, heading for the main roads. Pickup trucks went by loaded with Rockland's largesse—weapons, radio equipment, food supplies— primed for the crusade. The militia on horseback broke off at the fork, made their way into the trees, the meadow lanes beyond. Dust and exhaust rose.

With them went the other camps—hundreds of soldiers from disparate communities, allying under one banner, prepared to put aside their differences to take down a system that had long ago cast them all into the wilderness.

"What's our course?" Jake said.

Rockland's cavernous tone was an engine starting. "Horse riders are going in pairs, through the forests. There's a couple of security bases adjacent to the Fence—their first line of defence. We'll hit those first. We have hackers already in the servers and auxiliary tech teams making their way in. They'll shut down the power grids and the communication networks as soon as we give the order, open the gates for the rest of our road-forces coming in through the motorways. Meanwhile, our underground units are spreading out below the city and should start popping up as soon as they get the nod."

Jake hadn't expected to hear the detail.

He said, "What do you want me to do?"

"Follow my lead, son. Keep your eyes open and make sure you stay out of harm's way if things start getting dicey."

"And then?"

"Troops keep moving forward and you keep following. Don't worry, you'll pick it up."

"Easier said than done."

"Ah, you'll be fine. That or you'll find yourself in Abraham's bosom soon enough."

He winked, let Jake know he was kidding. Sort of.

Jake's horse pulled on the reins, wanting to dip its head to chew grass. Jake let it take a bite.

Oscar came driving up the path in a four-by-four, a solemn wave as he went by. Sadie rode with him. She did not wave. She and Jake stared it out until the vehicle disappeared into the tall haze. A flatbed truck went by—Wyatt sitting in the box with a platoon of other soldiers, an RPG resting in his lap. He looked happy.

"You're scared," Rockland observed.

Jake shook his head. "I wouldn't say scared. Nervous, sure. What if this goes wrong?"

"You could ask yourself that. Or you could ask yourself, 'what if it all works out?'"

Jake thought about that.

"You feel like this world was never meant for you, Jacob?"

"Every day since they took me from my home."

"I understand. Often feels like I have no expectations of it—that it likely has none of us, either. I see it as a place I used to live in but have since left and, if the universe deems it right and fair, I'll create something new so I don't have to feel that way anymore. That none of us do. 'Between me and thee will be a great gulf fixed'. Do you get what I'm saying?"

"I do."

He was a man who at once made Jake feel ease and fear. Jake could envisage Rockland in battle, here or at any other time in history.

Rockland pulled his steed eastwards, broke into a gallop.

CHAPTER SIXTY-SEVEN

Festival atmosphere. The only time of year the Privet was opened up, when Out-Zoners could wander through without paperwork. Droves of spectators made the most of it, going south on Regent Street, all the way through Piccadilly Circus, towards the square. Yellow and orange. Banners and umbrellas at the ready. Bubble machines.

A few of them had spoken to him on the way, pulled him aside to ask for directions and other details. *Are there toilets, officer? How many people are you expecting to show up to this thing? Who are you voting for, officer? Harr-dee-harr-harr.*

The uniform was transformational. *Drew public attention where his last get-up shied it off. Looked great on him, too, it had to be said. A tad snug in obvious places but the rookie had otherwise been of a similar height.* On the streets, the non-binarists acted comfortable around her. The CisHets looked down when they saw him, even crossed the road. *Didn't want any trouble.*

They would be overflowing at this rate, into Whitehall and the Strand. *The late ones still hoping to soak up some atmosphere even if they had no chance of seeing anyone famous in the flesh.*

Pall Mall. Where the motorcade was scheduled to pass, on its way to deliver the prime minister and her no doubt vitriolic speech. He had spent months obsessing over the street and its details, reviewing the photos, taking the virtual tours, sketching the buildings and side roads on napkins. Since arriving in the ISZ he'd been able to put sole to pavement, walk through the neighbourhood, see it up close for the first time. The PM and her Tribe wouldn't travel it again. Their green room at Portcullis House would be a hole in the ground by two o'clock. *Hallow's Eve fireworks direct from the Big Smoke.*

The spectacle would be impressive. *A real window-shaker.*

He stopped at a datapoint, touched the cadet's badge to the reader, accessed the Central Network, requested information on the security details around the area, on the approach to Parliament Street. He absorbed the intel, caught his reflection in the screen.

Damn, girl.

Fire engine red smile. That lipstick found in the cadet's utility pouch. A cute tribute to a cute officer.

The emergency access points to Portcullis were guarded, but not well. Not according to the system logs seized by the intelligence team. They had scrambled when the order to initiate Gunpowder early came in, set him up with the access codes, the work-shift timings, the names of individual officers on rotation. In with a grin. Out with a pout.

Music. Bombastic brass. He turned to see a teen trans girl with speakers strapped to her back, blasting 'Here Come the Girls'. Four-hundred unfuckable freaks and fatties wooed at once, flung their hands up, made little half-dance motions.

Ew-kay. Now entering Cringe Town.

The sooner this was over, the better.

CHAPTER SIXTY-EIGHT

Supporters of the Diversity and Inclusion Party had already set up camp two hours before Mary Gallard's special address. Three until the prime minister would try to minimise the damage with a speech of her own. The most ardent—those claiming territory at the foot of the steps to the National Gallery—wore t-shirts emblazoned with catchphrases. Words by Maria Suarez-Adarsha. Words by Mary Gallard. Bordering problematic, but nothing extreme enough to risk arrest.

Breathing space in the square only evident by spectators unfurling banners, unpacking neon bracelets, unleashing balloons. Children ate toffee apples, waved fibre optic glow wands, watched drag queens writhing on poles. Equality officers and censors patrolled the perimeter, hyped on nerves, eagled the slogans for anything offensive. Sky-eyes roved on drift-mode. Treatment stations set up early, ready to release herds of hi-vis therapists if it all became too triggering. Emotional support dogs waited and wagged.

Where the stone column once stood, the statue of Suarez-Adarsha gleamed an effervescent black, marble rivulets snaking like superheroine electricity around her chiselled limbs. Her stone eyes ignored the crowd, gazed instead at the stars somewhere beyond the screen of afternoon cloud. No one dared to touch the plinth. The lionesses at her feet remained unstraddled.

On the terrace, a rainbow of heads vied for inches, strained for a view, faces resembling the hundreds of feral pigeons displaced to the ledges where they watched the throngs with dumb captivation. Food stands encouraged the festival mood, hawked vegan tacos, buckets of melted cheese, Belgian waffles that oozed ersatz chocolate. A band on the Gallery promenade pumped transcore pop-punk. Cloud spit bounced off instruments, off plastic cagoules.

Despite the ripple of energy pulsing through the masses, Zoe Urwin was happy to note the atmosphere was nothing compared to the typical TEP gathering. The voters here were less verbose, less volatile, less likely to form a screaming circle when confronted by a difference of opinion. Watching them on the surveillance monitors from the comfort of zer office, zie caught zerself smiling.

They were there to witness a *zistoric* day, though not in the way they hoped.

Zoe pictured the panic, wondered if the barriers would hold, if the officers would maintain control.

Zie asked zer voxchat for a location update for the TEP volunteers—buses of supporters being shipped in from all corners of the city. Vital. They would be the ones who would tell the story. Their eye-witness accounts, shaped and moulded in the coming weeks, would become the trusted narrative, would lay the blame where needed.

Two hours until showtime.

Zoe called Dennehy. Dominic was right. The sergeant had to be checked up on, managed carefully.

Dennehy appeared on screen, perched on a crate in full uniform, accessorised with white ceremony gloves. "Ma'am-sir?"

"Give me an update."

"Not much to report. No disturbances. I can see the Gallery steps clear as crystal. It's a waiting game now, Minister."

The officer took a glance through the magnification lens she had set on a tripod by the window.

Zoe said, "Tech working?"

The sergeant picked up the sky-eye remote, checked the battery life, tested the display, confirmed it all looked good. The blast they had in mind would certainly wipe the smile off Gallard's face. Probably wipe her head clear off her neck.

"What about our guest?" Zoe said.

A smirk. "He doesn't have much to say, either."

The sergeant twisted the voxcam, showed him lying on the floor, tape around his mouth, motionless in his bonds, baby blues wide as plates.

Peter Cobbleswan would have something to offer the world after all.

CHAPTER SIXTY-NINE

Digital access was cream cheese. His handlers' work, not his. The biometric pass scanned without incident. He was inside the building in minutes, under the immense glass roof, the place big enough to house rows of trees and eateries along the arcade, upkeep courtesy of the CisHet Tax and endless penalties.

But physical access—the ability to enter without causing suspicion—that was his gig. A trans female walking through the piazza was one thing. An equality officer, another. Staff fell over themselves to wish him a nice day, to allow him to pass. Other officers—real ones—gave him an accepting nod.

Avoid them.

No, without making it look like you're avoiding them.

Can't risk it. The wrong question, the hint of a flaw in his character...

The meeting room. What was it called, again? The sign by the stairs listed all the names on little bronze plaques.

Right! There. Floor Three of Six.

The Kinsey Suite.

He waited by the lifts until a suit came through and swiped her badge for Third. He followed her in, spent his time fluffing his eyelashes in the mirrored wall to swerve eye contact.

Elevator music, vintage racket, auto-tuned and awful.

Third floor was a henhouse. Clucking staffers and secretaries and security all vying for air in the corridor. The echo on elevator-watch nodded him through, assumed he was escorting the suit.

No need to correct him. This was already hard enough.

The Kinsey was on the west wing, a one-hundred yard walk along plum carpet, past people looking for any reason to be suspicious.

Look purposeful. Pick up the pace.

He targeted the adjacent suite—the one with double oak doors, a framed oil of some former TEP figure. All smarm, no charm. And no echoes guarding that one.

He reached the entrance ahead of a woman trolleying fresh flowers to the Kinsey, didn't stop, went right in, closed the doors, flipped the bolts at floor and ceiling.

Ho-ly crap.

He was in. On the other side of the wall from where the delegations would meet. Near enough for the shockwave to take them out, maybe the entire wing fifty metres up, down and across. Brick and plaster would turn into shrapnel moving twenty-six thousand feet per second. The fireball would do the rest.

Project Gunpowder was clown cake, baby. Project Gunpowder was a mindjob.

Where to stow it? Somewhere by the wall nearest to the Kinsey, every inch a factor.

An antique bureau there, glass cabinet atop, unlocked, full of legal books—trans/genderqueer authors only. Still heavily censored, no doubt. He pulled a few of them forward to create a gap wide enough.

A pause to listen out. Hard to tell.

Hurry it up.

The tape pulled at the skin of his abdomen. His choice to go with something reliable—but damn, good thing he waxed. The device off now, its pocket-size composition disguising its power. He used the tape to jam it to the backboard, re-positioned the books a little. They bulged, not too noticeable. Unlikely anyone would clock it.

He tucked his shirt back in, thought about safe ground, about remote detonation, signal proximity. Far enough to not be deafened, not so far as to miss the fireworks. Wouldn't miss that for the round wide world.

Time to dip.

Hadn't heard them come in. Not the man in the skirt. Not his security officers. Heard the echoes flanking them, sure, but too late to matter.

Heard the bloke say now, "Glad you could make it."

Saw them come down on him, both sides, black and blue and heavy. Strange. Couldn't feel it. Couldn't feel anything. Couldn't breathe.

"Bigot, you think we didn't know you were coming?" said the Amazon kneeling on his neck. "Ooh, you're done, bigot, you're done."

The crossdresser swung the cabinet open, pulled the books out, let them land on the floor near his head.

It was over.

Project Gunpowder was Elvis.

CHAPTER SEVENTY

Rockland glanced at his watch again, stretched his neck over the barrier, scratched his jaw.

The lookout tower was built in the image of the broadcast tower in the Compound, air just as fresh. Had them all across the Heaths, he said. Vantage points on the road to invasion. The horses waited at ground-level, picked at the sward.

Jake took another look through the monocular. The wild landscape hit a stop where the concrete of civilisation began. A curl of blue smoke on the eastern skyline marked the route into London. Red smoke on either side showed where some of the other troops were being directed to flank the nearest security base. Once they rode down into the flat land, even with the help of a lookout tower, it would be difficult to see anything beyond the interminable road, the innumerable concrete ruins.

The clink-grind of Rockland's lighter broke the stillness. The man in charge heated his cigar, checked his watch again, shook his head, snapped open the saddlebag. The radio came out.

"Alpha-One to Charlie-One," Rockland said. "Do you read?"

Oscar came through fuzzy. "Charlie-One. Reading loud and clear, chief."

"Anything yet?"

"Negative."

"What about the police frequencies?"

"Business as usual."

"Huh." The cigar moved from one side of his mouth to the other and back.

"What's your thinking?" Oscar asked.

"Another twenty minutes."

"And if we have nothing by then?"

The radio hissed.

"Rock, something's wrong!" Jake recognised Sadie's voice, fragmented by poor reception. "I can feel it…stinks to high heaven.

They know what's happening…insider intel, maybe…trying to stop the revolution…"

"Relax," Oscar said into the handset. He shot a glance Jake's way.

"It's bad news, I'm tellin' ya…walking into a trap…the two of them are in it tog—"

"Don't waver on me now, Sadie. I need you good and frosty."

"But Rock—"

"Man-up. This second, sweetheart. Man-up." He waited for a response, didn't hear one. "We're going to be fine. Whether they know we're coming or not, what do they have that can match our firepower?"

Oscar again. "Nothing, chief."

"Not a damn thing. So, twenty minutes. If we still hear nothing from Winter, move into formation two and wait for my order."

A chatter of overlapping confirmation. Rockland tossed the radio back in the bag. He stayed looking out at the expanse.

"I'm not working against you," Jake said. "I don't know what's going on."

"I believe you."

"But in case there's any doubt—"

"Not from me, there's not."

Jake inhaled. "You're trusting."

"Jacob," he said, taking out the cigar. "Few realise their life—the absolute essence of their character, their capabilities and their audacities—is only the expression of their belief in the safety of their surroundings."

Jake nodded.

"This is the test of our mettle, how we respond in moments of doubt. We are not fair-weather folk, are we? Are *you*?"

"No."

Rockland limbered his arms, headed for the stairs.

CHAPTER SEVENTY-ONE

Chrissie edged her way through the crush of damp shirts and humid bodies. The thick clothes they had provided her at the Compound were stifling. She pulled off the parka, left it over the back of a bench, let her hair hang loose, hoped she could blend in.

Armoured echoes milled about the throng like cattle herders, taze sticks drawn. The steps of the National Gallery were at the opposite side of the square, supporting a grandstand. Microphones and videyes fringed the terrace where the VIP area had been cordoned off.

The One Strand office building stood to the east. Dennehy would be in there, somewhere on the fourth floor, positioned, waiting. Hints of movement behind several of the windows, too distant to make out any detail. Clearer to see was the security presence along the pavement—a twenty-strong line of Amazons, fully kitted up, blocking the entrance.

An impossible route.

Chrissie pushed instead towards the VIP area, not knowing what her plan would be once there, only knowing there might be the chance of someone in Gallard's team to walk along the area, close enough to wander within earshot. Might be enough. Couldn't trust the police or the dark-suited security staff to hear her out. They'd have her tits in a vice in some covert facility before she could eek out an explanation.

Wasn't that the likely outcome anyway? With no way of knowing where Gallard was, she needed a messenger, someone with a direct line to the top who would take her warning seriously. But what were the odds she could tell some staff member that their leader was about to be publicly executed and then slip away unnoticed?

No choice. No time. Had to try, had to keep moving. The fate of the country relying on her to throw her immense spanner of information in the works. No turning back now.

A press section, right by the stage. Journos with lapel mics coiffed their hair in lenses, streamed early insider footage on their smartpalms. A red carpet ran adjacent, designed to give the politicians face-time as if they were Hollywood stars. Best seats in the house. Maybe that would help…

A familiar whir shaved the air above her. Chrissie dipped her head, planted her hand over her face. The insectoid sky-eye skimmed the crowd, a single unblinking eyeball. They would have a recognition bulletin out for her. One accidental glance into a surveillance asset and all local equality systems would home in on her position, flag the find to all echoes within a five-mile radius.

The stench of anxious people hung in the air like a film. Chrissie kept elbowing through until she reached the press barrier. Security manned the entrances, scanned irises, squeezed voxcoms.

Now what?

She stood there asking herself the same question on repeat until a netwire crew from *The Independent* showed up. Chrissie recognised the field reporter—a pixie-haired hackette who never let the truth get in the way of her personal opinion. Jenny something. The reporter took up the lead, barged through spectators, ignored the handlers carrying her handbag and mid-morning latte, demanded the security staff move aside. Behind her came makeup people, lighting engineers, sound technicians, all lugging broadcast equipment.

Chrissie waited until they were waved through en masse. She slid in, tagged onto the back of the group, stuck close, lightly grasped the end of a tripod being hauled by a clueless engineer.

No one raised an eyebrow.

The hard part done. She slipped away among the other media teams. She had nothing to do now but wait, hope someone—anyone—from the DIP stopped near the press pit before the clock ran down.

Minutes stretched. Producers mingled. Technicians tinkered. Reporters made sure everyone knew they were as important as they were irritable. The band on the Gallery promenade struck up a rendition of *Fanny Fandango*'s greatest trans punk hits.

CHAPTER SEVENTY-TWO

Chaos churned like an undercurrent at Portcullis House. More security staff than Tavistock had ever seen in one building. Amazon officers grouped at every door and escalator.

Hannah held up her hand, stopped her cohort of staff in its tracks, took a voxcall in her earpiece. Tavistock knew her protection chief well enough to spot the difference in how she moved, head whipping side to side, shoulders lifting. A cat confronted.

Hannah pulled one of her deputies to the side, leaned in close to talk to her, came back to the group. "Ma'am, small change of plan. We're to go to the Chapel."

"Why?"

Hannah didn't answer, strode towards the private elevator. Her team steered the ministerial staff behind her in that gentle yet forceful way to which the prime minister had become accustomed over the years. The Chapel was beneath the ground floor, a suite of dim conference rooms far beneath the airy, skylit lounges and cafés of the foyer. Down there, ISZ tube carriages rumbled behind the walls. The undercurrent pulled at her. The elevator descended. Tavistock stared at the digital countdown, bounced her foot against the carpet.

Zoe Urwin, in the Chapel, slouched in an executive office chair. Made sense. Someone had to have pulled the emergency cord. Not alone, either. Dominic Kimmel behind zer, as ever, his chest a little puffed, smile a little too proud to suit him. A host of other cabinet familiars at the boardroom table. Members of her Tribe. Ezra Kennedy, the trade secretary. Nola Olufemi, the education minister. Belinda Marsh, the TEP's chief scientist, not looking herself without her lab coat. Echoes filed into the room, hustled for standing space in the wings.

"What is this?" Tavistock asked, finding most of her voice again.

As soon as she asked, the line of Amazon officers at the opposite end of the table ruffled, parted to give her view. A dishevelled uniform, bruised cheekbones, bloodied lip, mascara streaked cheeks, tragedy in colour.

"Where is he?" Tavistock said.

Urwin swivelled in zer chair. "Minister?"

"The priv. The priv who did this, who hurt this officer—"

The equality minister shook her globular head. "No priv did this."

Back at the victim—the limp frame, the torn attire. The poor thing was taking an unusual stance, a sort of half crouch. No. Not exactly. The officer was bound—plasticuffs lashing her wrists behind her to the wall-mounted radiator panels. Tavistock drew in for a closer look. Her security staff stepped out of her way. The cuffs were echo standard issue.

"Then who is she?" Tavistock said.

"Now that's the question you should be asking." An edge to Zoe's voice the PM hadn't heard zer use in open conversation before. "The one we should all be asking."

"I want an answer."

"I warned you, Minister, of what would happen if we allowed ourselves to relax—to let them play their dirty tricks, to let radical binarism thinking infiltrate our society."

"The privs?"

"The savages out there in the Heaths. The vicious, vile bigots. Who else? They sent this—" she jabbed her finger at the beaten figure, "—to be our undoing. To destroy us and everything we've spent years building."

Tavistock edged closer. "I asked you—who is she?"

Zoe's chins pendulated. "An illusion. An abomination. A subterfuge sniffed out only thanks to the brave and fierce efforts of the Ministry's intelligence services."

Dominic approached the table, said, "Our surveillance proved to be flawless, Minister. We caught them in the act—"

"Hush, Dominic," Zoe said. "Hannah and her team led the counteroperation. Let her explain."

Dominic shrank back to his corner. The security chief strode forward. The room a hot-box, smaller by the second.

Hannah said, "We've known for some time, ma'am. They were planning a large-scale attack. I hope you'll understand that we had to keep that information private but for a select few."

"What on earth are you talking about? What attack?"

"They made a last-minute change of tact. We've been tracking this individual since their arrival in the ISZ. They planted an explosive near the Kinsey Suite. They intended to assassinate you and the others— everyone attending the meeting."

The conspirator blinked, grimaced, brown eyes closing.

"She's not an echo?" Tavistock asked no one in particular, now only a stride away from the pathetic captive.

"Not even an ally, ma'am."

Seething, Tavistock closed the gap, swung her open hand hard across the captive's head. "How did you get in here? Tell me! Tell me, you ghastly woman!"

The captive rolled her head back, peered out through puffy eyes. Blood trickled from her lips. The voice fought through pain to get out. "Fuck...you..."

Tavistock turned to Urwin for help, waited for her enormous colleague to stagger out of the chair, squeeze past security towards her. The EQM's hand on her shoulder, righting her balance. Other than the uneven breath of the would-be assassin, no one in the room made a sound.

"This isn't easy to explain," Urwin said. "Better if you see it for yourself—the depths of their deceit, the extent the binarists are willing to go to ruin us."

See what? she wanted to say. *Please, Zoe, don't make this harder than it has to be.*

Zoe Urwin gestured to the voxchat orb at the centre of the boardroom table. The display blew up a mugshot into giant proportions—an intake record from one of the Coolers, dated ten years. The inmate's vitals rolled down the visual: his name, age, ethnicity, eye colour, a dozen other facts. The 3D scan of the new joiner's face rotated slowly. A young cis male, stubble-chinned and hard-boned. Pretty typical. He didn't look familiar.

"Who is he?" Tavistock said.

Zoe pulled up another display, this time one of the standard Safe Zone passes issued to trans and genderqueer citizens—the Key to the

City, as some called it. Like the mugshot, the pass came with its own head scan. The Prime Minister watched the feminine features turn, as if in a slow orbit. A beautiful trans woman. Plump lips. Dark almond eyes. Cheekbones to die for. It took a moment, but Tavistock recognised her now.

The prisoner.

The assassin.

There, two feet away from her. Not a woman after all. Not as flawless in the real world. Certainly not with the bruises she'd been given.

Zoe sighed. The display screen bleeped. The two 3D scans centred, overlaid, ghosted against each other.

A facial match.

The undercurrent in the room surfaced, rolled through the attendees in the form of a collective scream.

The sight of it didn't make sense to the prime minister. It made dark, secretive memories skewer her reality, took the breath out of her like she had been kicked off her feet, pummelled in the solar plexus.

Impossible. *Disgraceful.*

This thing. An insult to their kind. An insider. A fraud.

Tavistock turned away, found others in the room doing the same. Amy Lovelace looked grey. Hardened echoes and Amazons wailed. Someone among them was chanting under their breath, praying to the Goddess of the Pool.

Marsh said. "A CisHet male augmented to appear as one of us. Silicone breasts. Fat-grafted buttocks. The process short of genital surgery but enough for him to blend in amongst us."

Zoe's hand back on the prime minister's shoulder. "They're infiltrating us. These are the lengths they'll go to. No one can be trusted."

Tavistock wanted to be sick. "Disgusting…I can't…"

"It's all right, Minister. We've stopped them in their tracks. Do you see now? Do you understand?"

"Gallard…where is she?"

"On her way to Trafalgar Square."

"I want to watch it. The speech. I want to see it."

Zoe snorted. "You deserve to, Minister. We deserve to watch it together."

The captive made a sound, shoulders shaking. Silence fell on the room again.

"I'm…" the captive said. "I'm…no…woman…"

"Yes," Tavistock said. "I bloody well know that."

"…And neither…are you…"

The captive spit blood, grinned through broken teeth, laughed like the whole thing was some comic send-up.

Zoe motioned to the Amazons, "Officers, take this *thing* away."

Tavistock stepped back. The team of elite guards unfastened the imposter, grasped it by the hair and arms, dragged it across the room with its synthetic augmentations scraping against the Berber carpet.

Tavistock said, "Where are you taking him?"

Marsh followed behind them. "Disposal, ma'am."

CHAPTER SEVENTY-THREE

He came back up the knoll. Jake got the sense from the way he moved—kind of heavy, kind of casual—that all was fine and the plan was on track and their man on the inside had reported in. So it was a surprise when Rockland told him.

"Lost contact with our agent," he said. "One who was going to be our distraction, create the void we were going to fill. Either bailed on us last minute or got caught. Probably the latter."

"I'm guessing we're not calling the insurrection off."

"We planned for this possibility. If their leaders are still active, it makes this harder, but it certainly doesn't make it impossible."

Rockland kicked debris away from a patch of ground, crouched, set down the rifle and his bag, stood the radio equipment up. He had brought dry wood back with him, used it now to cobble together a little pyre, added a pinch of tinder, sparked it with a ferro rod and striker, the kind Jake's father used to insist on using even when they had matches or a lighter. It caught in seconds. Jake followed his instructions to keep building it up until it was about shoulder-width wide.

As the fire grew, Jake said, "If they caught your saboteur, they probably know we're coming, right?"

"Not necessarily."

"But they would make them talk, wouldn't they? Interrogate them for information?"

He shrugged. "Not interrogate. Torture. That's why we never told him everything we'd planned out."

Jake was surprised by the man's indifference, speaking like he was counting clouds.

"The authorities only know," Rockland continued, "that the honest people of this nation lie quietly no more. Be interesting to see how they respond. For us, it's still an advantage—not having them know what we're doing, what we're planning next. Conjure all sorts of things in their imagination, let them build it up into a panic."

Jake had to ask, had to confirm what he thought was true. It had been building up all this time, back since the workshops, when the big guns were first out on show. "You're banking on them surrendering quickly."

"For the most part."

Jake nodded. "And for the least part?"

"Few years' back, the Heaths weren't so organised, I can tell you. Took some doing to connect all the colonies and compounds and camps into one unified force. When we were divided, we were vulnerable. They knew that fact better than we did. And fuck me if they didn't act on it. The shock troop tactics they sent to decimate your home were happening all over the country back then. But eventually the Resistance started getting itself together. I was fortunate to be part of one of the first major counter operations."

He stopped for a moment, plucked the cigar from his breast pocket, inspected it, rolled it between his thumb and forefinger.

"We set up a dummy town," Rockland went on. "Made it look like we had a new settlement in the works and didn't bother trying to hide it much from aerial view. Our unit mustered arms and protective gear, made sure we were water-tight on security, then bunkered down a few klicks away. A few weeks passed and we got wind of a convoy heading in from the east, moving towards the town. We lay in wait, let them make themselves at home. The look on their faces when they found no one there…" He smiled, shaking his head. "…And the look on their faces when we showed up. Trannies are always more like girls than they are boys. They tend to scream when they're surprised, have you noticed that? Even if they claim that's an old stereotype, it's true. Cry, too, for the most part. Anyway, it didn't take long for us to disarm them, round them up."

Rockland leaned forward, held his cigar to the flames, singed the end back to life. Jake said nothing. He knew there was more.

"Their commanding officer—good-looking she was for an ally. Rare among that lot. But delusional. Fancied herself a tough one, demanded we release them all immediately. Suppose she'd only ever known simps her whole life, beta boy allies who'd jump at the snap of her fingers. Our company commander ignored her demands, of course. Instead he made a few of his own." He dragged on the cigar, exhaled slowly. "She didn't seem so tough having to eat her own shit in front of her troops. Hell of a sight to behold, though. Could barely stomach it myself. Still, credit to her—through sweat and tears, she choked it all down somehow. After that, every damn one of them couldn't wait to renounce the TEP, promising to do whatever we asked. A whole Amazon ground force bawling like babies, pleading for mercy. To be honest, I believe that's what we gave them in the end. Once their fallen captain had picked the corn out of her teeth, we allowed her to contact their base, tell them what had happened and request help. We cleared out right after that."

"That's it? You didn't…corpse them?"

"No, Jacob. We didn't. We got a roll of steel wire, tied them all together nice and tight, like you would a bale a' hay. Left them like that in one of the main tents and watched from the hills as their people came in and…" He swooped his fist downward, opened it up, raised it to the sky. "Hit the damn thing with an airstrike. Their people did not give one casual crap. Remember thinking they probably wanted them gone, too. Like a bad memory. A stain on their character. Because that's who we're dealing with, Jacob. People who'd just as quickly roll over their own to keep their lie alive."

The fire popped. The heat drifted back onto Jake's face. He said, "You're planning on blood today, aren't you?"

"We're planning on striking hard, putting an end to all this quickly, and not giving them time to hit the kill switch."

Jake's knee bounced. He turned away from the pyre. "Or any real time to surrender…"

"There's logistics to consider, Jacob. Holding prisoners takes resources. We don't have time for that while we're on the move. Afterwards? Yeah, sure. There'll be prisoners. A whole ton of 'em. The good news is we'll keep them safe from their own this time." He made a sound like a laugh. "After all, they've kept their re-education camps and youth institutes nice and ready to welcome new tenants."

Like for like. Tit for tat.

Jake said, "So all that stuff about the guns only being a scare tactic…"

Rockland stared back at him across the fire, not afraid of eye contact, not hiding a damn thing now.

"We're sending a message, son. They have to be reminded what we can do. They want to be treated like kings and queens? We'll be happy to oblige. Same as the French did in the eighteenth century." He picked up his radio, hit the button. "Alpha-One to Charlie-One."

"*Charlie-One. I read you.*"

"Cyber team in place?"

"*Ready to rock an' roll, chief.*"

"Then let there be dark."

CHAPTER SEVENTY-FOUR

Above the stage, a giant screen broadcast the empty podium, transmitted the live build-up to living rooms across the country. Chrissie stared up at it, imagined the horror that would unfold if she failed.

As she stood there, picturing the blast and the blood, it came to her. Nice and neat. Obvious now.

She didn't have to wait.

The podium was garnished with four microphones, clustered there like a chrome bouquet. They were connected to the immense speakers situated around the square, plugged into soundboards and satellite feeds, ready to fill the netwaves with all sorts of prose and propaganda. Anyone at the podium would be seen by multiple cameras broadcasting in real-time, streaming live and uncensored. Any words spoken into the mics would fall on the ears of millions. Right there in front of her this whole time—one big, bold, gaping security flaw.

Chrissie estimated the distance between her and the mics—sixteen or seventeen concrete steps, some of them wide like walkways to add a few more yards. She could probably get to the podium in under ten seconds at full sprint. Add one or two for hopping the barricade. Add another few to climb the stage rigging.

They would be on her fast, coming at her in the first five seconds. But if she waited until there was enough distance between the nearest echo and the stage, she could keep them at bay for longer—ten seconds maybe. A handful of precious moments then needed to figure out what was happening, to get the bundle on her.

Echoes, teams of two, milled about, watched the crowd, ignored the press pit. When the VIPs would get to the square, the officers would be everywhere, would probably form a human barrier at the edge of the steps. Until then, they had no need to be up there, had no thought at all towards protecting the broadcast equipment. Someone else's job.

Think first. What would she need to say?

One sentence. Maybe not even that. Enough words in the right order for an alert to flag up among Gallard's staff, prompt them to change plans. They would have to.

There was a chance the taze sticks wouldn't even hurt. Not at first. Not with the adrenalin in her.

Chrissie planted her hands on the railing, shook it gently to test its bearing. It would hold her for the hop.

Gearing herself up now, taking deep breaths, knowing she was about to push her body to the limit, move quicker than she had ever had to move.

This was it.

The last few seconds of freedom.

This was everything.

Fingers tight around the metal bar, waiting for the techies to be looking at their tech, waiting for the nearest echoes to shuffle a few more paces away. She gave one last glance at the giant screen.

It winked off, dead pixels stopping her as she bent her knees, balanced on the balls of her feet.

Daniel's smartnet show had done the same thing, days earlier. That hacked broadcast had replaced those frenetic puppets. That deep voice had promised a revolution. The thought of home hit her square in the ribs, took all the torque out of her legs.

Shrieks from the crowd.

Chrissie spun. So did half the people in the press area. Sky-eyes dropped out of the air like they were caught in a duck shoot. The drones plummeted without sound, crashed onto heads, threw screams up. The music cut off mid-beat. One came down not far from the press pit, arms and propellers breaking on impact with the paving stone, sending people scattering.

The mob got spooked, launched a new kind of noise.

Around the square, digital billboards went dark. Autocars on the main stretch rolled to a stop, shunted each other bumper to bumper, caromed into curb barriers.

A blackout. A big one.

Chrissie turned back to the steps. The stage seemed much smaller now without the screen to inflate its image. Whatever had killed the power would have killed the mics too.

Amid the chaos, dark blue—the colour of her old uniform—in her peripheral. Rough hands on her, tugged, pulled at her elbows, kept her from running.

"Just come quietly, TERF," one of the Amazons said in her ear. "You're surrounded by reporters. Best not to cause a scene."

She couldn't if she tried.

CHAPTER SEVENTY-FIVE

Over the radio, Oscar confirmed the servers were fried, estimated they had maybe an hour before the city got its backup networks hooked in.

They listened to the chatter over the frequencies for a few minutes, different team leaders checking in, each one moving towards their targets, working to take control of security bases and core infrastructure at all four corners of London. Jake tried to make sense of the noise in the background whenever a transmission came in— couldn't tell if the yelling was man or woman, offender or defender, couldn't tell if the rattling was gunfire.

"You okay?" Rockland asked him from the other side of the flames.

"Might be getting cold feet."

Rockland turned away, began to pack the radio up, preparing to join the troops. "Thing about cold feet, Jacob, is that we all get cold feet eventually. Stone cold, if you get what I'm saying? So in the meantime, why worry about the things that seem scary? There's always more to gain from doing those things, right?"

"There's another way we can do this," Jake said. "Non-violent. Disarm the security forces, by all means, but the civilians—most of them are just allies, only doing what they're told, what they think is right. We can change their thinking. Show them…"

"Show them the error of their ways? Win their hearts and minds?" The way he said it, he made it sound absurd. A child's idea.

"Why not?" Jake said, trying to stay calm, keeping each word even. "We have a chance here to show them all a better moral standard, not a twist on the old one. Whose heart will we ever change that way? We'd be continuing the cycle."

"Trust me, Jacob, the cycle ends here. You are the end of the cycle. You are the break pad. You are Shiva. By the time we're finished, no non-binarist freak in this country is ever going to think about trying to oppress us again. Not for a hundred years. Not for a thousand. We'll never let them forget. And we'll never let their deviant nonsense pervert our world again."

"If not gender, it will be something else. Race. Social status. You've seen it in action, Rock. It's all an endless play for power. Unless you change something fundamental about the moral standard—"

"Moral standard? You're starting to sound like Kolbeck. And look where all his philosophising has got him. The man lives in a cave, obsessed with the past, decaying like his books. Action trumps ideas, Jacob. Every ding-dong day."

"And actions can have an impact on our culture for decades. What do you think the next generation will do if we resort to their tactics?"

Rockland stood, kicked his pack hard. The radio handset skittered in the dirt. "Shit, Jake, what makes you think there'll be much of a next generation left if we don't?"

Jake met his eye but refused to move, concerned that if he did, the man's boot might come for him next.

Rockland stood there, his chest rising and falling. He said, "I had a kid once. A little girl. Beautiful, she was."

Jake felt the sweat bead on his hairline.

"Three years' old, taught her to play pirates," the man continued. "Sword fighting, shooting muskets, swinging from ropes—all that. Had the hats and eyepatches…" He chuckled at the memory, stopped himself fast. "We were playing outside one day when some random person came over, said they thought my daughter was male-identifying and that I should get her looked at. I said that was nonsense. She's just a kid playing a game, for Christ's sake. And there were female pirates anyhow—it's not like men had a monopoly on piracy. That conversation should have ended there, but that same random stranger—you know what they did?"

Jake shook his head.

"They reported it. Within days, Social Services was round, telling me my daughter needed to be started on puberty blockers immediately and if I didn't do it, they'd take her away. Of course, I wouldn't do it. I wouldn't let them. So they took me away instead. Lost all my rights to see her. Her mother, scared as she was, allowed them to start the treatment. I never saw either of them again. I got word a few years' back, when my little girl turned fifteen—when she should have been doing dance classes and having fun with her friends and discovering boys—that she hanged herself. They'd ruined her. My only child. My beautiful girl."

Even in the open air, Jake was suffocating. His skin prickled. His sight misted.

"And you know something, lad? It wasn't just her. Countless others across the country. Across the world." Rockland drew the strings on his pack tight, checked the rifle scope. "So unless you have some way of bringing them kids home, you and I—we have work to do."

Playing his last card, Jake said, "You'll be proving them right. Justifying the atrocities they've committed. There used to be a saying, back when the world made sense—an eye for an eye will make us all blind."

Rockland, this harbinger, this latter-day warrior, stood, brushed the dust off his knees, straightened up, said, "Used to be another saying, too, before they banned it from being said: In the land of the blind, the one-eyed man is king."

And with that he closed one of his, gave Jake a strange sort of smile, looked off, out across the fields, his hands on his hips, ready to forge the future.

Jake stood too. His arm came up over the flames and smoke and he fired before he felt the rising heat. The horses staggered. The sound of it was everywhere.

Rockland didn't move at first—didn't fall, didn't look back over at him. The cloud of blood went out the other side of his body like pink chalk dust. The man still stood there, empty as the chamber in the old pistol. A fear rose up in Jake. Maybe he had missed. Maybe the man was so tough the shot hadn't bothered him and now he was going to take that knife and leap over the flames and jam it through Jake's heart.

As it all played out in his mind, the knees buckled. Rockland did fall. His chest smashed into the pyre, sent a volcanic blast of cinders into the sky.

Jake staggered back, shaking. The clothes caught, the body began to burn—this thing that had been like him a few seconds ago.

In some other life, under less strenuous circumstances, and despite his history, he might have wanted this man to be his friend. The horror of his decision welled in him. A scream he could not quite hear barrelled about his bones.

What did you do, Jake? What did you do?

His voice, different sounding.

Another voice—one that sounded like old Kolbeck—said, *It scatters you. You can never cross back.*

He forced his feet to move, backed up towards his horse, which was now looking at him accusingly. Rockland's beast was as calm as its owner—as calm in life as in death. Jake walked around the fire, took up the radio, climbed back in the saddle, pulled the animal to face east.

The ride was brutal, rough land potted with broken walls, rusting metal wreckage. He found much of the old towns still there in skeletal form, abandoned rather than destroyed. They blocked his view of the miles ahead. He kept looking up to find the blue signal smoke. He guessed if he stuck to the motorway, he could make it to London in a couple of hours at best.

All the while, the radio squawked—Oscar's voice trying the frequency. *Charlie-One to Alpha-One.* Each time sounding more desperate. Far enough from the fire he had helped to start, Jake opened the channel.

"Alpha-One to Charlie-One."

Static. Seconds.

"Charlie-One. Christ, that you, chief? Where you been?"

"No, this is Jake. Rockland's riding ahead. He said to tell you to keep going. We'll meet you in the city."

"Well, yeah…copy that."

"But he said to hold fire—do you hear me, Oscar? Hold fire. Don't corpse anyone. He says he wants to do this as cleanly as possible."

Thinking it through. Uncertain. "He said that?"

"Yes."

"What if we meet resistance? The plan was that we hit them hard if—"

"He's changed his mind. He said hold fire under all circumstances."

"He did?"

Jake ended the conversation before he tripped over his own lie. "Oscar, you're breaking up. Do you copy?"

"I heard you. Hold fire, roger that. Wait a minute—"

"Oscar, you there?"

"Jake, do you read me? Can I speak to him?"

"Oscar? Oscar?"

Jake turned the radio off before Oscar could respond, shoved the handset back in the bag. He picked up the reins in both hands, snapped them, at peace with exhausting the horse to an inch of its life if it meant shaving off even a second.

CHAPTER SEVENTY-SIX

Blacked-out windows framed the world in a smog. Even from inside the Amazon van, Chrissie could see the huddle of DIP staffers making their way towards the terrace of the National Gallery, shielding Mary Gallard from the rain with oversized umbrellas. The crowd—stunned silent, watching—made do with ponchos and slickers.

They hadn't cuffed her. No surprise. All the Amazons in the squad were biological males, each twice her size. Surprise was they hadn't tazed her once they'd got her into the privacy of the van. That was its own worry. It meant they wanted to question her while her head was clear, make sure she didn't have an excuse not to talk. It would be a while before they got to an interrogation room. The van was stuck at the square until the roads cleared. The smartnet servers hadn't yet been restored. Without the dazzling netscreens and streetlights, the city was a shell, the people lost sheep.

The opposition leader would have been left quiet too if someone in her team hadn't thought to improvise. Maybe they'd expected something like this. Abandoning the podium mics, Gallard took hold of a loudspeaker. Though her words crackled, they cut right over the square.

"This!" Gallard said. "This is how they try to silence us. These are the tricks they pull to stop the voice of the people from being heard. Silencing a genderqueer person, in violation of the Trans and Genderqueer Equality Act—their own rulebook!" Pausing on each line to let the boos and hollers breathe. "But we won't be silenced. We won't put up with the extremes of their authoritarian doctrine anymore. It has turned in on itself, has begun to eat its own, has failed to fulfil its foundations in inclusivity…"

She's taking the fight to them, Chrissie thought. No one had ever had the guts to speak out against the TEP like this. Gallard herself had always been controlled about her criticisms. Did she know? Did she suspect her life was in danger?

The Amazon sitting opposite sneered, swore. The long half of his undercut hairdo shook at the words being directed at his Dear Leader.

Chrissie became conscious again of the cuffs squeezing her wrists, cutting off feeling to her fingers, keeping her from defending herself if one of the officers kicked off, decided to take out their aggression on a traitor to the state.

Gallard went on. "We can't keep going down this path, my friends. Common sense has given way to reactionary policies. Freedom of debate and discussion has been replaced by unquestioned obedience to the ruling party line. We cannot become a nation that criminalises opinion. We cannot…"

Yells, distant but loud enough to interrupt the rallying words, to unsettle the crowd. Chrissie strained to see, could only make out the ripple of heads turning towards the commotion, the beginnings of people trying to move away from its source, panicky.

The officer guarding Chrissie got up, stacked boots shaking the steel tread floor, pressed her nose up at the grate where the driver was sitting. "Yo, that's them."

"Keep it down, hun," the driver said. "We ain't got the comms up yet. Peek out the back and make sure the others are on it."

"What about the fugitive?"

"I said peek out, not go out. Anyway, she ain't going anywhere."

The duty officer gave Chrissie a scowl as she went by, swung the doors back, hopped down, sat on the steel deck, legs hanging off the foot ramp. The view was enough now for Chrissie to see the little spots of trouble in the distance, bursting like furuncles, discharging more hate and anger than was commonplace.

The TRANARCHY gangs were maybe three or four to a team, raising their usual crude weapons as their alternatives to placards—planks, softball bats, bolas. Each gang wore the apparel of their respective corporate sponsor—Pizza Hut, TweetTube, Googlesoft, Xprez, Goldman Sachs. Their shrieks were familiar, disjointed. The rhyming chant was new: *"Anti-trans terrorists! The DIP are cissexists!"* Over and over, higher in volume as they bullied their way through the crowd.

Gallard tried to carry on, her speech freestyling in the moment. "Don't let them shout you down, my friends! They are tools of the state! Political puppets trying to create an undemocratic one-party system! They don't…I say they don't speak for…"

Chants synching together, forming a united rallying cry. *"Anti-trans terrorists! The DIP are cissexists!"*

Chrissie winced. The Amazon at the door edged further out, rubber soles hitting the paving. The Amazon looked all over, cradled his electrorifle, jumpy as the crowd.

On the podium, Gallard turned away from the loudspeaker, conversed with her staff. The screen above her blinked from black to grey, an error message flashing up. Fluorescent strips in the van flickered on.

The signal fixed. The blackout over.

"Anti-trans terrorists! The DIP are cissexists!"

The square, pressure rising, suffocating. The sky beyond the doors, still thick with cloud. One of the surviving sky-eyes lurched up from the horizon, steadied itself as it rose, renewed its patrol across the horde of wet spectators, came to keep the tensions from spilling over.

CHAPTER SEVENTY-SEVEN

The Fence was obsolete by the time he reached it. New plumes of smoke spiralled from the watchtowers, steel barriers left twisted, warped by the roadside.

Visible steam pumped from the horse's snout. Jake slowed the animal down to pass through the hole that had once been a security gate, saw no one as he went, heard nothing besides the rattle of bent hinges in the wind. No reason for them to hang about, he supposed. The fortress breached, the keep still to be conquered.

On the other side, streaks of deep red on the paving, charcoal shapes that could once have been people, looked like giant black bugs with their arms jutting skyward. He opened up the radio.

"Oscar, do you copy?"

"Jake…the…copy…"

A nudge of the dial. "Where are you?"

"Almost at the ISZ. It's been a wild trip."

"What do you mean? What's the damage?"

"Lost some of the men. Angus is gone. Truck got rammed by an AGV when they hit the security base. Our guys had no choice—had to open up on them."

Fuck's sake. "We were told to avoid killing!"

"We're doing our best. Most of these milquetoast security guards are surrendering easily, like Rock said they would. There were just a few allies on the perimeter that wouldn't listen. Fair play to them. Hardier than most of the others."

"Don't let this descend into mass violence, understand? That's not what we're doing here."

"Lemme tell you, man, the more prisoners we take, the more we're having to leave troops behind. I don't know if we can do this without—"

"Please, Oscar."

"I need to speak to Rockland."

Jake took a second to think. "We ran into some resistance before the Fence. Had to split up."

"Come again? You say he's off-grid? He okay?"

"Last I saw he was heading into the city. Hopefully we'll see him in Westminster."

A pause—the Oz-man either thinking hard or relaying the update to those around him. "Got it. Let's keep this thing moving."

"Remember what he told us."

Further along the road, women and men, allies living in the OSZ, stood dumbstruck, stared out at the path the rebels had torn through the neighbourhood. They scattered when they heard the hooves, squirreled back into their homes and offices, the last vestiges of safety.

Four men he thought he recognised from the Compound stood outside a police station car park, lined up, rifles in hand. Equality officers, most in uniform, sat on the ground together, cross-legged, arms bound behind them. Smoulder carried over them in the breeze. The echoes were mostly inert, silent. Some wept. Alive, at least. Probably wondering if it would remain that way.

The men watched Jake come by, didn't seem to know him. They nodded in his direction all the same. One of them winked, raised his flask up, celebrations kicking off early.

Another kid sat by a roadside fountain, gathering a small crowd of supporters. He was monkeying with a radio, trying to get a signal. This one Jake definitely recognised.

"Popeye!" the boy called out, the sound of the horse's approach drawing his attention, distracting him from his job. "I must be fizzin'!"

The other men glanced up, each of them bright-eyed, high energy. They stepped back, made room for him.

Jake said, "What are you doing here?"

"Part of the welcoming committee," Zeebrah said. "Me an' the boys are with Sigma Team, took down some of the internal defences so the troops could get through."

"Looks like you did your job."

Zeebrah laughed. "Boys are already on their way into the city centre. You're stragglin'."

Jake let his horse drink from the fountain.

"I'm on my own," Jake said, deciding to leave it at that. "You see Chrissie come through? Earlier on, I mean. Before the Fence came down."

"What? No. Nuh-uh. Who was she travelling with?"

"On her own, too, I guess."

Jake pressed himself against his mount's neck, appreciating he still had a hard journey ahead, still a trial in ever finding Chrissie again, if he wasn't already too late. He didn't know how she could have got through but he knew she was inventive, capable of all sorts.

"What's the fastest way to Trafalgar Square?" Jake said.

Zeebrah chewed the question, pulled up a map on his smartpalm, handed it up.

"You can stick to the mains or cut through the gardens," the boy said. "S'up to you. Quicker yet, you could follow the path of destruction. That's where they all headed anyway."

In the distance, whoops and cheers, men yelling, incomprehensible.

Jake handed the device back, pulled on the reins, picked up the pace.

CHAPTER SEVENTY-EIGHT

The restive vibration of the crowd, breath rising as one, a brume drifting above the plastic hoods like steam off an animal's back—every individual on it a tic, jittery, poised to get up and run. The TRANARCHY militants branched out, made their noise, their poison coursing through the square, through the city. The press salivated, trained their cameras on Gallard, wanted to capture her flustered, losing control.

That was the point, Chrissie had no doubt. Disrupt the speech. Make her look incompetent in front of the world.

The big screen winked out a second time. Groans and tuts at more government meddling. The powers that be trying to turn the whole affair into a joke.

People ducked, protected their heads, worried the sky-eyes would fall again. The machines remained airborne this time, above the craziness, waiting to see what happened next, where the trouble would start.

The big screen lit up now, struggled for reception. An aftershock maybe. Netwave signals trying to settle.

Instead of the stage and the podium, a room appeared—no, a cell. Looked a lot like one of the holding cells at the Mayfair Equality Station, all cinder block grey and windowless. The scene was fly-on-the-wall style, one of the new closed-circuit cams, high-def, full of colour. Only not on a wall—more like on a table, chest level and badly shot, like the camera had been left there, forgotten about.

Not much in the room. Medical equipment, possibly. Apparatus on stands, steel trays, trolleys. And the figure, female-presenting, in the centre of the frame, in a chair—or a bed?—elevated so the person in it was upright, strapped into it. The scene lingered for a while. No sound, no movement. A still photo, Chrissie thought. A snapshot. A snapshot of what?

The snapshot moved. Or at least the woman did. Stirred. As she did, Chrissie's skin goosed, a hot-cold crawl climbing up the back of her neck.

The noise of the crowd died down. People clocked the screen, caught off-guard by the strange footage that seemed more disturbing the longer it hung there, the more the woman in the gurney provoked questions, her head bowed, dark hair concealing her identity, thin arms bare. The TRANARCHY members had shut up too, taken aback, reduced to mere audience members. Gallard along with them. She turned from the podium to see what had stolen everyone's attention. Her staff looked up at this latest trick, this calculated interruption.

The speakers whined, sounded like a heavy door creaking. Because that's exactly what the sound was—clear now on the screen, the footage evolving, people entering the room, three, four. One at the front of the pack looking familiar. Fat and suited…

Chrissie tried to swallow, her throat drought-dry.

The hair wasn't quite the same—short back and sides. The frame was a few pounds lighter, though still huge, still shapeless. When she heard the voice, she knew it was impossible for it to be anyone else. All arrogance and attitude covered in artificial sweetener.

"Wake up, sleepy head. The verdict is in."

The woman in the gurney raised her head at that, hair falling back from her face. She too was unmistakeable were it not for the drained look about her.

A gasp in the square, a rising babble cut short only because the large individual on the screen was talking again, no one wanting to miss a word.

"The court has found you guilty on all charges. You've let us down. All of us. We believed in you and you betrayed the community."

The sad figure shuddered, tried to shake her head. *"But it's wrong. Listen to me. It's not what this was meant to be about.*

"Enough. You have lost sight of our goals."

"Zoe, we can't."

"Shush."

"We can't allow child lovers to become an accepted part of the community. It threatens the whole movement—"

"Minor attracted persons have every right to be accepted and included. Your bigotry in this matter is—"

"It's revolting."

"I said enough."

"People won't accept it. It'll tip public opinion against the movement."

"Silence." The presiding official slapped the prisoner across the face. "Given your own legislation, the judging panel believes a traitor of your influence is too dangerous to remain active in the re-education system. Nor will cancellation be enough to defuse the bigotry you have unexpectedly allowed to enter our society. I take no joy in telling you, dear, that while grateful for your zistorical work for the cause, we will not abide problematic thought within our society from anyone. I suggest you take a moment to atone for your wrongs and may our Great Birth-Giver show you the mercy we cannot."

The figure wailed, jerked in the gurney, screamed, "You can't do this to me! I am the Party! I am equality! You've taken it too far! Look at what you're doing! You're ruining it all. I am a qween! I am a qween!"

The official flicked a hand. Someone in a white coat and rubber gloves appeared in frame, took the accused by the arm, stuck her with a needle like it was an afterthought. The victim shrieked, lashed her head side to side, hair a whipping frenzy. In seconds that all stopped. The footage went quiet. The accused no longer moved or wailed or anything else.

"Take it to the furnace," said someone off-camera. "Quickly. Leave nothing."

CHAPTER SEVENTY-NINE

The screen flickered, stopped, went dark.

Chrissie scanned the square. No one spoke. Many in tears, huddled together, hair in fists, mouths hanging, as if the blackout had come again and this time had unplugged everyone in the world, turned the population into the living dead.

The press area, only moments before an arena of ravening predators, so eager to capture the arrival of the protestors, of Gallard's faltering speech, now funeral-silent. Reporters looked to each other for any hint of what to do next. Censors, those still responsive, demanded camera operators to shut down their equipment, erase their footage.

The statue of Suarez-Adarsha appeared different. A pathetic shadow of the person in the recording—a naïve trans girl who had so willingly helped start a fire she couldn't control. A fire that had ended up burning her alive. The mystery of her disappearance had been answered. The only mystery now was who had known about it, who had kept the charade alive.

Who had revealed the awful truth.

The TEP would never have released this footage. Something else was happening.

"Fakes!" someone yelled. "Manipulated media!"

The TRANARCHY soldier, decked out in a rainbow-washed crewcut and tattoos, had clambered up on one of the fountain walls, was trying to get the audience back on-side, trying to wrestle back the narrative.

Another voice, somewhere else in the crowd, hollered the same accusations, backed up her sister, still fighting the ugly fight.

The echo guard, shifty, wandered from the van to get a better view. Chrissie budged along the seat, leant her head half out the rear doors. A little more of the droves of people, the grey sky above them.

"Lies!" another called out, tried starting a chant with it. "Lies! Lies! Lies! Lies!"

"*Lies! Lies! Lies!*" Some of the spectators bought into it, not believing the footage—or not wanting to. Not wanting anyone else to. "*Lies! Lies! Lies!*"

The chant didn't possess everyone. She could see them here and there, turning away, keeping their heads down, whispering in their groups, edging away from the mob. If the TRANARCHY and the TEP supporters had been a poison, the video footage was a slow-acting antidote, its introduction already flushing the system before her eyes.

As the clamour rose, the screen came back. The eerie hush fell again, everyone afraid of what would come next.

A different room this time. Not a cell. A hotel room—immaculate quilts, overstuffed settees. Same kind of discreet camerawork. No mistaking the person in this frame. The prime minister was a media darling, an icon of her generation, her bearded face one of the most recognisable in the country, even when slathered in eyeshadow and blusher.

And the prime minister was not alone.

Children with her. A boy and girl, no older than ten, their faces blurred to protect their identity. They were drinking flutes of champagne. The prime minister, laughing and teasing and coddling. The prime minister, stripping out of her robe, flashing a hairy arse at the hidden camera, pulling the children towards the hotel bed.

The crowd gasped in unison—or maybe the sound had come from Chrissie's own mouth—a sharp inhale that brought with it a deep, uncontrolled revulsion. The monstrous truth piped through the screen, a hundred feet across in synth crystal quality, unbelievable at first glance, more real than real as the seconds passed.

Chrissie tore her gaze away. The crowd had become a pale collective, bound in horror, hands to their mouths and ears. Parents had their kids pinned against them, shielding their eyes. Some of the spectators found it too much—vomiting, passing out, curling up, breaking into sobbing spasms while the screams and wails from the amplifiers drowned the square. When she forced herself to look up again, the image on screen—mercifully—had been blurred in full. But the sounds had been left untouched. Aside the weeping of children, the prime minister's familiar voice relayed her terrible instructions, forceful and impatient.

The sky-eye, on the edge of her vision, made its way nearer. Chrissie didn't think much of it, barely even registered it, what with all the

333

drama unfolding around her. Something made her remember the danger, of Gallard still at the podium, head tilted to the screen, as much in shock as everyone else. As soon as she did, as soon as she looked at the stage, the sour spike came to the back of her throat. Time slowed to a crawl.

The drone drifted in front of the screen where the prime minister's giant face leered up at the man, mascara running, tongue extended, every super-high-def taste bud on display, begging for the big finale. It hovered, swayed as if balancing itself, descended at pace.

Gallard flinched, maybe got a sense of it, seemed to even turn towards it. Chrissie opened her mouth to yell, had a thought that it might somehow make a difference, but couldn't get the sound out, couldn't get her throat to catch up, couldn't do a damn thing except let the flash blind her and the thunder throw her to the ground.

CHAPTER EIGHTY

The blast was the last thing the screen captured before it took the camera out, leaving the conference room with nothing to display on the netscreen but a toppled close-up of the pavement, the screams of thousands of people coming through the speakers like the sound of a freight train derailing.

The prime minister barely registered it happening. Her thought process had ground to a full stop as soon as the hidden videye footage had started playing out, the footage beaming to screens across the country. The footage somehow filmed from inside her private hotel suite.

She had the urge to bring her hand to her mouth, found it was already there. She could taste metal, tried to focus on it. She had gnawed away the skin around her nails. The person in front of her gave her another jolt.

"Minister, can you hear me?"

"Hannah?" she said, seeing her security chief looming. "How..."

Tavistock turned her head. Amy, paler than usual, eyes bugged, trembling. Around her, others from the Tribe—her most loyal, her most trusted sisters—all sharing the same horrified expression. Hannah moved away, pressed her earpiece to her head. The scene played back in her mind, ran as vividly as if the screen was still televising the footage, repeated the shrill notes of her own commanding voice deep inside her skull. The full force of reality travelled into her, a liver shot. She stumbled from her chair, pitched forward, heaved half her vegan pasta salad on the carpet.

The room moaned, chairs rolled back, people staggered towards the doors.

"Minister, it's all right." Hannah, there again, one hand on her back, the other scooping her under the arm. "We need to leave. Right now."

"Oh, my Goddess," Tavistock squeaked. "Oh, my Goddess. Oh, my Goddess! Oh, my..."

"Minister, please!"

"I was just helping those children understand the beauty of genderqueer love. It's not wrong. They wanted it to happen. They—"

Hannah slapped her. Hannah lifted her to her feet, shoved her into a disjointed amble towards the doors. The Tribe split—half of them already spilling into the corridor, the others seized in their seats, gawping at their colleagues, immobilised by trauma. Tavistock would have been left sitting with them had she not been marched out of the suite, shoved into the emergency elevator. Her knees collapsed. Hannah held her up, shook her roughly.

"Get it together! We have to get to the car."

"They were trans-ageist. They identified as being adults. Yes, that's what it was. Completely legal…"

Hannah squeezed her voxcom, called for the limo to meet them on the ground floor exit, said something about saving time. Cold air came, a breeze whipping her face and ears, carrying with it the scent of smoke and petrol fumes. She ran because Hannah ran, no concept of where she was going.

Beyond the gates, people hurrying, major panic mode, and something else out there—huge shapes barrelling past in a blur. Closer up, thick, shimmering horses, tearing along the roads. A modern-day Mongol horde. Riders held the reins single-handed, brought with them flashes of black steel, flares that belched blue smoke behind them.

Privs. All of them, privs.

Goddess, no…

The picture sent terror through her, gave her pulse a defibrillator start, squeezed the dormant scream from her lungs.

"The car, ma'am. Get in."

Couldn't take her eyes off the riders, couldn't fathom the numbness setting into her limbs.

"Get in the fucking car!"

The ground disappeared beneath her feet. A force pushed her horizontal. Her face pancaked on leather. A door slammed behind her.

"Warning. Automatic driver disengaged."

Hannah landed in the driver's seat, grabbed the wheel, threw it hard into a turn. The tyres spun, the vehicle jumped. Tavistock jellified, compressed into the seat.

CHAPTER EIGHTY-ONE

The tuning fork tone of the blast hung in the air. Thousands still screaming, surging away from the steps of the National Gallery, where the podium had been blown to matchwood, where Mary Gallard and several of her team had been sent flying across the terrace, noodle limp, clothes charred, smouldering.

The van windows had splintered. Chrissie's eardrums ached.

TRANARCHY militants joined the retreat. Echoes abandoned their posts. Everyone in the square high-tailed it from the smoking wreck of the grandstand. Chrissie's guard had scarpered. She could see through the grate that the driver had gone too, the door sagging open, a breeze running through the van, a caustic bouquet of smoke and burning flesh.

If ever there was a sign.

She hopped to her feet, dropped down to the road, hit a puddle, nearly lost her balance, nearly took a face full of pavement.

The chaos all too clear at ground-level. The black serpent of smoke surged, rolled above the streets. A crush of plastic rainbow coats as people freaked, bid for a way out. Umbrellas and placards and bags and rubble littered the ground. She started to move, only in the opposite direction to the fleeing crowd, asked herself what the hell she was doing while she was doing it.

Get out of here, idiot! You won't get a second chance!

Or was it her third? Fourth? How much longer could she keep running? Not sure it even mattered now. The DIP in tatters. The TEP had done what they'd set out to do.

The truth—out now, unavoidable, clear as cut glass. Wouldn't that count for something?

Couldn't call it. Only certainty: more chaos, more confusion. All chips in for a full-blown societal collapse.

She reached the steps. Took all of two seconds to confirm Mary Gallard wouldn't be there to see the end result. The blast had disintegrated the stand, had scorched the surroundings, flattened the front railings of the press area where Chrissie had been standing when the Amazons picked her up. Broadcast equipment lay smashed, abandoned. Several bodies among them, dead or close enough. Support dogs reduced to fur and viscera.

A different chaos now, coming in hot: car horns from the distant streets, yells and—a staccato sound, like stones bouncing off plasterboard. *Pop-pop-pop. Pop-pop-pop.*

Gunfire.

Instinct triggered. Head ducked. Mind seized on something. The footage. The grand conspiracy. That's why all this was happening. The One Strand offices loomed large. The intimidating security presence had dispersed. She tried to make out the windows. The smoke wouldn't allow it. Feeling her dismay turn to anger, Chrissie ran towards the building in a stoop, hurdled debris, ignored the sting in her eyes, hoped she wasn't too late, only knowing she had to try.

People became obstacles. Their wails converged into a hell sound.

Before she reached the pavement, the sergeant emerged like a miracle. Her ex-partner's thick neck and bulky frame unmistakeable. Her red hair and redder face still had the stopping power of a hand cannon. Dennehy had a man in custody, had him cuffed at arm's length. Didn't take a second for Chrissie to recognise him. Peter Cobbleswan was pop-eyed and jumpy and green-gilled.

Their hostage. Their patsy about to make his televised debut.

Chrissie froze. Something about her presence must have raised Dennehy's hackles. The sergeant looked up, locked eyes for a double second. Her face melted slowly into an open-mouthed caricature. Chrissie's former partner tried to cycle through the possibilities in a handful of seconds—still came to naught. Whether she read Chrissie's intentions or the confusion threw her resolve off-kilter, Dennehy let go of Cobbleswan's collar and backed away.

Chrissie moved forward. Dennehy beat a retreat.

The chase had them swerving through terrified bystanders, shoving, tripping over feet. The smoke grew thicker, filling the gap between them. The sarge moved faster than Chrissie had ever seen, adrenalin giving her the gait of a charging rhino. But it would only delay the inevitable.

Dennehy bounded into the road. Chrissie, on her heels, veered to her left. With the full momentum of her run, Chrissie bowled shoulder into Dennehy's side, the shift enough to cause the big woman to pitch forward, chin-dive into the paving, roll twice over, washout on her back. Chrissie kept at her, dropped both knees into her ex-partner's gut, swung madly, flung palm strikes into both ears. Dennehy squealed and mewled. Dennehy snatched fistfuls of jacket, threw Chrissie to the ground. Dennehy found her taze stick. Chrissie scooted, took a glancing blow to the elbow, spun, took up a fighting stance.

The sergeant hauled to her knees, wheezing, face grazed, hair frizzed. She bled from the mouth, was probably missing at least one tooth from the tumble. She was animal-scared and lame but she was smiling. Smiling because she saw Chrissie was unarmed. The asp powered up, hummed, alive with current. Dennehy staggered forward, broke into a final charge.

The applause of its run was a locomotive clack, coming up fast from the side. The giant emerged from the smoke, dark and four-legged. Its rider whipped a leg out. Dennehy, mid-lunge, didn't even see the size-ten as it swung into her face. Cartilage cracked. Blood spurted. The sarge went down again—Donald Duck, out of control, arse-over-head. The giant disappeared back into the chaos. Dennehy stayed down.

CHAPTER EIGHTY-TWO

"Driver, how far from home?"

Zoe Urwin's government-issued autobile hit forty-five miles per hour and steadied itself, the in-built computer happy enough to break the speed limit but not prepared to endanger itself or its occupants in the middle of London's busy streets.

"Approximately fifty-five minutes from home. There are multiple traffic alerts reported on route."

Zoe slammed a fist against the leatherette armrest, gritted zer teeth at the pain it sent pulsing along zer carpal bones, pressed zer nose up against the one-way window. That sick feeling, making zer hands tremble, fright bunching in zer chest. Hadn't felt that in a while. How long? Not since zer teens, zie guessed. Not since the dark days before the TEP had taken control.

No warning. Not a fucking thing.

How was that even possible?

They had ears everywhere. TEP intelligence had sussed the bomb plot, intercepted communications between the bomber and his Resistance paymasters, cornered the would-be assassin like vermin in the exact place and time they knew he would be there.

Zoe's operatives had been blind to all this other shit. Stolen tapes. Secret recordings of the prime minister. Hacked closed-network display screens. The whole thing a mare's nest.

Something stank. Stank foul and unbearable.

Zoe loosened the tie, snatched the waistcoat open, lost a button, smoothed the edge of a hand under one breast, brought up the type of sweat that came with eating hot food. Zoe retrieved the vaparillo, took a hard chemical hit, filled the backseat with vapour, felt the nerves soften.

Dominic, pressed into the seat opposite, looked grey, shrunken. His lips moved as if trying to speak, only saliva and air escaping.

"This is your fault," Zoe said. "You've fucked up, Dominic. You've done something you shouldn't have. Or not done something you should have. I'll get to the bottom of this and when I do—"

Zoe stopped the indictment. He was pointing to the rear window with one quivering index finger. His right eyelid danced. Zoe struggled to turn in the seat, neck cranking, aching. Zoe gave up, leaned forward, adjusted the specs, craned for the narrow rearview mirror.

Zoe said, "Driver, open a window."

The smoke absconded. The mirror cleared. Zoe adjusted the specs again, blinked, let zer huge head move side to side, mouth flagging. It couldn't be possible.

It couldn't be.

The mirror showed cars and trucks coming from the end of the road—big ones, people standing up in pickup beds, coloured smoke choking the sky. They weren't driving, they were racing, closing the gap as if pursuing Zoe's sluggish vehicle.

The vaparillo rolled under the seat. Only one word came to mind: invasion.

"Dominic…Dominic?…"

The useless cretin, slack-jawed, his knees bouncing to a manic beat.

Think quickly. Drop the dead weight.

"Stop the car," Zoe said.

The autobile rapidly decelerated. Dominic lurched forward, fell off the edge of the seat, hands raked the floor for purchase, skirt tumbled over his lace underwear.

"Get out," Zoe told him. "Get in the driver's seat and take over the steering. We won't get far like this."

"I should stay here, ma'am-sir. I need to protect you."

Zoe ignored his protest, threw the door open, tugged hard at his collar, made him scrabble like a beaten dog until he fell out of the car, face grating the tarmac. Zoe booted him in the backside. He half-rolled, elicited a grunt. His head bounced, glasses snapped, body flopped onto the ground like an uncoordinated toddler.

Zoe raised every ounce of strength, pulled the door shut. "Driver, lock the doors. Top speed. Get us out of here."

The locks shucked. Zoe, thrown back in her seat, moaned like a shit ghost. The electric motor whined.

The rearview—Dominic, pulling himself to his feet, staggering after the car, his face contorted with distress, screaming something about love.

The first few cars in the roving convoy veered to avoid him. The ones behind didn't have time. The small figure, creamed by the grill of a pickup, turned the windscreen into a blue cobweb, entered a ragdoll spin, end over end, skirt flapping in the wind, a perfect acrobatic tumble over the roof of the vehicle, before dropping to earth again, somewhere far back amid the smoke and exhaust fumes and hot tyres.

Wouldn't slow them for long. At this speed, a retreat home was out of the question. There were other options, surely. Places close by, filled with allies and security.

Zoe said, "Driver, take me to Ru Paul's Cathedral."

CHAPTER EIGHTY-THREE

The square, cut off, every exit blocked by vintage vehicles lined bumper-to-bumper from one pavement to the next, parked in such a way to create choke points for those attempting to flee by foot or by autocar. Between wheeled barricades came more horses, more riders. They manoeuvred along the streets, hoisted their rifles and flares, spewed monkey tails of coloured smoke behind them.

The sound of howl and gunfire had been replaced with whistles and horns and engines and the bark of instructions from among the freedom fighters. It seemed they had met next to no resistance.

The TRANARCHY militants, rounded up, picked out easily from the crowd thanks to their imitation-punk regalia. Many were unceremoniously prodded, marched behind a row of pick-up trucks. Their arrogance and attitude given way to hacking sobs and pleas, once defiant faces now clown-like, stained with eyeliner. A few others—the ringleaders among them—trussed up, slung over the back of horses, trophy deer at the end of a hunt, their indignity paraded before the crowd.

Separated from them were the echoes. Amazons and patrol officers alike, marshalled into small groups, disarmed, ordered to sit two metres apart from the next. Like their TRANARCHY allies, they formed a pathetic collective now, their status flipped from voices of authority to criminals awaiting trial. Or worse. One of the rebels moved between them, a blade in her hand, sawing the Venus-Mars insignia from their uniforms, one by one, shoving the fabric scalps into the knapsack at her waist.

Where were the prisoners were being taken? Had Rockland even a plan for that?

Most of the civilians ignored, left milling dumb and dazed, left to organise their own little huddles in an attempt to keep themselves safe. Others still attempted an escape into the streets, only to be obstructed by soldiers with improvised riot shields who yelled at them to step back, but otherwise showed no desire to lash out in anger as Chrissie had feared. The streets were not running red after all.

Not yet.

How long until that changed?

Not worth waiting to find out, not worth staying stuck among the defenceless herd while the victors got bolder and restless. The trail of flares moved their way on the breeze, thickened the air, made it hard to see much beyond a few feet ahead. She could make out the tops of the buildings on the periphery, could picture the row of theatres on Haymarket, the ersatz cafés on the Strand. If any of the buildings were unlocked, somehow accessible, there was a chance she could find a way out by navigating through the buildings, or at least shelter inside one until things died down, until a better opportunity to escape presented itself.

"All right, guys," a voice cried out. "Looks secure. Give it some welly."

Up on the pedestal, the effigy of Suarez-Adarsha trembled. A band of rebels pulled in unison, taut chains linking them to the plinth, to the rigor mortis limbs of yesterday's agitator. The foundations buckled, whined. Fragments of black marble hit the ground. The statue leaned forward. A cheer arose. Another pull. Suarez-Adarsha swooned, somersaulted, landed on her head, cracked the pavement. The mob roared, descended on the carcass.

Making use of the distraction, Chrissie ran again. Her leg muscles, stiff and seizing, allowed her only to move in a lumber, barely dodging the people as they lurched out of the brume, nearly tripping several times over abandoned bags, left over carnival junk.

Somewhere behind the haze, motorcycles gunned, engines deafening on approach. Chrissie wheeled to her left, scared she would stumble into their path, heard the shrill whinny of the horse ahead, the gallop of hooves moving towards her.

She backed up, desperate not to be trampled, paralysed by dread, unable to coordinate herself into the simple decision of moving out of the way, left or right, right or left.

The beast's soles, almost on top of her. Its great head emerged from the fog, its nostrils flared, smoking craters. It pulled to the side in one sharp motion, momentarily raised its front legs, kicked the air, snorted as it came to a stop.

The man in the saddle bent low. His hand reached out to her. Chrissie looked up at the rider. Relief threw its embrace around her, extinguished the fear. She grabbed the hand, allowed herself to be lifted into the air as she swung onto the animal's back, pinned her arms around his waist.

Jake cried out, snapped the reins. The horse bolted forward, forced her to dig her fingers into his jacket to keep from falling.

When they made it through the smoke, the rebels on the ground parted, waved them through the barricades. Chrissie's grip didn't let up.

Neither of them said a word. They rode, watching the world change around them.

CHAPTER EIGHTY-FOUR

None of the normal meet-and-greet. The Baroque doors stood closed. Zoe hammered with elbows and feet, screamed into them. Behind the abandoned autobile, the security gates folded closed. They wouldn't hold forever. Had to hope no one would even think to look here.

"Open the fuck up! It's Zoe Urwin! For the love of our Great Birth-Giver, open this door!"

Someone did—one of the sisters who acted as resident caretaker. Zoe knocked her to the ground, pushed zer way inside, stepped over the sprawled legs and velvet robes.

"My child." The familiar, falsetto voice bounced along the walls as the figure approached, flanked by two of the lower priestesses, her cowl thrown back, turquoise hair stringy and matted, face purple-hot. "Thank Goddess you came. The great one must surely be listening to our prayers."

Zoe, barely registering the high priestesses' words, stormed forward into the cathedral-turned-temple, skidded along the historic stone.

"Sanctuary," Zoe said, wheezy. "I need sanctuary."

"What's happening out there?" Tsunami said, reaching out to help, grasping hold of her old friend. "The last we heard, the blasphemer had been dealt with. Surely it is over. Our plans must bear sweet fruit—"

"You'll look after me, won't you?" Zoe blubbed. "You won't let them get to me."

The high priestess let the fear sponge into her—eyes darted, fingers stiffened.

"Please, o wise one. Hide me."

Tsunami let go of Zoe's stout arms, looked at her assistants, made to go towards the doors, to investigate the world outside.

"No!" Zoe screamed. "Don't go out there! Don't ever—"

A boom rocked the walls, rained ancient dust around them, rattled the mosaics.

Voices and engines not far off, gathering, building towards their target.

The clatter of metal buckling, concrete cracking. Zoe pictured the security gates being rammed by something heavy. Zoe shoved the high priestess out of the way, made for the exit towards the courtyard, from where zie—if fast enough— could slip away into one of the many coven lounges or side rooms, perhaps conceal zerself in a wardrobe or behind a curtain until the enemy at the gates retreated or gave up and, yes, there zie could bide zer time, recover zer breath, plot zer escape, surely find some way—

Another rumble. A Marsha P Johnson mural dislodged, swan-dived, crashed into the pews. The sound of it rooted Zoe. The screams of the priestesses rang in its wake.

"They're coming through the South Door!" the warning wailed beyond the walls.

Great Birth-Giver! They would be inside the private chambers before zie could get to them.

Zoe backed up, stumbled back to the nave. No sanctuary here. Needed to get out. North Door, zie told herself, loping into a lummox run. Don't stop.

The sculpture of Hermaphroditus held sway before the high altar. The sight of her unapologetic pose momentarily imbued Zoe with hope, channelled a psychic vigour, reminded zer of who zie was, of what zie was capable.

Seeing the protruding phallus gave zer the thought that a weapon would help, if only to make zer feel safer. Zoe reached for zer waistband, pulled Jezebel free, gripped the handle hard enough to pale zer knuckles, held the rod out in front of zer like it was a duelling sword. Zoe stumbled along the main aisle, breath shortening.

The barbarians came through the North Transept as Zoe approached the centre of the temple. Stifling a scream, the equality minister fled towards the statue's pedestal, scampered up onto the makeshift sacrificial stage, towards the marble feet, like a small child seeking protection behind a parent.

"Thou who wakest in the waters…When the sun is sunk in slumber…"

Zoe mumbled the words aloud, hoped they would transmute into incantation, would become a charm, would fall around zer like an armoured cloak from the firmaments.

The horde appeared in the nave, privs among them, toting rifles and hatchets and swords, whooping and bellowing akin to animals, searching for victims.

"Though with moon upon my forehead…Thou with heaving breast…"

More of them. One at the head of the pack hoisted a heavy cylinder on his shoulder, pointed it towards the Goddess of the Pool, called to his fellow brutes to stand back.

"Most powerful…I pray thee think…upon us…"

Zoe scurried behind the plinth, hyperventilating. The drainage ducts still soiled black. Shrieks from the far end of the hall. Zoe peered out from zer cover. Figures in purple robes, dragged across the polished floor like velvet mop-ends, their cries of mercy disappearing through the doors, doors that had been flung open, inviting more of the soldiers inside.

"Blessed be!"

The hurricane came. A deafening rush of air filled the temple, replaced immediately by a roar that was everywhere at once. The burst of smoke above flung debris in all directions, seemed to erase the world in a heartbeat. Zoe's body gave out. Gravity spun zer into the ground. Zer organs flipped, skipped against her ribs.

The temple on its side. Zer mind, somehow separated from zer body. Jezebel, inches away, amid the dust, broken in two. Feelings of despair and anger at once, tasting like bile in zer mouth, that same feeling zie had felt nearing zer ninth birthday. Zer father's voice, Big Daddy Julian Urwin, telling zer they simply couldn't afford a pony, that zie would have to ask for *something more sensible, darling.* The hate rose, hot and acidic.

Then Hermaphroditus, coming towards zer, immense and white, cock stiff, and for a moment Zoe thought zie had crossed over, that this was zer welcoming parade into eternal glory, that the Great Birth-Giver was approaching to embrace zer, had chosen zer, was inviting zer now into the great pantheon of trans and genderqueer icons so as to take zer rightful place among the stars.

"Blessed be! Blessed—"

CHAPTER EIGHTY-FIVE

ARCHIVE OF THE NEW BRITISH LIBRARY
SUBJECT: RADIO TRANSMISSION ISSUED TO CIVIL FREQUENCIES
DURING THE EGALITARIAN REVOLUTION OF 2046 (RECORDING
#33)
RECORDING DATE: 31-10-46

This material is of important historical record and is therefore freely available to view, download, share, broadcast, republish and reprint by any citizen as a matter of constitutional right.

LT. OSCAR T. GRANT [member of the Individualist Libertarian Movement]: Look alive, all you erstwhile exiles! You quondam criminals! You past-life prisoners! Daddy's back, baby! This is Revolution Radio, coming at you hot from within the walls of Whitehall.

No, seriously, folks! The Oz-man is beaming directly to you from Downing Street. Hoo-boy! What a rush, man. What a day.

Here's the latest. If it wasn't obvious yet, London is now ours. Okay, sure, we've still got a clean-up job underway but most major government strongholds are reported to have been seized and I'm not hearing much in the way of resistance over the vox-chatter.

I can confirm that in the past hour several major cities have been officially liberated from TEP control. Birmingham. Newcastle. Leeds. Bristol. Liverpool. Edinburgh. Cambridge. The list goes on, man. No jest. I'm watching it all play out right here on—

Wait a sec, folks! New info just in. I'm being told…yep…

Yep…

We've secured Manchester. I repeat, Manchester has been secured. You heard that right. Manchester is binary-town.

My god. I never thought it…

Arrests. Arrests are being made as I speak. Ringleaders being ring-fenced. You'll know who they are—and if you don't, we're gonna make it easy for you to spot them. The politicians, the journo-frauds, the corpo-racketeers, the media-shills—you'll see their faces when you close your eyes, I swear. They won't get far. No Safe Zones to cower in now, man. It's a big, wide, open world.

Speaking of which, if you're not one of them and you're listening to this while hunkered down in your homes, scared to look out your window—don't worry. You have nothing to fear. The transition of power is peaceful. It will remain peaceful. So he has ordered, so shall it be done. Our people have strict instructions to keep…

Hold on…

This just in. Sheffield should be…should be liberated by nightfall. That's what I'm hearing. Yes. The gates are about to give on the Steel City…

My god.

Stay tuned. We'll be broadcasting on this digital frequency and on every major NetTube feed tonight at Nine for an update on the situation and for a special message about the future of our nation.

And on a personal note—Rock, if you're out there, if you can hear us…get in touch, man. If you need help, tell us where we can find you.

Ominous spiritus. Oz-man out.

END OF RECORDING

CHAPTER EIGHTY-SIX

Oscar stood up from his broadcast desk, flexed his fingers. His rifle swung at his hip, energy still up, adrenaline still surging. His radio fizzed, squad leaders buzzing in with their SITREPs. They came through every minute or so like sports-score bulletins.

Between the radio babble, his attention was glued to the stack of netscreens pulling in live surveillance footage of London's major landmarks and transport routes, flicking multi-angles of the reclaimed streets, of the old guard being rounded up, the new guard setting up armed watch on roundabouts and Thames bridges.

"Squadron Alpha-Tango, make sure the south end of that road is secure and position another watch on that hotel there."

The guy was a machine. Chrissie was dumbfounded by the generalship of this unassuming young man. If not for the brutal success of the operation, she would think him a kid playing toy soldiers.

But here they were.

Hard to comprehend how she had got here. No more than fourteen hours since she had fled the Compound. Sitting here now, in the centre of zis—

Of *history*.

The Cabinet Office was said to be strewn with overturned filing cabinets, tech teams and analysts already poring over files and net tabs, picking apart the flesh of TEP activity from the inside. Voices and radio static filled the corridors of most buildings along Whitehall. The Downing Street Cabinet Room was less chaotic, allocated for the time being as an improvised command centre, the green velvet of the conference table cluttered with seized paperwork, electronics, firearms, boxes of unspent ammunition.

Jake prodded his boot into the burning timber of the fireplace, releasing a hiss of new flame. He stood there staring into it for a while. She had yet to ask him what he had seen on his way into the city, how exactly the security forces were defeated, what hand he had played in overthrowing the regime. All she knew was the new guard had been expecting them, had waved them inside into the inner most sanctum of authority, had told them to wait.

No, Jake assured her, she was not about to be arrested again. There was an *understanding*. Whatever that meant.

"Had my doubts," said a voice from the door. "But I suppose things sometimes have a way of coming together even when not everything goes to plan."

Chrissie squinted against the light from the videye screens and the flickering fire. The thin frame of the man seemed taller now than when she had met him in the cave. He stepped into the room, almost apologetically.

Oscar muted his radio, came over, big beam. He slung his rifle behind his hip, grasped Jake by the shoulder, flashed Chrissie a wink. "Not exactly as we'd planned, no. All that matters is the outcome, right?"

Jake gathered himself, breathed a heavy sigh, gave Professor Kolbeck's hand a spirited shake.

"You did it," Jake told him.

"No, no," said the professor. "We've done nothing yet. This is only the start." Kolbeck flexed his freed hand. "Truth be told, there were a number of people without whom we would not even have achieved that. I consider you all on that list."

"The footage," Jake said, turning to Chrissie, "of your partner and the equality minister discussing *Cockleshells*. Rockland said it wouldn't make a difference. The professor believes otherwise, says it could help persuade the country their image of the TEP isn't what they thought. Assassinations of people in their own community, conspiracies to hoodwink the public—they won't be able to censor any of it anymore."

"We'll be airing it this evening for the public to see in full," Kolbeck added. "Part of our work now will be to bring people back on-side, voluntarily, give them a chance to understand what we need to consign to the past. That footage you salvaged is the capstone of a body of evidence we have of the TEP's corruption, of human rights violations spanning years. We've been slowly building that data with the help of our friends on the inside."

He gestured to the door, to the woman lingering at the threshold. She gave them both a curt smile, said nothing.

"Speaking of which," Kolbeck said, "Hannah here requires your time, Miss Tieman. A few questions to help with the enquiries."

"Enquiries?" Chrissie said, taking a step closer to Jake.

"One of our patrols picked up Abigail Dennehy. She's been charged with Gallard's assassination and of being involved in the wider plot to impose laws on the population that may border on genocide. Even so, there'll be no bloody kangaroo courts or atonement sessions under the new administration, mark my words. She'll undergo fair trial. To make that happen, we ask you take the stand as a witness for the prosecution."

Chrissie pulled her arms around herself. "I'm exhausted. All I want to do right now is find my family. I need to know they're okay."

"They're fine." Hannah, finally speaking up, her tone even, her eyes soft in spite of the militaristic edge of her black suit and tight ponytail.

"How do you know?"

Hannah stepped away from the door.

"Aunt Chrissie!" The boy, tearing into the room, a torpedo on legs, throwing himself into her, hugging her knees.

Chrissie clasped him, fingers sinking into his thick hair, feeling him sob. Charlotte a few paces behind, already in floods, her hair a greasy mess, eyebags like bee stings.

The tears came to Chrissie, too. "I'm sorry. I'm sorry."

Charlotte hurried in, grabbed Chrissie in her arms, squeezed the three of them together for a long embrace.

"Our team traced them to a holding cell in Lambeth," said Hannah. "They were a few hours away from consignment to one of the experimentation centres in the West Country. We got lucky."

"Thank you," Chrissie said over Charlotte's wet shoulder. "Thank you."

Charlotte let go. Chrissie wiped her sister's face.

"My family's out there, too," Jake said, almost a whisper, not wanting to ruin the moment. "You have access to their records now, right? Believe we had a deal, Professor."

"Don't worry, son," Kolbeck said. "The search has begun. Let the team work. Meantime, as you can imagine, you and I have some catching up to do. Let's tie up these loose ends first, ay?"

Jake looked at the boot prints left on the cream carpet. He nodded, pulled an abraded pistol from his belt, held it out in offering to the old man. Kolbeck smiled, shook his head as if he was declining a vaparillo.

"I've no need," Kolbeck said. "You keep it."

Chrissie noted the little exchange, was about to ask what was behind it when Hannah put a hand on Chrissie's elbow, invited her to follow her out. On the surveillance screens, people were still being detained, ushered along the roads, ordered to keep their distance from crudely constructed barricades.

Hannah said, "The real work begins here. Rebuilding this nation will need us all to step up and confront what's happened."

"People won't change easily," Chrissie said, ignoring the woman's gesture. "You can put away the ringleaders but everyone else will still be left picking up the pieces. My testimony would be a drop in the ocean. It's a war out there. They're still divided, still angry at each other."

"Exactly why they need good people to show them the way."

"Good luck finding any."

Kolbeck's smile was the same one her grandfather would show her. Its curve conjured memories of shaving foam and tinned mints.

"They're out there," he said. "People who accept their vulnerabilities and don't punish others when they feel vulnerable. People who are honest with themselves about their limits and don't lash out, who work harder to meet their potential. People—like you, Christina—who hold themselves responsible. Who believe they can bring reality into being by doing the things they know are right, even if they don't always know they're doing it. It is *those* people. Those are the people who'll transform what is not yet into what will be."

"I don't know…"

"My god! Look at what you've already accomplished. Don't underestimate how much more you can still shape the future."

"Listen to him," Charlotte said, hoarse. "Do what they need you to do."

She looked at her sister, the precious big sister she thought she would never see again, who only ever wanted what was best for her. She looked at the professor, this man she barely knew. He believed what he was saying, no doubt of that. The conviction of his words set in her a deep relief. The raw bluntness of them, the validity of his presence, made her feel liberated in a sudden, incontestable way. It pushed the tiredness and anxiety into some recess of her brain. It awoke her to the reality that she was not only free but alive—and that alive was a good thing to be. A wonderful thing. A miracle. The past few days of tension and trauma, culminating into a hard knot, was pulled loose. The force of its release arrived all at once, unexpected.

Without thinking, she threw her arms around the professor's slight frame. Her hands pressed at his back, afraid to let go. She pressed her cheek into his chest. She tried not to cry again.

He returned the embrace, his fingertips tentative, quietly pressing her shoulders, patient, not letting go until she moved to release him. When she did, she felt embarrassed. But he looked directly at her, his expression one of pride, pulling creases around the edge of his eyes, and there were tears there too.

"Tell me what you need me to do," Christina said.

"Have the courage to tell the truth," Kolbeck replied. "That's all any of us ever need to do anymore."

Of course. She would have her day in court. She would make her story count. She would say all the things she had wanted to say for so long.

"They'll need a leader," she said, dragging a sleeve across her cheek. "Someone who knows the past. Who can make sure this never happens again."

"I'm not sure any one person can do that," Kolbeck said. "It's up to us all to resist, Christina. It's up to us all."

Chrissie nodded. She went with Hannah, her sister and nephew holding onto each hand. She stopped at the door, turned back to check.

"You'll still be here?" she said to Jake.

"I'm not going anywhere without you," he said.

Yes, the truth. The truth was beautiful.

CHAPTER EIGHTY-SEVEN

It was the smell that woke zer.

A pungent, chemical smell. At once sharp and stale. Not unfamiliar.

Eyelids prised themselves apart in an effort to glimpse the source of the odour, struggled to free themselves of gunk as thick and dry as bark, only to find the world still dim.

Shifting, squeaking noises. Hands on zer face, delicate hands, peeling at tape, making gentle tugs at the skin around the forehead. The light came, weak at first, filtered through cotton, then hard and white and painful. Eyelids scrunched again, retreated involuntarily. The hands applied more softness, wetness, wiped the frightened eyes, sponged the rheum away, soothed the stung corneas with their chill.

Zoe tried to speak. Lips imitated eyelids, pulled sticky and crusted against the other. Parched throat fought to cough up a word, pushed only a wheeze of stale air against the back of her tongue.

"Ehh…ehhhhrr…ang…"

Where am I? zie wanted to say.

Zoe remembered only running and being afraid. The boom of an explosion. The gale of dust. Nothing else.

The longer the time passed, the more the light eased, the more the headache subsided. Tried again, forcing the eyelids open. The lights formed a great globe looking down on zer. Something else looking down on zer—a long shadow. Two shadows. Voices talking so low all zie could hear was the clicking of spit separating in their mouths.

"Welcome, Miss Urwin," one shadow said.

Urwin. Yes. That's right. But not Miss…

Was this light the embrace of eternity? Was this welcome part of zer coronation into the everlasting glory of the universe?

"We missed you," the other shadow said.

This voice, not smooth or sweet or warm. Deep. Emotionless. Zer sight adjusted. The suggestion of a chrome lamp around the light, the hint of faces imprinted among the shadows, strands of purple hair falling lank around zer eyes. Zer head turned side to side. Zer neck protested, stiffened, elicited a faint crackle.

"Ehhrr…ang…"

"Don't try to speak," the first shadow said. The shadow was not all that dark. It had transmogrified into a solid, a person with shape and clothes and hair. The person had an instrument around their shoulders—a stethoscope.

That's it. A hospital. But no ocean sounds. No lavender oil. The smell was clinical. Had something to do with antiseptic or irrigation or some such…

"You've said about enough as it is," the figure continued. "That poisoned tongue of yours. Tsk-tsk. Such hatred. Contemptibility. If ever there was any justification for censoring free speech, that tongue may be the best excuse. Then again, maybe it's had enough of causing trouble. We'll give it time to cool off. Re-educate it. How does that sound?"

The CisHet male—as that's what the shadow undeniably was, as unbelievable as it was—leaned, disappeared, reappeared holding a mason jar between his fingers. He held it to the light, inspected it like one would a specimen.

When was the last time a CisHet male doctor had been licensed to work in a Safe Zone? To work at all?

"What do you think, little one? Feeling a tad less angry these days?" he asked the thing in the jar.

He brought the vessel closer to zer, rotated it with deft, surgical hands. Mesmerised, Zoe could see the twinkle of the glass, the yellowish-brown liquid inside, and at the base, as if shy, lay a blubbery mollusc-like lump, pink as prime ferm-fillet, bloated from its submersion, ragged with sinew at one end.

The male jiggled his wrist. The liquid frothed. The appendage bobbed. He grinned.

"Look at the bright side," the other figure chimed in. "You won't have a taste for the sweet things anymore. Maybe that'll help you lose some weight."

"She's already lost quite a bit," said the first.

A snicker, from somewhere else in the room.

"Right you are." The other male peered closer, gave zer a wink. "Need to be careful, love. Wouldn't want you to waste away to nothing now, would we?"

Seeing them up close, hearing them misgender her, hearing their jibes riding on the ends of their words, their oh-so problematic words, set her heart pounding. She was in the wrong place. This hospital was no sanctuary, no centre for healing or comfort.

Have to get out. Have to move.

Best zie could do was twitch. Torso strained. Spine bucked.

Zoe looked down. Zer body was nothing but the spherical mass of zer trunk, sunken against the bedsheet. Bandages rolled tightly around short, broad stumps. Zer breathing caught. A low gurgling sound emanated from somewhere within the remains of zer flesh.

The doctors beamed, satisfied.

"We've been working overtime to keep you alive," said one of them, though Zoe didn't look up from the absence of zer limbs to see which. "Wouldn't have been fair to deprive the jury of their trial, not after they've spent so long preparing for it, giving good thought to the sentence."

Movement from across the room. Shoes squeaking on linoleum. The beat of doors flapping back and forth on dual-swing hinges.

The doctors scraped their chairs back, moved away, let the others come forward.

Therianthropes. That was what Marsh had called them. A beautiful word.

The figures were not beautiful, nor much like the ones in her recollection. More disturbing up close, without the shield of an acrylic window in front of them. Healthier, better fed, browner of skin. Hair had begun to grow out as stubble around their heads and brows. No longer naked but clothed in loose fitting scrubs. Strangest of all, they had traded their blank misery for expressions of vague anticipation.

"Think of it as an atonement session, Minister Urwin," said one of the doctors. "And for your sake, I suggest you atone generously."

The other, at zer side, pulled wires from a machine. "Not sure how that's going to work without being able to talk, but that's for you to figure out. Best of luck, sweetheart." Then to the mob: "She's all yours."

The doctors faded away. The doors beat. The test subjects crowded the bed. One of them Zoe remembered, the one zie had seen being prepared for surgery, however long ago that was. He hobbled closer. His look suggested he knew zer as well. His arm shot out, seized belly flab, fingers clamped, twisted with zombie strength.

Zoe Urwin drooled, pissed, shook on zer sheets. Zer bulk lurched—a giant tumbler doll, unable to rock zerself away from the hands descending on zer, grasping at whatever mass they could. Took four of them to hoist zer up, one winching zer entirely by the hair, the others digging their broken nails into zer skin. Zoe swayed between them as they limped towards the doors, hauled zer like a refuse sack. Zer effort to scream raised only a wet rasp.

"Utt...ut, my...po...owns...!...My po...owns!..."

EPILOGUE

Spring came around like that, the months gone by like days within a dream.

A newly restored Great Britain had its work cut out. Revival of a dying economy. Reestablishment of diplomatic talks with the rest of the world. Restoration of culture over cult. Resurrection of forgiveness and of understanding, virtues that had long been left to rot in the ground.

Peace, a distant goal. Bringing the nation back, let alone back together, would be gruelling.

In those early days, Chrissie became obsessed with watching the netwires. She sat transfixed, her legs tucked under her, a cushion pressed against her like a security blanket, as Prime Minister Tavistock's surrender and proceeding impeachment were streamed into living rooms across the world. The capitulation of power became another episode in a series of humiliations for the fallen leader. Pundits dissected her actions at all hours, her crimes, her misconducts, her complicities, her impending sentence. The arrest of other high-ranking ministers, officials and enablers followed swiftly, their courtroom appearances covered in granular detail, discussed in every op-ed, in every voxchat, over every garden fence.

The event proved a catalyst, sparked uprisings in other corners of the world, though details of those were harder to come by. Grains of reliable information would occasionally come out of the rumour mills—of CisHet prisons in Berlin being taken over by the inmates, of a nationwide strike in Sweden forcing a new civil rights movement, of provincial rebellions in Canada, of armed revolts along the west coast of the United States, of multinational corporations across Europe getting hacked and bankrupted by their own employees.

Jake didn't care to follow the politics, actively avoided it where he could. He only gave his time to the stories of the families reunited, the children freed from captivity, the liberation of the many re-education centres, watching silently and still, the scars reopening each time.

With December came Chrissie's turn on the stand. Her testimony, treated as a defining moment of the revolution, the symbolic culmination of decades of pain and division, the denouement of all that was. Reports hailed her a national hero. Talk shows flooded her with invitations to speak. Grateful strangers gathered outside her apartment building, shouted up well-wishes. Anonymous death threats arrived every few days. The new government issued her a security team.

Talking about her experience allowed Chrissie to open doors within her that had for years remained closed. She had been exhausting herself in locking the truth away, suppressing her doubts, afraid even to think about betraying her former taskmasters. The unignorable rumblings from behind those doors had shaped her actions, a subconscious climax destined to erupt someday, somehow. More importantly, taking the stand helped her realise she was—had always been—a product of her choices, not a victim of her circumstances. She vowed to never relinquish her autonomy again.

The new mindset helped her deal with the guilt. Knowing now how much abuse her complicity had enabled was a tough pill. She wasn't alone—millions of others who had conformed and collaborated with the regime had begun to see the true nature of what had been happening behind the curtain. Ironic as it was, a programme of atonement swept the country. From the banning of puberty blockers to the permanent suspension of all gender affirming surgeries on children, a raft of new measures heralded the start of a nation's penance.

Amidst the overhaul of the old regime, Christmas was decriminalised and began supplanting the Yule-branded festivities once forced on the population. Regardless of creed, much of the country undertook the celebrations as a symbolic milestone, a day of homage to the freedoms that had been returned, and a time for the nation to grieve together. Inseparable since their ordeal, Chrissie spent it with Jake. They attempted a joint family gathering, but other than Daniel's innocent joy towards his gifts—not a doll among them—towards his mother's undivided love and attention, the celebrations were hushed, tainted with heartache.

The incoming government traced Jake's parents to a re-education facility up north. Kolbeck personally arranged for staff to transport Jake out there so he could bring his mother back to London, an event that brought as much sorrow as it did joy. It was discovered his father had perished less than a year before the revolution. Worked to death, though resistant to the end, his files said.

Word came not long after that an official investigation had begun to find Rockland. Teams of trackers were said to be scouring the countryside west of the city. They found no trace of him other than a hunting knife and crushed radio components. Some men came to speak to Jake in private, presumably to form a picture of his last known whereabouts. Chrissie wasn't party to the conversations, but the men stopped coming after a while and nothing more was said, publicly or otherwise.

Jake shut down a little through the winter. The spark in him dimmed. He appeared detached from the renewed optimism spreading through the country. Chrissie did what she could, nursed him with intimacy, healed him with touch, gave him the space to talk, even though the words were rare and few and guarded. He reciprocated her touch, hinted he was still there somewhere underneath it all, even if he spent most of the time staring into the distance, trapped alone with his buried thoughts.

He tried to track down his old cellmate from his time in the Cooler, said the guy always had a way of making him laugh. Chrissie and Charlotte threw themselves into the search, even called in support from their friends in the new ruling party. No one could trace him. The weeks passed. Jake stayed quiet.

With the intensity of change in the city, Chrissie suggested they move out, for at least a while. The two of them could hide away in the Heaths again, disconnect the voxcom, ditch the protection detail that sat outside the flat all day. Hannah said she could pull some strings, provide them an ideal spot. Jake agreed.

The change helped, began to wheedle him back. They went to the coast, watched the boats, ate at newly-licensed pubs, made untrained love, read each other books, gazed at the stars. By the time the blossoms arrived, his smile had become another guest in the house, infrequent but welcome.

He came to her one morning, laced his arms around her waist, kissed her by the ear. She softened, could tell it was one of his good days, that he was drawing on that internal well that seemed to fill a little more each day.

She said, "How about a walk?"

He said, "How about a drive?"

Through the bay windows, the hills were full. A lustre had been left on the road by the overnight downpour. The sun had disrobed, the air warming.

"Don't mind," she said. "Only question is where."

"I know where."

She looked at him and he delighted in her moment of confusion. Before he would say another word, he took her hand, led her out the kitchen door, into the car. They drove, followed the endless old roads still in disrepair, weed-treacherous and coruscating in the sunlight. He didn't let go of her hand. They rumbled onto a track, through a field, through another. They got out at the lake by a weeping cherry blossom tree.

Up close, the limbs and branches ranged above, pregnant with florets. He cradled his hands, coaxed her boot in, hoisted her up. She reached for him. He followed, used her for balance, sprung effortlessly onto the same bough, his feet scrabbling for purchase. They said nothing still as they climbed together, man and woman, high as they could go, neither one ever thinking about the drop. Only the climb.

Printed in Great Britain
by Amazon

20973656R00212